The Last Lover

BOOKS BY CAN XUE IN ENGLISH TRANSLATION

The Last Lover

CAN XUE

TRANSLATED BY ANNELISE FINEGAN WASMOEN

YALE UNIVERSITY PRESS ■ NEW HAVEN & LONDON

A MARGELLOS
WORLD REPUBLIC OF LETTERS BOOK

The Margellos World Republic of Letters is dedicated to making literary works
from around the globe available in English through translation. It brings to the
English-speaking world the work of leading poets, novelists, essayists, philosophers,
and playwrights from Europe, Latin America, Africa, Asia, and the Middle East to
stimulate international discourse and creative exchange.

Yale University Press books may be purchased in quantity for educational, business, or
promotional use. For information, please e-mail sales.press@yale.edu (U.S. office) or
sales@yaleup.co.uk (U.K. office).

Set in Electra type by Tseng Information Systems, Inc.
Printed in the United States of America.

Library of Congress Cataloging-in-Publication Data

Canxue, 1953–
[Zui hou de qing ren. English]
The last lover / Can Xue ; translated by Annelise Finegan Wasmoen.
pages cm. — (The Margellos World Republic of Letters)
"Originally published in Chinese under the title Zuihou de qingren in 2005" —
Verso title page.
ISBN 978-0-300-15332-3 (pbk.)
1. Husband and wife — Fiction. 2. Paramours — Fiction. 3. Unrequited love — Fiction.
I. Wasmoen, Annelise Finegan, 1953– II. Title.
PL2912.A5174Z45513 2014
895.13′52 — dc23

2013048362

A catalogue record for this book is available from the British Library.
This paper meets the requirements of ANSI/NISO Z39.48-1992
(Permanence of Paper).

10 9 8 7 6 5 4 3 2 1

CONTENTS

The Last Lover

JOE AND HIS BOOKS

Joe, the manager of the Rose Clothing Company's sales department, clamps a briefcase under his arm as he passes through the narrow streets that lead to his office. He is a small, conservative man
between middle and old age, meticulous in his dress, with shoes
invariably spotless, his beard and hair regularly trimmed. His pale
green eyes sometimes have a blank expression, either because he's
absentminded or because he's eccentric. He often harbors thoughts
of madness. Joe has a mania for reading, and for years he's read one
book after another, muddling all the stories in his mind. His memory
is of the kind that's excellent at making choices—a grafting memory—so the pathway of his thought is always clear. He usually sits in
his office in City B with a novel hidden under the files, trying to look
as if he's hard at work. In fact, he's reading all kinds of stories. As he
is circumspect and conservative, his clients over the years have never
discovered this secret. Joe's manner of reading allows him to practice
a singularly coherent method of linking his thoughts together. Every
day his job interrupts him countless times, but in the space of a second he can get back into the flow of a story.

Joe's home is on a small hill two streets from the office. From the
windows a stretch of blue sea is visible, over which seagulls hover. In
the light of an early dawn, he was already on the road to work. The
people of Country A rise very late, and there was no one on the quiet
street except a black woman, a street cleaner. Joe heard his footsteps
on the empty street sounding a hesitant note. To the right, the storefront windows reflected his tidy hair and necktie. Joe turned away

shyly and lowered his eyes to the ground when he caught sight of this distinct image of himself.

"Good morning!" he said.

"Good morning! You're out early." The slender woman leaned on her broom and observed him as he slipped by and disappeared little by little into the distance. Her large eyes blinked, as if she were lost deep in thought.

Joe reached his office, turned on the lights, and went to the kitchen to make a cup of coffee, then sat at his desk and continued with the story from yesterday. The book in front of him was very old, and its pages were yellowed; it must have been twenty years ago that he'd bought it. Joe had been purchasing books for three decades, and the house on the seafront was stuffed with them. He had taken all the beds and converted them into empty "chests" that sat on the floor loaded with books. Since the previous year Joe had been envisioning a magnificent plan: to reread all the novels and stories he'd ever read in his life, so that the stories would be connected together. That way, he could simply pick up any book and move without interruption from one story to another. And he himself would be drawn into it, until the outer world wouldn't be able to disturb him. Joe had put this plan into action, and after two months of persistence it was already producing results. For example, he could even talk business with a customer (he is, after all, the manager of the clothing company's sales department) and at the same time remain immersed in his stories. He would sometimes stealthily turn aside with a faint smile.

"Joe, my company would collapse without you," Joe's boss said when they met. He was the company's owner, a thin man of about sixty with white hair and wrinkles like canals across his face. "How do you know the secret of getting our customers to like you?" As he spoke he almost sounded sentimental, but at the same time he stealthily sized up Joe's reaction.

"I think it has something to do with my reading." Joe spoke slowly, deliberately weighing his words.

"Reading!" The wrinkles between his boss's eyebrows folded into an upside-down V.

"Yes, I read a lot of stories." Joe's speech quickened as a red flush spread over his face. "I, uh . . . I've even been thinking of resigning so I can read books all the time. Really. I've been thinking it over."

"Well, that would be a real loss for my company. You haven't made up your mind yet?"

It didn't seem as if his employer were urging Joe to stay; actually, he seemed hopeful that Joe meant what he said.

"No, not yet. I still have my wife and a child to support."

His boss peered into his face for a moment, shook his head slightly as though a little disappointed, and motioned with his hand for Joe to leave. Joe departed, pondering what his boss might mean by what he'd said, turning this over and over in his mind until his thoughts led to a dark tunnel. This man, whom he'd worked with for many years, clearly understood his employee. But as to how deep this understanding went, and what he thought of Joe's approach to life, and what hopes he had for him, Joe couldn't tell from his expression or speech. His behavior was equivocal and vague, in distinct contrast to the precise operation of his denim manufacturing company. Joe had the impression that his employer concerned himself very little with the company's day-to-day affairs, although he was interested in his employees' attitudes and the degree of their loyalty to the company. Joe wondered why his boss didn't seem to expect him to continue working there permanently. This was an insult to Joe's self-regard, especially since he was very conscientious about his work and had an intuitive knack for the proper arrangement of things. Joe himself had great respect for this capability. At this point in his thinking, Joe recalled his boss's wife. She was vivacious and clever, a gaudy woman of middle age. He thought this woman, Lisa, wasn't a good match for him, yet his boss treated her with constant affection. Joe thought of his own home, his plain and capable housewife, and their likable son, who was off at boarding school. By comparison, he could understand the harmonious relationship between the company's owner and his wife. But what did his boss think of him? What sort of expectations did he have for him? Joe was at a loss. There were occasional moments when Joe thought he might even tell his boss about how he read novels on the sly during office hours, but every time the words were on his lips he swallowed them back. Joe was a cautious man, circumspect to the point of being a touch pedantic. Once during a gathering at a restaurant his boss had gotten drunk and said, pointing at Joe's nose, "Don't think I don't know what you're up to!" Joe had turned white, thinking his life was about to undergo a great change. In fact, nothing happened, and his life went on as before.

After Joe left the owner's office and returned to his own, he felt a floating sensation pervade his body. He opened a book and followed its heroine through the alleyways of a slum. But today the small alleys didn't lead off in every direction. In one sunlit alley a fearful dark shadow appeared up ahead, with the *pa pa* flapping sound of a cloth fluttering in the wind, even though there was no sign of the wind blowing. Joe stopped in his tracks, frightened. At that very moment a telephone rang, and his secretary said a customer from the south was here to see him.

This man, named Reagan, had a square face and a stern expression. He wanted to sign a long-term contract with Joe. Joe figured that he would want to haggle as usual, and rapidly ran through a number of scenarios in his mind. But Reagan didn't open his mouth. Moving a chair over to the window, he gazed down at the people clumped together in twos and threes. He propped his very broad chin on his left hand as if he were calculating, but also as if he were thinking about something that had nothing to do with business matters. Joe was perplexed, and thought again of the alleyway in his book. When Reagan started talking, Joe jumped with fright because his voice was raised in a near scream.

"In the south, there are rubber tree groves and coconut palms everywhere. How much clothing do you think the workers need to wear? Haven't you ever thought of that? Do you have that much imagination? Yesterday two workers drowned in the bay because the clothes you make are too thick and heavy, and it's hard to get them off quickly . . . What kind of idiot designed these clothes? One of the workers who drowned was a girl. There were people who saw her leap out of the water like a fish and then sink back in. You fool!"

He held his head in both hands, looking unbearably vexed.

Joe was silent and reluctant to speak. He didn't know what he could say to make this better. He'd known Mr. Reagan for many years. He was an educated and highly cultivated farm owner—or, rather, he didn't come across as a farmer at all. He seemed more like the owner of an antiquarian bookstore. But today he displayed a violent temper.

"Do you really want to keep doing business with us?" Reagan looked contemptuously at Joe.

"We could design some light outerwear, pieces that can be taken off easily," Joe answered mechanically.

"I don't appreciate your way of thinking at all."

Joe was at a complete loss after Reagan tossed off this icy statement. When Reagan had visited his office in the past, a scent of the open country, of canola flowers, had emanated from him. Joe would inhale this odor keenly, and involuntarily he'd drawn the deeply tanned southerner into the network of his stories. He had never sensed that Reagan felt any hostility toward him, but today he knew that he did. Joe drew his arms in as if he felt a chill, and Reagan noticed the movement immediately. He asked whether Joe was tired of doing business with him. If so, they could break off the discussion.

"Like the two of us . . ." Reagan let out half a sentence and then swallowed it back.

Joe thought that he was trying to say that between two men like them it was difficult to reach an agreement. What was going on today? They had worked together for years; his figure often appeared in Joe's stories, with that square jaw reflected in the mirrors along the road, swaying back and forth . . . on the pathways in Joe's mind there were always mirrors hung on the tree trunks along every side. Not long ago, Reagan had given Joe a pair of wild birds, and their dazzling, variegated plumage had sent Joe into fantastical reveries. Then he had gazed at Reagan's expressionless face and felt that the man must be a conjurer with capabilities beyond anyone's expectations.

Reagan walked up and down Joe's office several times before asking Joe to hand him the contract. Then he signed several pages at lightning speed, so quickly that Joe couldn't see clearly what he was doing. His memory retained only an image of protruding blue veins and the long thin right hand. In his mind he marveled: How could a farm owner have a hand like that?

Reagan left after he'd finished signing the contract. As Joe showed him out, he caught sight of his boss's figure disappearing into the elevator. What was he doing on this side of the large building? Joe asked his secretary, Jenny, whether the boss had stopped by. Jenny stared at him for a moment and then slowly shook her head, disapproving of his neuroticism.

Joe had worked in this building for over a decade, and he was as familiar as anyone could be with his job and with the business of the company. Within his department, it would be almost impossible for anything out of the ordinary to happen without his knowledge. But today he realized that some things were getting out of hand. These things must have taken place outside of his awareness, and not even by racking his brains could he grasp the clues to what was happening.

That day, as Joe was on his way home from work, someone came up quickly behind him. It was the boss's wife.

"Vincent drinks heavily every day now. He made a spectacle of himself on the lawn right in front of our house." Lisa turned red in the face and she spoke a little bashfully. "He's not young anymore. I've been wondering what sort of influence all of you have on him. Hmm?" The woman swung around and glared at Joe. Sparks unlike anything he'd ever seen before flew from her eyes.

Joe could not answer. He couldn't even recognize the red-haired woman standing in front of him. The generally cheerful, gaudy Lisa was now shoving past him in a fit of rage, almost forcing him off the sidewalk. Like a gust of wind she was suddenly at a distance, her high heels energetically tapping the sidewalk. There were many people on the street at nightfall, all looking with surprise at the completely discomfited man. Joe saw an abyss open in the sidewalk ahead of him, and he walked toward it, thinking perhaps it would lead him into the web of the story he had recently constructed. But that large black open mouth wasn't an abyss after all—it was an underground pedestrian crossing. And just as he reached the entrance to the underground walkway, Lisa rushed out from the shadows.

"Vincent's mad! He's crazy! Damn it, how could this have happened!"

The expression in her eyes was frantic. A strong hand grasped Joe's arm and shook it, and Joe caught the smell of liquor on her breath.

"Hey, Lisa. Try to explain more slowly." Joe spat out these few words with difficulty. A fury—at what, he couldn't place—sprang up in his gut, and he felt disgusted with the small-framed woman.

But Lisa disappeared just as abruptly as she'd appeared. Thinking over the day's strange occurrences, Joe felt his head buzzing with confusion.

Joe's wife, Maria, was at her loom weaving a tapestry. It was her favorite pastime, and also a means of supplementing the household income. Almost all the homes in the neighborhood had samples of her handiwork hanging in them. Today Maria was weaving a scorpion design. With the deep brown insect hiding among exotic flowers, it looked original, fresh, provocative. Maria's body was strong and well-proportioned, and her hands, with the fingernails cut short, were dexterous at any kind of craft. Although she was almost fifty, her eyesight was very good, and she wore her thick brown hair drawn up in a bun.

On the lawn outside, two cats from Africa yowled without stopping, but it didn't sound like their mating call. Maria had bought these cats. Usually they made little noise, appearing and disappearing from the area around the house like ghosts.

"There were some problems at the office today." Joe felt weighed down by care.

"I heard about that." Maria glanced at her husband.

"You? Who told you?"

"Lisa. She stopped by."

"Don't listen to her gossip." Joe impatiently threw his briefcase onto the sofa.

Maria rose from the side of the loom and walked past the dining table to Joe's side, helping him put the briefcase on its stand. Afterward she laid her hand on Joe's shoulder.

"Don't be irritable, it's nothing serious. You're an old employee at the company. How could that old fox Vincent manage without you? Besides, Lisa came here for another reason. She's having trouble at home."

This was an odd thing, that Maria always called Vincent "old fox." Joe had never understood his wife's intuition about him. Joe didn't think his boss was at all cunning. It was just that he acted a bit indecisive. But if his wife wanted to call Vincent an old fox, then let her. Joe didn't care to question her about it.

"What's the problem?"

"According to Lisa, it's an Arab woman. Vincent has been hiding from his wife that he's living with a woman who wears a black veil."

"Living with? Doesn't he go back home after work? I see him there just about every day."

"That's right. But Lisa says other people see her husband at the Arab woman's house every day. How could that be? I think he must know some way to be two places at the same time."

Joe couldn't get used to Maria saying strange things, although she'd always had this habit. Her strangeness had been passed on to the two African cats. Not long before, the brown-striped female had even bitten their son.

"A man goes to work as usual, returns home on time, and has no vices, but is still seen every day at his mistress's house. Isn't this odd? Is it possible there's another man? Yet he's admitted to it. Lisa's desperate. She's up against something sinister."

Maria returned to her loom as she spoke, alternating her sentences with the weaving of a few strands. As Joe fixed his gaze on the enormous scorpion, he felt a gust of cold air at his back. The whole room was filled with dense, cold air. Maria began to rock back and forth in front of him as though she were floating in a thin mist, and at Joe's feet that treacherous cat was crouching. He staggered, trying to fight free of it so he could go upstairs to his study. Maria was mumbling to herself, but when Joe turned back to look, the seat next to the loom was empty. Where was her voice coming from?

It was only when he was seated at his writing desk opening a book by a Japanese author that Joe's head finally cleared. He read the story aloud at the top of his voice, with a profound feeling that his life of late had been reversed, and everyday life transformed into a dreamland, one that was like a chain of interlocking rings. Even though the story Joe was reading was set in the East, the young woman wearing geta sandals walked leisurely into a square that he had already constructed in his mind two months ago, a place surrounded by parasol trees. She hid behind the thick trunk of one of the trees, and only a triangle from the lower hem of her kimono was revealed by the blowing wind. Joe read until his eyes grew dim and he had to stop.

As Joe and Maria sat together in the kitchen eating dinner, the cat ran over to them unexpectedly and wound itself around Joe's legs, rubbing back and forth against his trousers and purring, *wu wu*. Maria's gray eyes were calm and shone with light as she gazed directly at Joe. He was bending over to pat the cat on the back when his hand burst out in pricks of heat. Was it possible for the cat's body to be electrified? Did Maria have such mystical power? Joe looked at his wife, puzzled. Her expression was rapt. Was she waiting for something to happen? What did she actually do at home all day, aside from household tasks? It seemed that his energetic wife had already made this house into a small personal kingdom.

Joe's son Daniel was seventeen years old. He was at boarding school out west and came home only twice a year. It wasn't clear exactly why, but the relationship between father and son was one of indifference, in part at least because each was inclined to be absorbed in his own little world. Joe didn't know what his son's interests were, but in Daniel's vacant gray eyes he recognized the yellowed photographs of his own early youth. In general, Daniel was more at ease with his mother, and this was apparent also from his relationship with the two cats. It was as if the ghostly animals played the leading roles in a conspiracy planned by Maria and her son—Joe couldn't help harboring this suspicion. He once encountered mother and son squatting under the flower trellis behind the house, discussing the two cats in voices alternately raised and lowered. Meanwhile, the cats crouched proudly on top of a stone table, holding their bodies very straight, as if they wouldn't deign to pay the slightest attention to the talk of the humans. When Joe appeared, the conversation broke off short.

"My uncle's family is taking this tapestry. Tomorrow they'll be here to pick it up. Now I feel an emptiness in my heart."

Maria cleared away the plates as she spoke.

"Why don't you weave a story? One that contains all possible designs, where there's nothing that can't be worked in?" Joe said the first thing that came into his head, and regretted it immediately. He worried that his wife might question him more closely.

"I don't have any such story in my mind, so how could I weave it? Watch out. You're stepping on the cat's tail."

The cat shrieked in pain and ducked away. Joe stood awkwardly, then returned to his study upstairs. He carried the book by the Japanese author to the bathroom and continued to read on the toilet. There was a sumo match in the book. The huge body of a wrestler from the north, Xiao Jing, was pushed off the stage and his young son was crushed to death. The wrestler's mournful silhouette disappeared into the dense mass of spectators. The loudspeakers started to broadcast an amazing sort of dirge. The music wasn't sorrowful—it sounded like joyousness that was being firmly repressed by something. When he'd read this far, Joe's eyes grew dim. Returning to the study, he became aware of how the story he'd been reading, set in the East, and the West, where he was in person, were converging on each other to form a separate, alternative space. He closed the book and turned his exhausted face to look behind him and up. This time a different story flourished in that different place, and a triangle of azure kimono hovered in midair. He heard the cat scratching at the door of the study, and it occurred to him: let the cat go ahead into this square, too . . . where a rank of black dogs crouched in stillness off to the side.

Joe's room was a typical bachelor's bedroom. There were no pictures on the walls, no decorations, and only a few unconnected yellowed photographs set in copper frames. Of the photos, one was of a hat, another of a walking stick, another a tobacco pipe, and still others were enlargements of objects like false teeth or screws. There were some photographs where you simply couldn't tell what they were supposed to be, such as a rectangular picture that looked like a brown path with something a little bit like porridge and a little bit like pigment flowing out of it. It left you feeling ignorant. The furnishings in Joe's bedroom were conservative and compact, and no one could have discovered from them that their owner was a man of complex thoughts. Joe didn't smoke, but there was an ashtray on the bedstand, and inside the ashtray a few small bones from when he'd had an operation on his knee. About five or six years earlier Maria had developed insomnia, and the couple now kept separate rooms. With Maria gone, Joe had quietly remade the bedroom into a bachelor pad. No cats or dogs were allowed inside. He realized that he was growing more eccentric as time passed. Maria's bedroom was on the far side of his study. Before it had been bright and spacious, but Maria had taken dark curtains and shaded the two windows, and even during the day she kept a small purple lamp lit. One day Joe found himself thinking of her, and he walked over to her room. It was filled with a perfume that was familiar to him. Maria was just getting up and dressing. Without turning around she said to Joe: "You've come too late, Joe. How can you keep these things in your mind constantly? Look at this lamp: it burns day and night in my heart, making the pitch-black places shine brightly."

They still went to bed together, and Joe was astonished by his wife's fervor. There were even some things she desired that were unfamiliar to him, and at the height of her excitement her body stiffened upward and Joe saw two small purple lights shining in her deep, indistinct gray eyes. From that time on, Joe had not entered his wife's bedroom. He was frightened of the abyss of her desire, and even thinking of it made his spine turn cold. "How can Maria be like this? She doesn't love me at all." Occasionally Joe would be sick at heart, thinking, "And then, she's so lonely, although there's Daniel. But he doesn't call or write from school."

Joe's bedroom and study made up his own little world. The books in the study were piled up to the ceiling. Once in a while he would climb a staircase to vacuum up the dust. In the *weng weng* buzzing of the vacuum, Joe's stories became like fishnets in the sun, fluttering in the wind. Recently he'd been coming across a lot of people from Japan, and these narrow-eyed visitors from the East would come and go at the edge of the square. If it was the height of the day's heat, they would evaporate like water droplets. "Evaporate like water droplets, a beautiful metaphor," Joe said to himself. About once a month, Joe straightened his books, placing them one by one on the floor and then putting them back on the wooden shelves in a new order. He didn't have actual bookcases, so all the books sat on open racks. They weren't particularly neat. Sometimes he would bring a book to bed and place it under the pillow. These were usually horror stories. He thought, by putting the book under his pillow, to suppress the disturbing violence of its contents. On such nights Joe's dreams were filled with tempests, as though doomsday had arrived. Joe, who was normally a calm spirit, didn't care for this feeling at all. But he still read thrillers one after another, sometimes even in the office, where his customers were able to see the fear written on his face.

Was Maria's fondness for mystical things due to his influence? Or, conversely, was it Joe who was affected by her? When he'd calmed down, Joe thought back on the two lamps reflected in her eyes. The roses in the backyard also seemed to be electrified, and his hand recoiled like lightning from the petals. He even heard the slight sound of sparks flying. Those roses were in a large patch of bushes Maria had planted, where she and Daniel sat among the flowering shrubs in summer drinking tea. As Joe looked down on them from the terrace, their voices floated up into the air. Daniel said, "Mama, once you pass the well you'll see the quarry." Maria's arid voice answered, "Everything is possible right here if you stay at home." Joe sighed, thinking of what kindred spirits the mother and son were. But one evening Joe saw Daniel wrecking the rosebushes. It was the day before he was going back to campus. Daniel was like a terrifying ghost in the moonlight, his movements irresolute and hasty as he mucked in the soil until it covered his body. Joe couldn't bear to call out to him, and so stood off to one side watching. Finally Daniel wore himself out, and covered his face with both hands. Was he crying? Joe knew that even as a child he'd never cried. The lamps in Maria's room dimmed, then brightened. Against the curtains a long, thin silhouette appeared where someone must be standing. In this southern town everyone went to sleep very early and fell to dreaming . . . Was this why they were all on the brink of madness?

When Joe was young, his father had looked him over without blinking. "Joe, Joe, how are you going to support yourself?" When his father said this, Joe had felt unbearable shame. He didn't know what he would do to get by. Daniel was much stronger than he'd been then, and this could be seen in his movements as he uprooted the roses and tossed them in the air. In his heart Joe envied him a little. The son was much more like his mother.

Joe wanted to draw a picture, to make a rough sketch outlining the story that lay deep in his mind. Time after time he worked out the composition, and time after time he rejected it. One day, he summoned his courage and picked up a pen, but what he ultimately drew was just a line that looked like an earthworm. It was completely meaningless. The day he finished reading the Japanese book, Joe was seized with an impulse to visit Daniel's campus and speak with him. It was a Thursday, and he needed to wait until Saturday to go, and by then his intention was already worn away from waiting. Even though he hadn't seen his son, Daniel's image slipped into Joe's dreams. It was a body without a head, with a rose on the shoulders in its place. Joe drew a picture of his son from the dream. He showed this picture to Maria, who said, "I've seen this person you've drawn before, it's an uncle on my mother's side."

The Rose Clothing Company didn't get caught up in Vincent's domestic difficulty, and its business wasn't affected. The prevailing spirit was in fact one of success. Even if Reagan grumbled, his farm still needed the company's clothing. He had just signed another contract with Joe for a not inconsiderable sum. Joe sat at the window of his office watching Reagan's form disappear around a corner and imagined the natural scenery of that small place in the far south called the Cape. Reagan had to rush back that very day. He was always hurried like this, and Joe had the impression that his life was full of vigorous activity. Out in the corridor there was a ceaseless crowd of people coming and going, accompanied by the *weng weng* buzz of their conversation. Joe knew his boss hadn't come to work that day. Everyone in the building knew it, too, but people avoided discussing it.

Taking advantage of the racket outside his door, Joe drew a new book from his bag. After reading a page, he was enveloped by drowsiness. The opening of this novel was very strange. It told of a large palace with a few guards standing about in the doorway. An old fellow carrying charcoal was trying to enter the gates to deliver it, but he was continually driven out. The old fellow saw a man who looked like a steward rush out as if to meet him and bring him in. But in his hurry he fell to the ground, and for all his effort he couldn't reach the old man's side. The guards stuck out thick arms and swept the old fellow away. He tumbled down with the coal he was carrying onto the stairs outside the palace gates. He could dimly hear voices calling from inside, "The emperor is arriving." As Joe ruminated on the murky scene on the steps, someone outside knocked twice on his door. Joe didn't acknowledge the knock. His eyes continued to rest on the page because of an illustration of a cat on the left-hand side. This cat wasn't like those cats from Africa; it looked a little like the indigenous cats of Country F. Many years earlier, Joe had visited that country and seen the far too numerous breed of yellow-eyed cats popping out of the cracks in the earth. There were few tourists who hadn't encountered them. What did the cats of Country F and that old man delivering coal have to do with each other? The knocks on the door grew louder. The doorbell rang. Why couldn't this guy call for an appointment? Joe had no choice but to stow his book in a drawer and answer the door.

"Vincent! What's the matter?"

Joe looked at his boss in panic.

"Everything's fine. It's just that Lisa's become paranoid. I came to see you to avoid her. God, what are you thinking of, shut up in here like this?"

He was asking Joe and himself at the same time.

"Me? I like getting lost in my thoughts. It doesn't affect my work, does it?"

"No, it's quite helpful for your work. You also just signed a big contract. How could we get by without people like you in this company?"

He watched Joe with an expression of sincerity. Joe felt that his glance was overbearing, but in the depths of Vincent's pupils he saw rays of light like those emanating from the eyes of the cat in the book he'd just been reading, a stern look of repressed bitterness. Maybe Vincent had some connection to that archaic nation? Maybe his Arab woman wasn't an Arab woman at all, but an even more mysterious woman of Country F? Joe lowered his eyes, not daring to look at his boss, and he became the old coal bearer in the book he'd just been reading: he collapsed on the stairs, his ears strained to hear the people inside the palace gates, the footsteps of groups running back and forth, back and forth.

Vincent continued, "So, what about that thing we were talking about earlier? What are you thinking? I've been to places like that. I mean a thatched hut in the wilderness, and from its doorway you can see the mountaintops burned by wildfires. You should consider things like this seriously. Don't give up thinking about them just because you're indispensable to the company."

Joe's boss was plainly standing right in front of him, but Joe felt more and more as though his voice was emanating from another room.

"You might end up like me," Vincent said, repeating himself so Joe would hear.

Joe was surprised and disturbed to discover that Vincent was smiling.

"Lisa came by my house." He struggled to get the sentence out.

Vincent stood up, releasing his breath, walked around the room once, and stopped in front of the window.

"Today it looks like rain, so Lisa went out with her umbrella. No matter what she's doing she always thinks ahead. How do men with wives like this live? I honestly can't imagine what I'd do without her . . . just as this office couldn't manage without you."

"So you're still hiding from her?"

"Yes, you know everything. Now I need to go back and check on things. If she can't find me she'll toss all my files into the stairwell. Then I'll have to send workers down to save them."

Vincent slipped out without a sound, so quietly that Joe wondered if he'd even been real. To get at the reason he felt this way, Joe opened his book again and read a page of it. The story sank into confusion. This time the person falling down the steps wasn't even the coal bearer; it was five palace maids. The maids were in disarray, climbing the stairs over and over, and each time they were pushed back by two fiendish guards. Joe's eyes were drawn in fascination to the scenery within the palace gates. The interior was, oddly enough, an uncultivated flower garden filled with withered bamboo stalks. "The maids will never abandon their attempt." Joe read up to this sentence. He recalled that his boss, Vincent, had just said a similar thing. He turned back to the beginning of the book and looked at the illustration of the cat on the first page. He found that the cat had lost its enchanting quality. The yellow eyes were lusterless. Returning to the previous passage, he read about the fountains in the garden. They were not manmade fountains; water from underground spontaneously leapt up through fissures in the earth. Some of the geysers were between ten and twenty meters high. The maids rushed up once again and were dashed back down, and the guards forced the palace gates shut. A gust of wind blew the maids' long hair loose, tangling it and obscuring their eyes. An image rose up in Joe's mind of a day in April, and an event that had taken place on the street in front of his house. That day, when he returned from work he saw his neighbors standing in twos and threes at the side of the road, looking ill at ease. Turning to catch what they were staring at, Joe saw a man and a woman dressed in rags walking slowly past, one before and one behind, looking straight ahead. What discomfited Joe wasn't this sight but rather the feeling of his neighbors' eyes on his back, as if their gaze could bore inside him. The couple walked on, but after a little while they returned. Joe felt the tension in the strained atmosphere, and he heard the creaking sound made by a kneading fist. The odor of spring rose from the damp earth.

"What's the matter?" Joe couldn't help questioning the old woman at his side.

"It was an earthquake. Didn't you feel it? Everyone came outside."

"But those two people . . ."

"They're not from around here. Shhh, be quiet."

There hadn't been an earthquake that day, so why were all these people deathly pale? The peaceful side street where Joe lived was full of secrets. Even Maria felt that the atmosphere there was oppressive. Her favorite platitude was, "Once something gets started, you might as well finish it." It meant that she could take all the craziness around them and make things even crazier. That's why in their house every object she touched was electrically charged, to some extent or other, and sometimes sparks burst out. What would the street look like if it really were fluctuating in an earthquake?

"Joe! Joe . . ." Someone was calling him.

He opened his office door and saw Lisa, her face gray and filthy with dirt. Although she had lost her customary glamor, she showed a kind of touching charm.

"Did Vincent come looking for you? I just can't catch up with him. Look at me in this state—you can see he's done for."

"No, Lisa, that's not it. You need to be a little more patient. He loves you."

"I'm not talking about that. Who said he has to love me? I'm talking about him. He's scared to show his face—what's he so afraid of? And there's his disgusting behavior out on the lawn . . . He was dressed up in formal wear and rolling around in the grass. His spirit's shattered, but I wanted to help him recover. Now it's too late."

Lisa hopped up onto Joe's desk and perched there swinging her legs provocatively. Yet the expression on her face was entirely serious, something you didn't see often. She listened attentively, concentrating for a moment, then said to Joe, "There's a magnetic field in your office. Vincent has known about it for a long time. He's mentioned it to me several times. So I went to find Maria. Maria is a remarkable woman. As soon as I entered your house I felt like I was walking on thin ice. Maria, Maria, she's exceptional!" Her husky voice sounded as if she were singing.

As she didn't get down from the desk, Joe began to feel terribly awkward. Although the difference in their ages wasn't very great, she was his superior's wife. Joe had no idea how to deal with her frivolous manner; furtively, he hoped that someone would enter the room. But no one did. Lisa sat planted on that high perch. Already she'd forgotten Joe's existence as she glanced back and forth along the cluster of buildings outside. Perhaps she was looking for her husband. Joe stealthily snuck to the doorway, opened the door a bit, and sidled out into the hallway. His secretary looked at him sympathetically: "That woman's out for blood."

Joe returned to his office, after taking a turn at the bottom of the stairs, to find Lisa already gone. What door had she used? She must have taken the elevator. She'd pulled out the book Joe had thrust under a pile of contracts and left a peculiar bookmark between pages 50 and 51: the shriveled corpse of a mantis. Joe set the rather large mantis at eye level and scrutinized it. Its yellow, jadelike eyes gave off a gleam he was already familiar with. He even felt its stabbing legs move between his fingers. On the surface of page 50, it looked like something had bitten a few holes in the letters. Could the mantis have done this? It had been dead for a long time. Well then, Lisa must have dug out the words with her sharp fingernails. While she did this she would have worn a look of rapacious concentration. What kind of woman had Vincent married? Joe put down the book, pressing the mantis inside as before. Now the shape of that enormous story in his head seemed a little vague, as if everything in it were becoming tangled together. Yet there was a borderland, extending to the sky above the North Pole, with masses of frozen clouds. Was the story he'd just been reading a story of Country F? Or a Nepalese story? Joe hadn't gone over the details in the book's introduction. He always started right in on the first page of a book, and then slowly entered into its web. Often the story's background was one he developed for himself. Or perhaps it was all in his imagination. Invariably, as he reached the middle of the book, he began to suspect that the sentences were jumping from his head onto the page. Otherwise, why was it that when he assumed the story was set in Mongolia, the hunters wearing short gowns in the beginning section all began wearing long robes?

Vincent and Lisa vanished without a trace, all the way up to the end of the workday. Joe figured they must have gone someplace in the city, the two of them calling out unceasingly but extremely distant from each other. If they were to meet, they would have to cross a river. But the sky was already dark; the water was very deep; there were no boats on its banks. Joe walked to the bar on the corner. He looked inside and saw Reagan drinking alone at a table. Hadn't he gone back home earlier? Joe stood riveted in place, staring. Reagan chased one glass with another, as if he were drinking water. There were some papers spread out on the table that might be the contract they had signed in the morning. He remembered what Reagan had said at the time, "The reenactment of tragedy is sometimes necessary." Afterward, he'd affixed his signature to the agreement. Now he had spread the contract out on the table in the bar to look it over, but what was he after? Was he still thinking of those two workers drowned at the farm? His jacket had a dark stain on it. Probably he'd vomited. Even then the barkeeper didn't make him leave. Maybe he needed customers; the place was really desolate. He stood behind the counter, obviously watching every movement of this drunkard, so as to intervene at any moment. Joe didn't want to go in because in their relationship Reagan always took the role of the leader. When Joe thought of that scorching, glittering farmland, he grew dizzy, feeling himself inferior. Reagan lived there year in and year out, but he still ran to the gloomy city every so often. On the surface he came to do business and sign contracts, but who knew what he really came for? Every time he proclaimed that he was going back that same day. Could it be that every time was like today, when he didn't go back but came instead to this low kind of place to soak himself in liquor? Reagan raised his blood-red eyes and stared in Joe's direction. Joe knew Reagan hadn't discovered him standing outside the window; he was terribly drunk.

"Do you remember Reagan, the farmer from the rubber tree plantation in the south?" he asked Maria.

"Yes, he's a real man."

Maria was putting a finished piece of tapestry into her chest. Joe realized that she had been selling fewer pieces. She seemed to be storing up tapestries. And she couldn't afford to spend money as freely as before. Joe couldn't help feeling sorry for her because she was giving up a few of her favorite extravagances.

"The sun must have fried that man's brains," Joe said.

"Nonsense. He's a born thief, I can tell. He doesn't have any brains."

Maria locked the small trunk and drew out the key. Joe saw electric sparks, this time breaking out from the key. Maria made a sign to Joe, then turned and went out to the garden. He followed her closely.

A small table was set among the rosebushes, and a large pot of tea was set on the table.

Maria drank a sip of tea and said, "Did you know that from here Daniel and I can see everything in your study clearly?"

Joe was surprised and craned his neck in that direction, but he couldn't see anything except a dark red brick wall and the creamy white balcony.

"Spectators have the clearest view of what goes on." Maria smiled.

The Maria who lived in that house with its own garden wasn't content with her middle-class existence, so she had developed a fascination with mystical experiments. Joe realized that she was conducting these experiments almost every minute of the day, and he also realized that they intimidated him. This was probably why he had hidden himself in his stories in the first place. There was another thing that bothered Joe, which was that after she started the experiments — with the tapestries, the roses, the cats all becoming her props — Maria grew extremely independent. Now even if Joe were to leave her and live elsewhere, she probably wouldn't care much. Her relationship with Daniel was comparatively close. Joe believed that information often passed between them even though they were rarely together. Take the roses: to those two they acted as a magnetic field, but they had no such effect on Joe. The day when Maria sat there with Daniel and Joe had stuck his head out from the study, listening to their voices floating in midair, he was simply amazed. But today, as Joe listened to Maria, there was something masking her voice. Her body wrapped in a blue checkered skirt looked fake. He listened to himself speaking, and his voice was rebuffed, blocked by a metal plate that left behind a *ca ca* screeching. Maria extended a hand and held Joe tight when she saw he was trembling.

"Joe, how many years has this been going on?" She squinted her slightly narrow eyes, with an expression of one doing her utmost to remember something.

Joe mused that the answer she was seeking lay in his unfinished story. Maria held some event deep in her heart, such that every few years, no matter what decade it was, she would ask this same question. Perhaps that event hadn't even taken place at a given time. All the periods of time she referred to were only periods that she differentiated for herself.

"I don't know. I want my voice to carry, but it just makes a din around my ears." Joe forced a smile. He was still trembling. He couldn't remember his story.

Not long after they ate dinner, Maria disappeared into her room. Joe noticed that she'd even turned out the lamps. Joe knew she wasn't asleep: she had a habit of mulling over her secrets in the dark. He had once compared her way of thinking to a tuberose coming into full bloom. Joe sat in his study and continued reading the third page of his book, gently fiddling with the mantis in his hand. The sentences snuck past his eyes until he felt he was being separated from the story. Joe too shut off the lights and sat in the lonesome dark thinking of Reagan's rubber tree plantation. He had a sudden intuition that Reagan still hadn't left. The bar was already closed, so where would the drunk have gone?

Joe emerged onto the street. He didn't find Reagan, but he did run into the black woman he saw every morning.

"Sir, are you looking for someone?" the woman stopped walking to ask, furrowing her eyebrows as she spoke.

"Yes. He's not from around here, and he's drunk."

"Go look in the underground crosswalk. He's there crying."

The woman walked away.

But the underpass was empty. It looked like Reagan had already left. The underground crosswalk was very gloomy at night; it brought out thoughts of homicide. It must have been an extreme compulsion from his heart that drove Reagan to pass from the magnificent sky of the south to this kind of place. When Maria said he was "a real man," this was what she meant. Joe recalled Reagan's appearance when he'd come to the office in years past, when Joe had thought of him as an optimist.

Coming out of the walkway, Joe took a few deep breaths in the damp night air. He felt he could go back to the story he'd just abandoned.

2

MR. REAGAN

On the plantation of rubber trees in the south, under the scorching summer sun, Reagan realized that little by little he was losing his mind. Reagan was an orphan. In his youth he'd gone into the tobacco business with his uncle, earned a bit of money, and bought this farm. He hadn't been able to finish school, so his knowledge was earned through tenacious self-study. Still, without formal teaching this autodidact had become an educated man, a stern but commonsensical farm owner. He enjoyed physical labor and at times went out himself to tap rubber, gather lotuses, and the like. Although women tended to indulge him, he was already fifty and still alone in the world. Reagan felt that his body was encased in a hard kind of shell, and that his motions toward socializing could not break through because the shell had grown along with his body. He suspected that his heart, too, had grown a hard shell.

Ida was an Asian woman, brown-skinned with wavy black hair. She was also an orphan, fled from an island nation in Southeast Asia to seek refuge with an aunt she'd never met before. Afterward she'd settled down on Reagan's farm. At first Reagan hadn't found her beautiful. She looked a bit like an orangutan, and her arms were far too long. Even so, Ida was an unusually conscientious worker. She had a good hand for technical tasks, and the farm tools she used became one with her body. In his heart Reagan quickly developed a fatherly sort of affection for her, always thinking to take care of this "orangutan." But Ida was reluctant to accept his care. She hadn't the slightest fear of her employer, and at moments she even mocked him.

All Reagan could do was angrily set aside his kind intentions and observe her from a distance.

About the time of Ida's second year on the farm, her aunt, her only relative, passed away. In Reagan's estimation the aunt was an unfeeling woman. She had never, not even once, visited Ida on the farm. According to Ida her aunt was wealthy and had three sons. So to avoid the sons' "misunderstanding" her, Ida hadn't visited the aunt either. Ida requested two days' leave to go to her aunt's home and help make arrangements for the funeral. It was late at night on the third day when she finally returned to the farm. Reagan was at the lakeside fishing. He heard a call for help from the opposite shore—someone had fallen into the water. He threw down his fishing rod and ran across to the other side. It took him five minutes to reach the scene.

It was Ida, but she hadn't fallen into the water at all. Instead she'd taken a lap around the lake and come back out. By the time Reagan reached her, she had already changed her clothes and was wringing the water from her hair. Under the dim moonlight she looked up at him a few times, flashing the large whites of her eyes, as if to reproach him.

"Is everything with your aunt taken care of?" He struggled for a long time before bursting out with this question.

"She suffered. You can't even imagine the pain. I can't imagine it either. So I went into the lake to try to experience it. But I couldn't feel as much pain as she did. Isn't that right?"

She hastily finished these few words with the opposite of her usual arrogance. She stood there with no suggestion of leaving, reaching up and grabbing at the air with her hands as if she were catching a butterfly.

"Ida, your aunt is gone."

"No. For everyone who dies, there is always someone else who remembers that person in his heart. Isn't that the same as still living?"

"Ida is very clever."

"Some people think they know everything."

Reagan felt his face burning. He couldn't get used to this girl's way of speaking. Could it be that he was too educated? Or was he making overtures to her in an evasive way? What odd ideas filled the head of the little orangutan who'd run away from the rainforest?

Because she stood there saying nothing, Reagan had no excuse to keep standing around. So he took his leave, telling her that he would go back to his fishing. At this, Ida grinned bitterly and turned her back on him.

On the way back, Reagan saw the rubber trees' appearance altered by the moonlight. The short trees were like row on row of dwarves, the ground under the trees was very smooth, with no shadows. Along the border of the rubber tree plantation were a few coconut palms. Their tops reached high up into the clouds, and as long as Reagan looked up at them the ground under his feet refused to stay firm. He thought he was like those chaotic shadows, without substance, while Ida was like the rubber trees, solid and firmly set on the earth, distinct but unable to lay bare the riddle inside her.

That time he'd gone to take care of business in the city, Reagan never thought he'd come across Ida in a pub. At the bar her appearance was entirely different, attractive and full of a tropical flavor, like a lemon. The desire hidden in Reagan's heart was suddenly brought out by her.

"Ida, what are you doing here?"

"Can't you see? I'm serving customers, to help out a friend. Today is my day off."

She passed among the tables, her long arms nimbly transporting glasses and dishes. The customers all craned their necks to admire her dancelike movements. Reagan sat by awkwardly. It felt as if there'd been an earthquake in his heart.

Reagan left the bar without ordering a drink. He turned into a long, dark street, and thought back to the sales manager at the clothing company. He was a highly self-assured man, whose heart hid unfathomable depths behind his bright, shining, pale green eyes. Each time Reagan sat in the man's office he became his quarry. Suddenly, Reagan found his way blocked by a young black woman with long curved eyebrows and large eyes revolving in their sockets. She calmly stood facing him, obstructing his way along the narrow sidewalk. Reagan's face reddened, and he almost turned to walk away.

"Stay there!" she said, her voice sharp and clear. "I've met plenty of people like you before."

"And what of it?"

Reagan looked at her curiously, but she merely flashed the whites of her eyes resentfully toward him.

"Southern men like you are all alike, running desperately into dark corners. I wouldn't even think of doing business with people like you. I have a job. I'm the cleaner for this street. During the day I keep watch to see if there's any business I can do. But I don't need southerners like you here. Go to hell!"

She stamped her foot, then abandoned him, disappearing into a florist's shop. The fine and delicate curves of her receding figure appeared vexed.

Reagan looked at the potted flowers. Before his eyes the image blurred: were these real flowers or paper? And then all at once he was shocked to see three pairs of eyes staring at him from inside the darkened room. His heart leapt crazily as he took a step back and walked away. He didn't care to linger in the city.

Exhausted in mind and body, Reagan stepped onto the train and took a seat in a corner of the back row, where no one else was sitting. He held up a newspaper to cover the bewildered expression on his face. There was someone in front of him laughing loudly. The voice sounded familiar.

"And he snuck away just like that?"

"I'm not worried about it. This place is so small, he'll turn up again within a few days."

"He's a crafty bastard."

It was a man and a woman over at the window on the left side who were talking. They were kissing openly and probably doing even more outrageous things. They seemed unconcerned about the racket they were making.

Hidden behind his newspaper, Reagan felt his whole body turn hot and dry. He looked toward his rigid reflection in the windowpane, staring at it. It looked like a dead man's face, especially about the right nostril, as if the corner of the mouth were already drooping. It was terrifying. He did not want to look, but he couldn't bear not to. The expression of the man in the glass was extremely eager. It also looked like he was suffering.

"You're convinced he's hiding around here?" the man said.

"There are clear signs," the woman answered, as if desperately holding back a laugh.

As the train was going through a mountain tunnel, Reagan felt someone gently stroking his face. He reached out in the dark to touch this person, but there was nothing for his hand to touch. Moreover, the touch of the person's hand on his face wasn't much like a hand, but rather like some kind of soft thing, maybe fur? The hand as soft as fur suddenly covered his nostrils. Reagan was suffocating. He let out a shout. He heard the young woman up front say: "This man can't be one of the crowd. It's possible he came from an ancient village."

The mountain tunnel was left behind. Reagan looked toward the window to discover his face covered in specks of blood; he looked at the floor, and saw a few white plumes. Could that have been a bird just now? He'd plainly felt it to be a person and had heard a man's heavy breathing.

When Reagan got back to the farm, he ran into a thunderstorm. His car passed through a thick curtain of rain, then stopped in front of the small gray building where the cook, Ali, was coming out to welcome him.

"You're back. A lightning strike just burned out the electricity. I thought I'd passed over into hell. How could this have happened?"

She was behaving oddly, not coming over to help carry his things. Then, twisting her obese frame, she disappeared inside the building. She must have been badly shaken. Reagan was surprised, too: how could this have happened? Wasn't there a lightning rod plainly standing on his rooftop?

As he headed upstairs, Reagan's head felt heavy and his feet light. He felt as if he were swimming along the ocean floor.

That night all kinds of crazed voices shouted in the blackness of the rainstorm. Reagan heard someone discussing how high the water would rise.

In the morning the garden was filled with bright sunlight, but Reagan didn't wake from his deep sleep.

Ali stood in the doorway, flustered and busied with something. The driver was washing the car.

"Our employer hasn't gotten up? This is unusual," the driver said with a smile.

Ali looked at the young fellow sternly, but didn't respond.

Upstairs, Reagan's dreams sank to a depth they had never reached before. Deep, deep underneath the black soil, innumerable frenzied tree roots tangled together, making him abandon any idea of keeping his mind clear. He thought naively that he needed only to dig out a passageway, like an earthworm, and he'd be bound to get his head out eventually. With his skull pushed against the dirt, his mouth stuffed with mud, little by little he started to move. All around him there were things whispering, *cha cha cha*. Perhaps it was the lascivious tree roots. Between root and root were crevices, and even though these were frequently blocked up, in the end he could pass through. Reagan decided to take a rest on one of the roughest root tops. He placed his mud-stuffed ear against it and heard the sap inside thundering like rolling floodwater and shaking the root incessantly. He remembered Ida: her nimble body and these tree roots were so alike! But he found he was having trouble breathing. He wasn't suited to this dreamscape.

"If Mr. Reagan doesn't wake up from this long sleep, we'll both be free!" The driver shouted, paying no heed to Ali's manner. "Last night when he and I returned home, it was like crossing over the precipice of death!"

Ali ignored the troublesome young man and went back into the kitchen in disgust. From the wide-open door she looked off into the distance and watched the workers laboring under the sun. They wore work clothes and straw hats, and wrapped up their bodies tightly. Ali noticed the young girl who'd arrived two years earlier, Ida. Her face was already blackened by the sun. Ali was aware of Reagan's intentions toward Ida. She was like an old crocodile in the river, with a perfect and clear knowledge of everything that happened on this farm. Ali's manner toward her employer was conflicted: she defended him but wasn't satisfied with him. Sometimes her displeasure reached such a pitch that she had almost no choice but to abandon him altogether. This past year, in the season when the coconuts were ripening, a woman visited Reagan's house; she was none too young and oddly dressed. Reagan and this woman, who was clothed entirely in black, like a shadow, were inseparable. They kept close together for a week, then she suddenly disappeared. Reagan had seized his moment in the middle of the night when no one was around to see her off. Ali heard the sound of a car. It was Reagan himself driving. After the black-clad woman left, Reagan's mood improved. He developed a fascination with nighttime fishing, sometimes fishing the whole night through and only coming home in the morning. Ali suspected that the black-clad woman wouldn't be returning. She also suspected that Ida was her boss's secret concern, because she was the only nonnative on the whole farm, so the boss couldn't anticipate her every movement and action. This was how she'd finally touched his heart. Why did he go fishing? Wasn't it because the girl liked to wander around at night? When she couldn't sleep Ali often went for walks, and she'd already run into Ida several times. Sometimes Ida was with a companion, and other times it was Ida alone. Each time Ida greeted her absentmindedly, calling her "Mother." She walked quite slowly, shuffling. She appeared to be looking along the path for some object while muttering softly to herself. If her friend was along, she would help Ida search. At times the night was so black that only animals could possibly see anything. Yet Ida could still see. Oddly enough, her eyes gave off a green fluorescence. Ali had seen it twice, and she'd been so surprised that her mouth had hung wide open. She'd hidden this knowledge in her heart and never shared it with Reagan.

"What are you searching for out here?" Ali stood in the road, blocking the way.

"I'm looking for the diamond ring I lost during the day, Mother."

"Does Ida have a diamond ring?"

"Yes, I remember it clearly. I'm sure it slid off my finger."

Ali was sure that the girl was scenting at some odor, that her sense of smell, like a hound's, guided her along a trail in the dark of night. Ali thought of her own youthful period of wandering about like a homeless ghost. She couldn't help a small chuckle. She sighed: "Time moves along."

Ida's movements were as quick as a snake's. She ducked into the bushes and disappeared unexpectedly. Her companion stood in the middle of the road calling softly, "Ida! Ida!" Her voice was mournful.

In the room upstairs Reagan still lay in a deep sleep. The curtains were closed tightly, leaving the bedroom in a never-ending night.

Lying on her bed in the singles' lodging, Ida spat out indistinct words to her friend: "In my hometown, a cloudburst shattered hundreds of the mudbrick houses . . . all the leaves of the Chinese banana trees were beaten flat by the rain. That wasn't rain . . . it was like, it was like a flood rushing down from the sky. No one could hide from it. Don't you understand?"

"I think I understand. How did you escape?" her friend asked.

"Me? At first I didn't want to live, so instead I couldn't die. We had to withstand this test every year . . . I couldn't stay there my whole life. I will go home someday. And I'm afraid that the sun here will dissolve me."

As her friend answered, she discovered that Ida was already asleep and dreaming. The fragrance of coconuts rushed intermittently into the bedroom from the window. She saw that Ida's expression in her sleep was one of disgust.

"Mr. Reagan has been asleep for two days," the driver said. "Do we need to call a doctor?"

"Don't talk nonsense. He had me bring him meals twice. It's just that he doesn't feel like waking up. Everyone has the right to do that." Ali was deep in thought as she spoke.

Ali had met Vincent on the road into the city. She saw him walking, a solitary figure that the sun had burned to a stupor. He appeared to have heatstroke. He'd walk a few steps and then stop, gasping for air.

"Sir, do you need help?"

"My name is Vincent, I'm a friend of your employer. Please, tell me, how is he doing?"

He seemed unable to decide whether to keep on going. His gaze wavered. Ali thought he must be looking for a place to sit down.

"Mr. Reagan isn't ill."

"Of course he isn't. How could he be ill? He decides things for himself."

"Should I go back and send the car to get you? You look tired."

"No, no, no. Look, the sun will set behind the mountains soon. I'll just sit off to the side for a bit, under the Chinese banana tree. I'd like to see the evening in this place. A long time ago I heard that the sky here is green at night. I think this must be true. Ah, the sun's going behind the mountain, thank heaven."

After Ali left, the sun set behind the mountain. Vincent closed his eyes and meditated quietly in the shadow of the banana trees. He had come here chasing a woman from a dream. She had taken a red flower—he couldn't say what it was called—from her head, and placed it under his nose so he could smell it. Then she told him it was "plucked from the farthest south, a place called the Cape." When he woke Vincent pondered for a while before determining that the black-clad woman in his dream came from his client Reagan's farm. Out of curiosity he had once looked on a map to find the location of the farm. In the city, Vincent and the woman were "transported" by an overwhelming night together in a shabby hotel. Lying on a simple, crude bed, half-awake, she had brought him to climax again and again. The strange thing was that the woman was just a figure. There was no body belonging to her. When Vincent eagerly embraced her, as he entered her from underneath, she began to move, but her body itself had no weight to it. The climax she finally brought Vincent to was vigorous but extremely barren. Each time it was like this. It almost drove Vincent mad, because this strange kind of climax failed to bring him release: his desire could not subside and instead surged higher. For an entire night he existed on the terrace of climax. The Eastern woman was silent, tractable, and tantalizing. Vincent realized that the woman, whose age was impossible to fix with much certainty, held the dominating position in these sexual activities. At daybreak he lay on the bed, exhausted and worn out, as the woman quietly shut the door and left. Afterward Lisa saw him lying in front of their house behaving in a revolting manner. He'd never been able to decide whether he'd actually been in a shabby hotel and had a sexual experience that left his bones weak. The woman had come looking for him several times since, dressed in black, her face indistinct. Vincent had grasped her hand, but there was nothing for him to hold but empty air. Besides, she came secretly and left secretly, and never spent another "transporting" night with him. So Vincent suspected that even the one time hadn't been real. Now tomorrow would be his sixtieth birthday. Vincent was inwardly startled by the desire in his body: this was the first time in many years that he knew it as a lurking beast.

The sky gradually darkened, and the wind carried a touch of coolness. Vincent heard the sound of voices. It was two girls walking along the path. One was local, and the other was a brown-skinned Southeast Asian, with a delicate frame and very long arms. And behind the Southeast Asian girl, a woman dressed in black followed closely. Vincent was struck to the heart. But it appeared that the two girls hadn't detected the woman behind them. They were bent over at the waist, searching for something on the ground.

Vincent stood and greeted them. The girls replied with ambiguous sounds, too absorbed in their own activity to notice him much. Just as they were exchanging this question and answer, the black-clad woman disappeared like a shadow. Vincent stretched his arms out toward the place where she'd been standing, but there was nothing for his arms to enclose.

When Vincent entered Reagan's house, Reagan had already come downstairs, alert and refreshed. They greeted each other in the living room. As the two men embraced Vincent noticed his old friend's vigor. As a matter of fact, Vincent had met this old friend only twice before, ten years ago on a bench in a park. He didn't know how it happened that the two strangers greeted each other without any reason to do so. They had discussed the deep blackish-green lake in front of them. The second day they both went back to the park, continuing their conversation. And after that they hadn't met again. Vincent knew about it when Reagan signed a contract with his company and later became a regular client. Nonetheless, he had never since tried to meet him face to face, or even mentioned to Joe that he knew Reagan. Over the many years, this old friend became a shadow in his memory. At least until the black-clad woman from his dream offered him a scent of Reagan's farm, and the past events suddenly revived.

At Reagan's home Vincent ate a meal and showered, then sat on the roomy sofa and chatted for a while. Reagan spoke of a poisonous species of striped snake, even taking out a picture to show him and warning him to take extra care when walking outside. Vincent didn't notice the snake in the thick growth of grass — he saw only the image of the black-clad woman next to the snake. At the sight of her back his heart throbbed with terror and he almost let the photograph drop to the floor.

"She's someone you know. I've heard her speak of you." Reagan glanced at him attentively.

Vincent withdrew his gaze in discomfort and stared instead at the gray-papered walls, at a loss.

On the roomy bed in the guest room Vincent rolled back and forth, unable to sleep. Although the room had an air conditioner and remained cool, his heart churned alongside the waves of heat in the dark beyond the room. It was a long night of surging desire, somewhat like that amorous encounter in the shabby hotel. But there was no one else there.

Reagan had said, "She's already gone." What did that mean? That she'd died, or that she'd gone away? His tone of voice hadn't been sorrowful. Perhaps *gone* with respect to her was a commonplace. Perhaps she was always coming and going from these tropical regions, and only occasionally stopped over in the city where he lived? He'd tried to guess her nationality. At times he thought she was Arab, at times he thought she was Indian, but there was no way to settle this. Yet at this present moment he realized that for her nationality was entirely meaningless. Before he'd gone to sleep, the woman who'd made the bed for him, Ali, told him that his wife, Lisa, had already come to the farm during the day. Now he fancied that Lisa's body was everywhere, but there was still no way to expend his desire. Was it more like Lisa or that woman to come and go like a ghost?

After the old clock struck one, Vincent noticed the bedroom wall receding. He remembered that he was on the ground floor. It was possible that he was already sleeping among the rubber trees. He made up his mind: if the striped snakes crawled into the bed, he would play a sex game with them. That would thoroughly change his disposition. He opened his legs to welcome those lascivious small objects; he almost let out a groan.

"Does our guest need anything?" Ali's aged voice rang out from beyond the door.

Vincent heard her turn on the light in the hallway. She must have stayed outside his door. He wondered what whim had sent him rushing off to spend the night in this place. Was it merely because of the woman in his dream? He wasn't the sort of man to have affairs. The Arab woman had broken into his life by chance. Originally he'd thought he would be bound to forget about it afterward, but he was unable to.

He got out of bed, opened the door, and saw Ali sitting on a chair in the corridor.

"You're not sleeping, Mother?"

"Me? I keep watch at night, to stop all of you from running all over the place. Who understands things here? Maybe not even Mr. Reagan."

"What have you seen?"

"On a scorching night like this, any strange thing can happen. Your wife is a passionate woman."

"Did she leave right away?"

"I don't know. Maybe she went into the rubber tree groves. She's not afraid of the heat."

"I feel a little cold, in fact."

In fact he was shivering.

"What should I do, Mother?"

"You came here, didn't you? Just don't be afraid, and everything will be all right. Try to be like Lisa."

Vincent wanted to speak to Ali but she stood up, tottering, and said her employer was calling her from upstairs. Oddly enough, it was quiet on all sides and there was nothing to hear, yet she heard her employer's summons. It would seem that Ali had the hearing of an animal.

He returned to his room and lay down again. He was still in an overstimulated state from waiting for those snakes to come out. He didn't know when exactly it was, as he lay half-awake, half-asleep, that he heard someone arguing outside the window. Among the voices was Reagan's. He sounded irritated and dispirited. Vincent heard him say repeatedly, in a voice that was almost crying, "It will kill someone." Without knowing how, Vincent realized that Reagan was talking to a woman.

But when he got up, Ali told him that Reagan was still asleep. Vincent told her he'd heard Reagan talking in the night. Ali nodded several times: "Yes, he doesn't know his own limits. He's always wandering all over the place."

"Why did he say someone would die?" Vincent asked, uncomprehending.

"It's a premonition he's always had. Don't you realize that this farm sprang up out of his heart? Everything here is the opposite of what it should be."

Vincent realized only that her words made him feel strange. He finished eating the breakfast Ali had prepared for him and walked to the stairs leading to the house. Lowering his head, he suspected his eyes of playing tricks on him. In the thick grass close by the marble stairs, six or seven striped snakes were hiding. One look and he knew they were those poisonous little snakes.

"Reagan's pets." Ali spoke from behind him.

Vincent's legs buckled and he sat down on the steps. His gaze couldn't leave the snakes, and a bizarre desire rose up inside him. The sound of Reagan's voice in the night echoed in his ears: "It will kill someone." After a little while the snakes concealed themselves in the grass. Vincent knew they hadn't gone far. Couldn't anything happen here on this tropical farm? Concealed behind Mr. Reagan's stern outer appearance was a frightening landscape like this one. He hadn't expected it. Originally he'd thought he was tracking down the Arab woman, but now he had entered Reagan's demon-possessed realm. He'd often heard people speak of intersecting dreamworlds. At his own company Joe was involved in this shady kind of business and he was making experiments through reading.

The sun was beating down on the roof of the jeep when Vincent left, and he dozed off in the back seat. Drowsily he saw himself passing naked through a dark region where every single thing lost its form as his vision suddenly worsened.

At the same time, fat Ali and Reagan stood together on the stairs of the building. Each held a short stick with which they conducted the striped snakes in a dance on the grass. Ali was wearing a brightly colored, tropical-pattern robe and Reagan was wearing black, a suit for mourning.

"He left, damn him." Ali set down her stick then sat on the stairs gasping for breath.

"He and I are like twin brothers." Reagan wrinkled his brow as he spoke.

"Are you thinking of leaving?"

"Naturally. Although I made every brick and tile in this place."

Ali stood up with great effort and returned to the kitchen. After a while the smell of meat pies floated out. Reagan's appetite suddenly revived. He felt his whole body trembling.

3

WHAT HAPPENED ON THE RUBBER TREE PLANTATION

In the rubber tree forest Lisa saw the black-clad Arab woman. She saw a tall, black image drifting among the trees like a spurned woman, but none of the workers noticed her. Perhaps they didn't even see her. An idea sprang to Lisa's mind: "Vincent is done for."

The primitive power of the rubber tree plantation left Lisa fearful, and she lost all certainty about herself. She made up her mind to return home at once. On the road back she came across olive-skinned Ida. Ida had been bitten by a poisonous snake and was groaning, holding a calf that was swelling gradually. The girl's face grew red, as if she were about to faint. Lisa reached out a hand to prop her up, but was warded off. The strength in Ida's hands was extraordinary. She almost pushed Lisa down to the hot muddy ground. She managed to struggle to her feet and then walked off, limping at every other step. Lisa felt deeply that her action had violated some principle of this place. What principle? She stared after the girl's solitary receding figure, and failed to think of what that principle, after all, might be.

From a distance she saw Vincent walking toward a jeep on the road. Vincent's elderly bearing caught her by surprise. She almost called out to him. But the jeep started up, and in a moment it had disappeared in a burst of hot air. The events of last night were similarly strange, even unbelievable, and besides she remembered only a few fragmentary, incomplete interludes. Those events seemed to have something to do with Vincent, but then again they also seemed to have nothing to do with him and were instead merely her personal secrets. The sky was quickly growing dark as her driver, Booker, rushed over from the banana groves, wanting to take her to a nearby restaurant. He said the restaurants and hotels around here closed up early, so they shouldn't lose time. By the time they'd reached the thatch-roofed rural family restaurant, sure enough, it had already closed. Booker pounded on the door until a middle-aged woman, her eyes heavy with sleep, slowly opened it. She had to be told three times before she understood what Booker was asking and finally brought them into the hall. Lisa had just sat down when she felt something bite her ankle. After a while, she grew faint. In the dim lamplight she seemed to see Booker flirting with the middle-aged woman. Later on the two of them put a few small plates of food in front of her. She ate a large amount, but couldn't say what she was eating. She thought it might be leg of mutton or something like that. She drank a few glasses of the local wine, a kind of sweet liquor. Booker and the woman didn't eat. They merely stared at her without moving their eyes until she felt layer on layer of suspicion in her heart. She thought to look in her handbag for her purse, but her purse wasn't there. She lowered her head to look under the dining table and saw a snake coiled around its leg. At this she screamed in fear. Booker and the woman kept on talking as if nothing had happened and then asked her, more or less without interest, if she wanted to go outside to enjoy the night view. She grumbled out a few sentences about how she'd been bitten by a snake, but mechanically stood up and stepped outside. She even forgot to bring her handbag, but the woman followed and gave it to her. Booker was definitely fooling around with that woman. Just now they'd looked too eager to wait any longer. The banana grove was as painfully hot as before. The mosquitoes made surprise raids under her long skirt. She walked on for a while and then thought it was no good. She worried that the mosquitoes would suck all the blood out of her body. Fortuitously, at this moment she raised her head and saw what had long been in her dreams: the green sky. Even the moonlight and Milky Way were green. She wondered whether the snake's venom inside her was causing her vision to change. Then she heard someone calling her pet name from when she was a young girl. It was a woman whose voice seemed to be coming down from the tops of the tall coconut trees. Afterward she discovered that she had lost the road, and for the entire night she walked and then stopped, stopped and then walked. She made a circle around the lake, passing a low small hill; she circled the coconut groves for a long time; finally, she returned to the rubber tree forest. Although her head was heavy, she didn't feel the least bit tired. She was woken by the workers who tapped rubber. She opened her eyes, and the first thing she saw was the black-clad woman's skirt. Her cotton skirt seemed to have just swept past Lisa's face. As she leaned on a rubber tree to pull herself up, her head cleared. But the woman walked too fast, and in a moment she was at the edge of the forest.

Lisa stood as before, distracted. She watched a red light filling the sky and something awoke in her heart. "Vincent, that old fox." It was with a slight smile that she spoke to herself. This immediately led her to the thought: "Vincent is done for. He's happy to be done for. I can enjoy my life." She passed through the rubber trees and walked to the shore of the lake, where she stripped herself bare. She admired her own not-too-old nakedness before springing into the water. The water was extremely buoyant, and for a while it was as though the little waves were pushing her body to the surface. She was excited to the point of madness, so she started to swim with a butterfly stroke, which is the method of swimming that expends the most strength. When she was young she had often swum like this. She burst from the water and flapped ahead, quickly fluttering to the center of the lake. She turned back to look at the shore, where she saw three workers standing beside the lake smoking. The place where they stood was precisely where the pile of her brightly colored clothing lay. But evidently, these men didn't care about her nakedness, since they weren't turned toward her to look.

As she was swimming back, she felt little uneasy. Would these men confront her?

When she reached the shore she raised a loud racket. This surprised the three men, and they turned their heads toward her. Lisa provokingly set her hands on her waist and turned her body up toward the sun. But they didn't approach her—they merely made *ze ze* tongue-clicking sounds of admiration. Lisa shot a glance at them, discovering that the three men were all handsome young fellows. Even through the coarse cloth of their work clothes she could see the rising and falling of their muscles, like bodybuilders'. Standing for a moment, Lisa found this hard to bear, and she bent to gather up her clothes. By the time she'd put them on, the three men had already walked a distance away. Lisa felt this must be the greatest humiliation of her whole life. She also felt deeply aggrieved to think that perhaps she was old. Hadn't they been admiring her?

Lisa couldn't find an answer to this question. The reason she stayed on at the farm was in order to find out the answer. She burned with desire, walking back and forth under the sun like a beast. This was when she ran into Ida. She wanted to draw nearer to the girl, but Ida pushed her away.

Ali stood on the stairs looking outside. Between yesterday and today, she'd already seen Lisa pass in and out of that patch of banana trees three times. It was her driver who told Ali who she was. This woman with fire-red hair appeared to be in dire straits. Her brightly colored clothing was already covered in dust, and her face was filthy.

"She's staying behind, and her husband's left," Reagan said dryly.

"The fire in their hearts must be painful for both of them, to leave all their work at home and rush off to this kind of place chasing their dreams," Ali replied.

"They didn't just rush here on a sudden whim, of course."

Ali looked back over her shoulder, but Reagan had already gone inside. He was tinkering with his fishing gear. Ali saw sparks flickering in the depths of his icy eyes, and from this she knew in her heart that he was already awoken. A fifty-year-old man must have all sorts of desires, and Reagan always perfected his schemes in the lethargy of sleep.

"Are you going fishing?"

"Yes. Last night I fished for the entire night. I sat on the windowsill and stretched my fishing rod out from there. Working high above the ground is really frightening."

"Being suspended in the air always is. But how is the problem of transport resolved?"

"I don't bother with that anymore. Let things start getting out of order. In the beginning wasn't the farm in chaos?"

Reagan stood and hung his red fishing rod on a hook high up on the wall. Ali wondered why he would have painted his rod red. Perhaps he intended to frighten away the fish. Ali's sight was a little dim; she saw the fishing rod on the wall turn into a dripping skein of blood. She left in a worried fluster. As she entered the living room she saw the driver, Martin, just leaving Reagan's bedroom, with Reagan's hunting clothes draped over his body. He was always stealing Reagan's clothes to wear. This had become an open secret.

Martin ran with a thumping *dong dong dong* down the stairs, warding off Ali's obstructing arm, and rushed outside. Ali heard a dog bark ferociously. Maybe it had taken Martin for a thief or a murderer. Ali couldn't comprehend this habit of Martin's. She'd seen him wearing Reagan's black coat and trousers to a lawn picnic, where he stood around unsociably. Not only did he lack Reagan's grave demeanor, he'd even lost his own customary clever liveliness. At the picnic he looked like a marionette swaying back and forth, cracking lewd jokes and making himself distasteful to every person there. Did he think that by wearing Reagan's clothing he'd changed into a different Reagan?

One time he unexpectedly said, "Mr. Reagan's intentions are obscene."

"You work for him. How can you talk nonsense like this about your employer's character?"

Ali said this with her mouth, although in her heart she hoped he would furnish a bit more information. But Martin stopped speaking. He wrinkled his brow seriously, and put on the appearance of thinking over some problem.

When Ali warned Reagan that someone was taking his clothes, Reagan said he'd known for a long time.

"Actually, I want to watch how other people play my role. Otherwise I have no means with which to arrange my life. Mr. Vincent is quite capable of arranging his life: look at the remarkable performance of his wife!"

Reagan made a few trips to the lake in succession, each time sitting there for the whole night. A forest keeper always came by at two in the morning, before dawn, to chat. In the past this forest keeper had not been a forest keeper. He was the region's "wild man," who lived by the lake in a thatched hut he'd built himself. At that time there had been no farm. His hair was white as snow, and when he spoke it was indistinctly, through missing teeth. Once he sat down he'd say a few world-weary things, speaking of how he'd already had enough of living. Also, strangely, at the *weng weng* droning of his speech, small fish would come up to the hook, usually enough to fill a whole bucket. Reagan's gaze crossed his red fishing rod and fell on the opposite side of the lake, on those jet-black clumps of reeds, but Ida didn't emerge even once. She'd gone into hiding.

"Before, around here, if you wanted something you could have it. The girls, they were all mixed up with the sika deer and you couldn't tell them apart. They ran down from the side of that mountain in one big pack after another. Was it even girls or was it deer who carried on the war of the century with me in that shack?"

Reagan sensed that this old man had already seen through him. He hoped he would keep speaking, that he would bring up Ida, but he persisted in only speaking of the past century's business.

Ida stepped on the body of the small snake intentionally; last week she had also been bitten once. Previously she had witnessed with her own eyes the death of a youth, not a local one, from a snakebite. What fear she'd been in then! Little by little she discovered that the farm people weren't afraid of the snakes. Her next door neighbor Mina had a series of scars on her calves and arms but didn't take a day of rest because of them. After a snakebite, there was a burst of red, a burst of swelling, and after that nothing at all.

Once she had left the dirty woman who was wearing a long, gaudy skirt, the soreness in her ankle lightened. As she passed through the banana groves, the forest keeper called out a greeting from his small wood hut. Ida was familiar with this old man, and she followed him inside.

She sat on a wooden stool, stretching out her right leg for him to see. He applied a few damp tea leaves to the wounded spot for her.

"Ida is already coming to terms with the snakes, little by little," he said, lisping. "Here is your homeland. Right? You and that, that whoever, Mr. Reagan, you get together somewhere every night. I've seen everything. That one time, you wore black clothes to squeeze into his house, and fooled around with him there for a week. After that . . . What am I talking about? Yes, you two are people who come from the same place."

Ida was astonished at the old man's acute memory. She couldn't think of anything to say to refute him. Perhaps what he'd said had actually happened, who knew? It was the way of this forest keeper to not differentiate between things. It astounded Ida, while also enchanting her. Before she'd lived here very long she'd gotten to know the forest keeper. He told her he had seen her before, that she and the deer had lived together and often come to his shed. Each time, he spoke of Mr. Reagan as her lover. At first Ida found this this strange, but because the old man's way of speaking about it was so particular, she was unknowingly drawn in. He often spoke of how Reagan had changed everything. Reagan had deprived him of his birthplace by force. He hated him. These snakes that bit but didn't kill people, these rubber trees without even shadows were wholly unfamiliar. Yet Reagan swam back and forth, like a fish in water. "You are different," he turned to say to Ida. "You and that man are the same sort of goods. You come from the same place and your homeland is connected to this place here. Everywhere waterwheels are turning. I tell you, after Reagan came, the lake had no wild ducks anymore."

Ida could never figure out whether the old man really hated the changes to his environment. He used an enchanting intonation to describe things of the past, but what Ida heard was rather praising the present. He repeatedly said that this farm was Reagan's farm, but Ida firmly set in her mind that he was the thick black shadow behind Reagan. When Reagan left his house, Ida saw numerous shadows dragging behind him. These shadows made his face as white as a dead man's. Ida felt it was only at these moments that Reagan could finally draw her in.

The tea leaves applied to her leg only irritated the wound. Ida felt throes of pain. She reached out her hand to wipe the leaves off, but the old man blocked it.

"This effect is what's wanted, you stupid girl. Think of the old toads in the swamp, think of them and you'll be fine."

Ida, in the midst of her pain, felt a sexual desire leap up inside her body. It was like that feeling just after being bitten by the snake. With her face reddening she strained to her feet and struggled to walk outside.

"That's right, girl, but don't fall down," the old man said from behind her.

That night, she tested the lake's depth once more. She was an expert diver, and without expending much effort she reached the center. After that she floated up to the surface of the water, and repeated this a few times. In the green sky there were all sorts of shouting sounds. She heard them all, and she knew that the person fishing on the shore heard them also. If not, why did he press down the reeds so that they kept making noise? Next, she heard her aunt speaking to her from underneath the water. In the past this aunt had often told people as a joke that Ida was too clever, she could calculate the moment of her own death. "A person of barely twenty who calculates the moment of her death—isn't this abnormal? I won't think of leaving Ida an inheritance. That would be the same as murdering her." When her aunt had said this, Ida's two older cousins were at her side, covering the smiles on their faces. Ida reached a hand down into the water and thought that she touched her aunt's hard, prickly hair. Her heart was pained by love and pity.

"You really reached the bottom of the lake?" After a long while Reagan finally asked her, stammering.

The sudden sex caught him unprepared and afterward he couldn't find the heap of clothing he'd tossed beside the lake. Fortunately his eyesight wasn't as good as Ida's: he couldn't see anything clearly. In his head an unsuitable metaphor relentlessly appeared: "war between man and snake." Sometimes he thought he was a snake, sometimes he thought his partner was a snake. At the beginning of their lovemaking Ida's body swiftly disappeared. The snakes' *si si* hissing was everywhere. Reagan hung struggling on a plateau of continuous climax. From start to finish he couldn't find release. He recalled a sentence he seemed to have said: "Ida, you're too frightening." Afterward he was gasping for air. However, what he might, perhaps, have said was: "Ida, you're too beautiful."

Ida ran away on bare feet, carrying her shoes in her hand.

Reagan groped around on the ground for a long time before finally finding his clothes.

He faced the mirror in his bedroom. Inside the mirror was a blurring mist, and no matter how much he wiped it he couldn't get it clean. He had no way to see his own face. Last night, his clothes had been wet through and full of mud, and Ali said he'd turned into a clay statue. But he didn't think to change his clothes. His whole body burned like a flame as he paced, like a lunatic, back and forth across the bedroom. Ali kept on from outside, indomitably knocking at the door.

"Help find me a mirror." He opened the door slightly, exposing half his face.

Ali returned shortly, and from outside the room she held aloft a round, antiquated mirror, which decades ago had been part of her dowry. Reagan looked into it, but the depths of the indistinct mirror were empty. After that Ali hid the mirror behind her back. "You've no need to look at this," she said. "All things are hidden under this bit of land. Once it's nighttime there are things that come out, and sometimes at noon, when the sun is right overhead, they also come out."

Ali's cumbersome body swayed like an old duck as she left. Reagan heard her going downstairs. At the same time he heard the sound of the desire inside his body ebbing, like unnumbered bubbles bursting in the water all at once. The first things to appear in the mirror were his two green eyes, before his entire aged face gradually emerged. Only in the deep recesses was there still a faintly discernable fog. "Ida, Ida . . ." Reagan's voice was at a crying pitch. Beyond the windows it was cloudless for miles. The burning rays of fierce sunlight opened cracks in the earth, while the workers wearing straw hats hid in twos and threes among the banana trees. There was a moment when he thought he'd discovered Ida. She was among those workers. He thought of going out, under the scorching sun, but his body trembled so fiercely he couldn't stand up straight. He could not leave the house. "I've come to this," he thought. "Why don't I return to dreams?"

And like this he wore his filthy clothes, and fell asleep rolled up on the floor.

"Mr. Reagan took great pains in building up this farm, for more than twenty years?" asked Martin, feigning experience.

Ali looked at him disdainfully, as she heard right away the implication behind his words.

"Everything here is prospering. I'd think he could retire. Sleeping all day like this, not taking notice of anything, is about the same as retirement. He's too hard on himself."

"What if he gave his place to you?" Ali asked in return.

"Me? Sorry, I'm not interested. This business drives you to death. I haven't been bitten by a snake, not even once, and I don't want to be. Look at that window—isn't that our boss standing there? Sometimes he doesn't sleep at all, he's surveying things instead. He's been aging quickly, and soon he'll have white hair."

"Mr. Reagan is in love."

"God, that's frightening. I thought the farm was getting out of order."

"Lately I've been worried about a fire. I stuck the fire department's phone number on the wall."

Martin went over to the well, pulled up a bucket of water, and splashed it head-first over himself so his whole body was left dripping. Yesterday he'd been loafing around outside wearing Reagan's hunting gear when the outer jacket suddenly hooped around his neck so he couldn't breathe. When he'd opened the buttons and thrown it to the ground, the feeling of suffocation grew even worse. He'd run, tumbling headlong into the lake. Immediately—the water hadn't even reached his neck—his suffocation was alleviated. Water had had this capacity before. Just now when he'd been speaking with Lisa, he'd broken out gasping again, and cold water had come to his aid. How could this be happening? He'd never had asthma before. Martin had worked for Reagan for five years, and he'd long since grown accustomed to his employer's eccentricities. He formulated a principle: meet the frightening without fear, the strange without wonder. He believed that he shouldn't approach his employer in the same way he approached most people. So without the least care he did a few things out of the ordinary, including stealing the clothes and so on. When his conduct met with Ali's rebuke, he was even a little pleased because it meant he wasn't going unnoticed. But there was the asthma. Martin remembered something. Once, on the way back from a long drive, when they reached the farm Reagan said that he wanted to get out of the car to look around. So Martin stopped the car under the trees, and leaned against a tree trunk to nap. Suddenly, a pair of strong hands stretched out from the tree trunk and locked around his throat. His eyes flipped to white and his legs kicked blindly. He thought his day of judgment had come. He could see nothing. Without knowing how long he struggled, he heard the sound of Reagan's voice by his ear. He opened his eyes. Nothing had happened at all. He was sitting in perfectly good shape under an old poplar tree. "You're having bad dreams again," Reagan said as he got into the car, glancing at him insidiously. When Martin started the car, he smelled his employer's body giving off an unexpected, intense, thick odor of anesthetic, a smell strong enough to make him dizzy. On the road, still confused, he reflected that Mr. Reagan was the kind of man to firmly control his domain. His domain was his farm, and every matter here was decided by him.

In the past Martin had also thought of changing himself into someone like Ali. That way he could get used to being on the farm.

But it was no good: his natural instincts were too crooked, so he was constantly punished. He knew that he was violating the customs of this place. It brought him happiness; still more the dread of death. Who could figure it out? It was impossible to say on what day the sorcery of Reagan's farm would call for his life: think of those disgusting little snakes. Sometimes driving the car at night he'd crushed more than twenty to death all at once! After crushing the snakes, he always hallucinated, seeing the windshield crawling so full of them that he couldn't make out the road signs. When he'd first come to the farm to take this job, Reagan had asked him whether he was allergic to pollen. He still remembered Reagan somberly staring at him as he asked this. At that time he took Reagan to be a bachelor with an obstructed heart, a man with a cheerless disposition. But events quickly proved him mistaken. His employer's capabilities left Martin's eyes wide and his mouth gaping. Although he couldn't exactly say what kind of capabilities these were, nevertheless he always felt himself firmly drawn in, then afterward exploited. Martin wondered if he was harming himself by his own rash, rebellious nature. Otherwise, why was he always uneasy?

"Look at him, it's like he's stuck to the window," Martin warned Ali.

Ali took the woven stuff in her hands and placed it on the bench in the arbor, stood up, and furiously criticized him:

"What nonsense are you talking about? Look, isn't Mr. Reagan eating downstairs?"

Martin blinked. Mr. Reagan really was sitting right in the dining room. Through the glass door Martin saw two snakes crawling onto his back, although Reagan stretched and seemed quite pleased. Martin was about to enter the room, but was shouted back by Ali.

"Stay there! You'd better stand there, don't move. What can you see, child? You can only see things that are already obsolete. Go change those wet clothes, you stink."

Martin didn't go to change his clothes. He went outside. Beside the old poplar tree where he'd leaned on the trunk to rest, he ran into Ida.

"Ida, are you looking for my boss?" He brazenly moved closer.

"I am looking for my diamond ring."

"You have a diamond ring?"

"I don't remember. If I find it then I have one."

Ida used a sharp knife to poke a hole in the tree. Wood scraps scattered in all directions. Martin hadn't realized the girl's arms were so strong and he quickly backed away.

"Ida, that day when I fell asleep against the tree trunk, was it you who clutched my neck?" Martin shouted at her.

But Ida appeared not to have heard. After a short while she'd bored out a hole as big as a shot glass. Martin saw the tree branches violently shaking and the leaves rustled with a *sha sha* sound.

"Ida, Ida! Stop that!"

He didn't know why he needed to call out.

"If you don't stop, I'll go get Mr. Reagan!"

Ida seemed to tremble. She disdainfully threw the knife to the ground and stood with both hands on her waist, looking at Martin. Then she squeezed out one word from between the cracks in her teeth: "Out!"

Martin took to his heels in fright, because he saw a poisonous striped snake on Ida's shoulder.

He ran a long way, with Ida's voice following him. It sounded like a stream of lascivious teasing, mingled with a few filthy words. Martin found her voice difficult to understand. He ran and ran again, his damp clothing sticking to his body. He became a drowning dog.

"Your diamond ring is inside the snake's stomach, I'm sure of it."

Ida's friend made this statement to Ida while asleep, but tightly holding her hand as if she were wide awake. Ida knew it was dream-talk. She gently withdrew her hand and slid across to the screened window to look outside. The afternoon sun was at its most poisonous. Flies and mosquitoes surged in a frenzied chorus. Out on the road, an army of snakes braved the scorching sun and headed toward the apartment building. A few had already entered the main gate. Ida thought to herself that a large group of the snakes must be inside the building already. She certainly couldn't go back to her own room now, because once she opened the door she would be besieged from all sides. The others must be taking afternoon naps. At this time of day, everything on the farm fell into a lethargic sleep, except the snakes.

Ida only indistinctly remembered that night with Reagan and the scene of the chaotic snake dance. The recollection of sex was almost horrible because it wasn't clear if it was persons or snakes, with the soil underneath her body becoming quite hot, swelling and undulating . . . Afterward it seemed that she had slunk away first, because desire is a valley that is impossible to fill, or that, in other words, she gave rein in order to capture. She heard Reagan murmuring a sentence from underneath her: "An orangutan in heat." After he said this, his skull suddenly dissolved; the body without a head shook with a convulsion. This man was everywhere but also had no substance. Ida felt the wide mouth of her womb already incredibly frenzied . . .

She wasn't willing to renew these old dreams: she knew old dreams couldn't fulfill her. From the moment the mountain torrent engulfed her small house she'd known this, so she had no way to make sense of what happened that night. Only if she built up a new dreamscape again, like the poisonous snakes doing tricks and striking attack poses outside the door. The first day she arrived on the farm, as she unfolded her young body under its tallest coconut palm, she saw those flickering snakes among the clumps of grass, and her intuition told her: this is your homeland and also your burial ground. At the time she still didn't know who dominated this land, but she thought it would all make itself clear. Ali asked her, "How were you able to escape that place? It's hard to imagine." At first Ida hadn't consciously observed Reagan, with his insidious green eyes. She thought of him as a depressing old bachelor. Until the time she discovered him fishing by the lakeside, when the evening mist mottled the image of his unmoving back, when she suddenly comprehended: in fact, all of this belonged to that somber fellow. This was the reason for that charade in the pub. Reagan erred in thinking their meeting there was by chance. It was directed with deep and considered care. Watching the man in flight, Ida knew her plot had already succeeded. Even so, the nearness of her target did not bring her the joy of victory. Those unsleeping nights, those lascivious voices deep in the earth, and the violent imprecations coming from the lake at times almost drove Ida to complete collapse. She'd dreamt of that business with the diamond ring, and after the dream she started searching for it outside. She had found many small jewels, sometimes in the gutters, sometimes beside the coconut shells people had thrown out, sometimes among the gladiolus petals, and sometimes inlaid into the scars on the tree trunks. The sky lightened, and placing them in the sunlight to look them over Ida made out that these were manmade jewels. Who was patiently going around in circles to toy with her? Regardless, Ida couldn't shake off the seduction of discovering rare things. Besides, perhaps these jewels changed into real diamonds at night. On this farm, nothing was too strange.

Reagan really was in the dining room, but at the same time he was upstairs in the bedroom. He was with the black-clad Middle Eastern woman (here she is Middle Eastern) standing in front of the window and observing the movements in the thick grass below. As the woman walked about, her clothing made a *sha sha* rustle, like the falling of a rain shower. They didn't speak. For Reagan, it was because he could hear all along the woman's unceasing speech. He heard all of it, but didn't understand what he heard.

As Reagan sat down to a meal at the table, he saw them. They'd heard a summoning call and slipped into the dining room, five of them altogether. One was especially impudent, and went so far as to latch onto Reagan's throat. The black grain on its body matched the pattern on that woman's skirt. No wonder that when the woman summoned the snake, it came. The egg in Reagan's mouth proved hard to swallow because the snake had locked on tight. Heavy footsteps upstairs could be heard downstairs. Someone seemed to be taking off into the air. Reagan stood up from the table, then tumbled down. As he tumbled with a muffled *peng*, the snake wound around his neck released him, and it flew toward the foot of the wall. In a moment it disappeared.

The sound of irregular footsteps came down the stairwell.

"Mr. Reagan fell down." Martin craned his neck to see inside the dining room.

"Don't worry about him." Ali spoke one word at a time.

She was watching the shadow of the black-clad woman in the distance, and she lowered her head as if lost in thought.

"Do you recognize this woman?"

"Why should I recognize her? She isn't from the farm."

The two of them watched the snakes gnawing at each other in the thick grass. Martin murmured, "A mess, a mess." What he thought to himself was, "How can Ali let her employer lie there on the ground? She's cold-blooded. She could be a poisoner."

That was when Ali and Martin heard, at the same moment, a voice calling for help. They learned only afterward that two female workers drowned in the bay. One died right away. The thick heavy waterlogged work clothes cost her her life. There was a froth of blood in the nostrils of the dead woman.

Lying on the floor of the dining room, Reagan heard the news of the worker's death in his dream. He stood in a dark, gloomy attic. Someone entered to report this event to him. He heard the man with a head like a mushroom say that the dead one was Ida, the girl from an island in Southeast Asia. At this Reagan heard thunder outside, then rain struck the leaves of the Chinese banana trees. He wondered: On this farm where there were no high mountains, could there be a sudden, torrential mountain flood? The mushroom-headed man went downstairs. Oddly, though, Reagan didn't hear the sound of footsteps. There were a few old books in the attic. Reagan casually caught up a small volume with a colorful cover and opened it to its first page, which was printed with an engraving of the owner of the attic—a small portrait of the proprietor. The man's deep-set gray eyes revealed a deep world-weariness, and his arms were covered with long, thick hair like an animal's. The owner of the attic had signed an agreement with Reagan so he could stay on Reagan's farm and build a house there. Reagan remembered that this deal was also struck in a dream. At the time he'd had a vague notion that this man's building might become his own refuge, and for this reason he agreed to allow him to build a small house on the low hill next to the bay.

When Reagan woke up, Ali had already tidied up the dining room. Reagan asked her about this business with Ida. Ali raised her eyebrows in astonishment, saying, "Ida just came by to borrow a sickle from me."

"Did someone from the farm fall into the water?"

"The message was a mistake. Rumors are flying everywhere these days."

The image of Ida carrying a sickle in her hand floated into Reagan's brain, and his heart palpitated nervously.

"Ali, have I signed a sort of agreement with someone, I mean, an agreement to let a man build a house on the farm? I'm concerned about this."

"Yes, you have. Do you regret it?"

"Oh, not at all. Doesn't this kind of life need a force from outside to break through it?"

He glanced toward the window, and saw outside that the sun was still shining brightly. There were several hawks wheeling in the sky. Was it because they'd discovered a corpse? For the first time in his life, he felt that his farm was too large. To oversee it from every angle would be simply impossible. A few years ago he'd bought the bordering farm, connecting it with his own rubber tree plantation to form a single piece of land. It was originally a farm for many kinds of industrial crops, and as soon as he bought it he'd regretted it. From then on, he hadn't gone once to inspect it. He had handed the entire place over to a manager for supervision. He felt he was already aging. He couldn't manage as many things. Why did he go on buying land? It seemed as though this decision to purchase would be his lifelong riddle. The hawks flew over from that farm, so they must have heard, too, the news of their new master. Before this they had never flown into his airspace. He knew that at the same time he expanded his territory a kind of expansion was progressing underground. It wasn't something people knew about. He could sense this expansion that couldn't be seen; however, it was hard to describe. When he went to the city on business, the feeling of expansion became incredibly intense. On its dark and narrow streets, he walked into a different world. For example, that African woman, the street cleaner, belonged to a different world. Reagan at any rate was unable to understand her kinds of desire and her disdain for him.

"What did Ida borrow a sickle for?"

"She said it was to cut grass. She's always doing strange things." Ali sighed.

"Why is Ali sighing?"

"When I think of this child running away from a place like that, it just seems unbelievable. Can you imagine the sight of a rushing mountain flood?"

"I can't. In a dream I was saying, Fall, fall, let loose the mountain torrents. But here there are only low hills. How could there be a mountain flood? You'd have to ask Ida."

"Ida forgot about it, a long time ago. There's no way of remembering an event like that."

Lisa flew past along the asphalt road. The skirt she wore was already so dirty you couldn't make out the color. Reagan thought she was running without a goal. Heavy clouds floated on Ali's face as she silently walked into the kitchen, thinking of the woman's grievous story.

The two of them heard, at the same moment, the sound of steps upstairs, although there was no one upstairs. They looked with care and listened with care, one standing on the stairs, one standing in the kitchen. It didn't sound like a person's footsteps. It sounded more like a large bird, perhaps a hawk. Reagan wondered if it could be the smell of a corpse spreading from upstairs. Someone flew down the steps. This was a person. It was Martin.

"Martin!"

"What is it, Mr. Reagan?" He blushed, hiding the large bag in his hands behind his back.

"You aren't afraid of hawks?"

"Of course I'm afraid." He laughed, "But there's nowhere to hide. It drops like a guillotine, cutting your body. Your body and your head are separated instantly. You don't have time to reflect on it." With this last sentence he raised his voice, as if making a joke.

It was Reagan's turn to blush. On the open expanses of the flatlands, he had been pursued by hawks before. He thought once again of Ida borrowing the sickle. That dark, dusky night, a muffled thunderclap under the earth had shaken his mind into a black pitch. He said to himself: "Climax is an inferno. Because the delight of not reaching release is in the elimination of the body."

"Good, good." Martin smiled again, seeming to see into Reagan's thoughts.

Lisa fled swiftly from the scorching sun. Her feet were blistered with walking, but still she couldn't stop. Everywhere, underneath the soil of the farm, there were people conversing, all kinds of people, all kinds of voices. She thought it wouldn't take even a few days before she grew used to these voices under the ground. At night she sometimes slept underneath the rubber trees, and at other times at the lakeside. The snakes had stopped encroaching on her and stayed far away. Even so she distinctly heard the sound of their slinking in one group after another as they dove to the earth's core. She thought of Vincent. What was Vincent? He was her dream, the dream she hadn't woken from for many years. And Vincent also lived inside of a dream. She remembered him saying to her that he was going to the farm he'd seen in his dream. Because of the dream he came here, and then he left. But she, following the landscape of his dream, remained lost inside that landscape. Now she was so strong Vincent wouldn't even recognize her. Just before dawn, she carried on a conversation with Ida.

The two women did not speak about their own homelands. They talked rather of the great deserts in Africa and life in tents in the desert. The two of them cherished an unusually strong aspiration toward a way of life they'd never experienced. Ida wielded a large sickle in her hands, moving back and forth across the clumps of reed. Lisa asked her what she was cutting.

"Whatever's there I'm cutting. At least, I want to cut down a few things."

Lisa lowered her head and saw that her own shoe was almost chopped in two.

"Before much time passes you won't need these shoes," Ida said, unconcerned.

Her words amazed Lisa. She sat there lost in thought, and didn't notice that the girl had left.

In the distance there was a car driving toward her, like a blue-shelled insect. Against the golden ground it was utterly conspicuous. Lisa grew a little nervous, without any reason to be. She stood still since there was no way to walk with that shoe. The car gradually came to a stop beside her. The driver Booker's straw hat extended from the window. This wasn't her car, her car was a milky yellow color. But she got in anyway.

"Where did our car go?"

"This is our car," Booker said.

"How come it's this color then?"

"You're going color-blind. It happens to everyone who stays here for a long time."

"You've been here before?" She was surprised.

"Yes. This is practically my homeland. Is it like that for you? They all say the farm owner went mad ten years ago."

Lisa recalled the cheerless gentleman in the sales office and couldn't help a bitter smile.

When the car drove past the entrance to Reagan's house, Booker stretched his head out the window. His face showed his confusion. As if absorbed by his thoughts, he whistled. Lisa saw Reagan walking out of the building. His figure was cut in two at the waist and in the middle was a section of blank space. In his hands he carried fishing tackle.

"We all turn toward this place, because the soil here can catch fire," Booker said.

"How do you know?" Lisa asked curiously.

"Yesterday I tested it. The golden earth is just like coal. Miraculous earth!"

He suddenly looked heavy with drowsiness. Lisa worried that he might overturn the car in a ditch.

The car accelerated. It was like a bullet running madly along the burning soil, yet Booker, uncaring, bent snoring over the steering wheel. Lisa's body sweated like rainfall. She realized the car was no longer on the road, which could be felt from the bumping of the wheels. She shoved Booker. Booker kept sleeping. She looked at the speedometer and found that the needle was broken. "Will we plunge into the gulf?" Her mind oozed this thought. She couldn't make out the landscape outside for the sea of fire that filled her eyes. The car was unbearably hot inside.

"Booker! Booker!" She screamed until her voice was exhausted.

Booker moved a bit, and murmured, "Don't get so excited, this will be over soon . . ."

Lisa thought he was trying to kill himself. In desperation she tried jumping from the car, but the door wouldn't open.

As she flailed frantically, the car came to a stop with a thud, *dong*. Booker still hadn't woken up. All at once she could open the door. A burst of hot air blew in from the still-fierce sun. Their car had stopped in a patch of peach trees that were all on fire; the light from the flames lit up the sky. Lisa promptly hid herself in the car.

"Every so often they catch fire," Booker said, with an expression of remorse. "We'll leave the farm soon. Everyone is saying that a worker died. She must have jumped into the lake because her body caught on fire."

On the road home Lisa fell asleep. She had many dreams, but the backdrop of her dreams was too dark, and nothing could be seen clearly. When she woke Booker told her she had been calling for a girl named Ida. He asked her who this girl was. The name sounded familiar. She told him it was Reagan's girlfriend. On hearing this Booker was struck with wonder and couldn't close his mouth for smiling. "Everyone knows that man has no substance. Just ask anyone on the farm and you'll learn." Lisa wondered dispassionately what it must be like to have no substance. Booker seemed to hear the words in her heart, and went on to say, "With no substance, he can pass through a sea of flames."

Lisa sighed. "What kind of woman is Ida?"

She and Booker returned home, but Vincent wasn't there. The rooms retained the look they'd had when she left. There was no apparent sign that anyone had come through. Lisa thought that Vincent might have already disappeared from their house and become a man without a home. Although he wasn't there, Lisa could still smell his odor, a smell she hadn't perceived before, which hinted of anesthetic. Shrouded in this smell, she and her husband were closer at a distance. Perhaps Vincent was staying in the slum district, in the underground tunnel shaped like a well that slanted as it extended into the depths of the earth, with a few lit candles along the way.

Lisa entered a dream. In the dream she had no need to go looking for Vincent because, like a hound following its quarry, he pursued her. Where Vincent was were also beggars, beggars eying Lisa greedily and menacingly, but they didn't want anything from her. Lisa strove in desperation to enter the small crisscrossing and interlocking alleyways. She was conducting a battle of wits with Vincent. But Vincent met each changing situation with one response. He oozed out from underground like a rising mushroom cloud; the cloud dispersed, and he stood surrounded by a crowd of beggars. Halfway through Lisa woke and saw the palm tree–patterned curtains shaking, intermittently rolling like the high tide, before she tumbled back into the dimly lit midst of unreality.

"Vincent! Vincent! Aren't you lonely?" She strained to shout, but had no voice.

She remembered that a vacuum doesn't transmit sound. She almost despaired.

But from a distance Vincent raised his eyebrows at her and made an ambiguous gesture. The beggars turned toward her with loud lewd laughter. Lisa suspected that she wasn't clothed. She couldn't confirm this, because she couldn't see her own body. She remembered that episode of nakedness on the farm, although the feeling then had been entirely different. Why must Vincent be among those beggars? When he approached, Lisa saw that he, like the beggars, wore a lewd expression. She couldn't keep her face from reddening. Vincent stopped in his steps. It appeared he didn't wish to approach her too closely. What was he thinking? Vincent, the owner of that immense and orderly clothing business, had unexpectedly hid himself in dark causeways, associating with beggars! Lisa thought with apprehension of the recent torrent of order forms . . .

Outside the window there were water birds calling. Their house was in the center of the city, so where had the birds come from?

"Ma'am, those aren't birds. It's me mimicking them outside your window."

Booker, his whole face filled with a smile, sat opposite her. He had obviously recovered from the fatigue of the previous day. His appearance was a little eccentric: a large specimen of a spider was stuck to his forehead.

"A gift from the farm. Night and day I am inside a spider's web now. I managed to catch it at the door of a restaurant; once I caught it, it died. My lover and I made it into a specimen together. Its gigantic web is just like mosquito netting!"

Vincent was in fact working at the company's head office, just as before. After returning from the farm, he described his mental outlook as being "as calm as water." The Chinese woman (here she is Chinese) came to his office once. She wasn't wearing a satin qipao, but was dressed like a worker who cleaned the streets, with a pen stuck in the pocket of her jacket. On entering she rounded the desk with practiced movements and sat on Vincent's knee. She drew the pen from her pocket and wrote characters on the desktop. The characters she drew were like square rooms, stably nailed to the paper; each single one was correspondingly independent. As Vincent leaned in to look, he saw there was nothing on the paper. Vincent felt the woman's body to be unusually light. When she twisted around to stare at him, he saw square rooms in her black eyes.

His desire was aroused again by this peculiar woman, but he sat there without moving. He thought if he moved even just a bit the woman would disappear. He thought of how this was another form of being "as calm as water." The crows on the rooftop across the street made a sudden, slight sound. The woman stood with a start, and walked outside, and Vincent went with her. Later they went to her home. Vincent believed it was her home—if not, then what place could it be? It was a dark room on the twenty-fourth floor. In the corner was a gigantic spider weaving a web. He reflected that the gray spider looked familiar. Vincent and the woman lay down on the double bed, but their bodies did not touch.

Afterward, he went daily to the twenty-fourth floor after getting off work, forgetting that he should return home. During the day his job was very busy. The company was expanding daily. Inside the factory the machines roared, and outside the factory there was heavy traffic. Vincent hadn't intended to expand the business. The circumstances of its development were beyond his control. He saw that his enterprise was spreading in all directions, like the background of the stories Joe had divulged to him. These days when he saw Joe in his office, Vincent felt perplexed: how did his business come to have an employee like Joe? All along he'd referred to Joe in his heart as "a two-faced man." On Reagan's farm, when in the midst of unreality his passion caused him unbearable suffering, he had thought more than once of Joe, as well as of those books hidden in his office. Perhaps it wasn't by chance that Joe had taken a job in his company? But he did not remember that event from twenty years ago too clearly. The sole impression he retained was that at the time Joe didn't like to speak. When he opened his mouth he grew very anxious.

The Chinese woman had never spoken before. Vincent surmised that she used a different system of language. The door to her room was always unlatched, so he pushed it open and went in. At times she sat next to the bed, at times she sat before the window, and when she sat by the window, Vincent stood behind her and saw numerous square-shaped characters in the sky outside. The pieces of the characters kept shifting, seemingly very busy. The woman was evenly proportioned and of average height, and, as before with the black-clad woman, he couldn't determine her age. Vincent saw her as his lover, but he wasn't eager to touch her body. He thought, for no reason, that if he touched her he would drop into a depthless void. Although he saw her sitting in the old twenty-four-story high-rise every day, he still couldn't refrain from suspicion: was she from Reagan's farm in the south? Although the geographical location of Reagan's farm was in the West, the landscape had a concentrated flavor of the East; therefore, he could go there to pursue the Eastern woman from his dream. She looked so lonely, with a mind clear of desires, just like a dream. Perhaps she truly was a different woman's (for example, the Arab woman's) dream? Vincent thought that many such women must be hidden within this overcast city. Hadn't he already known quite a few of them? Some of these women stayed for a while in shabby hotels, some rambled around in remote side streets, and some, like this Chinese woman, had a room in some tall high-rise . . . Vincent was a little distracted in his mind, a little dizzy in his head. He came to a stop leaning his hand for support on a large cabinet. He saw the woman showing her teeth as she smiled at him. Her teeth were slightly yellow, as if from smoking, although there was no smell of cigarettes in the room. The woman made a sign for him to sit by the bed.

As soon as he sat down, the woman came over and embraced him, sitting on his knee. Vincent was immediately excited. As their naked bodies stuck together, he heard the sound of flowing waves inside her body. Then he was lost in the incessant up-and-down motions of deep water. This one time, Vincent's bodily desire was finally released. This kind of release wasn't gained through reaching climax, but rather was in a change of direction halfway through. As for Vincent, in this sexual encounter he lost all his perception. Before, with Lisa, he used to imagine himself as a tropical animal, like a zebra, and through that kind of fantasy he grew thousands of times more amorous. But with this woman it was a different matter. He abandoned fantasies about himself, following her into a drifting world of water. Together they entered dark ravines and made love there. A voice was always in his ear: "Is this the sea or is this a lake? Is this the sea or a lake? . . ." He thought it ought to be the woman speaking, but she'd shut her lips and eyes tightly in the deep, swaying water, and was not inclined to speak at all. Vincent's fervor ran high as he felt himself using his mind to make love. He tried his utmost to recover his amorousness, but he was defeated. The undulation of the water favored their sexual rhythm. The manifestation of his flesh and blood became unimportant. There was a brief time when Mr. Reagan's rhythmic groans could be heard from some distant place. Once Vincent heard them he understood the implication of the groans. Could it be that this was the lake on the farm? The Chinese woman's body was agile as she constantly varied her position. Vincent's own body, in these peculiar movements, also became young. Yet there was no climax of flesh. He suddenly understood one thing: the reason there was no obvious climax was in order to avoid the listlessness following climax.

He didn't want to leave the bed. He reached out a hand and kneaded the woman's breast with his fingers. But at once he felt a sliding under his hand and the woman disappeared. On the empty large bed it was only himself left over.

He left the tall building still endlessly agitated and unable to reflect. But his desire wasn't entirely for sex. What was the impulse then?

When Vincent raised his head, he saw crows. What startled him was that the crows' bodies were soaking wet. They lined up in a long row on the banister of the balcony, combing their feathers with their beaks. Was it possible they had also just swum in the waterways of love? A woman wearing a white skirt appeared on the balcony, and the birds, *hu*, with a caw, all flew away. The woman leant her head down and saw Vincent. She made a face at him and, turning her back, dampened a few potted flowers on the balcony with her watering can. Evidently, she didn't notice the drenched crows. The woman's face was ruddy and filled with the freshness of morning; Vincent noticed her chest was shapely, the sort that sets men off on flights of fantasy. But Vincent's flight of fantasy was about another woman, with a foreign kind of sex appeal that couldn't be seen from outward appearance. Only on reaching the water did it finally take on a different look. Using Vincent's poor words to describe it: "Lascivious and ethereal. Greedy as a valley that can never be filled; but pure of heart, with few desires . . ." He suddenly thought of Reagan in the south, thought of him in the water, emitting painful but longing groans. Was the blazing sun of the south mending the wound in his soul? What kind of injury was it?

When he reached the office, Reagan was already sitting in the reception room. His appearance was greatly altered, his thin haggard face covered in sunspots. An injured eye twitched incessantly.

"Mr. Reagan, your eye . . ." Vincent looked at his friend anxiously.

"A souvenir left by my pets," Reagan answered.

He stood before the gigantic window of the round office. His formerly tall figure seemed suddenly to have shriveled. His leather shoes were covered in dust.

"I'm not here because of business."

"Of course not." Vincent spoke with understanding, watching him with still eyes.

"The whole farm is catching on fire. I think I've lost control of it."

"This morning I saw wet crows . . ." Vincent irresolutely mentioned.

"Of course, I saw them, too!" Reagan grew agitated. "A thick mass of crows, like a black cloud, dove from midair down into the lake. It was a collective suicide, a truly magnificent sight. But they didn't really die, did they?"

Vincent thought to himself that people and animals who harbored astonishing ideas were not able to die so easily.

Reagan abruptly invited Vincent to go with him to a bar. Vincent hesitated, because he never went to such places. But then he felt ashamed of his hesitation.

When the two of them sat down on the bar's high stools, some young people in the room were quarreling. Reagan glanced sharply at Vincent with his dropsied eye. It was as if Vincent's cheek had been bitten by a snake. He let out a shout of pain.

But Reagan didn't drink. Vincent finished two beers while the level of Reagan's brandy didn't move. Vincent wondered what he'd come here for, since he was not drinking. He watched the hairy backs of Reagan's hands traveling back and forth along the tabletop, trembling awfully as if from anxiety. Suddenly he must have thought of something, because he got up and walked away without looking back. Vincent promptly paid the check and went out. When he drew abreast of him, Reagan asked, "Do you know the cleaner for this street? A beautiful black woman."

"Joyner? You're looking for her?"

"No, not looking for her, only asking some questions about her homeland. You are close by, haven't you ever seen her in a dream?"

"Why would I see her in a dream?" Vincent asked curiously.

"Because . . . because so many memories are written on her face that no one can succeed in escaping her. Sooner or later you'll have to deal with her. Look, could she be hiding in this flower shop?"

The two walked in unison into the darkened shop. They heard a burst of confused sound behind the shop and then it was motionless and quiet.

"Something terrifying happened here, in this room!" Reagan spoke in a low, panicked voice.

Vincent wasn't nervous. He was thinking of his Chinese woman. Could she have some implied relationship to this "beautiful black woman," like intertwining vines? They didn't live far apart, so it was quite possible the women knew each other. People on this street all knew warm, eccentric Joyner. Vincent's company often ordered flowers from her. But Reagan continued sniffing back and forth in the air, his whole body shivering with fear.

Vincent could smell only the fragrance of the potted flowers. In the dark he couldn't even see what kind of flowers they were. Reagan passed the flowerpots and walked to the rear of the room. By the time Vincent made up his mind to follow him, Reagan had already disappeared. Behind the room was a small, narrow courtyard with a staircase leading up to the building. Vincent stood in the courtyard, lit a cigarette, inhaled, and fell into heavy thought.

There was no doubt that he had been to this place before. It was yesterday. Those steep and narrow steps led to a balcony above. He'd stood on a diving board on the balcony's edge, closed his eyes, and jumped down, reaching the deep water. It was just then that he discovered he could breathe like a fish. How had he forgotten all this? The "entrance" was actually here, and Reagan had known this for a long while. It was possible that his Chinese women also went into the world of water through this entrance. He thought again of Lisa; he thought of the Arab woman; he thought it possible they had all come to this place. Joyner's greenhouse was the genuine entrance to the world. And the beautiful black woman was the gatekeeper to this world. On this small side street, Vincent had once seen her eagerly seize a customer's jacket. The two had almost come to blows.

Vincent, in the midst of his confused fantasy, heard the sound of footsteps on the staircase—not just one person, but the sound of many footsteps. The footfalls came closer and closer, but only one person came down.

"Who came down with you? Those women?"

"Them? There's no one there, they're only a few shadows," Reagan said despondently.

"What is upstairs?"

"Upstairs? Everything is upstairs. But I can't remember. Tell me, what is this place?"

He grew agitated and left the flower shop without turning back to look. Following him, Vincent heard a loud upheaval in the dark behind him. The flowerpots tipped over one after the other. Vincent couldn't stand to look back. All of a sudden he saw a row of wet crows settling on the broad windowsill of the flower shop. A black hand stretched out from within, unhurriedly setting down birdseed. "So the crows flew off from here!" Vincent exclaimed. His spine ran cold.

"Hui Mingxia!" Joyner's clear, sharp voice flew out from the window. The name she called was Chinese.

Vincent kept a tight watch on the window. He believed Joyner was calling to his Chinese woman. But no one answered.

Reagan walked on at a distance. Vincent ran urgently to catch up with him.

"I'm going to the train station and returning to the south." Reagan's voice had a derisive overtone.

"Well, I'll see you off."

"You should pay more attention to people like Joyner. You are so close to each other. She and I are very close, too. Every time I come to the city I discover this."

At the train station Reagan stepped onto the northbound train. He'd said to Vincent beforehand, "I always get onto a train at random. And, randomly, whatever train it is reaches home."

On the road back to the office, Vincent reminded himself by saying: "Hui Mingxia, Hui Mingxia . . ." In front of the office building he saw Joe and asked him where he was going. Joe said he was going to meet his client Reagan, who was on the train to arrive in the city at three in the afternoon.

"People from places like that enjoy making sudden attacks." Joe looked troubled.

Vincent saw that Joe was putting a thick book into his briefcase.

4

KIM'S PASTURE

The scale of the Rose Clothing Company's business grew larger and larger. Joe's customers were increasing, and these were all large-scale transactions. This left almost no time now for reading, and his business trips grew more frequent.

Once he went to a large pastureland in the north, where the owner's house sat halfway up a mountain. Although it was the height of summer, when night came to the mountain it turned cold. Even wrapped up inside the thick pajamas his host had given him, Joe still felt a little cold. The owner, Mr. Kim, was a Korean. In his youth he had emigrated with his parents.

"I own ten thousand sheep, and cows and deer, too," Kim said. "I don't bother about the business side of the farm. I live like a retired king on this mountain. When I heard you were coming, I knew my opportunity had come. Now, let's empty our cups together. This is good liquor, and tonight it might make you realize your desires."

Outside the sky was already dark. Joe saw that within the room there were many big, human shadows walking back and forth, yet Kim didn't seem to see them. Joe was afraid, but he still had to feign composure. Kim told him how several years ago his wife and son had both died of pneumonia, one after the other. They couldn't endure the severe climate of this place. But he was himself loath to depart. It was as if a demon possessed him: the place was too beautiful. If it were morning, he would climb with Joe to the mountain's frozen peak to see the scenery.

"Do other people live in this building?" Joe couldn't help asking. He thought of the horror novel he'd brought along.

"Ah, yes. I have two guests. Many years ago they came to my house for a visit, then they went missing. I sense that they are inside the house. I've gotten used to it."

Joe discovered that when he said these words Kim's face had a cruel expression. A head of black hair shone under the lamplight, making Joe think of a black wolf. Fearful, Joe didn't pursue his questioning. He saw a dark, unmoving shadow behind Kim's back, and the lenses of Kim's glasses sent out an insidious reflected light. Joe said he had drunk too much and should go to bed.

Joe went to the guest room, bringing the alcohol fumes with him. Half awake, half asleep, he realized that it was a luxurious bedroom. But why were there so many black cats on the bed? Altogether there were five of them, all lying stretched out on the silk-and-satin quilt spread over the bed. Small green lamps were lit in the bedroom. It seemed much colder than the living room had been. Joe felt a shiver run through him. He swiftly dug into the quilts, and the cats seized their chance to squeeze in, too, furry but in fact comfortable. Lying down, Joe sobered up. Someone was knocking lightly at the door, but he didn't have the courage to answer. He decided to keep the lights shining continuously. Just now, in the living room, Kim had spoken of Joe's company. He said that the Rose Clothing Company was a monster, but if Joe could only escape to an Eastern country he'd be able to struggle out of the beast's claws. Kim from start to finish of his speech had watched Joe coldly from behind his lenses, watching until Joe recoiled. Deep in his heart, Joe didn't care about what Kim was saying. Although he seldom had time at present to read books, this didn't hamper his construction of his world of stories. On the road he'd already channeled this journey into the web of his story. And so, despite the terror in his heart, he was excited.

This enormous pastureland, named Dangulan or Red Old Blue, was so beautiful. Joe, getting out of the taxi, had stood there stupefied. It was a beauty that would keep others at a thousand kilometers' distance, a stern beauty. That silent and unbroken grassland;

that arrogant, ice-capped mountain without signs of habitation; also that house built halfway up the mountain, only the one and no second house — all these without speech closely pressed Joe's spirit. Joe couldn't help cowering, but there'd been no trace of the taxi for some time. Kim, wearing pajamas and holding a pipe in his mouth, came down the steps of the large building and casually shook hands. Joe noticed that his hands were extremely strong. They even had a sort of magnetism, as if hinting to Joe, telling him that he'd already entered Kim's realm.

Kim's household included only a female cook past her prime. There were no servants — or perhaps none of the servants appeared on the scene. At meals the cook sat off to one side, but from first to last she didn't speak a single word. Judging from her countenance, with its severely shut mouth, she apparently looked down on Joe. Joe was disheartened, and wanted to go to the guest room early, then shut the door and read that horror novel he'd brought along. But Kim suddenly started talking to him of his homeland, Korea, with his voice both sharp and urgent, as if he would open wide his inmost heart to his guest on their first meeting. In Joe's impression, Kim's homeland seemed to be floating, a dancing single-story building in midair. In this building the men and women had stopped cultivating crops or buying and selling. Yet these people's hearts held surprising lusts. They were capable of long periods of sex in dreams, not waking from lethargic sleep . . . "Yellow roses are in full bloom at the foot of the iceberg." When Kim spoke this ambiguous sentence, Joe saw that he had bleeding red gums and his whole face looked a bit like a tiger. But Kim suddenly stopped in the center of the room, his voice again an ear-piercing scream: "So many years have passed. Does the sun still hang in the East?"

Listening and listening, Joe entered into Kim's story. Even afterward, Joe couldn't really distinguish between the boundaries of Kim's story and his own. Kim's matchbox-like single-story houses always exploded open all at once, and from inside all sorts of ghosts flew out. The ghosts scattered in midair and disappeared into the human world, endangering people's lives. "Korea is a balloon in a boundless ocean," he told Joe in affirmative tones. Joe lowered his head to see his own sleeping robe embroidered with many foxes, but only felt desire leaping up between his legs. The more he listened, the more interesting he found Kim to be. In his heart he called this short man "a hawk"; he did not know why he named him this.

Outside it grew windy, with howling gusts, and the building started rocking as if the wind would smash the whole thing. Joe was scared, and he curled up in a ball, prepared to get under the table. Kim stood solidly on the floor. Perhaps he took this building to be a large ship on a billowing sea. He leaned close to Joe's ear, telling him a secret: "My house was built with no foundation. This building is in the style of my homeland." After a while the building became steady, yet the storm winds gusted even more violently, and it sounded as though hailstones were striking the tin sheet roof. Kim reached out an arm and hung it over Joe's shoulder. Joe once again exclaimed at the magnetism in his body. "Who would come here? Other than you," Kim said.

The stormy wind and the icy hail outside the room only intensified the seething desire in Joe's body. Amid the groaning sounds of the black cats copulating, Joe thought of a sexual partner who wasn't Maria and also wasn't the Kim in this house. It was apparently a person of indeterminate gender, covered in long black hair from head to foot. Joe felt dread at this unfamiliar and intense desire. He thought that perhaps the black cats were inducing these latent sexual fantasies. Midway, he climbed out from underneath the quilt and stood in the center of the room. The black cats followed him down onto the floor. One of them bit his calf, and when this fresh sense of pain again provoked his desire, Joe felt he would soon go mad. Concentrated hailstones struck the tin roof deafeningly loud, and the building looked ready to collapse. A knocking on the door sounded again and again in the pauses between the hailstones. He saw the peacock-embroidered quilt he'd slept in bulging up high. Was it possible there was still a cat inside, and that the cat had rapidly grown this large? He walked over and pulled off the quilt; inside was nothing. Joe lay down again. The black cats hid in the corners of the room and even more lascivious groans sprang up from their direction. Kim shouted from outside the door:

"Open the door! It's Kim. Years ago, I was in your hometown. Did you forget all about it?"

He yelled again and again until Joe finally lost patience, got up, and opened the door. However, it was the fat cook standing outside. The cook's garlic-bud eyes weren't focused on Joe. She was looking amiably at a small mouse at her bosom. The white mouse was one breath away from death. Joe didn't know whether she understood his words, so he used hand signs to gesture, saying to her:

"Kim . . . Kim, Kim!"

The woman immediately looked apprehensive. She tossed the mouse down on the floor, and left.

Kim finally appeared in the morning when the sun shone brightly. Joe saw that his face was a waxy yellow, and every movement of his hands and feet was unsure. He had changed into yet another embroidered sleeping robe, one printed with gold ingots. This get-up made him look unctuous.

"Did you realize your desires during the night?" He stroked his extremely glossy black hair.

Joe thought back to his high-surging passion throughout the odd night, and didn't know how to answer.

"The contract is already signed, but you still haven't made up your mind!" Kim said.

He called his wolfhound in from outside, and lightly stroked the dog, which was about as tall as himself. He told Joe that the dog's mother had died the year before last, died on the mountaintop. "I sealed her up inside an ice cave. When I turned to look out into the distance, do you know what I saw?"

"What?"

"The East! I saw it clearly, that place where the sun rises. Everything is there!"

"But a man like me cannot see that far," Joe said in disappointment.

"Ah, no! You're completely wrong. Yesterday for example, you went there, you were like an emperor . . ."

"I never went to the place you're talking about. I was inside the building the whole time, suffering from the attacks of those black cats."

"You're not pleased with the cats?"

When Kim spoke he again displayed his bloody gums, very displeasing to Joe. He felt that the man's body had the characteristics of a predator, one that seemed like it could break loose at any moment. Kim leisurely lit his pipe. After he'd smoked a few puffs, a thin flush spread over his face, and his black eyes shifted like a thief's behind his lenses. Joe drummed up his courage and asked whether Kim would be able to take him to the summit for a look around.

"I can't," Kim said outright. "All the roads are impassable. Japanese people came to this mountain before. The women changed into kimonos and geta sandals, then they disappeared into the snowfields."

Joe drank coffee, thinking to himself how lonesome Kim's life must be. Aside from that hometown floating among the clouds, his life was spent nearly cut off from the world. Kim read Joe's thoughts and responded, saying, no, he wasn't a bit lonesome, because everyone in the whole world could potentially pass through his residence. His house was like an entrance for getting into heaven. Joe, for example, whom he hadn't met before. Hadn't he hurried from so far away to be his guest? Although he hadn't known Joe before this, there was, in fact, a common communication of information between them.

"I don't at all . . ." Joe wanted to defend himself.

"Oh, no, no, no!" Kim waved his hands. "It's your doing. You send out messages, but you don't know it. Instead, I know you. Right when you set off I heard the sound of your footsteps."

Kim made Joe feel awkward, so he could only be silent. He saw a basket hanging down from the living-room ceiling. The hanging basket was piled up with wasps, and wasps were overflowing its edges. A few had dropped to the floor. Joe once again felt the house's perilous situation. In comparison to these wasps, which were as large as jujubes, last night's black cats really didn't count for anything. Kim's addictions were horrifying, but why on reaching here were his own desires so tempestuous? There had been one stretch of time when Joe had believed he was almost a hopeless case. Fortunately, afterward, reading had enchanted him. It was those fabricated stories that had saved him, that had brought changes to the look of his life. But stories were only a part of Joe's life, the sole part possessing meaning. Joe had not thought that in the world there could be a man like Kim, who lived altogether inside of fabrication. Clasping Kim's hand Joe realized his surpassing vigor. A wasp crawled onto the side of Joe's foot, so he hastily switched his seat. He saw a thread of mocking light at the edges of Kim's glasses.

"Your cook speaks very little."

"She is able to speak, she just doesn't want to is all. When she was young, her family turned her out for speaking out of turn. A few years ago she settled down at my place here."

Kim invited Joe to the greenhouse behind the building to see the "rare flowers" he cultivated.

"It is worth your making mental preparation. You need to have confidence," he said.

The so-called greenhouse was a large empty room. The room's windows were small, so that the rays of light inside were dim. After Joe stood for a while in the center of the room, he could make out the earthen bowls arrayed on the ground. There were no flowers, but rather a single type of coarse sand in the bowls. Kim squatted down and dug up a brown seed the size of an almond from a sand bowl. He placed it in the light to inspect it.

"Look, it's already burst open, but the shoots inside can't get out. All the seeds here are in the same condition. The flowers open inside of dreams. Surely you understand what I'm talking about? It's been more than ten years, and the seeds still keep this shape, neither sprouting nor decaying. Think about how surprising that is."

Kim continuously dug up all kinds of seeds for Joe to inspect. His voice sent out echoes into the empty room. Joe had the feeling of entering an enormous open grave; it was both curious and unfamiliar. A question repeatedly occurred to him: Were there any passages here leading to the mountaintop? The shadow of a person swayed in front of the windowpane. It was the cook, who was observing their movements from outside. It appeared that she was keeping watch over Joe at every moment, but why? Joe knit his eyebrows. Kim watched from the corners of his eyes.

"These flowers don't like the light. They are from my homeland. The buildings of our homeland have no windows, but every family still grows these kinds of flowers. Flowers raised in dark places have a slightly evil odor. Does your family grow flowers?"

"We grow roses." Joe thought of Maria's bewitched flowers, and abruptly grew sentimental.

"Roses, good, roses are flowers tended by people who regard themselves highly. A man who came here told me that his roses went crazy. They did not stop blooming, and so in all four seasons of the year his whole courtyard was bright red."

"You aren't speaking of me?"

"I don't know. Whether that person was you, you will be able to tell tonight. The fragrance of certain flowers can asphyxiate people. But they yearn for that wonderful moment."

Kim clapped the sand clean from his hands. In the obscure light his face looked like a rock, and his body also grew rigid. He did not move.

"Whenever you grasp hold of some object, other objects all change into unreal things," Joe said.

But Kim showed no reaction to his words, as though he really had changed into a stone. The nightclothes with gold ingots he wore fluctuated with an immeasurable light.

The door creaked with a *zhi ya* sound as the cook entered. She grasped Joe's arm, bringing him out of the room. She still didn't speak, but her movements were extremely confident. Joe indistinctly understood: she wanted Kim to stay inside alone. He remembered what Kim had said regarding confidence and comprehended it in his heart.

He walked into the living room and saw that the wasps had all fallen to the ground. They crawled on the floor in a large black mass, provoking disgust. Joe turned around and walked into the kitchen, but the cook flared up angrily and shooed him out, her face red all over. As she drove him out her mouth let out a sound like a wolf's howl.

Joe dodged into the bedroom where he'd slept during the night. He entered through the door and saw the cats occupying the large bed, sleeping peaceably on it. Joe quietly retreated from the room and slid out of the building.

At the far end of the grassland, the same as underneath a green sea, a human shadow wearing deep red clothing was heading straight toward him. The man was alternately hidden and visible, and so perhaps riding on the back of a horse. As he came closer and closer, Joe discovered with shock that the man was actually riding a leopard. When the leopard rose into the sky, the man's long hair flew up into the air. Joe watched until his eyes went blank. He nervously waited for the red-clad rider to climb the mountain. But when he was about to reach the mountain, Joe heard the deafening sound of a gun. The rider rolled down into the thick grass, and the leopard was nowhere to be seen. The scene from a moment ago was dissolving like a hallucination. Joe determined that the bullet was shot from near where he stood. Could it have been Kim? He turned around to look. The cook was just walking through the door, her ferocious eyes watching him.

Joe circled around to the "greenhouse" behind the building, but he saw no one there. He sat outside the building on a stone bench. A longing for his family gushed up in his heart. What was Maria doing at home? He thought Maria should come to this place. She and Kim were alike in many ways. There was someone following the stone steps up the mountain. It looked like the red-clad rider. Joe grew agitated. "Hey! Hello!" he shouted, not understanding why he shouted.

But the man wearing red was Kim. Kim's hair was a mess, his glasses were broken, and his left leg had been injured.

He walked limping into the building, refusing Joe's supporting hand. No one had helped him care for the wound. Blood already soaked a large patch of black onto the red trousers. Kim's blood looked like black blood.

"Who fired the gun?"

"Who fired the gun?" Kim repeated Joe's words. "It was me. I had the cook fire the gun."

Kim smiled coldly, grinding his teeth and showing his blood-red gums. That stoked Joe's horror again.

Kim sat in a reclining chair and closed his eyes to sleep, with his fists clenched tightly. Joe thought it looked like he was shivering.

"Your pastures are truly beautiful. I'd like to see your sheep."

"Other than me, who would come live in a fearful place like this? You speak of my sheep, but they're just a front. To make the people who listen to me misunderstand."

"Maybe your wound should be bandaged or have medicine put on it."

"No need. My body already has seven bullets in it. This sort of thing doesn't count for anything. The Japanese women wearing geta sandals were frozen in the ice caves. No one will be able to see those peerless, beautiful women again."

Now, especially, Joe wanted to start reading the horror novel he'd brought along. He abandoned Kim and went to the bedroom, pulled out his book from inside the leather briefcase hung on the clothes rack, then drew back the curtains, sat on the sofa, and began to read.

On the book's red cover was written: *This is a horror novel.* But at the precise center of the cover was a picture of a young girl. She was sitting embroidering in a tranquil boudoir. In the distance beyond her window were blue skies and white clouds. The beginning of the book introduced the childhood life of this young girl named Hailin. It seems she grew up in a lonely environment. Although she had parents, they abandoned her to do business in a far-off land. It was said that they'd gone to the East. Fortunately, the girl had a peaceful, even slightly indifferent, temperament, and so she didn't miss her parents much. She lived alone in an old house and took care of herself. After reading a few paragraphs, Joe grew interested in the book because behind its vapid writing he could again indistinctly see his familiar backdrop. He thought Hailin's household must have layered walls, and inside the layered walls would be underground tunnels. This girl must have a secret life. Continuing on, the depiction was an account of everyday life flowing like water. Her neighbors were a few names not to be remembered, and, later on, even the name Hailin became vaguely intermingled with them, and the descriptions changed to cloudy water. Also, he didn't know what were the intentions of the book's author, who suddenly dropped into a vulgar tone to start praising freedom. There appeared six or seven identical sentences in succession:

"Ah! The hovering of freedom! An unreachable height!"

"Ah! The hovering of freedom! An unreachable height!"

"..."

Reading this part of the book, Joe couldn't refrain from laughing. His laugh woke the cats, and they began their unbridled copulating. Strange calls came from the bed, a continuous disruption, and Joe feared they would bite him, so he went to sit at the window. On the roomy windowsill, he continued reading. In the second chapter the young girl, Hailin, suddenly disappeared, in what direction it wasn't known. The empty boudoir grew lively. Because she hadn't locked the door, all sorts of people entered: to gossip, to do a little business; umbrella fixers; farm-bird raisers; and so on. They carried a profusion of odors with them, and the boudoir's former ambience disappeared. But one day the young woman returned home. She had lost her right leg, and her appearance had grown unbearably coarse. There was a cruel, ruthless expression on her face. She drove away her neighbors, shut the main door of the old building, and began a life of deep meditation. At this point there appeared several vulgar and repeated sentences:

"What happened in the distant past? We will never know!"

"What happened in the distant past? We will never know!"

"..."

Joe could not smile now. A kind of yearning, similar to sexual desire, started to rise again inside his body. He leapt across obstacles and reached the kingdom of his stories. In its square, under the clinging roots of a banyan tree, he saw a multicolored kimono fluttering with the wind. "Hailin! Hailin!" he cried a few times in succession. He heard the book in his hand dropping to the floor with a thwack, *pa*.

When Kim picked up the book, Joe saw him snicker, his long hair shaking. He'd changed into a sleeping gown printed with a strange pattern. As he straightened up from the waist, Joe saw a black cat stretch out from inside his pajamas.

"Only this cat understands my state of mind," Kim said. "I've met the protagonist of your book before."

"Is there really such a person?"

"It's because what is written is the author's own life. She rested in my house for a night, then on the second day she went to the summit. That was where she lost her leg. Her appearance when she dragged her injured leg, howling, down the mountain I still see before my eyes today. You won't dare finish reading a book like this. If you read to the end, you'll be dragged in and never come back out. That is a true ice cave, much deeper than on the mountaintop."

The kimono disappeared before Joe's eyes, changing into a patch of vast whiteness. He thought of discussing the novel with Kim, but he felt he had nothing to say: the book had nearly no plot, and no imagery. Even so Kim bore out that Hailin was a real person in the world. "How was her leg cut off?" Joe sank back into a reverie without borders. He heard Kim's voice as if it were coming from inside the walls. The voice was ambiguous, and Joe didn't know what it was saying.

The room quickly grew dark. The cats were nowhere to be seen, and Kim also wasn't to be seen. The curtains shut of their own accord. Beyond the window a woman was crying. Joe groped his way to the bed, and in the dimness he quickly climbed the palace stairs and entered an uncultivated garden. On reaching it he realized that the garden wasn't in fact uncultivated. Many different kinds of animals made a racket inside, and the people were not few either. They all stood silently underneath a large tree. Their expressions were difficult to fathom, as if they were not of this world. Joe thought that perhaps they were ancients who'd lived several centuries ago. There was one youth standing under a cedar tree who appeared extremely troubled. Joe asked him where he was from. He said he'd come from home. His accent was strange, he was a foreigner. Joe asked him again where his home was, and he said the East.

"But this place isn't the East?" Joe assessed the mud-red palace walls and spoke in a loud voice.

The young man turned an expressionless face toward him and didn't respond to his question. Then Joe finally noticed that the youth was wearing prison clothes and, surprisingly, had shackles on his feet. Looking next at a few of the others, he saw that they, too, appeared to be wearing prison clothes. Joe suddenly, without reason, felt incredibly ashamed. A squirrel scurried between his legs. The squirrel belonged in this garden. Joe didn't belong here.

"My wife, Maria, planted many rosebushes at home," Joe said, as though debating.

The young fellow's face promptly showed a seemingly curious expression. But he still didn't open his mouth, only making an occasional sound with his shackles and turning his ear toward where Joe was speaking. What was it he actually heard? Joe felt unsure on this point. Then there was a sound near Joe's ear—it was the sound of Kim's voice.

"The entire garden is inside my house. A book is buried under the palace wall on the western side."

Joe deduced the location of the western side from the sun's bearing. The western part of the palace wall was burning as if with fire. Joe watched until his eyes stung. He thought that since the garden was inside Kim's building, there was no need to walk around futilely. He sat down on the grass. To his right under the cedar tree the young man held a book close to his chest. Joe thought the red cover looked familiar. He stood back up and walked over to him.

"This is your book. Inside is a cruel murder story, but I've already decided not to finish reading it. Who can finish a book like this?"

As he spoke he made a string of noises with his shackles.

"My book is about a young girl named Hailin. If I recall, she wasn't ugly, her parents did business, were never at home . . ." Joe said.

"Ah, you only read the beginning? That was a false semblance. The real story is afterward. This kind of story doesn't have a protagonist. Take your book and leave."

He handed the book over to Joe. Joe felt the book light and buoyant in his hand. Flipping it open he saw that it was, as a matter of fact, only an envelope. On the front cover the young girl Hailin had an unsightly open-mouthed smile.

Joe followed along the palace wall. In his ears Kim's voice grew louder and clearer. This led him to realize that he was merely circling Kim's building. Afterward, the voice grew quiet, and the wailing, desolate howls of the cats shook Joe's head into a daze. "Maria, Maria, forgive me, forgive me, what have I come to?" Joe spoke to himself incoherently. The grass lawn and the cedars disappeared and the palace walls were intermittent in the duskiness. Even so, up ahead he saw from behind Japanese women wearing cumbersome kimonos. There appeared to be three of them.

"You've been turning about in this room for a whole day. You actually can walk and read a book at the same time. This is a masterful skill."

When he spoke Kim's face again displayed that cruel smile. Joe tried as best as he could not to look at his face.

"I always keep a respectful distance from horror novels," Kim said.

Joe took the book in his hand and turned to the middle. Stepping in front of the window, he read a paragraph. It still told Hailin's story. The middle-aged Hailin sat in her sewing room embroidering a red spider. Upstairs the fretful sound of her parents' footsteps rang out. Her parents were now two old people who had lost their memories. On the third day after they returned from that distant place, Hailin with no irresoluteness at all had imprisoned them inside one of the building's large rooms. "No irresoluteness at all," these four words were underlined with a mark of emphasis. Joe read this sentence again and again, in order to comprehend its meaning from many angles.

"Joe, once you return home, will you or will you not commit yourself to growing roses?" Kim asked him.

As he drew nearer, Joe saw more clearly the design on his dark-colored pajamas. It was the savage faces of traditional theater masks, without any gleeful faces at all. Some of their mouths had long sharp teeth, with blood on them. Joe also heard the wail of an infant.

Because Joe didn't answer, Kim again examined him closely:

"If you read them repeatedly, can you make the stories become reality?"

When Kim leaned in close, exposing strange, long teeth such as Joe had never seen before and stretching his right hand toward Joe's face, Joe finally let out a shout. Then all went black before his eyes.

After a spell, Joe slowly recovered consciousness. He recalled that all along he'd been reading that horror novel, all along sitting at the windowsill. In the exact center of the house, Kim and the cook were in the middle of watching a seed inside a large flower bowl. A seed as large as a fava bean lay in the cook's fat palm. It wasn't clear what kind of flower it was. She raised her palm toward the light from the window. Joe saw clearly now that the plump brown seed had a termite-like insect popping its head out from inside. Kim laughed, *hei hei*, and showed Joe two other seeds he'd dug out from the flowerpot. Inside these were two similar insects.

"They are cultivated in our greenhouse. These small things don't affect the blooming of the flowers, and who's to say, the flowers may even benefit from them! Those roses at your house in reality open inside our dreams. You see them in full bloom, but that's only a false semblance. It's written clearly in the novel you're reading."

"I'm too timid," Joe said. "I can only stand outside the palace walls, beneath the stairs."

As they talked, the cook bent down to pick up the flower bowls and carried them away. Kim watched her obese receding back, nodding his head in commendation. He told Joe that last night a visitor had arrived. It was a woman. This guest wasn't planning to go up the mountain, but had rather come only to see his grasslands. Hearing Kim describe his guest's appearance, Joe thought that this arrival might be Maria. But Kim spoke a different name, and also said the woman had eccentricities, was an Eastern woman, and did not easily show her face to strangers.

"Ah, again it's the East!" Joe sighed.

But Kim, staring at him, spoke one word at a time:

"Afraid she's looking for you?"

"Impossible, impossible. I don't know any Eastern women." Joe forcefully shook his head.

"You have, however, been to her country."

"That's not possible."

Joe lowered his head to mull this over. Was Kim pointing to his years of reading? If so, he certainly had been to Eastern countries. It could be said that he had a singular feeling for Eastern stories. When he took all the stories and combined them into a web, in the square at its center appeared a kimono and peonies. At that time, in the midst of his busy marketing work, he'd still been able to enter lightly into his own stories, seemingly in large part because of the kimonos and peonies. In everyday life, he had never known women from the East, and due to his conservative nature, he also never had vain sexual hopes about strange women. But once inside his stories it was a different matter. More than once he'd had intense feelings for young women and mature women wearing kimonos.

But how did Kim come to know this? Perhaps he really had met him before? Before this Joe did not expect that there would be anyone in his country who could have fabricated a story like his own. Based on his observations, Vincent and Reagan were aware of the dual nature of the world, but they seemed to have no way of fully entering into his story. They were in too much daily contact and unable to wholly open up their hearts. And aside from work friends, Joe didn't have other types of friends. Joe thought again of Maria. For the past several years Maria had also fabricated her own world. Maria's and Joe's were parallel developments. But occasionally, Joe felt himself to be in her grasp, and in the blink of an eye this was enough to depress him. Kim, who was a longtime client of Joe's, lived in a way that was difficult to interpret. He was unfettered, and for a long time he had constructed his own complex, interconnected world. By coming here Joe felt that he'd thrown himself into a trap. Even so, he was happy to sacrifice himself. This really was his own story. Could that be?

A whispered conversation was taking place in the kitchen. Kim said that the woman guest was talking to the cook. They'd already conversed for a long time: they shared an aspiration for exchange. So the cook was speaking? Joe asked. No, the cook didn't speak. It was only the one woman speaking. She had the aspiration to speak, the cook had the aspiration to listen. As Kim spoke this sentence, the two of them walked into the dining room. While they ate, Kim told Joe, the women would eat in the kitchen. Joe thought this was a pity. He'd hoped the woman would reveal her face, and he would know whether she wore a kimono. And now he listened to Kim in discomfort.

"During the hailstorm, she was on the road. Her jeep broke down. Then she came up with a way to fix the vehicle herself. An estimable woman! Eastern women don't give up if they don't achieve their purpose."

"What is her purpose?"

"To come see my grasslands. Possibly also to ride the leopard. I've never seen her, not even this time, because she is covered in black cloth. Had you expected that?"

Kim seemed unsettled as he spoke. His whole countenance grew stiff. At this moment there was a loud burst of noise from the kitchen. Kim jumped up in surprise, his face turning a deathly white.

The cook looked in, then entered. She'd come to tidy up the dishes. She walked falteringly. Joe thought, mistakenly, that she would gather the plates and bowls, but she stood unmoving next to the table, her eyes staring at nothing. After a moment, she slowly collapsed beside the table. Joe tried to prop her up, but Kim grabbed him, saying, "Don't move her, her spirit has suffered an attack. Allow her to recover.

"In fact, she and I are from the same village. My village and hers were only separated by one kilometer. Every time there's a windstorm, we are both distressed, but we're the sort of people who make up our minds and never look back. She left her terminally ill father to escape to this country, and I, after accompanying my parents here, never thought afterward of going back. I'd rather climb to the mountain's summit, stand in the ice and snow, and look out from a high place toward my homeland. The woman who arrived yesterday told the cook that she is her stepmother, and at her father's dying wish she came looking for this pastureland. At first I thought that she was lying because the cook's father must have died a long time ago. Even if he hadn't contracted a fatal illness, he couldn't have lived this long. And as for this woman wrapped in black cloth, judging from her exposed hands and feet she's not that old. How could she be the stepmother? Then, a thing I never could have predicted happened. This woman stood there speaking to the cook, and she told the whole thing, all of the particulars, and the cook's eyes filled with tears . . . Ah, how can there be such extraordinary things on the earth? In short, between yesterday and today the two longtime residents of this house are learning from strange experiences. Because through this woman, we meet the history discarded behind us. This isn't good."

Kim's face recovered its color and his hands stopped trembling. He seemed to have decided on a plan.

"So, what is she really here to do?" Joe asked.

"Her? She's seeking repayment for a debt. She's already gone. My house is therefore brought into darkness."

When they left the dining room, the cook still lay on the floor. Kim said that the woman had carried away the cook's soul. It was difficult to imagine how the cook's prolonged days would be passed after this. However, it was no use to worry, because he had ordered many more flower seeds, and the present greenhouse would be enlarged. These flowers alone would be enough for her to work on, without too much time for recollecting things of the past. Further, the climate was already changing, as storms grew windier and more frequent. He said this, and those potted flower seeds containing insects appeared in Joe's mind. He immediately felt an itch on his neck, and the skin all over his body felt uncomfortable.

Kim at long last led Joe to tour his pastures. As they lay on the grass, watching the hawks gliding in the air overhead, Kim again revealed his blood-red gums, with the expression of a predator.

"Where are those sheep of yours?"

"Oh!" He answered as if waking from a dream. "Don't you understand yet? They are in my dreams."

"So it's like that." Joe was a bit disappointed.

Afterward they drove in an old clunker, stopping and starting. The grasslands were certainly large enough, nearly without borders, and the plains were the same. Seen from a distance, the large mountain where Kim's house sat appeared utterly monstrous, lonely as it broke up from the ground, in its surrounding pastureland. Joe looked back and forth, but from beginning to end discovered no waterways. Could the piled-up snow on the mountaintop have never melted? Looking at this cold, still, solitary mountain peak, Joe felt his eyesight growing blurred. Several decades ago, Kim's whole family had immigrated to this country. What were the actual circumstances? Kim said he did not have sheep or cattle, nor did he have workers, so why did he order so much workers' clothing? Perhaps Kim's parents were wealthy, and he could arrange for a home in this strange place? In Kim's words, living here was "not in order to break off from other people, but in order to merge into the midst of other people." This sophistry in his way of speaking made Joe laugh.

"Your house is truly beautiful, built here, like a kind of magic." Joe gasped in admiration.

"That isn't my house. I am no more than a guest." Kim wrinkled his eyebrows as if lost in thought. "I've already told you, the house has no foundation. That is to say, it isn't built up—it was originally here. You, for example, if you are willing, can become a tenant, too."

"But I have my own house. My wife is named Maria. My son is

named Daniel. I have to go out and sell clothing every day. I have to make a living." Joe felt falseness in his voice.

Kim glanced at him, saying, "That won't hinder you. Don't you already practice the skill of reading at work? I, too, had a job originally. I was a gardening specialist."

Joe thought of those insects with a burst of disgust, and he couldn't help inquiring about them.

"The flower seeds had worms inside them to start. I only use special methods to make them develop. I love working in the greenhouse. When I was a horticulturalist I did only surface handiwork, but now my work grows more and more interesting. Have you seen a wild hare before? It has a battle of intelligence with the hawks. I sought the home of the hawks. I have never found it. It isn't on the cliffs overhanging this mountain. It's in a place no one has thought of. For example, the East."

"Where do you buy the flower seeds from?"

"I don't know. I found the nursery in the local newspaper. But the address was fake. There's no such place in existence. The strange thing is that I sent a letter there, and they shipped me all varieties of seeds. This has something to do with my homeland. That's how I think of it."

Another day had passed. This place had no dusk, and night fell suddenly. In an instant, Joe could see nothing. Kim pulled him into the car. The car lights cut into the black in all directions as they drove ahead, and shortly they reached the house.

Kim's pace quickened as he entered the dining room. Joe went in with him. They saw the cook lying as before on the floor. Kim bent down to look at her, saying to Joe, "She's suffered a serious blow." Then he went to the liquor cabinet and brought out the liquor they'd drunk earlier. He gave Joe a large glass. Joe drank a few mouthfuls, and saw the dark shadows appearing in the room. These shadows were all excessively large men, and their heads butted the ceiling. One of them stretched out his hand and smashed a basket filled with wasps over his head. Immediately the room filled with crazily flying wasps. Joe shed his coat and used it to wrap his head tightly. He squatted, leaning on the wall. He heard the fellow next to him say:

"It's so comfortable. Why are there people who refuse this happiness?"

Joe suspected that the bodies of the men in the room must be crawling with venomous wasps because they were groaning as if in pain. Someone was yelling "Mama, get up," probably referring to the cook. It did mean her, and Joe heard her roar, like the howl of a beast he couldn't name, both painful and longing. Joe was deeply affected. He picked up his jacket and rose to his feet. There was no one in the room, only the black mass of wasps madly flying. His face swelled up before long, and his head felt dizzy. A pair of hands dragged him into the dining room. His eyes swelled into a narrow slit, and through the slit he saw the disheveled hair of the cook.

He was led into the guestroom, where a fragrant lotion was spread on his face.

"People who come here are never afraid of the wasp attacks."

The one speaking was in fact Kim. Strangely enough, though, it was the cook who'd led Joe into the room.

"Where is the cook?" he asked.

"She's still sleeping on the floor of the dining room, accepting the consolation of the wasps."

Joe stroked his face, which was swollen out of recognition. He heard a beastlike howl again. Moreover, the cry was not the same as before: it was like the sound a beast made when baited. Kim also listened closely. He said, "The cook is the kind of woman who's able to give up her life. Her homeland left her with a nightmare, for decades she's lived inside a nightmare, and she told me she never wanted to wake up." He also said, "She isn't unable to speak—she isn't willing to speak. Is it possible that someone able to howl like this would still be willing to speak? So she became a tenant here."

Kim made him lie down on the bed, but the bed was already occupied by those black cats. There were more than ten altogether, squatting on top of the quilt. "There is no picking and choosing in life," Kim said, at the same time pushing him toward the bed. Once

Joe fell down, the cats crowded around and licked his face where it had been stung. Their scorching, prickly tongues made him extremely nauseous. He wanted to howl, too, and he did howl, twice.

"That's right," said Kim from off to the side.

He heard Kim quietly leaving, shutting the door to the room. But he did not go. He spoke with someone at the door. Every time Kim's voice rose a little, the cats crazily licked Joe's face. Two of them even tried to bite his cheeks and wrists. So he dared to howl twice again. Joe had never liked to go too near cats, and when he was at home he felt that these somber animals hid an incalculable will. But now his whole body, from head to toe, lacked strength. He was oppressively tired and could only let them manipulate him. He did receive one benefit: the pain in the stung places lessened.

He couldn't remember when he went to sleep. On entering a dream the feeling of nausea disappeared. There was someone beside him who urged him to go look at the snow lotuses and, without reflecting, he went with him. The two men climbed the mountain on a single road. The mountain was steep and slippery, requiring both hands and feet in many places. At his side Kim cautioned, "Meet a man and casually go along with him, and in the long run you will be the one who meets with disaster." Joe disregarded the question of whether there would be a disaster, because once they reached the steep slope, if he drew back he would have fallen into a bottomless abyss. But he couldn't go up either. There was some object tangled around his foot. The man turned his head to tell him two cats were tangling up his feet, and added that if he'd escaped those two cats when he was at home, with his wife, Maria, all would be well. Now it was too late. "That time when you ate turkey, why didn't you think of what the cats wanted?" The fellow, with his head wrapped in a scarf and his face obscured, started to complain to Joe. Joe felt his feet slipping down. He couldn't stop, he simply closed his eyes and didn't mind anything . . .

Joe sat in the back seat of a taxi. He lay down and pulled the horror novel out of his leather briefcase, turning to the first page. The novel's conclusion suddenly appeared between the written lines. A white-haired Hailin sat in the kitchen peeling potatoes. A vampire spied on her from outside the window. Hailin raised her head, saw the vampire. Her eyeballs suddenly couldn't move. Later she discovered that, aside from her eyeballs not moving, her body was unaffected. She had no discomfort. She still peeled the potatoes, took out the roasted fish and put it on the plate, and decorated it with cherries. Passing through the drawing room, she unintentionally looked at the mirror and discovered blood dripping from the corners of her mouth. Her neighbors opened the door and came in, letting out surprised cries and then hurriedly fleeing. Hailin thought she had probably changed into a vampire. With this thought, she had a feeling of freedom.

"Reading that kind of book on a journey is not a good idea." The driver spoke without turning his head.

"Why do I feel like the car is going back and forth, and still hasn't left the pastureland?" Joe asked.

"With a place like this, once you enter you can't leave again. It isn't a bad thing, either. Close your eyes, and you can always reach home. Didn't you give me your address?"

"I gave it to you?"

"Yes. What you gave me was an incorrect address. There is no such place. Then your host gave me another address, written quite clearly. Your host is the kind of person who even plans out what to dream. For decades I've been making trips back and forth through this area, and I've figured out his disposition. Just think, why would someone want to live halfway up a mountain? That fat cook, I heard she murdered her own sick father and then fled here. Now she messes around with caterpillars all day to atone."

Joe heard this chatter and found the man disagreeable. He picked up his book to read again. He couldn't understand its contents, and even the characters' names had changed. The plot seemed to speak of a serving cook avenging herself on her unfaithful lover. The cook's name was also strange, Yi Zhi Mei (or Iljimae, "a plum branch"). The lover went to eat at a small restaurant. Yi Zhi Mei threw a bowl of boiling soup at him. The soup didn't touch the man; all of it splashed onto her own body. Within a second, her skin and flesh fell to the floor and all that was left was a skeleton standing in the restaurant. The man stared fixedly at the bones in front of him . . . Continuing, there was an explanation of the name Yi Zhi Mei. The book said that it was "Eastern." The serving cook came from some island nation in the East, these things had happened in ancient times, the cook's status was somewhere between a prostitute and a respectable woman, and the lover was in truth a patron of brothels. That lover, after seeing the cook's accident, went completely insane. He brought the cook's bones back home, made a glass cabinet, put them inside, and locked it from outside. From then on every time the lover fooled around with a woman, his eyes saw the objects inside of the glass cabinet. The glass cabinet was set next to the bed for a long period. Joe read this and started to smile. He felt that the novel was too hyperbolic. However, he still wanted to know the whereabouts of that glass case, and imagined the look of the skeleton wearing a light, graceful summer kimono.

The car went faster and faster. Joe couldn't sit securely in the back seat. He realized that the driver was making maneuvers, and thought he must have some insidious motive. He feared something would happen. There was one moment when Joe saw him call out to a person through the car window. Joe hurriedly looked outside and saw to his surprise that it was Kim. Kim stood in grass as high as his waist, dressed up to look like a hunter, with peacock feathers stuck in his hat.

"You've left me no way to rest," Joe complained.

He let down the velvet curtain over the car window, deciding that no matter what, he wouldn't care or notice. He wouldn't even care about his own life. He reflected that the driver had no reason to be after his life, altogether no reason. If he wanted to make a point, then he'd made it. Perhaps that person in the grass masquerading as a peacock was his audience. At this time, Joe's longing for Maria was more intense than at any other. He recalled that night in her room with its small purple lamps shimmering like fireflies; even her slightly aging slackness filled his body with longing. The occasion had made him embarrassed. Strenuously, he would not think of that scene. Over the days, he'd nearly forgotten the events of that night. But now, Maria's body overbore him. Her breasts with their erect nipples would block his nostrils, stifle him. Joe's body quickly shriveled. He hid in the darkness of the back seat, and did not notice when the car reached a dangerous speed again. He heard the driver curse, then suddenly the car stopped.

"That day you weren't at home, there was a hailstorm. The second day, in the morning, the roses opened even more exuberantly. Can you tell me what happened, Joe?"

"I can't, my dear."

Maria left the side of his bed and quietly went downstairs. Joe lifted his head from the pillow, looking at the wall in front of him. To his astonishment he discovered a new tapestry on the wall. It was a human skeleton wearing a kimono, and the flowers of springtime bloomed on the kimono. The tapestry was so large it covered almost half the wall. When had she started weaving it? Joe's heart was full of gratitude, but the impulse for sex completely disappeared.

5

The day Joe left for the north on a business trip, Maria was like a small brook rising in the springtime, cheerfully welling up with hope. Joe had taken a taxi at dawn. The previous evening they'd already said their good-byes, so Maria didn't see him off. She stood at the window of her bedroom on the second floor, listening with minute attention to the sound of the taxi's motor, watching Joe get into the car, his briefcase with the words "Rose Clothing Company" printed on it clamped under his arm. For a long time after the car drove off Maria still stood there, smoking a cigarette and reflecting on the Rose Clothing Company's situation. She thought of how the company's business had spread across the entire country, and was now even expanding to a few countries in Africa. But what kind of people was it relying on to prop it up? Everyone said her husband was the backbone of the company, an employee who'd given outstanding service, but as for Maria, she'd truly thought about it in a hundred ways and still couldn't understand. She knew that Joe had some natural talent for the business trade, yet she knew his thoughts didn't lie there. Joe's thoughts all lay with his books, and because of this the essential life between husband and wife had begun separating years ago, moving little by little onto different paths. This had continued until two years ago, when Maria had grown nervy in the process of weaving those odd tapestries. Then a subtle communication had begun between them again. Maria hoped Joe would go on business trips. She was pleased with his frequently leaving home for a few days at a time. But this wasn't because she wanted to have affairs of her own; it was rather a thirst for change. Every time Joe went away for a spell, the house grew clamorous, on the brink of something happening. For example, at this moment she heard the two cats in the backyard shrieking in a frenzy; a large flock of sparrows followed them onto the steps; and in the southern wind there was a cloth flapping with a *pa pa* sound. Even her tapestry loom downstairs began making a rhythmic noise.

There was someone coming along the path leading to the garden. It was her son, Daniel. Daniel had long since stopped going to school, but the two of them kept Joe blind to this fact. Maria had her son stay at her friend's house two streets away. Daniel did nothing all day now. The times when Joe wasn't at home, he snuck back secretly to help Maria tend the garden. Recently he'd brought home a Great Dane of enormous build, and had made a doghouse for it with his own hands. He proved quite skillful at these things. The Great Dane was extraordinarily gloomy. Perhaps this had to do with the climate of its homeland. But after the dog arrived at their home it appeared quite comfortable. Although it didn't heed either the family or the two cats, they could see it was vigilant and much affected by its new environment. The better part of the day it lay dozing among the roses. Daniel christened it "Pirate."

"Mama! Pirate took our spot. Can we still drink our tea there?" Daniel shouted into the house.

"No, child," Maria, her hands covered in flour, came out and answered. "It might make Pirate unhappy. Don't you see he's trembling? Nightmares from the past still hover around him. Think about where Pirate came from, a place where there's no daylight half the year."

Maria put an apple cake in the oven and sat down in a chair, recalling the circumstances of her own girlhood. This had been a small town then. A few shops were scattered thinly along the streets and only one bar was open until two in the morning. Maria's parents taught at an out-of-town school. She had passed an incomparably lonely youth in this town with her paternal grandfather. She had also been to college and been an office worker at a bank, but in the end she had returned in weariness to her hometown. By then the town had already developed into a midsized city, and that was where she came across Joe. Joe's eccentricity attracted her. She felt this man was a bit like a cat, and he more or less conformed to the type she favored. The lovers built their present house on the old site of her former home. She resigned from her job and became a housewife. In Maria's eyes, Joe had been changing all along. The first few years they were together, even though Joe liked to be silent, and when talking liked to "absent his spirit," she never foresaw that he'd develop into his present state. In recent years, along with the city's large-scale expansion, Maria realized that her husband's "soul had left its home." And she, who didn't care to go outside, nowadays felt her own hometown grown unfamiliar. There were some streets, some buildings, that she had never been to and didn't want to visit. One day, however, inside a newly opened bookstore—it was her first visit there— she saw her husband facing a bookcase. Maria didn't know why her face reddened. As quick as flight she snuck out of the store. After returning home, she hadn't mentioned this to Joe. It was only in the late night, when everyone was quiet, that she envisioned Joe hidden in some place she didn't know about, perhaps in the basement of a bookstore, or perhaps beside a water tank on the roof of a highrise restaurant. Or even on the sidewalk of a recently repaired road, reading books by the bright light of the streetlamps. Maria watched passively as Joe's interest in books swallowed up everything else, destroying their married life. These past few years, her husband was "journeying in spirit" at nearly every moment. Even when he spoke exuberantly about business at his office, Maria, with perceptive insight, realized that her husband was actually exuberant about something else. Not only did Joe's changes depress her, but also, at bottom, wasn't she by nature a woman who liked "something new every day and night"? What Joe's changes brought out in Maria was a sudden change in herself. Her own changing was not an expansion toward the outside but was rather confined to the family, taking their house as its boundary. Maria wasn't clear about what she had done in concrete terms. She only felt that now she was like Joe, often able to enter an unusually intense, approximately hallucinatory state. At first this state occurred only when she was weaving tapestries, but slowly things became more complex. In the past two years, she suspected she'd become like her husband, sinking into the snare of "mental journeys," while this house, and her son, Daniel, accompanied her into the snare. Sometimes, Maria was so frustrated by this feeling of unreality she wanted to scream. Sometimes, instead, she was extremely content. There were a few times, when she was sitting in the house or sitting in the garden, that she clearly heard the voices of her ancestors speaking, her parents and her father's parents. They seemed to be expressing their objections to her extravagant way of life and their disgust at her immoderate spending.

Maria was a woman who liked extravagance. She had an especially excessive fondness for jewelry. She generally spent as much money as Joe brought in, and the better part of it went to the jeweler. But she didn't adorn herself with the ornaments she purchased. Instead, she locked them out of the way in a jewelry case. Yet she also bought insurance for the valuable pieces. Joe believed her to be a woman who liked possession. He also knew she didn't like long-term possession. She only liked the joy produced in the blink of an eye by a purchase. But then why buy insurance? Joe believed that she was compromising to some notion. In addition to jewelry, she bought valuable Persian rugs. When she'd bought so many there was no place left to spread them out, she simply took a few of the rugs that were still quite new and threw them into the garage. Joe had no way to share in the joy of her purchases because every time she went to the shops it was by herself, and after the things were bought and brought back he couldn't see that there was any special expression on her face. If what she bought was jewels, she locked them in the gigantic jewelry case and that was it; if it was a rug, she spread it out on the floor at once, switching it with the old one. With whatever remained of that day, she did what she needed to do and never spoke of the things she'd bought. Joe sometimes reflected with hatred that she truly was a selfish woman. But on further thought, didn't he also buy books? Besides, he never discussed his reading with her. At this his anger would disappear.

When Daniel was about ten years old, Maria's lust for shopping swelled until Joe's income nearly wasn't enough to support it. One time she bought an expensive diamond brooch, costing nearly six months of Joe's salary, and they even took out a small loan. Luckily, Maria wasn't the sort of housewife to eat an entire mountain of wealth. Later on she began developing her own interests, buying a knitting machine and weaving lambswool tapestries. (Perhaps it was those beautiful Persian rugs that gave her the inspiration?) She was the sort of person who had a talent for real solid work, so from the start there were people who placed orders with her. Since she had begun to weave tapestries, Maria's desire for shopping had abated somewhat. She grew absorbed in small matters, and inside the house she discovered a few odd signs she'd never noticed before. The very first strange thing she discovered was that the bodies of their two cats carried electricity. When they were in heat, it was so strong she suspected that the electric shock would kill her if she touched them. Was it because the house's foundations were so ancient that strange things appeared there? The things that couldn't be explained followed one after another. The roses, the noodle-making machine, the hose irrigating the garden, the stairs to the house all became unreliable. The time when there was a problem with the stairs, Maria, by coincidence, wasn't wearing her glasses. To her eyes every stair slanted down in the same way. Her legs gave way under her, she sat down, and slid all the way downstairs. When she had collected herself and looked back up, she discovered that the staircase was now fine. These accidents around the house were inconvenient, but on the whole she harbored a kind of nameless and surprised pleasure at them. When she saw Joe getting an electric shock from touching the cats, her heart was also glad. Joe never discussed the strange occurrences with her, and Maria didn't bring them up either. But when Maria and Daniel were together, the two of them talked over these events spiritedly. One time, when Joe wasn't at home, mother and son spent the entire day out by the old well in the backyard without intending to. They even ate their meals next to the well. This was because Daniel had witnessed with his own eyes one of the African cats fall into the well, then emerge later from a tunnel that no one had known about. That day the two of them saw no further marvels, but their mood was unusually elated.

"Mother, do you think Pirate is tired of living?" Daniel seemed concerned.

"That's not so, child. Pirate's just too absorbed in things, like nighttime animals are by nature. Have you ever seen a smiling dog? But Pirate is able to smile. He practiced this skill in the dark."

"His master drove him out of the house because of his smile. I don't think he can tell how much light there is. In his eyes, it's nighttime here where we are. Pirate dreams both day and night."

Daniel was tall and thin and looked a little like a heron. Although there was nothing Maria and he didn't talk about, she still felt that his nature contained some obscure thing. That obscurity originated with Joe. For example, Daniel hid at Maria's friend's house, overly cautious and circumspect, seldom going out, appearing to be extremely bashful, ordinary, but she knew he wasn't an artless child. He had plans that would be difficult to realize; he was unable to abandon these plans.

Daniel arranged the garden systematically. He did such things almost without effort, but he was always nervous and unable to relax. This was the reason he ran away from boarding school. People said he was an excellent, self-disciplined student. But his mind was not on his schoolwork, and this was something only he knew. Maria wondered what this child's mind was set on. Once she visited his school, where she watched her son from a distance, seeing him standing like a heron in the midst of many people. She suddenly felt that she was looking at Joe in his early youth. The sensation of it was distinct before her eyes. How could that be? Wasn't Joe a short fellow?

When the two sat down together in the house and drank their coffee, Maria had Daniel look at the new tapestry on the wall. On it was woven a whirlpool, circle after circle whirling into its bottomless depths.

"This is a young woman wearing a kimono. I already saw her once, in Father's study."

Maria was inwardly startled.

"You read the same books as your father?"

"No, I only read travel stories. I like traveling."

"Would you like to go abroad? To countries in the East, for example?"

"No, I'd just like to stay at home."

Probably it was only Maria who could understand her son's words.

One of the African cats passed quietly between their feet, its fur rubbing their pants legs and making *pa pa* crackling noises. The other cat, the yellow-and-white one, came over. Daniel called it "Beauty." Beauty's body was not electrified at present. She was a bit irritable, and apparently searching for something. Maria asked Daniel whether he heard his grandfather speaking inside the house. Daniel responded that he heard him every day. Maria asked him whether he was afraid. He said he'd been used to it from when he was little. What was there to be afraid of? Besides, being afraid was no use.

"If Father doesn't like his work, he can come back here. Why does he have to go to the office every day? Couldn't you sell all that jewelry you have? I've been to a dealer to ask, and the market value isn't bad."

"It's exactly the opposite: he does like his work. Look, he's off on a business trip again. If he didn't work, he wouldn't come into contact with all different kinds of customers. He was happy when he left in the morning."

"So that's how it is."

Daniel was silent. He bent over, placing a piece of chocolate candy in the mouth of Beauty. Beauty ate the candy with a gloomy expression, and walked off haughtily when it was finished. The other, brown-striped cat, however, rubbed back and forth across their pants legs, seemingly to tell them something.

"I understand. Father is supposed to be far away from home, but he's really returned to you here?"

"It may be. But what do Grandfather and those other people want to say? That he shouldn't go far away? Like when we were drinking tea on the lawn and watched him appear in midair?"

Daniel didn't answer. Maria also didn't wish for her son to answer.

For many years, she'd been awaiting a solution that was difficult to fix on, an unreckonable thing, proved only by action. She was in a confused state when she wove this whirlpool tapestry. Her son voiced her premonition, that the composition of this pattern came from Joe's recent reading of a book by a Japanese person. Maria had never read the book, but she had captured Joe's soul. And Daniel, without much effort, entered this unreal world.

"Daniel, later on won't you need a profession?"

"I can help people as a gardener."

He added sugar to his coffee with assurance, altogether unconcerned about this issue. After becoming a private gardener, he could be like Joe, coming into contact with all different kinds of people. Now Maria realized that her son and his father were the same type of person, and had no fundamental use for the pains she took. Maria also realized that he did not really need to hide from Joe. Joe probably wouldn't be angry that he had left school. But Daniel didn't seem to be afraid of Joe's anger. Rather, he was purposely maintaining an estranged relationship with Joe. What for? Perhaps he didn't want too much daily contact with his father, but preferred to meet him in some subtle moment and place?

In Maria's bedroom was a portrait of her father. She'd put the portrait down at the back of a wardrobe, and only when she was getting dressed did she face her father in its dimness. The father's face in that portrait appeared arrogant, with bright, piercing eyes. Maria found it difficult to counter his look. In the beginning she had hung him on the wall. Later she detected that her father was staring at her, and she unexpectedly lost her competence in life. At this she finally invited the portrait into the wardrobe. The day her father entered the wardrobe was the day she started to weave tapestries. The communication taking place in the dark redoubled her confidence. In reality, her childhood memories relating to her father had practically all disappeared or been wiped out. The vanished father turned into the spiritual support of the father in the portrait. Maria thought: This is the meaning of so-called adulthood. What was a father? A father was a kind of negation, his strict eye making Maria's life into a string of illogical marvels, and even indirectly affecting Joe's life. In the night after the day when the roses were blooming like crazy she had seen with her own eyes how Joe, like a crazed man, rushed downstairs, seeming to want to take in the entire courtyard, looking left, looking right, looking everywhere.

Joe had also seen Maria's portrait of her father, which formerly had been placed in the corner of the living room. Although he had never met her father, Joe said he wasn't a stranger to his father-in-law. He also said that all the stories he read concerned her father. "You have a legendary father." Joe made this statement casually, but Maria was greatly shaken. Perhaps it was Joe's urging that gave her a little faith in this father who did not exist. Maria's intoxication in daydreams these past few years probably had much to do with the father in the portrait. If even her father could be revived in a fabrication, what couldn't be fabricated? An elderly neighbor, after seeing her tapestries, said that the design on one of them gave him a feeling "like dropping into an abyss." Yet he bought that smallish tapestry. Evidently he wished to experience what it was like to drop into an abyss. Deep at night when everyone was silent, her father was able to talk; his speech couldn't be heard clearly. He seemed to be speaking to her mother, but the talk between them was mixed up with her grandfather's chatter. Her grandfather and mother's talk could be heard more clearly. They usually offered her stern criticisms. Maria was already used to such criticism, although she was not used to her father's vague voice hidden behind it. She would often wonder why she believed she was the daughter of that man. She was also gratified by her relationship with Joe: she'd settled on Joe all at once, but it was because she'd had that kind of father. The composition of the world was truly marvelous.

When Maria saw her gray-and-white hair in the mirror, she thought of her old age. She'd never expected that her life when she was elderly would be as active as the present. Many years back she had already planned to pass peaceful waning years in this ancient house.

"Maria, Maria," she said to herself, "In fact, you aren't your father's daughter, and you aren't any man's daughter—you are this town's daughter. This small town has already disappeared, sunk underground, and so your train of thought transfers to underground. You've become an unearthed archaeological relic."

She was imagining herself with her whole body verdigris, sitting among the rosebushes and basking in the sun. Perhaps Daniel saw on her face, on her neck, that copper-green. Daniel was her son, and from the day he was conceived, the small town's ill wind had brushed his immature cheeks. Maria recalled something that had happened when Daniel was three years old. One day at dawn her son had escaped from her care, walked to the neighbor's garden, got into the doghouse, and squatted inside, completely still. Maria went mad, embracing her lost but recovered son and wailing and crying. Maria knew Daniel loved her, but his kind of love was too gray, even old, and this pained her heart. She was unsure of whether her son actually loved his father. She felt that the father-son relationship between them was of a rare kind, as was apparent when Daniel could see from a glance the Japanese woman's kimono inside her tapestry's whirlpool. This earth holds some people who, although not through language, and not through close association and exchange of emotions, can still, from estranged distance and silence, reach deeper levels of communication. At this point, Maria seemed to see the verdigris of her body giving off a flickering light.

Maria's short gray hair stood up straight in the mirror. Her expression was apprehensive. Was this, or was it not, some kind of awakening? Would the restlessness that came with the nearing of old age be able to bring her in the end into eternal serenity?

That evening, when Joe was away, Maria turned off all of the lights in the house. On a night like this, even her parents and grandfather were not talking. But she collided with her son in the living room, and was frightened into a cold sweat all over her body.

"I heard you call me, so I came back," Daniel said.

"I didn't call you."

"Maybe you didn't know you called me. The night is very beautiful, and our house is like a bay laurel. Mama, what do you say, should

I follow the path leading to the mountaintop, uphill all the way? The snow piled on the summit is eye-piercing."

Maria heard her son's voice shaking. She thought, He truly is a passionate young man.

"Mother, today I helped the Vietnamese family, over on the street where the church is, put their garden in order. After it rained, millions of earthworms gushed out of the ground. The family didn't react. They stood in the doorway drinking tea."

"You found a job, child."

"Where is Vietnam? I was thinking about it while I was hoeing, but I couldn't think clearly. Just now, when you called me, on the way here I suddenly thought of Vietnam. I saw the family escaping from the rain into darkened houses. Young girls with bare feet, their feet crawling with leeches . . . They don't react to these kinds of things."

"Daniel, are you in love?"

"I entered a dead-end street. I went mad seeing the earthworms."

"Daniel, let me touch your face."

Maria stretched out her hand toward her son, but there was nothing to touch. She knew the Vietnamese family. They'd opened a laundromat; the faces of the adults and children had assured expressions; the girl went to the public school and walked in the street with a careful look, not anything like the girls around here.

Daniel left the house without a sound, like a cat, and Maria was immersed in the complete stillness. After midnight, a hailstorm woke her. That hail fell strangely. Hailstones as large as eggs shot toward her window and fell to the ground. Afterward she used a washbasin to gather them up, enough to fill it. The window of Joe's bedroom was shut tightly, and the glass had not been shattered. Maria lay down on Joe's bed, covered with a quilt, her ears full of the sharp call of the mad gale wind. In her mind acts from her and Joe's shared life swept past. She saw clearly how daily life had shifted underground, how their surface exchanges had changed before her eyes into this mystical relationship. She remembered in early years Joe making a joke to her: "With all your energy, you're itching to move the jewelry store into your strongbox." But Joe was also full of energy. This short man, without meaning to, had built up alongside her a fortress to re-sist the invasions of daily life. But in the passing of months and years, their life inside was eroding little by little, changing into something unrecognizable.

She lay on Joe's bed. This was the bed he'd slept in for many years since they had moved to separate rooms. Occasionally, Joe came to her room, but for several years she had never been in this bed. She opened her eyes wide, trying to see anything at all, but it was a wasted effort. Only if she closed her eyes did she feel that there were shad-ows in the room. The smell of Joe's body could still make her excited, but inside that odor was a poison which could destroy the seething desire in her body. Those few times making love in the past few years didn't bear looking back on. When she imagined herself a lioness, Joe became a vapor . . .

It was only at this moment, on the night of the hailstorm, that Maria's shapely body finally embraced Joe, tumbling onto that large old bed. She let out a lion's roar, and from a remote place came a faint echo. This was the night of Maria's inferno, as the body's tor-ment freed the spirit from its home.

6

LISA'S SECRETS

Lisa, who came from a gambling town, was like sunshine on a summer's day drying the layers of mold from Vincent's hidden life. She, who'd lost both parents to the slot machines, with her shining eyes, her loud voice, her coarse, stiff red hair flying in all directions, was like an exploding bomb. She was a consummately skilled administrator, and very few people could manage what she held in her head, the method and keenness. She could make decisions swift as lightning. Many years ago, this daughter of a gambling family had wandered into this small city and fallen in with Vincent. The two of them had established the clothing company together.

She had retired from management of the company when its business was thriving and expanding because she feared the battles of the business world. Its battling reverberated with the lingering sound of her dead parents. From that day forward, she lived inside the enormous shadow of Vincent's inner world. When she was still young, Lisa came to think of herself as vulgar, and she didn't intend to change this part of herself. She wore colorful, gaudy clothes, spoke coarsely, and sometimes got drunk. After she married Vincent these traits became slightly restrained, but it wasn't an alteration in essence. She knew Vincent appreciated her.

Their house had reddish-orange outer walls and was situated behind the trees on a hillside. In front of the house lay an enormous flower garden and lawn, with a light-blue swimming pool like a beautiful jade under the sky. Vincent had designed this wealth-symbolizing residence on an impulse in his youth. The building had four stories. Although its furnishings were contrastingly thrifty, the several oil paintings that hung on its walls were quite valuable. Even so, after they had lived there for a year, they both started to neglect the upkeep of their house. For the sake of privacy they dismissed nearly all the servants, only retaining a cook. The sturdy fellow was also in charge of cleaning the swimming pool and the interior of the house. Fortunately the owners didn't bring guests home. The garden quickly became an uncultivated plot. All kinds of birds came to make their nests among its overgrown flowers, grass, trees. This, too, lent a peculiar air to the residence. What secrets did the husband and wife keep? For Lisa, their so-called secret was actually a riddle, something that couldn't be explained but rather was a longing buried away from beginning to end in the depths of their hearts. They both fostered this kind of secret. Especially at periods when business picked up and communication with the outside world became more frequent.

Once they were fully familiar with each other's bodies, after their enthusiasm for frenzied lovemaking had long since receded, the two, independent of each other, began searching in the nighttime. It was on a summer night that Lisa, waking from an apprehensive dream, turned on the light and discovered that it was exactly one in the morning. So as not to disturb Vincent sleeping beside her, she hurriedly turned off the light, and walked outside on bare feet. Sitting on the stairs was a playmate from her childhood, a dwarf nicknamed "Dummy." Lisa was pleasantly surprised to see him.

"Dummy, where did you come from?" She grasped his hand. His palm was rough, like a file.

"I took a fork in the road that leads from here to your hometown. It only takes half an hour." When he said this, Dummy appeared to be making a joke. Even after the passing of so many years his voice was clear and loud; his chest had a good resonance.

"Tell me about it. I want to go back, too."

Lisa plainly knew that this was dream-talk, but she was willing to keep talking.

"I walked here from there. But if you want me to go back on the same road, that's impossible. Everything changes after time. I'd need to search for it again. You also need to search. In your house there is a road leading to the gambling city. You cannot see the road, because it disappears in the daytime. It really only took me half an hour to get here, but what does that prove? It proves that there is a road . . ."

He would have kept on like a tongue-twister, but Lisa cut him off . . .

Dummy said he was only passing by, and now he had to leave. He walked down the stairs mumbling something to himself. Lisa saw his small body disappear into the shadows of a cluster of peach trees.

She didn't know when Vincent had also sat down on the steps. Vincent said, "Lisa, won't you go out searching for a bit? I'm going to."

He, too, walked down the stairs, disappearing into the shadows of the peach trees. At first Lisa heard bumping sounds among the branches. After, she didn't hear anything.

He returned in the morning. Lisa asked him where he'd gone. He was unable to say, only that the more he walked the less confident he felt, so he'd had to return home.

During the daytime, Lisa went back and forth among the trees, but failed to discover anything. It was then she was most puzzled because she discovered that as Vincent's work grew busier, he slept less at night. He would tumble out of bed, head to the closed-in untended garden, and not come back out. And Lisa herself walked back and forth along the periphery of the garden. This went on until she learned that her husband had appeared in a garden at a street corner at midnight. She finally had her suspicions.

"I was tired of walking, so I went to that garden to rest for a while." He spoke vaguely. "To me, she is you, and in a place like this, nothing is too strange."

"You've found a new companion."

"Nonsense, you are who I found. Lisa, if it wasn't for you, I could sleep at night like a corpse."

They drank underneath the grapevines. They were both drunk, falling on the ground.

"Vincent, Vincent, did you grow up out of the grass?" Lisa asked, her eyes blurry with drink. She saw meteors falling from the sky, and her red skirt had already caught fire.

"Lisa, I saw you setting a fire in the abyss." Vincent spread his arms and legs wide. His green eyes lost their light as his gaze settled on a clump of grapes. "It's so hot. Is your gambling city full of stone mountains? I know you're not afraid of fire, dear . . ."

After Lisa sobered up, she saw Vincent lying in a small rivulet, the mountain spring rinsing his short hair. All his clothing was soaked. She called to him again and again, but still he slept like death. Afterward the cook came out and shouldered his unwaking employer, carrying him back to the house.

When Lisa retired to their home, weary of work, she began her life of reverie. Or, you could say, she continued her life of reverie.

When Lisa was young, no one foresaw that this scarlet-cheeked, incredibly driven young woman would be one for reverie. During her roving period she had tried every kind of work: housemaid, waitress, car washer, tour guide, office secretary, typist, department store bookkeeper, warehouse custodian, radio broadcaster, and even a short time as a weather announcer. She was multi-talented and multi-skilled, free from worry, even-tempered, with a remarkable appearance, slightly vulgar, a common woman. But there truly was a reverie belonging to her. Every day it took place at a set time in the middle of the night, a secret of which no one was aware.

Every night after midnight, at the time of utter silence, a few strange people assembled at the walls of her bedroom and discussed the long march. By raising herself slightly from the bed Lisa could see their several black shadows, and their conversation also carried to her ears. The long march was their perpetual topic. All the apprehension, difficulty, loss of hope, feelings of defeat, and life-risking resurgence that this activity contained—these were not things ordinary people could understand. In the stifling silences, Lisa often shouted into the darkness. Thereupon the tall, thin figures would scurry over and clutch at her throat, rendering her unable to move. She vividly felt the nearness of death. After this recurred a few more times, Lisa gave up in fear. She would rather suffer the oppression of that silence, that not-yet-reached limit of sorrow. In those years she passed through many places, but whenever she reached a place, at midnight discussion of the long march would be, as before, the inevitable topic. What was the long march? Observing the shades assembled at the walls, with their unchanging, conspiratorial air, listening attentively to those tedious, nervous dialogues, and imagining the army's march through that endless hell, year after year, Lisa little by little came to understand that the long march was not another's; it was related only to her own life, something she should do her utmost to forget, but also a deep thought destined to be inscribed on her heart. There was a tragic night when an old woman in the shadows spoke of a member of the long march army, wounded and at the point of death. This young woman lay on a crude stretcher, imploring her companions to be merciful, to lift their hands and throw her into the river. Blood spurted from her mouth and her hands danced madly in the air like chicken feet. The troops silently followed the river. Their faces little by little grew incomparably savage. The black sky seemed to press down on each person's back. Suddenly, there was the sound of desolate crying, but it was not coming from within the army. Rather, it was coming from the sky itself . . . The old woman had told the story up to this point when her voice disappeared, and the whispering of the others surged up again. In Lisa's dream that night there was a continuous rainstorm lashing at her face like a whip. The strange thing was that this soul-corroding grief in the night did not wear down her body. It was even nourishing: she looked excessively healthy. Even the tragedy in the swamp at night when the whole army was destroyed, the cut-off cries reverberating through the air, the horror of the severed bridge, the struggle in the tiger's jaws, could not fade the rosiness of her cheeks. She thought that perhaps she was a compound body of two people. The one suffering hardships in these reveries nourished the other, who was leading a comfortable life.

Once, when she was working as a tour guide, an old man fell in love with her. As the cruise ship headed to a small tropical island, at midnight on the deck Lisa told this fatherlike white-bearded old man about the long march, her narration baffling and hurried, as if she were trying to catch hold of something.

"Lisa," the old Middle Eastern man, Yasin, said in her ear, "Come to me here, girl. I am the destination of your long march. Look there, it's a falling star, a happy star."

His body gave off an odor of sulfur. Lisa gave herself over to illusion.

Before dawn Yasin lay dead on the deck, his aquiline nose suggesting boundless dignity. The tour group continued on ahead, and Lisa, alone in the cabin, carried on the long march. She already felt deeply how remote she and the beautiful Yasin were from each other. Among the long march army, between the dusky sky and darkened land, who else would be able to see her destination? And so, for the first time in many years, she remembered her distant parents, discovering with panic how much she resembled them. In the ship's cabin the discussion reached a high point, because behind the long march army there appeared a pursuing army . . .

After she met Vincent, these ghosts no longer appeared to Lisa. From their first meeting she saw a heavy shadow behind him. That shadow would sometimes grow larger, shrouding the two of them inside it. Lisa thought that a man who could carry the black night on his body as he walked back and forth was her ideal of a man. The two discussed at length the matter of the long march. Lisa asked him, Had he been one of those ghosts in her bedroom? Vincent answered, Perhaps yes, but he couldn't remember things from the past, what a pity. As they spoke there came an intermittent smell of sulfur, making Lisa shudder uncontrollably. Vincent was not adept at description, and he only repeated, "Ah, Lisa, my ideal!" That sentence seemed unbearably crude. Lisa told him that the shadow behind his back was like a powerful black cloud. With him standing beside her, she felt as if she were living inside an imagination. But in this, wasn't she too lazy?

In the city, among crowds of people, Lisa always kept one eye on her husband. Often, as she ran to his side, her high heels snapped off.

In recent years Lisa had observed with panic as the shadow behind Vincent grew darker and darker. At times his whole person unexpectedly disappeared inside it, without leaving an image or trace.

"Vincent, Vincent, have you abandoned Lisa?" She worried over this sentence.

Originally, when they married, Vincent's world became her world. The two of them passed many unforgettable days in a shared refuge. But now Lisa was suddenly again a solitary person.

The nighttime became a trial of tortured nerves. Especially on rainy evenings.

The day she retired Vincent asked her what she was going to do, and she responded, "Start the real long march." Vincent felt a little surprised at first, but soon he was relieved, saying, "You'll settle everything for the two of us." That evening they got drunk to celebrate Lisa's return to the home.

Afterward the period of waiting seemed endless. The ghosts didn't appear in her room any more. She tried a room separate from Vincent's, but they didn't come. Later she realized that there was no need for separate rooms, because it was quite possible Vincent was one of the shades. The searching activity was thus begun. The dwarf, Dummy, had told her that on the plot of their house there was a road leading to the gambling city. Lisa thought, without any reason to, that by finding this road she could join the long march army. But Vincent's searching had its own method. Once he headed into the thick groves and tangled grasses, Lisa could no longer find him. Lisa could not help suspecting that building this house on a hillside and buying this enormous garden in the middle of the city was something Vincent had premeditated long ago.

Sometimes Lisa went to the office to observe her husband closely. But she couldn't see the slightest marks of his nighttime activities on him. Where did he actually go at night? She said to him, "We can return together to my hometown." Vincent said, however: "I'm also searching for you. I've reached the long march campsite. The fires are not put out, the troops have not yet departed."

When Vincent and his co-workers got into a car, Lisa saw the black shadow behind him remain outside it. The car started off, and the shadow floated on top of the car roof like a black hot-air balloon. Lisa could only stare, but the faces of the people next to her had no expression at all. Perhaps they saw it, too.

The night without Vincent was a night without anything at all, other than the *yi ya* babbling of an infant learning to speak. Perhaps it was their punishment for leaving no descendants . . . their two-person world couldn't contain a new life. Lisa still harbored a desire to develop on her own. One time she thought that it might be worthwhile if she walked to the head of the mountain stream, because recently a species of small fish had appeared in the rivulet, like a piece of news from the outside world rushing in. She changed into high boots and groped her way along the gully holding a flashlight. The moon was dark and the wind high as Lisa heard the faint sound of the army's bugle, and smelled a pungent smoke. Her pulse grew wild. The gully bent and curved. She thought she was already behind the mountain, and up ahead was the side of a large road. But the gully unexpectedly cut short and the babbling spring, *chan chan*, ran down into a natural well. This well was not far from the road. It actually looked more like a puddle than a well. She could imagine that it was very deep underneath its commonplace appearance. Lisa didn't have the courage to jump into the well. Although she was able to swim, as soon as she thought of the bottomless abyss and the narrow entrance she became so afraid that her mind went numb. Besides, who could guarantee that Dummy had taken this road? Vincent was even less likely to have. Hadn't people seen him sitting in a coffee shop off the street? She stood beside the road in her boots, sweat pouring like rain all over her body. The second night she practiced again. This time she hadn't walked far before the rivulet disappeared, its running water seeping into the ground. She realized that the earth on which she stood was soft. She was sinking down. She grew anxious and began to churn up the ground, reckless of everything, turning up the piece of land. Then someone was in front of her, speaking to her. It was Vincent, who seemed to have been there for a while.

"Lisa, go back. There won't be any results so quickly. Your hometown is more than five hundred kilometers away, in the mists and fog. How can it be found all at once?"

"But you, what are you looking for, Vincent?" she asked him, her mind in confusion.

"I'm not looking for anything, I was this way before I knew you. I can't always stay in one place. But we are together, aren't we?"

"Yes." She had to admit what he said was correct. Of course they were together, perhaps forever.

In the dark she saw Vincent reach out his hand toward her. Her hands held that familiar hand, bringing it to her face. Suddenly, she discovered it was a broken-off arm.

"Vincent!" she shouted desolately, and fainted.

The water from underground flooded her clothing. It was the mountain stream, the one which had just disappeared.

She returned to the house dripping wet. The driver told her Vincent had already gone to work. This driver, Booker, was a part-time employee. He looked so steadily at Lisa's body, which seemed almost nude, that her face reddened.

"Haven't you seen this before?" She forced herself to make a provocative look.

"I haven't. At least someone like you," he said resentfully.

"Huh, go back to your hometown and look around then."

Lisa realized that she wasn't making sense, saying this. Why tell him to go look around his "hometown"? Did he have a hometown? It seemed she was going too far with her obsession. But the young man had already walked off. She heard the cook cursing maliciously from inside the house, but she didn't know if he was cursing her or the driver.

She changed her clothes and went downstairs to eat breakfast.

"Who were you cursing at?"

"I don't know," said the cook, A Bing. "I just wanted to curse at someone. There's such a strong smell of gunpowder in the house."

"It's the smell of brimstone."

"You and Mr. Vincent are at war between yourselves. Am I right?"

"No. He and I are fighting a common battle. How can you get the most basic part wrong?"

"I think it comes to about the same thing. This morning when he was eating breakfast he had blood flowing over his hands."

Lisa covered a surprised shout with her hand. A Bing walked away, as though nothing had happened.

It was after this that Vincent fell asleep on the grass, behaving awfully. She looked carefully at his hairy wrists, but there were no scars on them. Then Vincent looked at her with lust-filled eyes, hazily saying, "Who are you? Are you a Moroccan?" Lisa shouted into his ear, "I come from the gambling city!" He turned, one side of his face stuck to the messy grass, and said, his voice distinct, "I need a woman of Arab and Japanese descent, or else you won't be able to see me." He finished this sentence and snored.

Lisa sought out Joe's wife, Maria, to talk about the situation. She didn't know why she needed to find someone to talk to, but since she needed to talk, she had to find Maria. She'd been to Maria's house, which she secretly called "the playground." Striding through the wooden gate set in a bamboo fence, she grew dizzy, with the clear feeling of a powerful magnetic field inside the building. That afternoon, drinking coffee among Maria's rosebushes, Lisa spoke to this woman, who had great wisdom and a cool head, about her own chaotic life. As she was speaking, Lisa realized that the roses had an unusual fragrance. She asked Maria where this variety came from. Maria said they were from a pastureland in the north, and that the flowering plants there were all cultivated in midair.

"I sit at home, but at any time I can see the snow piled on the mountaintops," Maria said, smiling with a slight squint.

Two cats scurried out from under the low table. Lisa's whole body tingled.

"Your cats, Maria?" she asked.

But Maria's silhouette grew dim, and after a bit Lisa could only hear her voice.

"Our long march requires an impetus that doesn't wear away," Lisa said hopelessly, in that direction. "Otherwise, on that great overcast river, the iron chains of the bridge will break, *hong*, with a crash. The whole army will be destroyed, doomed by fate."

Maria was smiling artificially. Lisa saw that her head and body were completely separated from each other. All at once her hair stood on end and her spine ran cold with fear.

Lisa walked straight to the wooden gate, still hearing Maria's voice continuing, following her.

This meeting left Lisa with an indelible impression. From then on she regarded Maria as being similar to herself. She often saw Maria's husband, a short, reticent man, but her impression of Joe was very hard to clarify. Today was the second time this month she'd come here. As for the period when she hadn't come, it was because she was a little scared.

"Hello, Lisa!"

Maria reached out strong, nimble hands and held her. Her thick gray hair was casually drawn back behind her head and her whole body gave off an inhibiting energy. She said she'd been weaving.

"Amazing!" Lisa said, leafing through the works piled up there. "Maybe you could guide me. I'm looking into these deep, deep whirlpools. My heart becomes a mirror . . ."

Abruptly her voice cut off, because she saw an extremely familiar picture. She'd seen this picture many years ago, when she was still a young girl, and in the days following she frequently met with it again. She clearly remembered, on the long march nights, how this picture would repeatedly appear in the dark. What Maria had woven was a scorpion, hidden in a deep clump of grass, a big fellow, faintly visible. This scorpion was red. The lambswool Maria used to knit it was dyed the color of flame.

"I can't see it clearly . . ." Lisa said, stammering, pointing to the picture.

"Oh, that design! It's nothing, that's Joe."

"Joe? Clearly it's a scorpion!"

"Yes, but it came out of his story, and Joe's stories are Joe himself

. . . I can't explain it. Have you really seen a fire-red scorpion before? I usually like to weave things that have never been seen before, like Joe."

Lisa believed what Maria said, because she'd never been an affected woman. She asked Maria whether she knew that Joe had a mysterious client in the north.

"I know. But why mysterious?" Maria was a bit alarmed.

"Because the man doesn't exist. Every year he orders clothing from our company for his workers at the pasture, but when our people make business trips there they discover that it's an abandoned quarry. He pays for the orders, but the clothes are piled in a warehouse to this day."

A slight smile floated on Maria's face.

"Ah, that's what you're talking about. That kind of man has no set home. Don't take him too seriously. And anyway, the company hasn't taken a loss, right?"

"I guess so. I really want to see him with my own eyes. Your husband is the only one who's met him."

Lisa watched this woman who in weaving transformed her husband into a scorpion in the grass. Abruptly, she felt unexpected passageways appear in her mind. Perhaps her long march at night should shift direction; perhaps she should change from expanding outward to becoming still?

Following Maria into the living room, she saw through the French windows a very thin boy wielding a hoe in the courtyard. The boy's face looked somewhat familiar.

"That is my son, Daniel."

"Oh!"

That day she sat with Maria in the kitchen. She talked all along about Vincent. Outside it was raining, with the constant sound of drops falling. Daniel often scurried in and out, his clothing soaked through, with a fugitive look. Lisa noticed that the boy made no sound when he walked. Lisa asked Maria what the Rose Clothing Company signified to Vincent. Its immense machinery working day and night seemed somehow separate from him. His world was a different place, at night among the trees in the garden, in the gloomy middle of the night in gardens at street intersections.

"The Rose Clothing Company," Maria lit a cigarette and spoke slowly, "to someone like Vincent, is everything. Maybe he thinks his life has already run its course."

"How strange!" Lisa sighed. "In your house nothing is peaceful," she spoke again.

For Lisa, Maria's house was a place that made her nervous. In its vicinity all sorts of voices were speaking, every object carried electricity, and then there was the son with the cruel expression. There were also the tapestries with their furtive meanings. But even so this woman was someone Lisa believed she could trust. Were Vincent and the company collecting this type of person? According to Maria's way of speaking, Vincent's life had already run its course, and so he began an absurd lifestyle, one without any sense of reality. Then why did she say the Rose Clothing Company was everything to him? Would he take this spectacular, human enterprise and make it into a ghost's stronghold? Lisa thought of the black-clad Eastern woman on the rubber tree plantation and her whole body broke out in goose bumps.

"The Rose Clothing Company's business is expanding to the north. Three batches of orders arrived in a row, each from eccentric clients. It was hard to get in touch with them. These days Joe has to spend all his time on business trips."

Maria's expression was extremely calm as she spoke. She was not making a large fuss over a small issue. Lisa thought, Maria's life has long since run its course. She saw now that Maria was like a goddess.

"There is an Eastern woman in Vincent's life, perhaps a Japanese woman," Lisa said.

"She lives on 13th Street in Building No. 2."

"You knew this already."

"No, I didn't. I only passed there by chance, and saw a woman covered in a black veil coming out of that building."

"Do I belong to Vincent's finished life?"

"Just the opposite, I feel you belong to his future. This means that you two will be isolated from each other, just like me and Joe. Actually, Vincent is looking for you everywhere, too."

Leaving Maria's house, Lisa seemed to have decided many matters. She also seemed to have decided nothing. Although her steps appeared careless, she felt that every step was along some invisible trajectory.

That night, when Lisa once again converged with the long march army, which she hadn't encountered for such a long time, when like blind men in the enormous dense fogs of a swamp they circled around and around, she realized that passageways were beginning to appear in her chaotic mind. The ghosts who'd come to her house many years before did not reappear, nor was the sound of their voices any no longer in her ears. She strode from the room, passing unhindered through the chaotic garden, and walked directly into the midst of the army.

"Lisa, Lisa, Vincent has been waiting for you a long time." They spoke in unison. "Go with him to the grass over there to make love. There is a zebra that will guard you."

But Lisa came to an iron cable bridge. Underneath were terrifying waters. Her bare feet stepped onto the rocking cables. She couldn't stop because the people behind her pressed her on. Her feet slipped again and again but never fell through. She heard herself shouting for help; her voice was drowned in the clamor of the waves. The people behind her were singing a strange song: "The long march, the long march."

Lisa finally lost control, and her numb hands loosened their hold on the iron chain. She closed her eyes. But she still proceeded with the army along the iron cable bridge between the two mountains. There was someone carrying her. She wanted to see who it was, but couldn't with the dense fog blocking everything from view.

"Ah, you've returned," Vincent said. He sat smoking a pipe in a small thatch-roofed pavilion.

"I've been looking for you everywhere. Here's my umbrella. How will you walk back with the rain coming down so hard?"

Lisa stood in the midst of the coiling smoke as Vincent's long arms, like a caveman's, embraced her. In her distraction, she realized that she was still on the long march. Seemingly, she and Vincent were at the camp cooking food for everyone. The firewood was wet through, choking the two of them and making them cough. Lisa stood up and went outside the canteen, panting for air. There was a fine drizzle on the plain, where among those sitting on the ground and those staggering along she saw to her surprise a woman in a black skirt shuttling back and forth. She recognized at a glance that tall and somewhat rigid posture.

"Her, her!" Lisa shouted incoherently.

"It doesn't matter, it doesn't matter. The army will set out soon." Vincent grasped her hands, pressing his lips to her ear as though making a promise to her.

She couldn't see Vincent's face clearly, yet she said to him, "I don't want to go back. Let's walk on a bit farther."

"We're already getting farther and farther from home." When Vincent said this, Lisa could no longer see him.

Continuing on she heard Maria's voice behind her. She returned to her own house, where she heard the driver and cook cursing at each other in the kitchen. Looking out through the French windows she could see the small pavilion and the smoke curling up, but she did not see Vincent. Was he still inside the pavilion?

"This unjust life!" The cook A Bing raised his voice and sighed.

"A Bing, A Bing, how fortunate, almost all of my friends live with cooks." Lisa stood at the door of the kitchen, addressing A Bing. "See, the title 'cook' is so attractive!"

But A Bing was in a very bad mood at the moment. He said fiercely: "For people like us, life is no better than death!"

When A Bing spoke, the driver Booker appeared distressed. The two of them evidently wanted to embarrass Lisa, but to what purpose? Lisa recalled Booker's dissolute life on the farm, and she reflected that this young fellow was also a riddle. Right now, for example, he'd rustled up an army uniform from somewhere and was wearing it, but the uniform didn't suit his languid bearing. Lisa believed that he was playing the part of a clown, and in her heart she loathed him. She wasn't someone who could be annoyed easily, so she sat down at the kitchen table, trying instead to see what tricks these guys were up to.

Once she'd sat down she felt very tired, and she fell asleep leaning on the kitchen table. Yet at the same time she heard Booker loudly discussing the long march. Lisa wanted to cut in, but her eyelids wouldn't stay open.

"When sinking into the swamp the best thing is not to struggle, otherwise it's all over."

She didn't know how long she slept, perhaps a very long time. When she woke, she heard them beside her still discussing the long march. The circumstances they spoke of were wholly familiar to her.

"Booker, are you on the long march at night?" she asked.

"No, I'm on the long march during the day," he answered haughtily, as if this gave him a higher status.

In his lazy way, he already lay face-up in an armchair, his legs propped up on the arm. Lisa truly could not connect him with the army, the fires of war, and the smell of gunpowder. But how did he come to have information about it? In her heart she had many suspicions.

"A Bing, I've seen you all day inside the house. Are you also on the long march?"

"Yes, Lisa." When he spoke as before it was with a distressed look. Then he cursed a few times.

Lisa thought, Is it possible every person is on a long march? Judging from the vast army she knew, this seemed a matter of course. In the blink of an eye, the magnificent spectacle of a global march welled up in her eyes. The spectacle shook like lightning, then quickly disappeared.

A Bing stood apart from the table and said to Booker, "I have a wife, and a child, but I haven't seen them in many years. I've climbed and climbed, and in the end how many mountains have I crossed? Just think, your wife pulls your daughter along, shading her eyes with her hand as she stands under the eaves, her gaze always trying to penetrate the thick mist before her. And me, I trudge along in the swamp. The rumor of catastrophe is becoming widely known in the ranks. There is a poisonous snake, and if someone's shoe is worn through he can be attacked."

Suddenly he covered his face with his broad palm and started to cry without shame. His violent wails appeared meant to drive Lisa away, and intended to make a powerful show of force. Booker stood up from his chair, looking indignantly at his employer.

Lisa left the dining room and headed upstairs to the bedroom. She shut the bedroom door, but could still hear the two men standing downstairs, their voices ferocious, like two savage wolves. She turned around and saw Vincent lying on the bed, still holding a pipe in his hand.

"Have you come to an agreement with them?"

"It counts as an agreement. In the dark, I must listen to their commands." Vincent's voice was a touch hoarse. "Those two are very powerful. Didn't you realize on the farm what Booker is capable of?"

Vincent put down his pipe and said lightly: "Come over here."

They tried a new position. Lisa asked Vincent where he had learned it. Vincent said he'd learned it yesterday from a group of animals. Last night he'd made his way alone into a great primeval forest. Lisa said that she'd felt like a cat, without a clear climax, but completely beside herself. Was this the tiger's way of sex? Vincent did not answer, but said: "Listen, the young men downstairs are completely silent."

Many years ago, in a small coffee shop in a poor neighborhood, Lisa had stared at the thick black shadow behind Vincent, lightly repeating: "Vincent, Vincent, I love you." The proprietor had come over with a strange look and asked Lisa, "Does this man live in a forest?"

"I am slowly changing into a tiger," Vincent answered for her.

When Vincent saw her onto the road back to her apartment, she did not walk beside him, but fell behind a little, stepping on the black shadow behind him. At the same time she made up her mind not to return to the apartment but to go to Vincent's hotel . . .

Now they lay side by side on the bed, and Vincent recalled this occurrence. Lisa asked him whether he was changing into a tiger. Vincent said yes. He also said he really did have the feeling of living in a forest. He started to speak to Lisa about what had happened on the farm. Accompanying his narrative, what Lisa discovered before her eyes was not the rubber tree plantation but rather a vast and borderless desert. The sand blown by the wind blotted out the sky. Without knowing how, Lisa realized that the feeling this desert gave her was the same feeling as the rubber tree plantation. She was stirred once more with the excitement of her whole body catching fire under the scorching sun. The suffocating sand and dust left her no way to draw near. Vincent handed the broken arm to her again.

She made an effort to distinguish the lines on the palm, but it was no good. Blood was already dripping down and sticking to everything. She had to bathe . . .

Maria said to Lisa, "You are Vincent's future. It isn't him disappearing in the night, it's you. You are the sound of nature, traveling without hindrance."

As Maria spoke, one of the African cats stared at Lisa guardedly. She saw that its tail was discharging electric sparks. In the sunlight a *pi pa* crackle issued from the rosebushes. Plainly they were on fire, only the flames couldn't be seen. Lisa mused that Maria had changed her house into the rubber tree plantation. This woman was capable of so much. What was her future? Lisa opened her mouth, wanting to ask her, but the question didn't come out.

"My future is Joe, of course," Maria said, smiling. "One day he will journey to some country in the East and settle there forever."

"That East is you then?" Lisa asked in confusion.

"Ah, that is a difficult question to answer!"

Maria walked into the room where the loom was set up. Lisa sat at her side. She heard the loom continuously repeating a word: "Joe, Joe, Joe . . ." Maria's agile hands wove a fluctuating design. It was impossible to name its shape: it could be called a whirlpool, or a snowy mountain, or even a square without edges.

"Joe said he was going to the north on business. How could I believe him?" she stopped.

"Yes, who can even believe her own heart?" Lisa echoed her.

Seeing the beautiful wool, there floated up in her mind the red sun of an early morning in the gambling city, where sprouting seeds, exhausted from a long night of breaking through, struggled out. Under the red sun there were human shapes like dewdrops. Her parents were two of those dewdrops. She couldn't remain seated. She stood up and took her leave. At that moment Maria hurriedly tugged at her, pursing her lips and signaling, but Lisa didn't understand. She didn't know why all of a sudden she threw off Maria and ran to the door. With shock she saw tall, thin Daniel making love to a small young woman among the rosebushes.

She rushed out the front door and ran far away, as if she'd committed a crime.

"What a beautiful day!" she said to herself.

YOUNG DANIEL

"All along you thought we were Vietnamese. Actually, we are from the ancient country Z, where our palaces have red walls and green tiles, and white hares run all over the gardens. There may be an emperor wearing a long satin robe of sapphire blue, but no one has seen him. My home is several thousand li from the capital city. I can't say exactly how far, because none of us has ever been to the capital."

The girl told Daniel these things in an arrogant tone. She said her name was "Amei," but she also said that all the girls of Country Z were named Amei. This was rather convenient. Once you heard the name you would know where they came from.

Amei stood naked among the flowering shrubs, her smooth body glistening under the flickering sunlight. Only the triangle between her legs was a shiny black. She greedily stretched out her long, thin arms, as if she wanted to fly away.

"Amei! Amei!" Daniel rushed in alarm to put on his clothes, tugging at one of her arms.

He stooped to pick up her skirt and give it to her, but she hit him, knocking him to the ground.

She stood with her arms akimbo, squinting at the sky. Daniel, however, thought she was like a hydrogen balloon rising upward. And so he embraced her body in his arms.

"I saw a camel carrying our village on its back. Wherever the camel stopped, we landed there and put down roots. Daniel, have you ever ridden a camel before?"

"No, I haven't. My dear, I love you," Daniel murmured, kissing the hollow at the nape of the girl's neck.

"I love you, too, Daniel. But I must fly away soon. Your country has no camels, and you cannot look out on the landscape from high places. I can't stay here without moving. Look, your mother is coming."

Daniel released her, and turning toward the house he saw Maria walking down the stairs. When he turned back around, Amei was already gone. A white thread ran across the crystalline sky. Daniel was terribly annoyed. He wondered, staring at the ground, where her clothes had gone.

Maria did not come over. She returned inside, where she was working. Daniel didn't want his mother to see him looking like this, so he quietly slipped out of the yard.

Daniel returned to the house of the Russian woman, Zhenya. Zhenya was Maria's friend, a fat, fiery-hearted widow. She let Daniel live on the second floor of her home in a small room with a window facing the sea. Zhenya sold fruit to make a living, and her house was her storefront. Daniel also helped her at this trade. His own business began with Zhenya's customers, because among the people living nearby every house had its own garden, and all needed care. Zhenya said she was forty, but Daniel believed she was at least fifty-three.

Zhenya sat in the shadow of the fruit baskets, sunk in thought.

"Zhenya, do you have a fiancé?" Daniel asked her.

"Oh, yes. He's in Siberia. We haven't seen each other for twenty years. He doesn't even have a telephone there, so we pass information through business groups as they come and go. Young man, why do you ask about this?"

"How do you two address the question of sex?" Daniel's face reddened, but fortunately the light in the room was dim, and Zhenya did not raise her head to look at him.

"That is a secret between the two of us, one we can't tell other people."

"Do you still intend to get married?"

"Of course! Otherwise what am I doing all this hard work for? He hasn't come to see me once, and I have never once been to see him. See how we toil!"

"Do you plan to make money and then go to Siberia?"

"That is impossible!" She stood in surprise, looking at Daniel. "How can you speak of money? A little business like this can't make money. He was very clear on this point . . ."

Daniel lowered his head in concern. He felt as if he were living inside an unsolved mystery. Zhenya was like a bread oven, hot from head to toe, and her days were so difficult! Even so, what in essence distinguished those two from people like Amei and himself, who were so near, meeting daily? Like his father, such an able, a talented man . . . He thought this and then stopped, because he respected his father too much. At present Daniel had five customers. He planned to expand to ten customers, so he would be much too busy. He liked working in the gardens and he knew that the garden of every house held its own secrets. And if you didn't go there to work, you would never know these secrets. This was the kind of thing Daniel had observed since he was young, and so, in the end, he chose the profession of gardening. In his own home, it was only his father who didn't understand this secret. His thoughts lay in other places.

Today when he was selling fruit, Daniel had recruited another customer. It was a disabled man, with a handsome face and a golden beard on that face. He lived in the middle part of the street in a white house. The family was wealthy. His wheelchair stopped in front of the shop. He was only looking around, not buying any fruit, as if he were waiting for Daniel to come out and speak with him. Daniel went over, and they quickly struck up a conversation.

This young man, Nick, appeared to have a violent temper. He spoke incoherently, one hand waving back and forth as though he were having an argument with someone. It cost Daniel great effort to understand that, in fact, Nick was an insomniac. He stayed out in his family's garden all night long. But the layout of the garden drove him mad. He'd made up his mind to ask someone to help him disrupt it. For a long time, he had dreamed of a stretch of uncultivated land

and the full wheel of the moon slowly rising there. He hoped Daniel could help him realize this dream.

The impression Daniel had of Nick's house was of a white building which could be seen from the street. It was a long, four-story building, taking up almost a quarter of the block. Because the white edifice beyond the iron fence was so close to the street, and so immense, Daniel had never thought of there being a garden behind it. As to the garden, he had in fact heard Maria speak of it. But he had never seen it with his own eyes. Maria had told him that Nick's family were old residents of the area. The family business was large, its foundations deep. But since the middle of the last century the family had been in decline. She didn't know why. Its members had dispersed, and now at the house there remained only Nick, who was disabled, an old grandfather, a cook, and an old servant who had something wrong with his eyes. The building contained more than a hundred rooms. It was a long walk from the east end to the west end. A city census taker once went to their house, a young man, who passed back and forth through the building. He said that he'd looked into all the rooms and was positive no one from the household was there. Where were they actually living?

Daniel accompanied Nick through his family's house and reached an enormous brown transparent tent. He had never in his life seen such a large tent, like a small square inside. Moreover, the tent was constructed of a material he had never seen before: it was neither cloth nor plastic, but was almost like a transparent animal membrane. Yet he couldn't think of what animal had this kind of membrane. There was an orange hot air balloon in the center of the tent. Stepping closer to look, he saw pots of nearly dead orchids in the basket under the balloon.

"This is my family's garden." As soon as Nick spoke, a *weng weng* buzzing sounded from every direction.

Daniel turned back and discovered Nick's wheelchair floating in the air and, further, that the head of the man sitting in the wheelchair hung down, that his handsome face was grayish, and the corners of his mouth drooped in an unsightly way. It seemed he had taken ill.

"Nick!" Daniel called out anxiously, and was soon frightened by the noise he raised. All around was a sound like the constant breaking of glass windows, and the hot air balloon began gradually to shift.

Daniel wanted to retreat from this unsettling place, but at the entrance where they had come in he saw a fiend, a man in his prime, who stood holding a large hatchet.

"Where should I work?" he mustered up the courage to ask. At once he felt a pain in his eardrums, as if they'd been punctured.

Nick's wheelchair moved in a circle through the air inside the tent. As it rose higher and higher, his voice carried down from overhead: "Start with the mud under your feet. It's grown over with Euphrates poplar."

Daniel climbed into the hot air balloon. The balloon leapt into the air, and before long it rushed out through a gap in the tent. It didn't rise very high, however, always traveling along at five or six meters up, and never leaving Nick's residence. Daniel saw the enormous tent bulging and shrinking like a frog's belly, and heard Nick shouting from inside. Under the blue sky, Nick's household did seem a bit unusual. Daniel had always believed his own to be the strangest house, and had never imagined this kind of situation. He forgot his original reason for coming.

Someone suddenly began speaking from a partition underneath the basket of the hot air balloon. Daniel leaned on the seam to look underneath, and saw two people on the level below the basket. They were very old men, with wrinkles like rock fissures on their faces. One was sleeping, the other wrapped in his thoughts.

"Hello," Daniel said, knocking on the partition. "Are you the owners of this house? Can you tell me where your garden is? I need to get to work! I can't fly back and forth in the air all day!"

Despite this long string of words, the old man, as he woke, only watched him guardedly and shrank back. He seemed to be trying to make his body appear as small as possible.

"Please, tell me, are you the owner?" Daniel roared.

The old man stood up, trembling and rustling, and with effort spat out the words:

"No need to shout . . . danger . . . cliff . . ."

The basket collided violently with something. Daniel's vision went dark. He got up and sat on a wooden chair. The hot air balloon still wheeled in the sky over the house. Daniel suddenly understood that this family spent the better part of their time in the hanging basket. This is why the city census taker had been unable to find them.

So why had Nick employed him to take care of the garden? Up till now he hadn't seen even the shadow of a garden. Aside from the large building, their residence consisted of only the enormous tent in the back and this unused space outside the tent. Perhaps the tent really was Nick's family's garden, and all the objects in it were things Daniel couldn't see. He couldn't see them because he was not as perceptive as Nick. Before Daniel's eyes appeared the image of Nick's wheelchair hovering inside the tent at around midnight. This was the anxious insomnia of which Nick had spoken. Now Daniel discovered a marvel: the bowls of orchids unexpectedly burst into full bloom. He counted twelve flowers, and also a few buds ready to blossom. Looking at them, Daniel couldn't help thinking, Did Nick intend him to care for the flowers in midair? Daniel did not like the feeling of suspension. He also could not think of how his work would progress in that kind of environment, where he couldn't even sit stably. As for the two old men under the partition, could they really believe that the hot air balloon was safer than the inside of the house?

Someone below was shouting. It was Nick, who'd reached the open space, waving his arms for Daniel to come down.

"Jump down, jump quickly! The balloon will explode!" His face was white.

Daniel heard a buzz, *weng*, in his head. He climbed over the side of the basket, closed his eyes, and toppled down.

Everything was fine. He fell on the mud, without any injuries. The earth of the open plot was soft.

"You've crushed a whole patch of violets!" Nick said.

Daniel discovered a knife wound on Nick's face. It was still bleeding. He let out a cry.

"It's nothing," Nick said. "It's from wrestling with the cook. This sort of thing is unavoidable. I wanted you to come down because the hot air balloon isn't able to bear too much weight. But it doesn't descend when you want it to, either, so you're forced to jump out. It's the same for me: entering the tent is easy, leaving the tent is hard. I have to fight with the cook. He's cut my wheelchair to pieces. You may find it strange: why do I want to have a garden inside the tent? It's to treat insomnia! I push the wheelchair along, traveling back and forth in midair, the nerves of my cranium get a rest, and the long, long night passes. There are several trees that have grown too tall and block my path, but that's no problem. Every time I encounter an obstacle, I become more agile. But I'm not satisfied with the grass and flowers of the garden below—always the same varieties, and all clear from a glance. I want transformation. You can help me, right? Daniel, I tell you, in the garden just a moment ago, I thought I would never wake up again. That way I wouldn't have insomnia. But I'm still unresigned; I cried out."

Daniel saw that as Nick spoke he was staring fixedly at one spot, so he turned around to look. What he saw almost made him vomit. The cook was standing inside the tent. He had sliced his stomach open and was pulling out his intestines.

"Don't be afraid." Nick pushed his wheelchair nearer, saying quietly, "We can take this opportunity to go examine the garden."

"I want to leave," Daniel said weakly.

"Good-bye then. Thank you for helping me arrange the garden."

Daniel was passing absentmindedly through the large white building, which was so still that even the crows and sparrows were quiet, when he bumped into two men in uniform. They grabbed his shoulders and shook him sternly, saying, "Wake up! Wake up, you!" Daniel told them that of course he was awake, but they didn't believe him. They said people who came here were never able to wake up. They asked Daniel where the family was hiding. He said they might be in the basement. The two men left him and ran downstairs.

He was leaving through the main entrance when Nick caught up to him again. Nick wanted him to promise never to speak of the place where his grandfather was hidden. He also said that if Daniel told, it would be the death of them. "Inside here is a paradise on earth," he explained.

Daniel returned to Zhenya's with his empty stomach rumbling. Zhenya gave him a large bowl of borscht and some veal. Daniel ate until his forehead sweated. His mind was greatly eased.

"Nick is a murderer," Zhenya said. "He kidnapped his grandfather, along with the manservant, and threw them in a dry well. Every day he throws some food down into it. He suffers from insomnia because his conscience is troubled."

"How do you know this?"

"Is there anything on earth I don't know? But this Nick, he isn't a bad person. He did it to save his grandfather's soul. Those two old men don't plan to ever come out from the well."

As Daniel helped Zhenya unload the fruit baskets from the car, he saw his father walking by, swaying as he walked. He carried a leather suitcase and appeared to be drunk. Daniel had never seen his father like this before. He remembered his mother saying that his father was on a business trip, so why would he still be loafing around here? Worried his father would recognize him, Daniel quickly turned his back and went into the building. Inside he stood at the window facing onto the street and saw his father place the suitcase on the ground, sit down on it, and read a book.

Zhenya quietly entered. She wanted to speak with Daniel about his father.

"Your whole family is very interesting, very difficult to fathom. So when your mother proposed that you stay at my house, I agreed right away. Buoyant people, like your family, are the kind I like to deal with the most."

Her heavy body pressed down on the sofa like a rock, so that the shape altered.

"Your mother's spirit is so light, she's truly happy! You've asked about my fiancé. Look at me, I'm so fat, so heavy, how could I go to him? If I was like your parents, who can make themselves invisible at any time, I would have returned to his side long ago. Look, your father isn't sitting on his suitcase, he's rising into the air. That's how focused he is!"

"My father is reading an Eastern detective story," Daniel mumbled.

"Of course, he's a great man."

Daniel noticed his father's hair was a mess, his clothing disarrayed. The strangest thing was that he was wearing a pair of garish leather shoes, the kind with pointed toes and a decorative pattern. Was this man actually his father?

"I like buoyant men the best." Zhenya's eyes suddenly shone lewdly.

As her voice fell Daniel turned to look at his father, but didn't see him.

"He never stays in one place," Zhenya said with admiration. "No one can be sure where he is."

The whole following afternoon Zhenya was tormented by a fearsome worry. She said that she had caught "gigantism," that the flesh of her body was expanding until she couldn't possibly survive it. "Daniel, Daniel, I'm going to die!" she hollered, flailing on the sofa. In her despair she refused to handle any of the business, so the troubled Daniel ran in and out, both selling fruit and comforting her.

When the sky was dark she finally calmed down. Staring into Daniel's eyes, in a daze, she asked, "Daniel, tell me the truth, am I completely hopeless?"

"How could that be? Zhenya, you are a beautiful woman. You're a little fat, but that doesn't affect your charm at all. You are the kind of—let me think a bit—right, you are the kind of person who can be in two places at the same time, like my parents." Daniel thought he'd said a clever thing.

"Really? Really?" Zhenya grew happier. "You're a good boy! Ha, I will let you meet my fiancé. I can't say for sure what day he will come with the business inspection group! Now I have a plan. I intend to make the sensation of my body disappear. Do you think I can manage it?"

"You certainly can." Daniel spoke in earnest.

Even so, that night Daniel, sitting before the window, saw a peculiar thing. His bedroom was on the second floor. He looked down and saw a man and a woman kissing under the streetlamp. At first he didn't notice, but then he thought the man looked familiar. He discovered that as a matter of fact the man was sitting in a wheelchair. It could only be Nick, Nick wearing a white sports shirt and looking like a vigorous young man with extremely well-developed muscles. The woman turned around, and her immense body was illuminated by the streetlamp. To his surprise, it was Zhenya. Daniel felt happy for her because she had a new love. Before, when he thought about her strange, possibly nonexistent fiancé, Daniel had felt uncomfortable. He believed that this man was merely an illusion depending on a few threads of information to preserve it. Although this was interesting, Zhenya had no need to renounce all life's pleasures because of him. But Daniel couldn't understand Zhenya's display downstairs, when he saw her sit on the stone steps and cry bitterly. Once she started crying, Nick, as though evading a contagion, fled, his wheelchair rocking.

Daniel ran downstairs to Zhenya's side.

"Daniel, I can't go on living!"

"What's the matter?"

"You must have seen what I just looked like. Aren't I like a pig? I'm so fat!"

"I looked down from upstairs. What I saw was a beautiful woman and a prince kissing." Daniel stroked her fleshy back and reassured her.

"I want to die!" she said loudly.

"Wait a bit, Zhenya. Wait, and you'll change your mind." Daniel raised his voice, too. "Once you see how he looks flying around in his tent, you'll love him even more!"

"He is a half-bodied devil."

Zhenya stood, with effort shifting her body. The two of them went inside and shut the shop door. Daniel smelled the thick stench of rotten fruit. The smell was more concentrated than at any other time. It was suffocating. Zhenya had not returned to her bedroom, but sat dully among the fruit baskets. Daniel thought she must be remembering something. He couldn't stand the smell, so he went upstairs.

Zhenya sat there the entire night, crying every so often. Daniel slept in his bedroom, hearing her crying and complaining, mingled, it seemed, with Nick's voice. Daniel didn't believe that Nick had really come to the shop. Rather, Zhenya was imitating Nick's voice. In this way she demonstrated that she surely loved him. But why had Nick run away?

"Is Nick here?" Daniel asked a red-eyed Zhenya in the morning.

"No. Everything you heard was him speaking from inside my body."

She had squashed a basket of apples, ruining it. The juice ran all over. Zhenya really was too heavy. Daniel wondered if she truly planned to die. Her disgust toward her body had reached the point of wanting to wipe it out altogether. Was a person like this still able to love someone else? Was her love genuine? Daniel suddenly understood: Zhenya simply wouldn't die. She had come here from remote Siberia, and had all but put down roots. Thus, she was unable to seek death; she would always live like this. In the dark storeroom with its rotten fruit smell, she made despairing moans. No one could have imagined her love to be so deep. Perhaps her lover was a Siberian with a beard, a man as shrewd as a thief. Perhaps it was Nick, who had no legs but could fly in the air. After all, it wasn't important who it was. The important thing was that antennae could stretch out from inside of this despairing body . . .

Daniel raised his head, and saw Amei standing in the doorway.

"Amei, Amei!" he called out in confusion.

"Here, where you are, is like heaven, Daniel." Amei made a lovely smile.

She caught sight of Zhenya, and her eyes immediately grew bright and shining. She walked timidly up to her and mumbled, "I've come here with Daniel, Auntie." Her voice carried a weeping note.

Zhenya glanced at her with an expressionless face.

Amei grew even more ashamed. She went out, her head lowered and her face turning red.

Zhenya, who had not slept all night, suddenly grew lively. She directed Daniel, and the two of them hustled, lifting the large basket of squashed apples and throwing them away. Afterward she rolled up her sleeves and went to make breakfast in the kitchen.

"This is living," Daniel sighed. In his heart he recalled Amei with concern. He didn't understand why a person like Amei would be ashamed to meet Zhenya. Thinking of Amei among the rosebushes, how abandoned she was, he still couldn't keep his heart from pounding with infatuation. Then he remembered his father. His mother probably thought, like Zhenya, that the farther away he went the better.

Daniel returned to his own home and saw his mother, as usual at this time of day, drinking tea in the garden. She beckoned Daniel to join her. The sky was overcast, and the two cats were again wailing beside the well.

"Your temper has grown steadier at Zhenya's house." Maria's face betrayed a smile.

"Father is walking back and forth out on the street. How is that possible?"

Maria snickered, *pu chi*, saying: "He said he was leaving on a business trip. If someone is too consumed with stories, he no longer has any sense of reality. Don't you agree?"

Daniel glanced at his mother, thinking that her eyes looked bright and shining.

He went upstairs to his father's study. As he sat down in the old-fashioned armchair, looking around at the bookshelves that filled the room, it occurred to him that his father had just been there. On the open page of an old book spread out on the table was a drawing of a cat, and beside the cat were the words *Turkish cat*. He examined it with care for a long time, but even then he couldn't tell what the characteristics of a Turkish cat were. This cat and the cats of his city were alike in every particular. When he was small, Daniel had sometimes snuck into this library for a look around. He didn't read books himself, but he had always been familiar with the smell of books. From the time he was six he had known that his silent father lived inside a completely different world. And although his father's world fascinated him, he had never thought of connecting with him through reading. In fact, Daniel thought he and his father were already in communication, only his father didn't think so. For example, he saw the cat on the page, saw the words *Turkish cat*, and felt that he already knew the book's meaning and was faintly agitated by it. To quiet his agitation, he moved the book a little aside. But at this movement, he felt in the right hand that lifted the book a numbness and weakness that rushed straight toward his heart. He had always believed that his father, absorbed by his many bookcases, must surely have a great and powerful mind. Daniel himself was thin, weak, and easily agitated. When he encountered a problem he was often unable to extricate himself. His worship of his father was thus natural.

Daniel took the books down from the shelves one by one and leafed through them, then restored them one by one. He was once again captivated by the smell issuing from the books. It was an extremely familiar smell, but also complex and hard to describe. It was like ice flowers on the windows on a snowy morning, or an old well with the moss of many years beside it. But what it was most like was the illustration in the book on the table—that Turkish cat. While he was absorbed in concentration, leafing through the book, someone slipped into the library and hid behind a bookcase. It was Amei. From her hiding place, Amei couldn't help sighing. She'd felt for a long time that it would be hard for a boy like Daniel to survive. His appearance now confirmed her view.

"Who's sighing over there?" Daniel asked. He couldn't see Amei.

He was suddenly upset. He replaced the book and went to find his mother.

But his mother was gone. It was Zhenya sitting at the table in the garden. She welcomed him over, smooth-browed and smiling.

"Every time I come to your house, I forget that I'm fat. I'm almost as light as a swallow now."

Daniel sat down across from the balcony of his father's library, staring at it in a daze. Amei's silhouette flashed for a moment on the balcony. His spirit was still immersed in the atmosphere of the books.

"Zhenya, tell me where my father really is."

"He and Maria are together. Those two can't be apart for a moment. Has Daniel thought of leaving home?"

"I've already decided to be a gardener here. So how could I leave?"

"Oh, that's no obstacle."

Zhenya hugged an African cat on her air cushion of a stomach. The cat tamely licked her stomach where her clothing parted.

"Daniel, I want to tell you about your mother," Zhenya said, watching the red dragonflies fly back and forth. "Maria is a remarkable woman. You can't find another woman like her nowadays. Think about how the small town she used to live in has been gone for so many years. Almost no one from it is left, but without changing her original plans she still speaks with them. In this city, who of us can build a house on a foundation passed down from our ancestors? I'm afraid there is only Maria. One night, my Siberian fiancé had entrusted someone with a letter for me, and the letter said he was tired of waiting. It said that since he couldn't touch my body, it was the same as not having a fiancée, so he planned to go roaming. After reading his letter, I wept and came crying to your mother. You were still at boarding school then. Your house was blazing with lights. Your father was on a business trip. I thought your mother was in the bedroom, but I looked all over and couldn't find her. But as I searched, the sorrow of my heart eased. I sat in your kitchen eating meat pies and my mind became entirely calm. Then I heard someone speaking in a low voice. I followed the voice and finally found it in the laundry room in the basement. Your mother was sleeping in the large tub, with dirty clothes piled around her. Her mouth moved continuously, calling out, in a quiet voice, a name unfamiliar to my ears. Every time she called out, a strange, hoarse voice sounded from the wall opposite her. I couldn't hear clearly what it said.

"'Zhenya, dear, do you love your fiancé?' She suddenly turned her head and looked earnestly into my eyes.

"I stood there, my brain completely numb, then I felt my heart surging. I piled up words: 'Maria, Maria, I love you! You cannot abandon me.'

"You see, Daniel, your mother and I are such kindred minds. Your mother told me later that on the night your father went away on a business trip, she was having 'true communication' with him through those ancestors. When your mother and I sat among the rosebushes drinking coffee, my body floated in the air. That really is a rare happiness! She sang 'The Small Village Bakery' for me. Every time I heard it I shed tears. The two cats ran back and forth, giving off electric sparks. If it wasn't for the sound of cars outside, we would have forgotten where we were. Daniel, I'm telling you this so you will know that your mother is a woman entrenched in older times. The origin of her family is complicated, which makes her proud but also makes her suffer. Yet she gave birth to you on this foundation. It's so strange!"

Zhenya's speech had just ended when Daniel again saw Amei. She went out quietly through the main gate. Daniel shouted to her. She did not answer.

"Life is so fine! Red dragonflies, girls!" Zhenya said.

That day the two of them returned to the shop arm in arm. On the road, Daniel smelled the icy wind blowing from Siberia, bitterly cold, but fresh and new.

8

MARIA TRAVELS

Standing in the southern wind that blew across the wilderness, Maria felt her mood brighten and expand. She had taken a late-night train. She'd slept in the car while the train rocked, and had many uncommonly strange dreams. When she awoke these were wholly forgotten. All she recalled was a dream about snakes. In her dream, nimble, delicate green snakes pushed into her room through every crack and crevice. Afterward, the sound of strangers' voices entered the room, and the snakes floated one by one into the air and disappeared. She didn't wake when the train reached the station. A train attendant woke her. The attendant was a young girl, with a freckled snub nose. She looked as though she might be Cambodian. She stood to one side and watched Maria collect her bags, as if there were something she wanted to say, but she held herself back from speaking. When Maria disembarked the girl also helped carry her luggage, warning her in a professional voice, "It's very chilly outside, take care not to catch a cold." Maria thought the girl was a bit unusual.

The place was called North Island. It was a place Maria had dreamt of as a child. Toward the end of his life her grandfather had told her about this place in a few spare words. Over the years that followed a notion often occurred to Maria: could North Island be her true hometown? At present she felt that her coming here wasn't a sudden whim she'd seized on, but rather that she'd arrived after several decades of premeditation. It was a secret journey. She hadn't even told Daniel.

There were buildings hidden among the bamboo groves. The village covered a considerable stretch of ground. Maria had never seen bamboo this large and tall before. Its height exceeded that of poplar trees, and the smooth trunks left one with a feeling of dread. The village was made up of earthen houses with grass-thatched roofs, scattered thinly over a large area.

The taxi driver brought her to the entrance of the village and departed. Maria looked toward a wilderness extending as far as the eye could see, and her heart brimmed with uncertainty: What did these villagers do for their livelihood?

Based on arrangements she'd made beforehand, she was met as a guest. A large, tall woman with a voice like a man's took her suitcase and led her through the bamboo groves. The woman was barefoot. She wore a dark blue linen gown, with her heavy bronze hair drawn up behind her head. Maria thought that the woman, whose name was Wula, was probably about forty years old. She also thought that Wula's whole body seemed flush with strength, like an animal's. The woman walked too fast for her and kept having to stop and wait. Maria felt apologetic.

They stopped at the door of one of the earthen houses. This building was a little larger than the others, but already old, having a look of decline about it. Even its wooden doors swayed. Just inside was a spacious central room with a number of giant ceramic water vats arranged around it. In the center of the building were an enormous square table and wooden chairs that were also large and rough but looked very comfortable. Maria thought that perhaps all the people here were incredibly tall and large. After she sat down in one of the chairs, Wula disappeared. Maria heard the water in the vats splashing, *ding dong,* against the sides as if they contained some kind of aquatic animal. Maria looked into the bedroom and saw that the bedding was done in very aggressive colors, a homespun cloth with a background dyed deep blue with a pattern of large gold flowers. In the dimness it gave off an ambiguous light. "How beautiful!" Maria was inwardly surprised, then her heart surged with a sort of regret, a pained feeling at the imperfect art of her own handmade weavings.

Someone knocked on the door. Maria stepped over, opened it, and saw a man with a body like a pylon and hair that was already white. He asked whether Wula was in. Maria said she had just left.

"That poor woman!" the man said, stooping and lifting the covers from the water vats to look inside.

The room was too dark for Maria to make out the animals in the water vats, but she saw indistinctly that there was something in every one. The vats were deep. The things attempted to climb out, but never succeeded.

"What are these animals?" Maria couldn't help asking.

"They're peculiar to this place. They used to be feral, but then, over many years, they became domesticated. At first they ran into the village in packs, jumped into our jars, and sat there without moving. Then, later on, we domesticated them. We named them golden tortoises, even though their bodies don't have shells. Wula raised all the ones here in this room. Before this, we planted rice paddies for our livelihood. After the tortoises came, no one planted any more. When you arrived you saw, too, how all the land lies uncultivated. They are really tortoises of desire! What's the old saying? 'Where there is desire, there is a wilderness,' is that right?"

When he spoke, his white teeth flashing, Maria grew alarmed. She sensed that he was a man inclined to violence. But she also thought his sort of violence was harmless.

"Why would the tortoises seek their own death?" Maria sank into confusion.

"Maybe they want a life of certainty. Every vat is a dungeon."

"What do they eat?"

"For a long time now they haven't eaten anything. They depend on nourishment from our bodies to live. Just think, who wouldn't want to run a business that required no investment? You only have to change the water once a day! And a tortoise sells for 200 yuan. As each day lengthens, the people of the village become like the tortoises. You didn't meet anyone on the road coming in, did you? It's because they were all lying down inside their houses. Except for small children, most people are lying down."

"Why are they lying down when they could go outside and play?"

"Who would be in the mood for play? They contemplate their life of suffering instead."

"Wula, too?"

"Wula is an exception. That's why I called her 'poor woman.' She has no time for contemplation. She's opened this hotel and she has to take in travelers from outside. My name is Qing. Didn't I tell you that already?"

After Qing had inspected the tortoises, he stood at the entrance smoking tobacco. Now Maria could see Qing's face. His expression was hard to describe because the left and right sides of his face could have belonged to two completely different persons. Maria was sitting directly opposite him, so she saw the left and right sides of his face at the same time. The left side was lively, and at the moment it wore a bitter expression, even though a second before it had looked full of energy and even slightly evil. The right side of his face had a somewhat frightening look, dead like a corpse or vampire, with a firmly shut mouth and an eye like a glass bead. Perhaps he knew that the right side of his face was frightening because he was apt to place his left side forward. Now he turned his face sideways. Maria saw his left eye blinking continuously. The muscles in his left cheek twitched.

Maria stood and walked to the doorway to see where he was looking, and discovered Wula already within his view. Maria was surprised: what a strong influence Wula had on him! Even the left side of his body began to twitch. It was an unbearably painful sight. When Wula walked in, her brow creased, Maria was even more surprised to see that her appearance had completely changed. She no longer looked forty years old, brimming with a natural wildness. She looked instead like a weathered old woman. Her long face, like old tree bark, made Maria wonder whether this was the same woman as before.

Wula entered the room, greeted Maria, and asked whether she'd rested well. Then she stiffened her face and, with her back turned to Qing, asked in a low voice from deep in her chest:

"Is there still something wrong?"

"No," Qing answered feebly, leaning against the earth wall as though he might faint.

Maria marveled at the way this pylon-like man had turned into a mashed cotton flower.

Wula led Maria by the hand into the bedroom, saying in her ear, "Don't mind him. He's here to cause trouble. I was to the east of the village visiting an invalid when someone told me he'd come here, so I hurried back. He hasn't said anything bad to you?" Maria answered, "No." Wula said, "He's a hollow man." She shut the bedroom door with force, and stuck close to the crack in the door, peering out to see whether Qing had left. She repeated this action for a while because Qing still hadn't gone. She started heaving sighs. Maria thought that at this moment she seemed at once old and impetuous. It was as if she had a secret hidden deep inside her, a secret of which she could not speak.

"Is Qing a local man?" Maria asked.

"I'm not sure." Wula waved her arms in vexation. "He says he is, but I don't see it. How could someone local have a face like his? But you can't say he isn't local, either. Many people here watched him grow up. I don't know why he despises our lives so much!"

Wula was indignant, and her face went red all over. Gnashing her teeth, she added: "He cut off our way of retreat."

Wula helped Maria turn down the bed, and said to her, "You should rest a while. I still have to go take care of the tortoises."

But after Maria lay down, Wula wasn't in a hurry to leave. She sat in a chair in front of the bed and started to tell Maria the story of her village.

"You've seen everything. The place has become a wilderness, and it's continued this way for decades. Before it wasn't like this at all. Before, this was a foggy region. Back then things were obscure and dim under the sky. People's temperaments were good, in a rare way. It was a good place for rice paddies, and you'd go outside and see paddy fields. The whole village was a cooperative business. Specialized merchants bought our produce. Our lives were peaceful. Think of it: through the fog, can we ever see clearly where our graves lie?"

After she spoke of these things, Wula was suddenly silent. There was a misty expression in her eyes. As Maria lay there she heard once again a familiar agitation coming from within the walls. Yet it wasn't the sound of voices. It was as though there were lots of mice scratching around inside. Although she was nodding off, she couldn't help asking Wula: "And then?"

"And then? After that, a hidden danger erupted in the village. The hidden danger was Qing. Qing's family was of a particular sort: they wanted to make things very, very clear. Even though they were born here, and grew up here, they were different from the rest of us. You could even say that they are foreigners, I think. For example, with selling grain—we never haggled. But his grandfather had to dispute with the buyers, asking one price and then getting a counteroffer. And as a result fewer and fewer people came to buy, until a part of our grain lay rotting on the ground. But fish and grain were plentiful in the village, and life at that time still went on. With the generation of Qing's parents the situation grew worse. The strange thing was that everyone wanted to see Qing's family as leaders. Everyone obeyed the family, probably because of our great inertia. Qing's parents were shrewd and demanding. Everyone said they laid schemes and plans far ahead. Once this husband and wife were in charge of the village's affairs, the rice paddies were neglected. This was because the parents insisted there was no reason to do hard manual labor, that we only needed to raise the asking price of the grain and everything would be fine. This tactic worked for the first few years; later it was a catastrophe because the dealers coming to buy grain grew scarce, less than half as many as before. The villagers were suddenly so poor they had to skimp on food and clothes. But that one household still appeared to be happy. Sometimes Qing and his little brother would belt out songs on the threshing floor, singing late into the night without going inside. Qing's parents both died on the same day. It's said they ate a poisonous mushroom, and they bled from the eyes, nose, mouth, and ears. Qing and his little brother almost collapsed with grief. After they buried their parents, Qing formally became the head of our village. He was opposed to us planting grain in particular. He had schemes to scare off the grain dealers. Later on he introduced the tortoises from somewhere. Even though no one saw it, I knew he brought these animals because before him there were none here. You noticed his face, of course—isn't it terrifying? But I've gotten used to it. A man with a face like that is capable of changing everything! So now there's no fog in the village. The sun comes out, and every object is very, very clear. In this environment everyone became ashamed, and then collapsed."

"Collapsed?" Maria asked, her eyes filled with sleep. She thought she was already dreaming, but she very much wanted to hear the story.

"Yes, collapsed . . ." Wula's voice lowered. "Dejection . . . disease, a trouble in the heart. You're an outsider, you can't see them, they don't come out. Some people . . . stay hidden inside their rooms until they die. Only Qing saunters around outside, Qing . . ."

In her dream Maria's mood also became one of dejection. She was following a path through an endless forest. The path was dark. Animals made suspicious sounds in the woods. She didn't know whether they were predators. She was tired, more tired than her heart could sustain, when an idea suddenly occurred to her: was this the village of the dead? At this thought, there were tears in her eyes. It surprised her. She'd never been one to form sentimental ties. How was it possible now? She stopped in her tracks, sat down on the grass, and listened to the calls of the wild animals. They came more and more frequently. She heard her own heart, too, beat twice, then stop once, with the sound of blood rushing through the ventricles. She thought her heart must be wrecked by the damage.

When Maria awoke she smelled the fresh scent of the grass and leaves. She remembered that in her dream she had been pulling up weeds from her own grave mound. Out in the central room Wula was talking to Qing. Waves of sound flowed in, their speech seeming intimate, with even a teasing note. Maria got dressed, made the bed, and then couldn't decide whether to go out into the hall. But Wula was calling her.

She sat in Qing's embrace, her pliant body incomparably bewitching. Maria stared blankly. Wula's bronze-colored hair swept down, plentiful and shining and filling the room with its luster.

"Come have some coffee," she said to Maria, with composure.

Qing stretched his face out from behind her shapely shoulders and looked mockingly at Maria.

Maria looked at the blue veins protruding from her own hands, so adept for manual work, and felt inferior. Some time passed, and she managed to raise her eyes, letting her gaze rest on the side of Qing's face that held no expression. That half-face recalled in her a kind of distant memory. She thought of paved granite roads and an elderly jewelry craftsman walking along them.

"She's bashful," Qing looked at her steadily.

Probably Wula also thought it was too much. She struggled out from Qing's embrace and poured coffee for Maria.

Maria noticed that the tortoises in the water vats had all grown quiet. Qing walked outside to smoke. Wula sat down next to Maria.

"So you two are lovers," Maria said dryly.

"I became his mistress because I was afraid. You don't know, Maria, how hard my life is. During the day, I go to each home and comfort the suffering people. Then I also have to take care of the tortoises and receive guests from distant places like yourself. I'm so busy, and yet I don't mind. But the night comes, when everything changes. Every night I go mad. Some nights, I think I've changed into a goat— I ate up a whole patch of the grass at the doorway! In the morning I was in such anguish that I wished I were dead. Then Qing came. He stood under the starlight, and under his gaze, like a wolf's, I became tranquil. So the two of us, neither with a home to return to, fell in together. Don't believe that I think well of him. Most of the time, he is my enemy."

The enthusiasm suddenly faded from Wula's eyes, replaced with an emerging desolation. She proposed taking Maria to tour the village.

"You will see a sight familiar to you." She smiled ingratiatingly.

They ate some bread and then went out. Qing, who stood at the door smoking, stared at Maria, which made her whole body tremble, her face burn.

"No one can resist his charm," Wula said proudly, tossing her hair.

They swiftly entered the dense bamboo forest. Although it was summer, Maria felt eerily cold. She kept breaking out in goose bumps, and regretted not dressing more warmly. It grew colder and colder, and her whole body shivered and shook.

"Wula, how do you know things about me?"

"We've had a connection for a long time. So for the past few years I've been sending you travel brochures."

Wula had not answered her question. Maria hoped they soon would reach a house where they could warm up for a bit. She thought the huge, towering bamboos were changing into icicles. If she kept on walking she would be stiff with cold. She looked at Wula by her side. The woman's face was ruddy and she was not feeling the cold even a little. Maria finally saw an earthen house. A dirty boy, his face plastered with mud, sat at the doorway to the house. He was stirring up the sewer water with a stick. Wula said they would go in to sit for a bit, and Maria immediately agreed. The boy slapped the dirty water with the stick so it splashed onto Maria's pants. Maria heard Wula call him a good boy.

On entering the house she warmed up a little. Inside three people were lying down, all in one room but on three cots. It didn't seem like a home. It was like a makeshift hotel. The three of them were not asleep. They stared, eyes wide, at the ceiling. The two older ones were the owners of the house, it seemed, and the other was a middle-aged woman. This woman's expression was one of sorrow. Her thin, bony hand dug at the metal rods on the side of the bed, nervously twitching. The two older people were comparatively quiet, their bodies covered by the same kind of thin quilt, with a blue background and gold flowers, that had covered Maria. They almost did not move.

Wula squatted by the bed, talking to the middle-aged woman in a near whisper. Maria struggled to hear her. As Wula spoke the woman's nervousness lightened and the hand digging tautly at the bed's iron rods loosened. After a time, Maria saw her face suddenly reveal the shyness of a young girl. She heaved a sigh and sat up in her bed. As she sat up, the two old people in their own beds raised their bodies slightly, in unison, reproaching her with a glare, as though she had just done something unseemly. The three of them faced each other awkwardly.

"Lila, this is Maria, the woman I told you about. Wasn't there something you wanted to ask her? Look, she came herself." Wula broke the impasse.

Lila, as if she were freed of a heavy burden, dressed and went outside with Wula.

The three of them stood by the doorway talking. Maria discovered that when she left the house Lila became youthful and vivacious. She no longer looked like a middle-aged woman but rather like someone about twenty years old; her brown hair also had life in it. She caught Maria's hand, and said impatiently:

"Maria, Auntie Maria! Are you really from that place? Can you tell me about what happened forty years ago in the locksmith's workshop? Oh, please don't be offended. That event is like an enormous rock pressing on my heart. God, there's something wrong with my throat, I can't speak . . . Wula! Wula . . ."

Her face swelled, turning red. Wula helped, obligingly thumping her on the back and comforting her, saying, "Don't worry, don't worry. Maria is here. She can tell you everything."

"What happened in the locksmith's workshop forty years ago was a murder that was desired by both parties," Maria said, carefully and cautiously. "So you really are the locksmith's daughter?"

When Lila heard this her face brightened. She made several "ah" sounds in surprise.

"Then Nick, the one who's lame, he's still there? That demon?" she asked, gnashing her teeth in rage.

"He's still there, but he didn't do this. Your father was a man who knew his own mind."

"I know," Lila quietly agreed, her gaze suddenly distracted.

"Before long, Lila came to North Island, and became the daughter-in-law of this family!" Wula said in a loud, celebratory voice. She raised one hand and made a strange gesture.

A gust of wind scraped past. Goose bumps covered Maria's body again. She couldn't hold back her complaint: "It's so cold here."

Lila and Wula smiled at her when she said this. Wula explained: "You aren't used to the weather yet. Here, our hearts each hold a ball of fire. If you want us to live like people in other places, that's difficult. To tell the truth, Qing couldn't deprive us of our right to farm all by himself. It is we ourselves who demanded it. The Qing family only saw through to the villagers' natural instincts, that's all."

As Wula spoke, Lila leaned against her, looking as if she couldn't bear to be parted from her.

A shout came from inside the building, a denunciation. Lila's face changed color and she rushed back inside.

Wula explained: "The two old people protect Lila. If it weren't for them, I'm afraid she wouldn't have lived to today. After her father died, she simply didn't want to live."

"Is her husband here?"

"That's a peculiar thing. No one has met her husband. He is a shadow, even Lila hasn't seen him. He only lives in the recollection of the old couple. Lila heard their story, was deeply moved by it, and stayed on with the family."

Maria felt a pair of eyes staring at her from the depths of the bamboo forest. The expression in these eyes was familiar to her. But just when she was about to see who it was, the person disappeared. She wrinkled her brow in an effort to recall who it was. Wula also looked in that direction, as if lost in thought.

"If you don't mind the cold, I will take you to Grandmother's. She lives alone in the depths of the bamboo forest. There's a small brook at her door. She is the only one in the whole village who doesn't raise tortoises."

"Is she your grandmother?"

"No, she is everyone's grandmother. They say she's almost a hundred, but she's still pretty nimble on her feet."

"I'd like to see her."

Wula made Maria walk faster, saying that this way their bodies would give off more heat. They'd walked for a while when the road before their eyes disappeared and they had to wind in and out among the bamboo. Maria became dizzy, but Wula grew energetic. If she hadn't had to slow her steps to accommodate Maria, she could have walked as swiftly as the wind through the thick bamboo groves. At the moment Maria grew so tired she was about to fall down, Wula stopped.

"We're there?" Maria asked listlessly.

"Yes. But we can't enter the building yet, because the old woman is sitting in the stream bathing. She'll be embarrassed if she sees that someone is here."

"On a day that's so cold?" Maria exclaimed.

"But she's not cold, she's so hot she can't stand it. Not many people come here, so Grandmother walks around outside naked. Every month the villagers give her grain. Look, she's coming over."

Maria saw that Grandmother was even shorter than a dwarf, and wrinkled all over. Grandmother ducked into the earthen house. This small, low building was set behind a few weeping willows. Unless one looked carefully it was difficult to discover.

"Grandma! Grandma!" Wula shouted loudly, as she passed through the door.

The old woman did not answer. The room was very dark, like entering the deepest part of an underground cave. Wula led Maria ahead. The strange thing was that they walked for a long time and never came to a wall. Apparently, the building only looked like a building from the outside. It was actually a tunnel.

"Grandma!" Wula shouted again.

In the dark a small light flashed. It was the old woman striking a match. She lit a pipe. In a short while a choking tobacco smell permeated the air. The spot where the old woman sat appeared to be a rock slab, on which were many curiously shaped pebbles. As Wula drew nearer, Grandma was playing with the pebbles. They made a *hua hua* sound, the sound of running water underneath the rock.

"Is it her?"

It was the old woman's hoarse voice.

"It's Maria, Grandma, she's come to see you."

Wula pulled Maria down next to her on the rock. Maria felt a pair of piping-hot hard small hands squeezing her arm. She stopped shivering and no longer felt the slightest cold.

"So this is what Joe's wife looks like." Her aged voice sounded again.

"Maria, Grandma knows your husband. When he was little, Grandma hugged him, and went with him into the river to bathe, but afterward Joe forgot all about it," Wula said gently.

"Oh—oh!" Maria couldn't speak.

"Grandma uses these pebbles to help her remember things. She cannot forget a single thing, not anything! Do you hear the sound of running water? That isn't water, it's the fluctuation of her thoughts. The place where Grandma lives is very special. People from outside can't find it." Wula's speech was full of adoration.

"Maria, do you understand Joe's work?" the old woman coughed as she asked this.

"I don't know, Grandma," Maria said, hesitating. "Are you talking about his sales work? I think I understand it. I always support his going on business trips, and wait at home for him to return."

"You really support him?" The voice became stern. "Listen, his work is only a pretense! He's a two-faced man."

"I thought as much." Maria summoned her courage and said, "I am also two-faced, so I came to North Island. I cannot forget the things of the past."

"Joe cannot forget them either," Wula cut in.

"My grandfather, in his story, mentioned a rock cave, but he didn't mention the bamboo forest. And yet once I got out of the car I recognized this place." Maria felt as if this were dream-talk. "It's so dark here."

Wula had Maria stand against the wall, to avoid stumbling over the small animals passing back and forth. But where was the wall? Wula said it was by her right hand. Maria groped to the right and went several steps without touching anything. Yet Wula said she was already touching the wall, it was only that she hadn't felt it. Every object in the room was like this. Take Grandma's pebbles. They looked like stones but were actually small animals, pets Grandma doted on.

Maria decided to go back, and she returned to Wula's side. Abruptly, she realized that Wula's voice was getting farther and farther away.

"You don't need to look for her. She can't leave this house," Grandma said. "Calm down. Think about your own mistakes."

"Mistakes?"

"Yes. If you're tired, you can even sleep. There are too many clamorous things in here. An old person like me can't sleep, I only doze."

"But you just wanted me to think about my mistakes."

"Did I say that? It's the same whether I said it or not. Put your hand here, feel this small mouse. What do you think of it?"

The small mouse was very hard. It was bouncing and bouncing, like a glass ball. Maria thought it was impossible to be sure that it was a mouse, but Grandma said it was. She also said it was the one she loved best because it stood for the greatest mistake of her life, a mistake that almost cost her her life.

"You used to live in a town where the roads were paved with granite, and later you could no longer find that town? The young always make mistakes, and always think of their mistakes when they grow older. Today my mouse is obedient."

"Wula!" Maria shouted in her direction.

"Don't bother, she is too ashamed. Besides, she's over there."

A feeling of panic rose in Maria's heart. What could she do in this expansive desolate "house," with no way to determine what anything inside it was? Wula had brought her here, but what did she expect from her? Now she, too, was ashamed, because she could not guess the meaning of the things before her eyes. She had always thought the meaning ought to be self-evident.

The old woman screamed. Maria would never have anticipated that she could let out such a sharp, thin sound, like a bird call. And then immediately she began to grumble because a small animal, probably a squirrel, had bitten her cheek. She said she was too fond of them, so they sometimes gave her lessons like this.

"It was a small town with dark clouds pressing down overhead." She suddenly sank back into her recollection.

"Wula!" Maria shouted again. She could hardly stand it any more.

Grandma was angry. Her voice became husky and confused. She loosed a string of curses, took the rocks and threw them on the ground. In a moment Maria felt the ground full of small animals scurrying madly. Maria thought, Grandma doesn't cherish these "pets" after all. In her state of frenzy she would not let Maria approach. Whenever Maria neared, she made a strange, low roar, as if she wanted to eat her. Maria was exhausted, almost collapsing. Her legs trembled with painful needle pricks. She sank to the ground and lay down, not caring whether the small animals ran back and forth across her body. Without caring or noticing, she closed her eyes.

But she couldn't sleep. In the dark she heard Wula talking with Grandma, and it sounded as though they had been talking for a long time. So in fact Wula had been nearby the whole time.

"You look at her, seeming so delicate she can't stand up in the wind, and you worry about her, but actually she can wrestle with evil people—jackals and wolves." It was Wula's voice. "At first I couldn't decide whether to let her come, but she was too persistent—it was beyond my control. And with her constitution, she can withstand anything."

"Wula, did you cry today?" Grandma's voice again became dignified. She was striking a match.

In a short while, Maria again smelled the tobacco, and this smell unexpectedly sent her to a small building with wind chimes hanging from it. She also saw a few fine books on the bookcases in the corridor. She didn't know how it happened, but in those books was Joe's handwriting. It gave her a very odd sort of feeling.

"Today I did not cry." Wula's voice sounded timid. "Because Lila kept pestering me to talk about her problems, I forgot my own. Grandma, do you think things are hopeless for Lila?"

"Yes, hopeless. She has to wait on her father- and mother-in-law to the grave. She is an ill-fated person. Who let her see what happened way back then?"

Wula began to sigh. Maria could hear that her sighs were rough and heavy, like a man's, and wondered how Wula could suffer so much over other people's problems. She thought again of Lila, of her appearance lying on the cot and her appearance outside. It seemed the faces of the people of North Island were not at all like those of people outside. They could change into something unrecognizable in a single day. You couldn't tell whether a person was twenty or forty years old—the age seemed to change depending on the situation. Take Grandma: at the moment her voice was just like a middle-aged woman's, but Wula had said she was almost a hundred. Grandma reached out her hand in the dark, and the hand was smooth, without any protruding veins on the back. But earlier, beside the stream, she had appeared extremely old. Was it that when one reached this "house," time flowed backward?

Now Grandma lit another match. The face that shone in the flame made Maria jump with fright. It was the face of a brown bear, behind which was the circle of a halo, and, finally, in this halo, Grandma's face. That is to say: the bear's face was real, the human face false. She tried to see which it actually was, but the flame went out.

"Grandma, which side of your face did the squirrel bite?" Maria asked.

"The right side. It doesn't matter, their bites do no harm because my face has so much hair on it."

"Maria, let's go." Wula walked over and gripped Maria's hand, saying to her in a low voice, "Grandma wants to talk with a little hedgehog, and she doesn't want us next to her listening. Be careful. Here's the small stream, we lean to the right side and walk along, all along keeping to the right, and we'll reach the outside of the building."

When she said "lean to the right," Maria felt Wula push her to the right. She asked Wula whether Grandma was one of those people who live inside stories, who have two lives at the same time. She was thinking of Joe's double life. Wula said no, that Grandma actually had only one life, the life in this house. People from outside enter the building, talk with her, and have the illusion that they are influencing her life. Her life in fact cannot be influenced. Maria went along with Wula, lifting one foot, then the other. She wanted to talk with this woman about Joe, but didn't know how to put things clearly. She believed Wula and Grandma already had a deep understanding of

Joe. If Maria questioned Wula, she would be ashamed of her own ignorance.

They walked a long way but still had not walked out of that "room." Maria asked how this was possible. Wula told her they'd already reached the hotel.

"There is a door at your right hand, it's the main door of the hotel."

Maria felt only empty air to her right. But all at once she came to her senses, turned and walked to the left. On the left was an opened door, with light shining through.

Qing sat smoking next to the large table. Maria faced the right side of his face. This time she discovered that the right side was not only expressionless like a corpse, but also showing signs of decomposition. The earlobe on the right side seemed to have rotted into a hole and swollen into a lump. And so Maria thought, What a poor woman, this Wula. Her life surely was as dark as if there were no sun or sky.

"You thought it was false, but actually it is real," Qing said.

Wula embraced his neck from behind, with an intoxicated look. Maria saw what she believed at this moment to be the left side of a man's face.

"The tortoises were so noisy it was hard to stand, so I changed all the water in the vats. Listen, they've calmed down."

"You're such a dear," Wula said, kissing his left cheek.

"I've been thinking about it but I can't understand," Maria raised her voice to speak, to avoid showing her uneasiness. "Is Grandma's house next door to yours? Is it just beyond this door?" She indicated with her hand the door through which she had just entered.

"Yes. Push open the door and take a look." The two stood up and spoke in unison.

Maria walked over and pushed the door open. Before her were the bamboo groves of North Island. A chill wind blew past and she promptly shut the door again.

The two of them, staring at her, loosed a sigh and sat back down. Wula whispered to Maria: "Actually, even a painstaking search won't locate her home. Most of the people in this village have never met

Grandma. Can you believe that? Everyone knows she lives behind a few weeping willows in the bamboo groves, but the building can only be found from time to time. When I took you there, I had no plan in mind. I was only walking at random, because I can't recognize the place. Even if I'd been there hundreds of times it wouldn't be possible."

"You think of something in your mind, and afterward that thing becomes real? Like in a dream?"

"When I get quite near Grandma's house I might feel a foreboding, but this kind of foreboding has no certainty. If you don't notice, it's the same as if there were none. When you reach her house, all the questions you ask are answered."

While saying these things, Wula again sat in Qing's embrace. With a change in position, Maria now saw the left side of Qing's face. She felt that this pair of lovers, fooling around together, was full of life. In their movements they seemed to want to swallow each other. Qing stretched out his long, long tongue and licked Wula's face and neck; Wula circled her strong arms tightly around him, her fingernails embedded in his flesh. It seemed that people here had no sense of shame. Now the two of them cast Maria wholly to the side. Moaning loudly in unison, they began to make love. Maria promptly rushed out, her face burning.

She walked in the bamboo grove for a while, and her heart finally calmed. No one from the village was to be seen. It was mealtime, but there was no cooking smoke. If it weren't for an earthen house dimly visible here and there among the trees, it wouldn't have seemed like a village at all. Thinking back to the scene she'd just seen, Maria found it incomprehensible. In this deathly still place, a corner of the world gone to waste and forgotten by the outside, how could desire continue?

"You're distracting me with your walking back and forth."

It was Lila speaking. The girl watched her with bitterness in her large brown eyes.

"How many years have you been here?" Maria asked her.

"I can't remember. Can you tell me about the lame man?"

"No, I can't. Only my son has been in contact with him. Lila, do you love your father?"

"I hate him. Auntie Maria, I suffer too much. Do you think I should go back to my hometown?"

Like a blind person Lila stretched out a hand into the air in front of her, scratching back and forth, bawling: "Go to hell! Go to hell!"

"What are you doing?"

"I need to claw these things, then it will be all right. They surround me day and night. I don't know what they are: sometimes they look like a spider's thread, like a gray tassel, something like that; sometimes there is nothing, only a terrifying black. Ah, there is something hiding in that bamboo tree."

Lila put her arms around the trunk of a bamboo, held it closely, and put her ear to it. Then she shook her head with all her strength. It appeared that not hearing anything made her agitated. Watching her frantic movements, Maria recalled Lila's father the locksmith. That man, back then, stuffed dynamite into the walls of his workshop and blew off his own leg. Maria was stroking Lila's back, thinking to comfort her, when she saw an old man and an old woman emerging from the bamboo. It was Lila's father- and mother-in-law. They looked lively and agile, the opposite of their former sickliness. The two separated, flanking Lila on the right and left, then suddenly pounced and caught her. They were seizing her to drag her back home. Lila struggled at first, but soon became obedient. When passing by Maria, she said in a loud voice: "Auntie Maria, I'm such a fool! If I go back with you, I might as well be dead!"

Her in-laws listened to this speech, then released their hands in unison, becoming affectionate, warmly restraining her, and comforting her with low, kind whispers: "That's right, that's right, a young girl who understands how things are."

The three of them walked closely together toward the house.

Maria returned to the entrance of the hotel. She remembered clearly the direction she'd been facing before when she'd headed into the depths of the bamboo, so how had she come back here?

She resolved to try once again, seeing as the two people were inside making love. Although they acted as if no one were present, Maria herself was terribly uncomfortable. This time she circled to face the rear of the building and walked in that direction. At the start lay a road, and farther on she reached a thick, cheerless wood. When she was cold enough to start shivering, she heard nearby, from inside a few bamboos with trunks as thick as basins, the *nan nan* muttering of low voices. They resembled somewhat the voices inside the walls at home, so she was not afraid. The difference was that these voices carried a sprightly note, full of praise and urging. Maria circled back and forth alone in the forest, listening to the low voices. Her mood suddenly changed for the better. She realized that she no longer feared losing her way. At the same time she felt amazement at her former misunderstanding of the concept of losing the way. How could she have misunderstood for decades?

Wula sat under a bamboo tree. Blood flowed from the side of her forehead and her hands were swollen up like steamed buns. She was crying.

"Wula, how did this happen to you?" Maria stooped and covered Wula's temple with her handkerchief.

"We fought. Every time we make love, we come to blows afterward. Qing says I am a tiger. I don't know how I got to be like this. But him, he is a wolf! Do you see the teeth marks on my forehead? I bit his finger!"

Saying these things, Wula appeared inspired, her eyes filled with anticipation.

"Let's go back to the hotel," Maria said.

"I want to go back, but I cannot find the road. My heart's in chaos."

Her hair spread down and covered her face. Maria saw that there was no shoe on one of her feet, and a bloodied wound on her ankle as well. Wula lifted her head, with tears in her eyes.

"Maria, go back home. If you don't go back, the road back won't be there. What can you do here? We all depend on raising the tortoises for our livelihood. These animals don't appear to eat or drink, but caring for them is not easy because they depend on the energy of our minds and bodies to live. If one day we no longer want this kind of life, then they'll disappear from the water vats. A few of Qing's relatives did this, and now they all lie in their homes on the brink of death. Without tortoises, they lose their means of support. What meaning does life still have for them? Maria, you would not like living here for long. Only people who grew up here, from the time they were small, like their lives here. Look at Lila, who's been here so many years: she cannot make up her mind."

"I still want to see the tortoises. I still haven't seen them clearly." The idea occurred suddenly to Maria.

"Walk toward the right, keep walking, and maybe you'll find yourself back at the hotel."

Maria turned around in the bamboo groves for a long, long time, until she grew disheartened, and then she began to be afraid: would she starve to death in the forest? When she truly could not walk any farther, she sat down and leaned on a bamboo tree, falling into a doze. As she slept, someone spoke, lover's talk, in her ear, sickeningly sweet and calling her "little nightingale."

"Are we going back?" said the taxi driver, who had thick eyebrows and big eyes, seeing her awaken.

"Where are we?" she asked, rubbing her eyes.

"At the edge of the bamboo forest. Look, up ahead is the wasteland you saw when you arrived." He pointed to the right.

"Oh, I didn't notice it! I still need to go to the hotel and pick up my luggage."

"Of course, the hotel is right ahead."

Maria got into the taxi, uneasily sizing up the driver and thinking that he didn't look like a local.

"You don't live on North Island?"

"Me? I come and go. I specialize in transporting guests like you."

After Maria entered her room and picked up her luggage, she stood for a while in the hallway. Finally she couldn't bear the curiosity. She edged toward the doorway and saw no one there, she returned and pulled open the lids of the water vats. It was amazing, every single vat was empty, without even any water.

"I just saw your village head Qing sitting in the wasteland and howling like a wolf."

As the taxi driver spoke his back was to Maria. She realized that all along he had averted his face from her. She was only ever able to see the back of his head.

"He isn't my village head, because I'm not from around here."

"It isn't so simple. I still regard him as your village head."

Maria saw that he was stealthily laughing. She imagined how Qing would look howling like a wolf. Would the right side of his face, where it was starting to decompose, be able to grow a wolf's fur?

Once the car started moving, the driver said to Maria:

"You didn't think I would come here, too?"

"Ha, you're Joe! How could I not have recognized your voice? You were wearing a mask? I thought that you were someone else. How did you find your way here?"

"Wula has been sending me travel brochures, too. She and Qing were woven into my story long ago. I told you just now that I come and go, transporting guests. I have done this for a long time. When I go on a business trip I come here, and in the future Daniel will also be able to come here. Look at those two white egrets in the sky, so free and unrestrained!"

Maria didn't see the egrets; she saw a granite path. Her heart surged up with a thousand kinds of tenderness, so she leaned her head on Joe's shoulder and shut her eyes. She heard many people all hailing her; most of the voices were familiar. Then she saw the square surrounded by cypresses, and a young woman wearing a kimono, and a spring in the center of the square. In her dream she said to Joe: "Joe, I've arrived in your story."

On the road Maria did not wake up. Even if Joe stopped the car for a meal, she ate and slept at the same time. She felt so weary she could die.

Even so she woke when they reached home. She saw Daniel busy in the garden, with small Amei working alongside him. Maria said to Joe:

"Could these two be a match made in heaven?"

Joe smiled serenely, answering:

"Just like the two of us back then."

9

IDA'S LIFE IN EXILE

Ida thought she had finally escaped Mr. Reagan's clutches. She sat at the bar counter, ordered a glass of red wine, lit a cigarette, and inhaled two puffs, feeling dizzy and elated.

The owner of the bar was her fellow townsman, a man a little over forty who looked like an old ape, with small eyes always staring straight ahead. The bar was a family business. The owner's wife and daughter both worked in the restaurant. On holidays Ida came here to help out. Ida's movements were nimble, her mind agile, and she attracted customers. The owner's wife wanted her to stay, to become a member of their household.

The bar was in an out-of-the-way spot. A green neon light, which flickered like ghostly eyes, was set on a grapevine trellis out in front of the restaurant. It was by chance that Ida had come here. Once she arrived she fell in love with the place, then, unexpectedly, discovered that the owner was from her hometown and the bar's customers were all to her liking. For the most part, customers arrived one after another around midnight. Almost everyone walked, very few of them drove. Without anyone realizing it, the seats at the counter and in the large dining room filled. People kept straight faces, spoke in lowered voices, and discussed serious issues in groups of two and three. The owner, Alvin, told Ida that the tone of the bar came about naturally, and only people who spent all day in illusions liked to come here. When they arrived, they poured out to each other the nightmares pent up in their hearts. Alvin called this "woe telling." Ida didn't come to the bar for woe telling; she had been attracted by the bar's name. From a distance she saw the neon lights on the dome spell out two words, Green Jade. She still remembered how things had been that night. She'd walked a long road, roaming nearly all the large streets and small alleys of the city, until at last she reached this corner. At that point she had already made up her mind. If this bar were still not what she was looking for, she would go instead to a certain storefront and sleep there, leaning against a marble wall. But her luck had found her.

Now, in the dim lamplight, with the sound of many whispering voices in her ears, the times she had made love with Reagan often floated up in her mind. The place was sometimes in the thick grass next to the lake, sometimes among the rubber trees, and once, to her surprise, in the middle of the main road. The time, however, was always the middle of the night, without exception. She was unwilling to go to Mr. Reagan's bedroom because she worried she might faint in a place like that. More than once she thought of how funny it was. What if people on the plantation knew that their boss turned into a beast at night? What would they think? A young woman, nearly drunk, greeted her. She was an old customer of Ida's. "I saw your old sweetheart," she leaned close and said in a low voice. "He's whiling away time in the city, too." The young woman applied purple lipstick. Ida felt fish scales growing all over her body. The owner busied himself behind the counter. When Ida first arrived, she had talked with him about the mudslide in her hometown. The man appeared calm, but in his memory the event was quite clear. His whole family had died. The owner's wife was a Western woman, and their daughter also looked entirely like someone from the West, but the closeness among the members of this family was of a kind that's quite rare. If they were apart even for a short time, they would call out, summoning each other. Perhaps because of this closeness, the daughter didn't go to school and served customers in the restaurant instead. This beautiful girl had a calm nature. Ida had never seen her go out on dates with boys. The decor of the bar was unusual, and imbued with a decadent air. The walls were hung all over with the bones of strange animals. Solemn classical music played on a record player. It wasn't very clean in the dining room, the dust seemed to get on everything. People coming in sneezed repeatedly at first. Yet this gray, fog-covered, dark environment had a special atmosphere, so over many years the family had kept up a good volume of business.

Starting yesterday, Ida was staying next door to the owner's daughter's room. Her room was on the second floor, down a long corridor crammed with ancient, dusty furniture. Little white mice scampered in and out of the furniture. It was said that the owner's wife raised them there. Every time Ida went upstairs the mice scurried in front of her feet, so she always took great care where she stepped. Each morning, when she was still in her room sleeping, slight sounds from the room next door would awaken her. It sounded like someone jumping from a high place, a moment would pass, then *tong*, coming down with a thump. One day Ida truly could not stand it. She got up, rubbing her eyes, and went next door to see. The young girl's door was wide open. The room was filled with mice, at least a hundred of them. She was sitting on a table.

"I jump down from the table, to train them in how to quickly flee for their lives," the girl said.

She stood on the tabletop again. The mice waiting on the ground had a look of alert terror. Ida saw they were all shaking with fear. The girl jumped like a diver, then dropped down. In a blink of an eye the mice scurried to the foot of the wall, quivering at the loud sound.

"My father hasn't told you my name yet. I'm Jade."

Her face reddened, and she knelt on the floor to kiss the frightened mice. Ida turned her head and saw Jade's mother, full of smiles for her daughter, holding a mouse in each of her hands.

"My husband talks on and on every day about returning to his hometown. My daughter and I can only make preparations. It's so strange that Ida really comes from that place we long for from dawn to dusk. Do you still remember things from when you were a child?"

When she spoke her eyes opened wide. Ida saw in them an infinite loneliness.

"When I was small, and thought every day about fleeing from the mudslides when they came, it was the same as with these mice. A moment ago I saw Jade's demonstration and felt as if I was returning to my hometown."

Mother and daughter hurried downstairs because the owner was calling them from below. Ida returned to her room, thinking she would go back to sleep. But once she shut her eyes she saw the mudslide, her body suspended in the air the whole time. So she sat up, and looking out the window she saw the tranquil, empty street. Ida reflected on how, even when staying in this dead corner of the city, she often felt an impulse to slink around the neighborhood like a snake. Especially at night, when those whispering customers arrived in twos and threes. There was a customer who was the owner's friend. He very seldom drank, but when his girlfriend drank beside him, he watched her admiringly, urging her to drink a little more. The girlfriend's face was often flushed. She would point into her glass, to make him look inside. At this, he would lean forward and earnestly look back and forth and all over the glass. This man was very much like a man from her hometown who grew vegetables and lived beside the rainforest. Perhaps it really was that vegetable farmer, although he appeared to be too young.

Ida thought, sentimentally, that she had finally escaped Mr. Reagan's clutches. If she were back on the plantation now, she would be busy at work among the rubber trees. For a long time she'd watched as Mr. Reagan enlarged his territory before her eyes, and for no reason she'd grown indignant. She thought he was a tyrant who would make everything disappear into nothingness. At night, among the mists, when the feeble moonlight did its best to struggle through the layers of cloud, Ida felt a desire for Mr. Reagan, perhaps even love. They were tangled together, and she was willing to disappear into nothingness, to disappear into nothingness together with him.

But now she hid in the bar. She thought that Mr. Reagan couldn't find this place. Making her way through the whispering customers, Ida would hallucinate just as if it were the plantation's unsteady land under her feet. "Ida!" the owner was calling her, because a group of people was coming in the door.

This crowd of customers held straw hats in their hands. Their bodies smelled of seawater and the sun. None of them spoke. One after another they silently sat down at the bar, then began to drink glass after glass. Ida was greatly surprised to see that one of the women was a neighbor from her lodging on the plantation.

"Can it be? Can he find any place?" Ida said to this customer.

"Yes, it is fate."

She saw Jade standing opposite, her face pale and expressionless. She might have been listening to the music. Her mother was a little farther away, with her face also turned in this direction. Mother and daughter were both wearing white jackets that were not at all in keeping with the old, dust-covered, decadent ambiance. Did they notice these "hunters"? Or grow uneasy at their arrival? Why did the mother have such a joyous expression on her face? For the first time in many days, Ida smelled the flavor of sunshine. Unable to control her emotion, she took a few deep breaths. As she inhaled deeply, she caught sight of that woman, her neighbor, smiling. Ida's face instantly reddened.

Jade and her mother both walked off, but they didn't go very far. At the end of the hall, at the stairwell, they glanced in Ida's direction.

Ida walked through the back door and stood in the small courtyard. A single raindrop fell on her forehead. Lowering her head, she saw the cobblestones also leaping with mice. The bar was set near the outskirts of the city, so the customers must have walked a long way to get here. Ida, imagining them hurrying along the road at night, imagining them harboring a thirst in their hearts, could not help being touched. She suddenly thought that if there had been a bar like this when the mudslides came, maybe people wouldn't have fled. Her hometown had teemed with mud frogs, and the walls of this bar were hung full of mud frog specimens. In the bar surely people wouldn't hear the rumbling of the mudslide outside, since they were only accustomed to listening to things inside. When the mudslides came, they would be chatting wisely in twos and threes at separate tables.

"Ida."

It was Jade. Two more raindrops fell on Ida's face.

"Ida," she said again.

"Oh, Jade. How are you feeling today?"

"I feel like I want to find a dark hole and go squat inside it to think things over. There are many dark holes in our bar, you slowly come to realize."

The young girl's face couldn't be seen clearly in the dimness. Her hoarse voice had a weathered tone. Ida remembered her astonishing beauty.

"Do you have a lover?" Ida asked.

"I do. But we meet very seldom, because I can't go outside. Oh, I haven't gone outside in over two years. He's my schoolmate. At nightfall he stands on the street waiting for me to come out, but I don't want to go. I'd rather get things done around the restaurant. That doesn't mean I'm not stuck on thinking about him. It's because I know that once I leave Green Jade disillusion will overwhelm me. I help out Father in the shop, thinking in my heart that someone is outside waiting for me. I almost hear the sound of his pacing, it does me such good. If I want to clear the thoughts in my head, I just find a dark hole to get into."

Ida reached out a hand, and held the young woman's ice-cold hand tightly. She felt sorry for Jade.

"And yet my lover became my foe," Ida said.

"It's so strange, I can't think of how that could be."

"That—that is to become a single body with someone, but also to become enemies with him. Even when I stand here, I can still see the crows on the farm spreading over the sky and covering the earth."

Jade's hand on Ida's large hand gradually grew warm again. Ida's heart rushed with the desire to kiss her.

"Jade! Ida!" It was the bar's owner calling.

Ida thought, her mood complicated, that she had finally escaped Mr. Reagan's clutches. She heard a constrained disturbance among the customers. Here and there were the sounds of stifled cries. Even though she made no effort to look, she still saw white mice scurrying madly among the customers. There really were too many of them. A boy came crashing and tumbling over and grabbed hold of her hand, then pounced into her arms, making a slight rustling sound with his trembling. The boy appeared to be younger than twenty. "They're coming again. How can this be? Oh? How can it?" he said. Ida remembered that she had just seen him talking to an older lady with an elegant manner, his eyes showing a maturity exceeding his years. "They call you Ida, are you really Ida? Damn it, they're scurrying over here again. You know how to cope with them."

Ida helped him into a chair, using her body to block the lamp-light so he was left in total darkness. She felt as if this boy were her little brother.

"Whose child are you?" she asked him warmly.

He drew both his legs all the way into the chair, and held his knees with his hands.

"If you leave me, I will never get up from this chair. Tonight there's a rainstorm."

Although people panicked, no one had fled. They formed a line standing next to the wall now, staring fixedly at the little animals running along the floor. Ida thought that they were in fact enjoying these little animals.

Jade walked over from the distant end of the hall, with a gait that looked like she was drunk. Ida had never seen her like this and couldn't help feeling curious. The boy took one look at her and tugged nervously at Ida's hem, saying over and over: "Her! She's coming! You have to hide me! She's coming!" He hid his head in his knee. But it was Jade who stopped her steps in the center of the hall, staring blankly at the animal specimens on the wall. A beam of green light seemed to cut off the other half of her face. In the blink of an eye, Ida understood the relationship between these two people.

When the music stopped, the mice were no longer to be seen. The entire hall became as still as death. At some point, people had taken their places. Perhaps it was the bar owner who'd stopped the music. Now, over by the counter, she could no longer see the figures of the owner and the two waiters; there was a patch of dark. Where had they gone? Ida looked again, and saw that Jade wasn't there either. After a bit, the room resumed its earlier scene of low whispering. But the whole time, the boy stayed in his chair. He grasped a corner of Ida's clothing in his hand.

Ida stood there awkwardly. Past events were before her eyes, an acute struggle in her heart.

Mr. Reagan had once poked fun at her: "Everywhere is your domain. Wherever you go, you make that place your home."

She had retorted: "I want to be free and unrestrained. I imagine drifting like a kite with the string broken off."

Someone reached out a hand from the dark and dragged her over, pulling her straight to the back door. It was Jade. Ida had realized this from the start.

"Don't pay attention to him. He'll bring you with him into an abyss. The boy has no taboos. He's not used to what our bar is like, his situation is miserable."

Jade's pale fingers fearfully twisted her brown hair.

When the mice were no longer making a disturbance and her father and mother went outside, Jade stood beside the ancient furniture covered in thick dust and told Ida of the hopeless love affair. It was Jade herself who'd pursued this Japanese boy. The boy liked to climb mountains. In the early days of their association, Jade had sensed dimly that his weak, brittle exterior was only a kind of disguise, that inside it was some wild thing, a thing that Jade feared from the bottom of her heart. At that time they were as inseparable as a body and its shadow. Finally, one day the boy invited Jade to climb a nearby mountain with him. The mountain wasn't very high. It was a bald rocky peak. Although Jade made ample preparations, she never imagined that midway up it would begin to rain. They lay prone on a steep, slippery cliff. The rain fell harder and harder. He entreated her not to look down, because "you would be able to see right through me." This sentence induced in Jade a desire like a reptile ready to strike. The seduction was too great for her. The result was that she fell into a stone cave grown thick with cogon grass and damaged her spine. During the half year Jade spent in the hospital, she felt that all her hopes were dashed, as though she had died. The boy also went missing. When youth at last triumphed over the spirit of death, when her physical strength was little by little recovered, Jade saw what she had seen that day looking down from the mountain. It was a mouse swimming along a current in midair. Jade regained her normal life, and the boy reappeared. She made up her mind to open up a distance between them, and to raise little white mice with her mother. Her mother, it seemed, grew ever more fascinated with raising mice, so within a short time their corridors were full of the little animals. But the boy didn't want to have a distance opened up between him and Jade. He knew perfectly well that Jade wouldn't leave the house, but he still went to wait for her every day at the old place. Sometimes, like yesterday, he burst headlong into the bar.

"The most frightening thing is the thing we most want to experience," Ida spoke with deep sympathy. "Your boy has a tenacious will."

"I know," Jade said distractedly. She kept looking toward the stairwell, seeming afraid her mother would appear there without warning.

"What are you afraid of?"

"My mother doesn't approve of my sentimental side. She thinks I should concentrate all my attention on handling these mice. Of course, she is right."

Days passed quickly at the bar. Although almost every day had the same substance, Ida still hoped to prolong each one as much as possible. When she had free time, she thought, harboring an infinite longing, that she had finally escaped Mr. Reagan's clutches, but what were things like in the south on that rubber tree plantation? Every day when the business of the bar began at midnight, when the guests came in one after another like shadows, Ida would hallucinate, thinking she was working as before on the rubber tree farm, and that these customers were her co-workers in disguise. Why did the bar owner always put on solemn, abstruse classical music? Could Mr. Reagan already be here, mixed in among the guests? Perhaps it was because of her longing that the days went so quickly, she thought. Escaping her own lover was a good thing. Hadn't Jade escaped hers? Before,

Ida had never known there was a kind of longing like this: longing for the thing or person one absolutely needed to escape. This new form of longing, while unable to bring her fulfillment, could fill out and enrich every day. Look, Jade was even more fulfilled.

Jade's mother was looking around at the end of the passage. She saw that her daughter's door was closed, and tiptoed over. Ida watched her place the object she was holding in her hand on the ground. It was a little white mouse.

"Ida, Ida, do you think Jade is happy?" she asked anxiously.

Ida saw the falling dust all over the woman's clothes, and her hair was a mess, but this could not conceal her innate beauty. That beauty was a bit like the green beauty of a newborn plant, quiet and noiseless, but astonishing. Ida avoided her ardent glance and answered indifferently: "I suppose she is happy. Every day she looks forward to the next, doesn't she? Her mother is truly daring. Who else is brave enough to raise so many little mice? This really is something like a dream becoming a reality."

The woman smiled, as if freed from a mass of worries. She reached out a fair hand and stroked the old pieces of furniture. It seemed they were like her infants.

"These were purchased at a secondhand store. Her father is set on believing that the furniture belonged to his former family, and was scattered after the mudslide. But I have two friends who happened to come upstairs to look at them, and they said these were their family's old things. What do you think, what is this memory then, after all?"

"Memory is the things people think up." Ida spoke too freely.

The woman looked at Ida with some surprise. She walked past and began to lightly knock on her daughter's door.

Ida thought it inappropriate to stand there, and went downstairs.

The bar owner was not downstairs. Someone else sat behind the bar counter, a waiter with an almost fierce expression. Ida had never understood why the owner had recruited someone who looked like this to work at the counter.

This waiter, Mark, was fiddling with the worn-out record player.

It was playing the same music Ida had listened to every day until it became familiar. But under Mark's hands the music became, at intermittent moments, strange sounding, and hearing it Ida's whole body broke out in goose bumps. She swiftly turned to go outside, but tripped over something. Lowering her head she saw that it was the bar owner. He was lying on the ground reading a book. From his appearance he seemed to focus his entire attention on it, and was undisturbed by the outer world. Because the light in the room was dim, Ida could not tell what book it was. Alvin sat up and asked Ida benignly, "Ida, do you still remember what it looked like at the very last moment right before the floodwater swallowed your home?"

"I've completely forgotten. It was chaotic then."

"All those things are written inside this book." With both hands he hugged the book, which was as thick as a brick, to his chest. "Only it doesn't say them openly. They are riddles, which I have to guess. That's what this sort of book is like. I carried several books here from my hometown. When there's nothing to do I lie on the floor and read. Why do I lie on the floor? For convenience' sake. I only need to place my ear against the floor and the things described in the book make all sorts of sounds. I call this 'listening to books.'"

"Could I listen to books?" Ida asked.

"You couldn't, Jade can't either, but Jade's mother can. This kind of thing requires reading experience. And there's that fellow Mark, he can, too. Look, isn't he lying on the floor? He's listening to music. What he hears and what you hear are completely different."

Ida walked over to the counter and looked behind it. She saw Mark's body curled up in a ball on the floor. He was crying.

"Mark is our restaurant's treasure. The customers say his entire body is musical."

Ida walked out the main door and stood under the Green Jade grape trellis, her whole body bathed in its light.

"Ida!" Jade called from the window of her bedroom, with tears in her voice. One of her hands caught at the clothes at her chest, and her eyes bulged with fear.

"Jade! Jade!" Ida waved toward the second floor. She remembered that Jade's mother was inside the building.

What was Jade's mother doing inside? Intimidating her daughter? It seemed the woman was always stealthily forcing her daughter to do something.

Jade's whole upper body extended from the window, as though she were going to jump from it. Once and then again she rushed toward the outside, but she could not get through. Ida understood that it was her mother pulling her back. Ida wondered, since it was like this, why did the mother continue to force her? Perhaps it was because mother and daughter were naturally too beautiful. Overly beautiful people often prefer an extreme sort of life. Something was thrown from the window. Oh, it was a little mouse!

"Ida, good-bye!" Jade shouted, her voice hoarse from the effort, and then drew back in. Immediately someone closed the window.

Ida looked up at the spot in confusion. Why was Jade saying good-bye?

But Jade had not gone anywhere. When night came, she appeared with her mother again at the bar. Mother and daughter looked serious, even somewhat desolate. But the owner was dressed in formal wear, with a bowtie, and beaming with high spirits. Who would have thought he bent to the ground to listen to books?

In the main hall, from a dim corner, came a voice that made Ida's heart leap and her flesh twitch. It was Reagan, Reagan was calling her; Ida heard him clearly.

"I'd like a brandy," said the stranger, who was sitting with a companion.

The world, after all, could have voices as similar as this.

"Miss, please look over to the right." He spoke again.

Ida saw a mouse on the wall. It squatted, gnawing, on the head of a deer. The sound of its tiny teeth scraping the bone was clear and piercing. Ida stared, the menus in her hand falling to the ground. She thought distinctly that she had seen this sight somewhere before, many years ago, with rain and seawater. It also had something to do with a strange man. But it wasn't the man in front of her. This man's voice sounded near to her ear: "Manila, Manila, floodwaters cover the open fields." She turned, but the two men at the table were no longer to be seen.

Jade came to her side and, leaning toward her, spoke: "Now we both have fallen into a cavern. Such an exciting night. Haven't you been out to see the sky? Right now the sky is purple and red."

Jade finished speaking and bent down, picked up the menus and handed them to Ida, then went to wait on guests. Ida observed in her movements as before a kind of bodily longing, just like the snakes in the wild. Where had her guests gone? There really was not the slightest trace left behind. Ida's heart shrank a little in pain. She thought, once again, that she had finally escaped Mr. Reagan's clutches, and perhaps because of this he sent his voice to cover the whole earth. The earth, after all, held a man this infatuated.

She attended to many guests. They all wore numb expressions, with a look of pretending to listen to the music. There was a woman whose jacket button unexpectedly fell off. She bent down to feel along the ground, filling her whole hand with dust. The man who'd come with her also helped her look. He shone a flashlight underneath the table for a long while, so long it seemed undignified. Now the guests close by all walked over to look, surrounding them in a semicircle. The man started crawling on the ground like a cat. He crawled through the empty spaces between the tables, with people giving way in turns.

"A dropped button amounts to upsetting the whole arrangement."

A woman wearing a dark-red coat said this in a low voice. Ida observed her excited eyes gleaming.

Ida was not herself. Wanting to avoid these people, she gathered the plates from a table and went into the kitchen. The cook at first was busy in front of the flame. When she heard Ida enter, she stopped the work in hand and turned around to face her. There was a buzzing *weng* in Ida's brain. Was this Ali?

"I didn't know you were here, that you worked here," she said, stammering.

"Are you new here? I heard there was a new person who'd come, but I hadn't met her. So it's you! It's good that you've come, though the work here isn't easy to get used to."

Ida was relieved. It wasn't Ali. She only resembled her a great deal.

"Oh, I made a mistake. But have you worked in a place like that before?"

"Are you talking about the rubber tree plantation? Of course, fat people like me have all worked in that kind of place. The scorching climate was unbearable for me. Besides, I thought there were too many snakes. They even got into the refrigerators. I would rather be here, missing that place, than stay there myself. I left ten years ago."

She guardedly looked toward the kitchen door, then walked over, closed it tightly, turned back and sat on a small wooden stool to peel potatoes. After a bit someone knocked at the door. She pursed her lips at Ida, saying: "Don't pay attention, it's the bar owner wanting to come in. Once he comes in he adds salt to the meat pies, he says it's to test the customers' sensitivity. He's really insane. I think his opening this bar was an insane gesture, don't you, Ida?"

"Maybe. I'm not sure." Ida listened to the owner's anxious yells.

"Lunatic, a complete lunatic! He wants to go back to that army camp!" The cook turned her fat body around indignantly, and waved a spatula menacingly at the door.

"Army camp?"

"Yes. Couldn't someone like him only have come from somewhere like that? A well-trained soldier. You haven't noticed that the atmosphere in this bar is like an army camp? This is a place that levels individuality."

She put down the spatula and stood there, huffing, clearly not working. Ida thought she was like an angry child. She reminded her of a penguin. In the kitchen, sounds from outside couldn't be heard, so it was a completely different scene. Someone was poking his head in at the window. It was Jade's boyfriend. What was he planning to ask about here? He looked extremely haggard standing under the lamp in the yard like a ghost.

"But someone like this boy ought to go to an army camp for training," the cook said.

Ida finally understood that Mr. Reagan was inescapable. In this unusual bar, far from the farm, Ida's mood had changed. She didn't think of returning to the farm at all. The place where she wanted to return was her old home. In her imagination it was a vague shadow. Actually, she didn't want to take a train there, either. She wanted to take a shortcut, and the shortcut was one of those dark holes in the bar that Jade had told her about.

One day, when music reverberated throughout the bar, Jade guided her into a dark hole. At the time they stood in the backyard talking. There was no rain, intermittent gusts of cool wind blew across the sky, the moonlight appeared clammy. By a pagoda tree someone whistled a hackneyed love song, flirtatiously. Suddenly Jade pressed a hand forcefully on her shoulder. Ida's feet slid, then she fell with Jade into a hole.

Ah, she was overwhelmed with so many thoughts and feelings! Thunderclaps and the smell of the damp mud immediately surrounded her. The sound of shouts spread out indistinctly from somewhere. They were all familiar voices. Jade was not in the same hole as she, but in one next to her. When Ida called, she made a muddled echo, as if she were almost asleep. Surely Ida stood on the mud of her hometown. That softness could not be forgotten in a lifetime. The rain carried a thick fish smell, and it fell without stopping. Soon her hair was wet through. By her ear, a man from her hometown said: "Manila, Manila, floodwaters cover the open fields." She remembered that she'd recently heard someone speak this same sentence. At this moment, she deeply sensed that the people of her hometown had an instinct for quick adaptation. Otherwise, in a place constantly assaulted by mountain floods, how could a race survive? Those people taking the night road, how forceful their steps were, with almost every step holding tight to the pulse of the land.

"Ida, Ida, have you seen the burning clouds of sunrise?" Jade mumbled in a low voice off to the side.

The music swelled, and the smell of the tropical rainforest grew thin. But a rooster still crowed at the light, starting and stopping, crowing and crowing.

Jade's hard, nervous fingers hooked Ida's fingers. They stood shoulder to shoulder. A man and woman, both drunk, supported each other home. Jade said that they had a long journey to make.

"They are returning to a house with a dungeon," Jade told her.

"But my dungeon has no boundaries," Ida said, disheartened.

Jade stifled a laugh. Ida had seldom heard her laugh in this elated way.

"Has your boyfriend come?" Ida asked.

"I can wait somewhere like this, and hear his footsteps traveling far from his hometown. This feeling is always so beautiful. I hear the sound of his instincts."

Ida thought she would go back to the farm tomorrow. There should be many holes like this there, too. She had completely mistaken them before.

Ida moaned. "My foot!" she said. Her foot was still stuck in the mud of her hometown. It was difficult to extract. Jade turned to look at her, and said it would be best to get used to it. She also said anything could be gotten used to. The door opened and Ida saw the bar owner hiding in the shadows. He lay under a table reading a book. It was very difficult to believe he could see anything clearly in such a dark place. Did the two drunken customers leaning on the table know that Alvin was underneath them?

"Jade, I really admire your father."

"So do I. You should know that the whole bar is his dungeon. Sometimes I think that I'm ridiculous compared to him! The best I can do is not leave my bedroom to go outside."

She circled around the counter and went to find Mark. Ida bent down to speak to the owner. He opened his mouth, but his gaze didn't move from his book.

"I've read this story for decades. Everything in the story is a trick.

Ida, have you made up your mind to go back? Tomorrow's train leaves at nine in the morning."

"How do you know I am going?"

"All things are written in this book. After you leave, you will not be able to find this bar again."

"Why not?"

"You bolted into it by chance. It's not easy to find, and if you don't pay attention then you miss it."

The owner placed the book like a pillow under his head, coiled his body, and appeared to be sleeping.

Jade and Mark stood dumbly under the lamplight of the counter. The record player was already mute. Almost everyone was drunk. A few people got up to leave, another few leaned on the bar top and tables fast asleep. Ida watched to see who woke up and then immediately she would run over, taking them by the arm to walk them outside. The people she led by the arm were often extremely grateful, calling Ida, "good little girl," "little angel," and so on. The look of affected seriousness when they'd entered the bar had disappeared, without leaving a shadow or trace. A woman staggered out the door, then suddenly turned around and called to Ida:

"Tonight we were lucky to meet, in days to come we will not forget each other. Good-bye!"

"Good-bye," Ida said mechanically. She hadn't even seen the woman's face clearly.

At dawn, Ida saw many gorgeous butterflies in her bedroom. They flew up and down in the lamplight and lined up to form letters. Watching them dully, Ida began to weep. At the same moment, she heard Jade in the neighboring room jump down from the table.

Ida left the Green Jade bar. When she turned back to look, the flickering neon light had receded into the distant end of the road.

10

REAGAN'S DIFFICULTIES

"A day without Ida is like a nightmare and like a liberation." This was what Reagan thought. He stood in the shallow water of the bay, watching the gray-green seawater, experiencing the enchantment of the sea's fullness and power. The year before, was it merely because she couldn't shed her cumbersome water-logged garments that a girl had drowned? He climbed to the shore while speculating on this question.

Fifty-year-old Reagan had achieved great success in his business. His rubber tree plantation made a continuous profit, which allowed him to buy up the large farms at its periphery and convert them into rubber tree plantations. Over the past few years, Reagan had gradually withdrawn from strenuous daily tasks and handed over work matters to a capable manager. The manager, Jin Xia, whose nationality was unknown, was an excellent administrator. He ran all Reagan's business affairs with clarity, without noise or bother, and, what was even more important, as regards the farm's expansion his every move was with an eye to the future. One night Reagan dreamt that this Eastern man had mastered the secret of turning stones into gold. He held a rod with a head inlaid with gems, and when he pointed to the piece of land where he stood, that land became Reagan's. Reagan stared for a long time into his narrow, cunning eyes. What he saw in them was not desire itself, but rather a changing form of absence.

"Jin Xia, do you still think Ida will come back?" Reagan was sitting by the sea when he asked this.

"She hasn't really left. You should know that it's only a question of perspective."

Jin Xia's long, thin body was like a shadow rising from the sea.

Reagan always needed to study his speech before he could understand it, and had first taken a liking to him because of this. Jin Xia and his family lived in an old house halfway up a mountain. It was the residence Jin Xia had chosen. He and his wife and their two sons always came and went alone. They didn't establish close relationships with the workers. At times the loneliness in the bones of this family even made Reagan afraid. He worried that they had thoughts of conspiring to undermine him. But later he would reprove himself for these misgivings. In fact, Jin Xia was his only confidant on the farm. He had poured out to him all of what weighed on his mind. At such times, Jin Xia smoked his cigarettes and seldom interrupted. Reagan wasn't sure whether he wanted to listen, but he certainly took it all in. For example, just now Reagan had mentioned Ida, and Jin Xia had produced a singular opinion on the spot.

"Will your sons be going to school in the north this fall?" Reagan asked.

"Yes, but they hate to leave the farm!"

"Oh?"

"The two of them made up their minds never to leave the farm in the future." Jin Xia expelled a mouthful of smoke, his tone growing boastful.

The mountain slope cut through the Chinese banana trees. Jin Xia's gray wooden house was set underneath a large banyan tree. The banyan was like a fierce-faced guardian spirit. Its enormous roots hung in the air, giving it a domineering aspect. Reagan knew that termites had attacked the wooden house, and it was already an endangered building. But Jin Xia's family didn't mind. Perhaps they didn't have long-term plans. Jin Xia's wife had a name that was pleasant to hear, a name Reagan had difficulty pronouncing. At present she was putting quilts out to dry in the sun, probably because the house was too damp inside. She nodded haughtily toward Reagan, which served as a greeting.

"Living on the mountainside, you must know what happens on the farm as if you held it in the palm of your hand," Reagan said, jokingly.

"The truth of the situation is that we have become outsiders." Jin Xia struck his hand on the table uneasily. "Is it because our family lacks ambition?"

Reagan heard a muffled howl from the inner room and jumped up in surprise.

"You can't be raising a wolf!" He felt his knees shaking.

"Yes," Jin Xia said, his expression fleeting, "my sons are raising it. They felt that life here was too superficial, they wanted to do something more stimulating. And then they brought back this little wolf. Don't be nervous, the wolf's chained up tightly. Sometimes I'm anxious about their hobby, too. After all, I am their father. Luckily they'll be going to the north soon . . ."

He raised a palm toward the sky as if wanting to make some gesture, but he couldn't make the gesture with his hand, which stayed awkwardly in the air. He looked more like a bachelor than a father.

Reagan turned to enter the inner room, but at the same time the two children rushed out, blocking him outside. He glanced in and saw the window covered by a black cloth. Nothing inside the room could be seen.

"Uncle, there's nothing inside!" they said in unison.

The two boys were dressed shabbily and their faces were dirty, completely out of keeping for a well-off family. Reagan observed that they had cunning expressions in their eyes, like their father. At this moment the children's mother entered. She whispered a few words to the children, who then both looked at Reagan with resentful eyes. It seemed they were interrogating him, asking why he'd come here to upset their lives.

Jin Xia still sat at the table as if nothing had happened.

"These children have no upbringing," he said, although he seemed to be showing off, not apologizing.

When the wind blew, the wooden walls of the building creaked, *zhi ya*, so much so that one could sense the building tilting in the wind. Jin Xia shut his eyes slightly, intoxicated by this ominous sound. His short, dark wife seemed not to have heard anything.

The wolf didn't make a sound, but the two children in the inner room began crying.

"They've injured the wolf, they are distressed, too, so they are crying. The little devils!" Jin Xia told Reagan.

But Reagan thought the sound of their crying had something not quite right inside it. Just how it wasn't right, he couldn't think of at the moment. Their cries weren't the cries of small children. Rather, they seemed to contain deliberate and shrewd hinting, transmitting to someone some information difficult to speak aloud. To whom? Reagan didn't understand the information the sound carried, and felt vexed. He looked at Jin Xia, at his happy, sated appearance. He was at the table arranging six small glasses into a plum flower shape. His long, thin, cigarette-stained fingers revealed his somber inner heart.

"Is your home always . . . always as lively as this?" Reagan couldn't think of a suitable description.

"Yes, I'm very sorry."

But he still did not appear sorry. This false affectation infuriated Reagan. But was it really affectation? Or maybe he simply had no affectations? His wife was bringing the quilts back in from drying in the sun. She said she feared it would rain. She made trip after trip, mechanically, appearing calm. The two children's strange crying couldn't vex her at all.

"At first, I didn't expect to set up house here. But once I saw this mountain, this banyan, this building, I didn't want to leave. It's hard to change your nature. There's something I want to ask you about, Mr. Reagan. Can you tell me how much area the farm covers? For the past few days I've been completely confused by this question."

"It's the same for me, Jin Xia. Sometimes I feel our land is limitless; sometimes I also feel that not even the place where I'm standing exists. Should we continue buying land?"

When the sound of the wind stopped, Reagan and Jin Xia walked outside and stood under the banyan tree. As they looked down from the mountainside, their field of vision widened. Over the farm was a stretch of gleaming sunshine. Why had Jin Xia's wife said it would rain? Reagan's gaze swept over the rubber trees, arriving at the lake. The land made him feel stifled. He had the impulse to flee — maybe he could leave, as Ida had. Maybe Jin Xia lived here in order to draw back a ways from Reagan's farm? But why did he so intently help Reagan enlarge his landholdings? Reagan could clearly remember how Jin Xia's eyes had flashed with a greedy light when he was discussing business. He had no way of knowing the nature of Jin Xia's delight. Judging from his spare lifestyle, he didn't care about money. Turning around, Reagan looked back at the house, that enormous termite nest, and an ominous premonition sprang up in his heart. Was it possible he was encountering his life's evil star? This taciturn man, whose nationality was unknown, and his strange family who lived in this wooden house built by a hunter many years ago, did they use the quiet pose of their lifestyle to influence him? Or was it to negate his existence? What was the meaning of the woman's arrogance, coming as it did from the depths of her heart?

The two boys stood at the main door watching him, raising small fists against him. Reagan thought that if he went inside again they might rush at him and strike. His gaze moved in the direction of his own home, but how strange, he couldn't see the building. The spot was bare, except for two electric poles. After a while, his yellow dog ran from somewhere into his field of vision.

"From here you can't see your house," Jin Xia said.

Reagan loathed the tone of his voice. He thought that this man had mastered everything of his and was using Reagan's own influence to eliminate him step by step. His house, everything in the house, had surely been eliminated, because looking toward the farm from this mountainside he could see no people and no buildings.

Depressed, he took his leave of Jin Xia and went down the mountain. He walked far away and turned back to look. He could still see Jin Xia standing under the banyan tree smoking his cigarette. Was he keeping an eye on Reagan? It seemed likely that, in that negating field of vision, Reagan's own form was also erased. At the thought of being thus "erased" himself, a wave of fear rushed through Reagan's heart. What kind of person was Jin Xia? Yesterday, Reagan was still telling himself to seize the opportunity, to continue enlarging the farm's holdings. "Take as much as can be taken," he'd said almost shamelessly. In fact, he'd also agreed to a large business deal in preparation for extending the rubber tree plantation to the north, near the sea. But seeing Jin Xia, Reagan somehow couldn't feel reassured. Jin Xia's tall, slender frame, his peculiar intonation, the gray shirt he wore were altogether too insubstantial. On many occasions Reagan wanted to ask about his nationality. But he only got out half of the question before drawing it back because he thought it was inappropriate. How could he inquire about the origins of someone like Jin Xia?

"Hi, Mr. Reagan!"

It was that girl, the one whose older sister had drowned in the bay. He meant at first to escape after a few perfunctory sentences, but discovered that the small girl looked at him avidly, as though she had something to ask of him. She was also a worker on the farm and wore the heavy work clothes, the uniform manufactured by Vincent, which had undergone improvements. Now there were almost no buttons on the garments and taking them off was extremely easy. Reagan remembered that on the day her sister was buried she had cried until her eyes bled.

"Is there something wrong, child?" he asked affably.

"My sister is an expert swimmer," she said, watching his eyes.

"Oh?" Reagan was suddenly dizzy.

"Everything on this farm goes to extremes, so does she. Our parents are rich, they've separated, they live in villas in the north. Your farm is truly beautiful, Mr. Reagan, too beautiful. My sister says so, too."

From her way of speaking it seemed her sister was still alive.

Reagan tried his best to think of her sister's face, but it was always vague. A young lady from a wealthy family who came to the farm to be a worker, and then, one day, wearing thick work clothes, swam into the open water. "Swam into the open water," this metaphor was too apt. The girl had stood there waiting for him so that she could talk about her sister. But why did she want to discuss her? Was she thinking of her, or sighing with grief? Or perhaps it was envy? Hadn't someone said that the nature of everyone who came here changed? This girl, too, had changed her nature. Disregarding everything, she lived in her imagination. It appeared that her sister's death held a kind of enticement for her. Now she probably thought her weeping at the time had been unnecessary.

"Mr. Reagan, I must go. I still want to ask you a question. Do you always stand outside when you're pondering things?"

"Can my thoughts be seen?" He was at a loss.

"In your shadow, the grass turns yellow. But you don't know it!" She ran away.

Reagan thought, gratified, that his farm wasn't a stretch of emptiness. Of course, he could not wholly comprehend what Jin Xia's intentions were. Even if nothing could be seen when he looked over here from under the banyan tree, once he came down the mountain, he ran into this girl, a girl who lived in the dream of the farm. Her suffering and that of her sister was concrete, it existed, and that dream-chasing sister had carelessly given up her life. To start with he had invited Jin Xia to the farm because of his working spirit. Or, you could say, because of his fanaticism for buying land. But Jin Xia didn't want to occupy land himself, and the impoverished life he led was difficult to make sense of. Reagan couldn't say what the fanaticism of his bamboo-like body aimed at. Reagan asked himself, Am I pondering things? The movement of his thoughts was like the turning of a millstone; it was no more than taking the outward appearance of things that happened and reviewing them once again. At root, it didn't count as real pondering.

Yesterday some people had returned from Vincent's city and told him they'd seen Ida. During the long, long night, he and Ida had dug their own deep caves, each listening to the sounds made by the other. "Ida, Ida!" he said. A chunk of earth fell down, striking his head. His movements became frenzied. Ida's movements were methodical, making Reagan think of her composure in escaping from the landslide. He heard her digging reach underneath his feet. And yet Ida was concealing herself at a bar in the city. Even as his farm grew larger, it still could not reach the city where she was.

"Mr. Reagan, Mr. Reagan, the sun is already cruel, come hide in the shade under the trees."

It was Ali.

"You look so depressed, you should come over and sit with me."

He walked over mechanically and sat next to her. The cook patted his knee with her rough hand. He turned around, and made a smiling face.

"So many small snakes crawled into the house. It made me think, I'm afraid the day Ida will return is not far off."

Reagan was unsure what type of person Ali really was, but he realized she wasn't someone who kept a quiet spirit or checked her passions. Although Ali's age was advanced, when she sat in the kitchen, thinking deeply, no slight stirring on the farm could escape those aged eyes.

"Ali, do you think I should continue buying land?"

"Of course you should. It can make your heart peaceful, can't it? Jin Xia understands your ideas best, you can trust him to the last."

"The last?"

"The last, you, I, we'll both see it. This morning, for instance, that old lizard came into the building again. Every time he does, a new round of desire rises."

Martin brought the jeep over. Reagan saw the young man's entire body, top to bottom, covered in his own clothes. Even the leather shoes on his feet were Reagan's. How had he grown so impudent? There was another person in the car, the younger sister of the girl who'd drowned. She was dressed up in gaudy clothes.

"Going home, Mr. Reagan?"

"No, I have no home," he unhappily answered.

"Sit in the dining room with the mad dancing snakes, and you can think things over, same as before."

The girl's mocking voice came from inside the car. She turned her head away and didn't look at Reagan.

"Elaine's so silly." Ali's deep voice was filled with intimations of disapproval.

Ali stood up from the stone bench by degrees. Reagan also stood and got into the car with her. The four of them drove home together.

As Reagan walked up the stairs to his house, a stranger's unfamiliar voice sounded by his ear:

"Manila, Manila, the floodwaters cover the fields . . ."

Reagan felt his legs go soft and he almost sat down on the stairs. He looked in all directions, but there were no unknown people there. Elaine and Martin stood to the side, nervously attentive to him. Evidently they had heard the voice. There was Ali, too, who was measuring him with her eyes.

"Probably some stranger inside the house?" He feigned relaxation, and stretched himself.

"What strangers could be here? Even the snakes are familiar visitors. Some people you think are unfamiliar because you don't often actually think of them. But they cannot forget you," Ali said as she went into the kitchen.

When Reagan went upstairs, Martin and Elaine closely tailed him. He walked into the bedroom, and the pair followed him in. Moreover, they immediately took possession of his bed, becoming heedlessly intimate. Reagan was just about to leave when they stopped moving. Martin said:

"Mr. Reagan, you're not used to looking at young people like us?"

"Please leave, both of you." He squeezed out these words between his teeth.

Martin got up from the bed with an aggrieved look, mumbling, "I don't understand you, Mr. Reagan, why do you wrap yourself up so tightly?" Elaine thumped furiously on the mattress and threw a pillow to the ground, then she jumped down from the bed and stepped on it.

As they left, Martin said directly to Reagan's face: "Even though you're my boss, I still want to tell you, Mr. Jin Xia has lost all hope in you."

Reagan walked to the French windows. In his field of vision, Jin Xia's lodging became a small gray speck in the distance while the farm looked like it had caught fire in the golden sunlight. He picked up the pillow from the floor, put it on the bed, and lay down with his head emptied of thought. His gaze rested on the open door of a cabinet—that bastard Martin had taken almost all the clothes and personal things from inside. Was Martin even his employee, or was he his master? Many years earlier, when Reagan discovered the young fellow taking his clothes, he'd initially been excited. At the time he thought he would influence this youth, but judging from circumstances today it was exactly the opposite. The two of them were challenging him to battle. The sister of the girl who'd died to follow a dream bared the vulgar desire of her body to him, and at the same time she disdained his lack of upbringing. He had seen Martin sitting in his dining room downstairs, his body wrapped in four or five small snakes. The snakes were not encircling him from outside, but had gotten into his body, entering from one side and exiting from another. The youth's countenance was like that of a man in a coma. After Reagan entered the dining room, the small snakes left Martin's body and slid away, following the base of the wall. Reagan was greatly surprised. He wanted Ali to guard against this youth.

"Don't take him to heart," Ali said. "He drifted here from an impoverished border region. The place where he was born had no material comforts. Everyone worked like convicts. Now he has an advantageous position. But people like him can't change the bearing of poverty."

Imagining life in that poverty-stricken border region, imagining this young fellow who, when necessary, let poisonous snakes enter his body, Reagan felt a kind of respect well up in his heart. It was for this reason that later, when Martin time and again took his clothes, Reagan did not object.

Was it possible that the shadowlike Jin Xia could have expectations of him? Jin Xia worked madly, but not to leave his specious mark on the face of the earth. Reagan thought of the collapsing "termite nest" where he lodged, and felt that Jin Xia would stand fast.

One afternoon, after Ida had left, Jin Xia quietly accompanied him to the lake, where they sat for a long time.

"Jin Xia, how large is our farm now?"

"A hundred and sixty square kilometers."

"I hadn't imagined it was so large."

"Taken all together, it's very large. That's why Ida left. She wants an honest man, not a shadowy landowner like you."

"You speak directly. The past few years I feel I've become more rarified. Look at that patch of reedy ground ahead. Ida and I made love there. A mouth opened up in the ground, crowds of water snakes poured out and wound around our bodies. My neck was looped tightly, I couldn't feel the slightest pleasure."

As Reagan spoke the lake water began to ripple, and he realized the embankment beneath him was also shaking slightly. He couldn't help being a little worried. But when he stealthily sized up Jin Xia, he saw him writing in a little notebook, his head lowered.

"What are you writing?"

"I'm calculating the surface area of the newly bought farms."

"You haven't been listening?"

"I've been listening. You often talk about this."

"But this is the first time I'm telling it to you!" Reagan was disappointed.

"That's not right, how could it be the first time? You've forgotten. I like Ida, too. But without her, what can you do? You are fortunate to have her. I knew early on that Ida was the master of this farm."

Jin Xia was always able to say the things Reagan most wanted to hear. Reagan called his words "a spirit-enchanting potion." If it weren't for Jin Xia, Reagan didn't know how he could have suffered through such days.

"But she didn't expect to stay here."

"Oh, you're mistaken, Mr. Reagan, you always make this mistake. You forget again, this is Ida, who escaped from the landslide."

The afternoon sun shone on the lake water, shining on the reeds. An occasional water bird flew past with a sharp cry. The place now seemed incomparably ancient. In Reagan's mind a fresh memory appeared. In this memory a young Jin Xia carried Reagan's little brother, running in the wind. His long, thin legs seemed to rise up into the air. He was wearing a strange black-and-white gown, and looked both Chinese and Japanese. Reagan almost let the question leave his mouth: "Jin Xia, where are you really from?" But what he actually asked was: "So how large is the farm?"

"The calculations differ a good deal, Mr. Reagan, sometimes by a multiple. However, this is normal. Surveys of the surface area can't be depended on, don't you agree?"

Reagan grew conscious of the reality that his farm could not be measured. He thought Jin Xia might also be conscious of this, so why would he still go to the trouble of taking measurements? One time Reagan woke from a dream and walked into the woods, where he saw his workers, all wearing straw hats, sitting in the moonlight like statues. He passed by these unmoving figures and immediately sensed the plane attained in their minds, one that took the rubber tree forest as its starting point, a limitlessly extending open sky. He rudely called out: "Ida." Immediately someone answered him, but the voice answering was a man's. Watching the groups of people like wooden statues, Reagan was afraid. He stepped back to walk out of the woods, wanting to break away from the feeling of stagnation they gave him. But the rubber tree forest was possessed. Even if he turned in a familiar direction, he could not reach the edge of the woods. On that occasion he exhausted himself to the point of collapse.

"Mr. Reagan, as I see it, as the farm grows larger, our hearts grow peaceful."

Jin Xia stood up, saying he needed to go manage a piece of work. Reagan saw that as he took a branch in the road, two fellows scurried out from the woods and propelled him away. Reagan wanted to shout but couldn't because he realized the scene taking place before his eyes was false. After a while he gradually recovered a sense of reality. He noticed a stain on his coat. He'd worn this gray-green garment for a long time. Ever since Martin had swept away his clothing, he'd had nothing else to change into. It all seemed so absurd. As the farm grew larger, the work of measuring had more reason to permanently continue. This was Jin Xia's scheme.

There were small birds—he didn't know their name—hidden in the clump of reeds. The number of them surprised him. As he passed the spot, small objects like locusts sprang from the grass into the air and flew high up into the clouds. He opened his mouth, making stupid "ah! ah!" sounds. He looked back at the ground, where everywhere was a mass of crows. Clearly the crows had just flown in from somewhere else. Where? From the city? He'd heard someone say that in the city the balcony of every house was packed full with crows, wet dripping crows.

Someone was calling him. It was Ali, panting as she came over. She said he might be drawn into a lawsuit. She'd heard that Jin Xia used improper methods to manage the farm.

"What does he mean to do?" Ali said, as if she were in the dark.

But Reagan saw that she wasn't really nervous. It seemed she was still looking forward to a certain event. He thought that this was a common mentality of people on the farm, they were all looking forward to a certain event.

"I don't entirely believe this. Is it a ruse, is he hurting himself to win us over?" Reagan said.

"Yes, is it a ruse?" Ali repeated his words excitedly, a light shining in her eyes.

"Jin Xia is a strange, unpredictable man."

When Reagan opened the curtains and looked outside, a woman appeared in his field of vision. This happened two days in succession. She was Jin Xia's wife. On the farm, covered everywhere with wind-blown sand, rumors flew in the air. Already several people had come to tell him rumors about a public sale. Already Jin Xia had avoided Reagan for days. Now his wife was digging in the soil next to the road. What was she digging up? Ali entered.

"She's already dug a lot of deep pits beside the road. She says she wants to examine the composition of the soil. This woman is a sorceress. I'm not afraid of her husband, I'm only afraid of her. Why would she examine the composition of the soil? She wants to dig down to the roots of things."

Reagan was surprised and turned around to question her, but Ali had already gone, taking his dirty clothes with her. Ali's talk made his spine run cold. For many years he'd seen his life as a perfect whole. This outlook was now thoroughly destroyed. Over there, halfway up a mountain, two pairs of eagle eyes observed the farm's fragile existence. Once they showed their strength, everything would return to a savage era. Despite the distance, the sound of the woman's digging in the earth still carried to where Reagan stood. She seemed to be digging at the foundation of his house. Even the glass in the windows trembled slightly. Reagan suddenly understood why when he went to her home she acted as if she despised him. Perhaps in her eyes, he was only an idiot. What did she see within layer on layer of soil? Her manner of grabbing tight, of not letting go, left Reagan with an indistinct feeling of hopelessness. He said to himself, over and over, "Ida, Ida, we're through."

This family was laying out schemes far in advance. Reagan's thoughts couldn't capture what they had planned. His heart leapt madly in his chest, as the hoe she raised resentfully seemed filled with hate, and stroke by stroke dug into his heart. He heard someone outside his door say, "Manila, Manila, waves from the sea flow into the distance." He ran over to open the door. Ali was standing outside.

"Is something wrong?" he asked her stiffly.

"I was worried that you might need something, so I've been waiting here." Her face seemed to redden, but it might have been the light playing a trick.

"Just now someone was talking outside the door."

"Impossible, I'm the only one here. Look, am I interfering too much? If she keeps digging like this, won't she control every last bit of the farm? After all, we are old residents, we should be respected."

"Why would you concern yourself with what that lunatic does?" he said, ill-temperedly. He closed the door in her face, irritated.

As for Jin Xia, who was addicted to buying land, and his "lunatic," perhaps they were playing at a two-person comedy. Just now Ali had said "old residents"—was this sarcasm? Reagan wasn't a true old resident. There was the forest keeper, and before the forest keeper, there were some people—he basically didn't know anything about them—but only they were the true old residents. Over so many years, Reagan had never run across people like that. To his surprise, he realized that by analyzing the soil's composition the farm's history could be known. It was a little like mythology. Why did this family want to seize the farm and hold it? Then there was Ali, who seemed to understand their situation as if she held it in the palm of her hand. Last night someone had walked into his house, someone a bit like the black-clad Eastern woman. But "she" was a young man walking over to face him. He held a round porcelain dish. He'd abruptly smashed the dish to the ground, where it broke into splinters, but made no sound whatsoever. Without knowing how, Reagan formed a kind of attachment to this black-clad youth. He wanted to pour out his feelings to him. The youth turned his white bony face toward Reagan, kicked at the smashed pieces of porcelain with his toes, and did not answer his questions. Reagan understood, he would never get an answer. Looking at this young man, an unusual desire rose in his heart, even more intense than his desire for Ida. This one time, Reagan terrified himself. The young man went outside. He followed but failed to catch him, because the young man strode like the wind. Recalling this event now, Reagan thought, for no reason, that it was actually Jin Xia pretending to be a youth. Although he had looked like an Eastern man, the impression he gave was also of someone of unclear nationality. But during the day, when he faced Jin Xia, Reagan didn't feel the slightest degree of desire. Jin Xia was certainly not the sort of person to make people desire him, if not to say, he was the sort of person to extinguish desire.

"Look, she's already found what she wanted. Her pose is so graceful."

Ali had come in again from somewhere without his noticing. They could see Jin Xia's wife shouldering her hoe and receding into the distance.

"How did you know this woman wanted something? You don't know her."

"In my hometown, there are many people like this. Once I saw this family I was sure they were the same kind of people. They absorb a few things from your body, and they pour a few things into your body. I'm speaking of Jin Xia's family. Mr. Reagan, from the day they arrived, the farm has been changing, but you haven't detected it."

As Ali was speaking her eyes looked to the ground. Reagan thought that surely she knew many more things. There was nothing hidden from this pair of aged eyes. He even suspected Ida's leaving had something to do with this loyal, faithful old servant. But why did he suspect her loyalty?

With these many contradictions rushing toward him, Reagan made up his mind to flow along with the current.

He stood in the garden wearing pajamas, because the driver Martin had taken all his coats. He turned his face to the autumn sun, figuring that it wasn't bad to be a child, to be unconcerned, and let this 160-square-kilometer farm return to its age of savagery. He didn't want to be concerned with the future any more. A few workers walked past. Were they going to work? No, they weren't going to work, they were playing a part. They each harbored their own ancient story, drifting along on his farm, searching for something.

In a spot where the grass and leaves reflected the light, underneath a palm tree, he saw his mother. His mother's appearance didn't show her age and there was no expression on her face. She held knitting in her hand, as if she were making wool socks. The sun shone on her body—wasn't she too warm? He didn't dare call out because the sight before his eyes was too fleeting. But his mother raised her head, looking at him inquiringly, as if to say, "Why are you wearing pajamas outside, little boy?"

His bare feet tread on a small snake. It was ice cold.

"Martin, Martin, you're always wearing my clothes. What are you thinking?"

"Me? I don't think about anything, I'm unable to think, so I wear your clothes. When I walk outside, I become another Mr. Reagan, and the knots in my heart disappear. I'm a rootless person, I always need to pull on a coat."

Martin made an exaggerated gesture. Elaine stood to one side covering the smile on her face.

"I think," she directed her words to Reagan. "I think Martin is like my sister. Someday he will swim into the sea wearing your clothes . . . Mr. Reagan, have you noticed that everyone on the farm looks the same? Only people harboring the same thoughts come here."

"There are two crows in the pockets of my hunting gear." Martin shrugged, and began to whistle.

Reagan followed the young man with his eyes as he walked, bouncing, into the distance. He was overwhelmed with many thoughts and feelings. The sunlight seemed to press down on his body, thousands of jin heavy. He lowered his head and saw the bottom hem of his pajamas torn and bloodstains on his bare feet. Before dawn, he'd heard the sound of the earth rising and falling, a *sha sha sha* rustling, like the movements of an enormous python. He'd thought then that the land was traveling away from him, that the crows would not wheel over his head. But now he saw Martin wearing his hunting clothes, saw him embracing the younger sister of the girl who had drowned, and the land came back under his feet. Elaine was not ordinary, either. Sometimes she loafed in front of his house, her eyes staring straight ahead. If he stepped in front of her to say hello, she would jump away, guardedly, reproaching him in a loud voice: "Who are you?"

She had said, "My sister gave me her place, but I'm not grateful for it."

A train's steam whistle sounded in the distance, he heard it clearly. Perhaps Ida had returned long ago, and was hiding somewhere. The longing in Reagan's heart was for the black-clad young man. That different impulse was hard to forget—could he be an incarnation of Ida? The discrepancy in sex didn't amount to anything. There was a photograph of a young man clipped in Reagan's sole photo album upstairs. His mother had said it was his older brother, but he had never met this black-clad man.

11

VINCENT VISITS THE GAMBLING CITY

In a room in the tall high-rise Vincent imagined the Chinese woman telling him that he should visit the gambling city to figure out a few things about his wife, Lisa. The Chinese woman sat with her back to him. She hadn't opened her mouth, but Vincent heard her thoughts. They came toward him as language, and so he formed this statement from her present thought.

Lisa had forgotten her birthplace entirely. She spoke incoherently of a grassy lawn. Retired grandmothers sit on the lawn in wicker chairs all in a row. Some read the papers, some nap. In the distance, a long snake slinks along in the deep grass. A silver-haired woman catches sight of the snake. She doesn't get up. Instead she covers her face with the paper and lies down in her chair.

"But you haven't spoken of the gambling city's most important feature," Vincent interrupted.

"The slot machines?" Lisa's eyebrows drew together in a line, betraying her ferocity. "I've seen many of them in that valley of death. If you go there, you'll see the blood-red sunsets. I cannot go with you because if I go to that place I won't be able to return. Poor Vincent, I'm uneasy about letting you go there."

But Vincent had his mind on the horse-racing tracks. He didn't take Lisa's prophecy to heart. Hadn't she come from that place? And hadn't she lived outside it for decades? Vincent had always envied his wife's origins. He thought of them as a legend that was true. He had never told her this, and if she heard him say as much she would be furious. Vincent had only passed by the gambling city once on a train, and had never stayed there. Every night he saw its rose-colored sky in his dreams. The domes of the gambling city appeared so dubious under this sky, so untrue. On a nearby mountainside, the bells of a cathedral tolled. There were no people in his dreams. He felt that the activity in the casinos had nothing to do with people. When he'd first known Lisa, her body's active, inexhaustible desire astonished him. He'd had so much happiness from it. For many years he'd wanted to explore the source of her vitality, but she kept her mouth closed like a stoppered bottle.

"I only remember that grass lawn. It was a home for the elderly," Lisa said, unbending. "The other things were like floating clouds, they weren't important. The selectivity of my memory is very strong."

"So you also think the casinos are empty?"

"Yes. Although they are full of people, in reality they are empty."

Vincent and Lisa's talk led to nothing. In fact, this situation was predictable. Vincent's company was expanding as before. His luck was so good it was hard to believe. He brought in several aides to develop two subsidiary companies. He asked Lisa whether he should retire. Lisa said people like him couldn't retire, so he should work up to the end. He thought about what she said and felt it to be correct. She was always right, as if she were his road sign. When she said, "Although they are full of people, in reality they are empty," Vincent felt as though he wanted to cry.

Recently, Lisa had undergone a transformation. She drifted around in dirty clothes, as if she had lost her awareness of the people surrounding her. But at night she didn't go outside any more. She slept heavily. One night at midnight, Vincent came home from a bar out on the street and walked into the bedroom. In the dark he felt the air in the room buzzing, *weng weng*, hurried and nervous, like an air-raid siren. He sat on the bed, collected himself, and clasped one of Lisa's hands as she slept. The situation didn't change. He said to himself, "Lisa, Lisa, you are capable of so much." In the dark Lisa suddenly spoke to him distinctly, "Vincent, after this don't cross over that little bridge. You have fallen from the bridge into the stream. The river water is shallow, shallow. Your head rests on a rock sticking out of the water, only your clothes are wet." Vincent turned on the light and discovered that Lisa was still dreaming. She no longer needed to move her body to seek those remote stories. Now she lived inside them, day and night. But he, as before, rose during the night and searched wildly until he wore himself out. Woman, woman, what kind of miracle was she? Had her birth in the gambling city determined everything about her? Sometimes Vincent saw the relationship between them as a race between competitors. This way of thinking even influenced his heart. Recently a stifling sensation grew more evident. But he already understood that no matter how hard he ran, he couldn't catch up to his wife asleep at home. He was no more than a shadow in the light of a streetlamp; she was a rock within history. Yet she was reluctant to part from him! What for? She didn't ask about the Rose Clothing Company's affairs, but Vincent had always felt that the business's prosperity bore a direct relation to her undertaking in the earth's deep core. Vincent wanted to comprehend how her desire was brought into being at that core, but his effort was futile.

"Vincent, are you still excavating that gully? There are more and more little fish, little shrimp."

Once she woke Lisa said this to Vincent, her face filled with the fatigue of her nighttime life. He could see that her rest was painful. He understood that the most active part of her life was now separated from him.

"This unforeseen gain from the stream gives me temporary satisfaction. Darling, I love you."

"I love you, too, Vincent. But I can't search on the earth's surface with you. There are problems emerging in my life. Now I'm on a drilling crew. Don't you think so?" Her expression was contented. "Have you heard the story of Maria's long march? She is also on a long march. How strange!"

Vincent had nothing to say. The noise of the air-raid siren disappeared from the bedroom, but his heart still leapt with a *peng peng* throbbing sound. He'd heard Joe's insinuating tone when he spoke of Maria's long march. In his memory it was a kind of sweet punishment since Joe, always stiff in conversation, grew red-faced and excited when he talked about it. Similarly, Vincent could not figure out what

Maria's activity was. But his wife could communicate with Maria, without their actually meeting. Everything was changing. Even this morning, he could no longer enjoy that strange territory with Lisa through the intercourse of their bodies.

The whistle of the train entering the station woke Vincent. He walked out onto the platform with no plan in mind. He left the station alone and discovered himself in a small rural town. The town had only one road, thinly dotted on both sides with shops and the residents' houses. As it was early in the morning, not a single person was out on the street. He thought, This is what the gambling city is like. Where were the casinos? He turned his gaze toward the distant stone mountains beyond the small town and saw low-hanging clouds covering their summits. He stood for a good while until a black woman, a street cleaner, appeared. The woman looked just like the street cleaner in his own city. She waved her broom, sweeping little by little over in his direction. The closer she came, the more Vincent felt that she was just like the beautiful street cleaner he'd seen so often before. He simply stared. Finally, she swept up right to his feet.

When her broom touched Vincent's leather shoes, he almost jumped.

"Welcome to the gambling city, Grandfather." The young woman smiled charmingly, showing her appealing teeth.

"Do you recognize me?"

"I've seen you on my sister's street. I knew you would come here."

"Why?"

"Because everyone comes to the gambling city. This road is covered with traveler's footprints. They've even worn down the granite pavement. Our place here is beautiful, isn't it? At dusk, it's like the whole city is filled with rose blooms . . . They say a white elephant will come to the city soon."

There weren't even many trees in the crude little town. He couldn't see the scene she spoke of, but the young woman's description of it enchanted him. What sort of migratory bird was she? He inquired about a hotel. She pointed out a stone building and said that was one, but she urged him not to stay there. She said that once he entered he would turn into a real gambler. After this, she suddenly became upset. Because talking delayed her work, she lowered her head to sweep the ground and didn't acknowledge Vincent again.

Vincent walked toward the stone building. First he rang the old-fashioned doorbell. It rang for a long time without anyone answering. Then he experimentally pushed the door, without thinking it would actually open. Inside was an empty parlor with a few sofas. Vincent went over and sat down on a sofa, waiting for someone to come. He waited a long time, yet no one came. Was it really a hotel?

Later someone finally came, but it turned out to be the same street cleaner. She had probably swept the entire road.

"Is this your home?" Vincent asked her, perplexed.

"No, this is my hotel, Grandfather. I'll take you to your room."

She led him to the rooms below ground. Vincent was a little unhappy, but she said, "In the gambling city, we have to have rooms underground, because of the daily earthquakes."

They followed the staircase down turn after turn in a spiral. The room he was going to appeared to be buried deep underground.

She turned her head and spoke vivaciously: "There will never be earthquakes down here. This has been proven. I am named Joyner, too. I am my mother's obedient daughter, and so is my older sister. I never thought you could love this place. All the people who come here come out of love. How else could it be? Or else why would they come?"

Joyner led Vincent into a large room. It was more like a bedroom at home than a hotel suite. The room was messy and smelled of cigarettes. It looked like a room an elderly bachelor might live in. Joyner gave him the key and told him that whenever there was an emergency, he should stay inside the room and not move around. She suddenly turned melancholy, adding to what she'd already said: "If it were any worse it would still only be suffocation; people here don't have bodily suffering." She went out in a hurry, shutting the door. A *tong tong tong* thumping sound followed as she ran upstairs.

Vincent felt that he was entering a murderous trap. He stuck his head outside to look around and saw three tightly shut doors in the hallway. He imagined what was going on behind the doors and suddenly felt afraid. He quickly closed the door, latched it from inside, and then went to shower.

When he'd finished his shower and came out of the bathroom, someone else was sitting in the room. The man had his back to him. Vincent could not see his face, only his brawny neck.

"I'm your neighbor," he said, "Don't be concerned. You don't need to be concerned here."

"How did you get in?"

He smiled slightly, then answered, "The locks are all for show, there aren't any rooms that can be locked. You must have thought that only a few people lived in this small town. No, the gamblers all live underground. We drink spring water. Listen, it's the sound of the spring."

What Vincent heard was the roar of floodwater. The sound was coming from the bathroom. He instinctively ran into the other room, thinking in confusion that he should shut off a faucet, but there was nothing wrong in the bathroom. When he came out, the man was nowhere to be seen and the door was locked shut, as though he'd never been there.

In exhaustion, Vincent lay down on the bed. He knew he wasn't in a deep sleep, but rather in a lethargic doze, because he was worried that some emergency would occur. There was a brief moment when he heard the whole floor of people in the underground rooms snoring. Altogether there were eight people—that is to say, in the other three rooms there were eight tenants. Vincent thought the gamblers must be truly happy to be sleeping so soundly. Where were the casinos? He struggled with his drowsy state, wanting to pick out through the thick black smoke the street where Lisa had lived, and wanting to find the dwarf. He walked, all the while asking in a loud voice, "Who? Who?" He thought there was bound to be someone who would come out and answer. But no one did.

When he woke up he saw Joyner, who looked miserable, sitting on the sofa and worrying over her own thoughts.

"Where is the dwarf?" Vincent asked.

"Are you asking about my husband? He never stays at home, he comes and goes between your city and my city, never resting. Grandfather, have you gotten used to the earthquakes?"

"I haven't felt any earthquakes. There's only a lot of smoke."

"That's an earthquake. You must be anxious? Earthquakes make people anxious. I sit here, thinking about your problems, then I also think of my sister's situation, and I become more and more pessimistic."

The expression in her eyes made her look as if she were not of this world.

"Grandfather, you know, my sister and I are both street cleaners. This is the only work we can do. But we love our work! Why? Because when we stand in the street nothing can escape our eyes. You, for example. You got off the train, walked over, and who did you run into? It could only be me. I brought you to my hotel, and you are staying here. Of course this isn't quite the same as your original travel plans. But now it's the only thing you can do—stay here underground. You could also go up to the surface, only that wouldn't result in anything. You already know that it's a deserted city. This is the privilege of a city's street cleaner!"

Vincent watched her recover her vivacity, speaking as she gestured with her hands, as if she would jump up from the sofa. He thought, This girl is too lonely.

In the hallway someone was calling her name. She stood up, excited, and walked away, saying, "Surely it's that old Tom. They can't organize their lives without me!"

For a while Vincent stood in the room, and then he decided to go to the surface.

As he climbed the stairs he couldn't open his eyes for the smog and smoke. On every floor he heard the sound of the tenants quarreling behind doors. When he finally reached the street again, he had a feeling of being released from the dark into the sunlight. He thought of Joyner's always calling him Grandfather. He was suspicious. Could he have gotten so old?

It was nearly noon. There were still no people in the town. In the distance the stone mountains were illuminated by the sun, with an unspeakably bleak air. Vincent reflected that his journey was not at all like what he'd envisaged beforehand. Not only had he not found any answers, his thoughts were even more constricted. He also suspected he had come to the wrong place. Or maybe this wasn't the gambling city where Lisa was born, but a smaller town near the gambling city? But the spot had been marked clearly on the map at home. A few decades ago Lisa had told him this was the place. It couldn't be a mistake. Besides, when he was at the train station, hadn't he seen that copper rooster beside the rails? This rooster was the most important sign, Lisa said. It symbolized the way the gamblers cherished time.

Vincent made a circuit of the street and finally heard a stirring. It was the sound of shattering glass from the window of a gray two-story building. A puff of thick smoke emerged. He thought of the warning about earthquakes and grew nervous. Yet no one ran out from the building. Joyner came over, her hair disheveled, with an angry expression.

"Don't you see, the people there are slowly dying! How can you be so unconcerned?"

A gust of wind swept past, mixed with thick smoke. Vincent sensed that something was about to go wrong.

"Joyner, what do you think I should do? Should I go back home? I can't understand anything here. I don't know the history of the gambling city. It's all Lisa's fault . . ."

He became incoherent. But Joyner sniggered, making his skin crawl.

"Joyner, I'm leaving."

"No, you can't leave!" She glared, her eyes wide.

"Why not? I'll just catch the train, I know where the station is."

"You can't leave," she said again, her tone relaxing. "Because, because of the earthquakes."

"But I can leave. Look, there's no effect at all."

"Fine, go, but you could die. When you get there you'll be done for."

"How do you know?"

"You're right, I don't know. It's just a feeling I have."

Joyner sighed and sat down on a stone bench at the side of the road, blankly staring at the thick smoke pouring from the broken windows. At this, Vincent felt again that he couldn't leave, at least not for a bit. He said to himself, "Lisa. Oh, Lisa, how come I can't understand even a little of what is in your heart?" Lisa, who'd been lovely like a flower in her youth, had grown up in this deathly quiet place. Maybe she was born deep underground! Had the city always been like this, or was it made this way by the people here? If it was made this way, what had it been like before?

"Joyner, why are you the only person who comes to the surface? Is everyone in the city underground?"

"It's because of the earthquakes. You still don't understand?"

"The earthquakes can't harm people if they come to the surface, so why do they hide underground?"

"Oh, you don't get it. You really don't understand anything. Hasn't Lisa told you? It is the principle of the gambling city. It will never change. Listen, they're crying in fear."

Joyner stirred herself, saying she had to work. Actually, the road was quite clean. There was no one to sully it. She lifted her broom and started to sweep. Vincent understood, she wasn't sweeping to keep things clean, she was there to receive visitors. Look at her expectant appearance, as if she's waiting for her boyfriend to appear.

"Joyner, who are you waiting for?"

"For anyone. Wasn't I waiting for you? Your arrival was my holiday."

Vincent sensed that she wasn't happy at his arrival. Her look was always heavy with care. As he and Joyner were speaking, a group of men came out of the two-story building with smoke pouring from it, forty- or fifty-year-old men in their underwear, looking like they hadn't woken up yet. Joyner flew toward them, raising her broom to strike, rebuking them as she drove them back into the building. At first they grumbled, then fearing her wild, violent look, they obediently went back inside.

Joyner's face ran with sweat. She spoke to Vincent, as if embarrassed: "Gamblers are always discontent."

"All these people are in your care?"

"Yes, my youth is wasted on things like this. It's not worth it, is it? Follow this road to the end, then turn right and you will see Lisa's home."

"Lisa's home! Didn't her parents die a long time ago?" Vincent was frightened.

"That was only an analogy, it's how people here look at things. Go, they are waiting for you."

He hadn't anticipated that Lisa's parents would be extremely wealthy. Although her elderly father and mother were seventy or eighty years old, their minds were clear and they looked quite spirited. The large, extravagantly decorated house had a number of servants. At Vincent's arrival, the old couple was guarded. They kept asking at first when he would be leaving, as though they took him to be a threat. Afterward, when they heard Vincent explain that this was only a short-term visit, they finally relaxed, and accordingly took no interest in him. They would let Vincent do what he liked, and said he could stay at their home as long as he wanted to stay. Then, not waiting for Vincent's reply, they lay down on the thick cushions of their respective rocking chairs, talking with an old parrot in a birdcage hanging under the chandelier. Vincent couldn't understand their conversation. It seemed they were debating the question of putting power lines on the stone mountains. It also seemed they were analyzing methods of tracking down criminals on the run. No matter what the old couple said, the old parrot always said, "Very good! Very good! A work of genius! A work of genius!" Vincent suspected that these words of praise were not the only things the ugly bird could say.

Vincent grew tired of listening. He also found a rocking chair to lie down in. There were many of these rocking chairs in the living room. He had just settled into one when he heard the manservant who had been standing at the door say in reproach: "This man doesn't have the status to lie there." Vincent found this amusing. A hurried burst from a buzzer rang out in the main hall. The elderly couple got up from their rocking chairs and went to an interior door, then thought of something and stopped again. Vincent's father-in-law turned back and said to him, "We need to go to the rooms underground. We don't know if we'll be able to come back up once we get there. You should do as you please, have fun. We hadn't imagined you'd come, it's one of Lisa's tricks."

Vincent wanted to tell them he would be leaving soon, but the old couple didn't want to listen. They hurried each other to the basement rooms. After they left, the servant, who before this had stood unmoving by the door, became animated. He ran over and hung two blankets over the old couple's rocking chairs, then took down the parrot's cage and stuffed it into the empty stove that sat in the fireplace. Vincent heard the old parrot shouting abuse: "Villain! Stuckup fiend!" When he shut the door to the stove, the bird couldn't be heard. Vincent smelled a strong, acrid tobacco. He turned and saw smoke pouring from the stairway leading to the basement entrance. The servant spoke from behind him:

"Where do you think you can run off to?"

"Are you talking about me?"

"Who else would I be talking about!"

"Why do you dislike me?"

"Because you are a cold-blooded man, never to come here in so many years."

"But I didn't know there was anyone here who wanted me to come. Lisa told me her whole family was dead. The gambling city she described was not like this place, either. What's gone wrong?"

"There's something wrong with you, of course. You fantasize. You can't see the essence of things."

The servant stood there haughtily, and Vincent saw his feet treading on a snake. It was the kind of small striped snake he'd seen at Reagan's farm. The snake was struggling to reach up and bite his ankles. The servant pulled a dagger from his pants pocket, took off the sheath, looked it up and down, inspecting the edge, then bent over and cut off the snake's head with a single stroke. The snake, its head and body in two places, wasn't dead. The head and the body seemed to have an invisible connection between them, and wriggled a retreat in unison to the door. In the wink of an eye they were out of sight. Vincent looked back to the ground and saw that there weren't even bloodstains left behind.

In the living room the smoke grew thicker. Vincent thought the servant would prevent him from leaving, so he stood without moving in his former place. The servant stooped to light the stove and immediately the sound of cursing flew out. Vincent took advantage of the servant's inattention to walk out. But the servant did not come after him. What did it mean when he'd said, "Where do you think you can run off to?"

Joyner stood by the road with a serious look. She still awaited visitors, not knowing the direction from which they would come. The street was already swept clean. Vincent looked in her direction, and gazing at this lonely girl, he felt an inexplicable sadness. He thought, perhaps, many years ago, his wife, Lisa, had occupied this girl's place. In fact, the first time he met Lisa he could see the shadows on her high-colored cheeks. But he would never have thought that she possessed such an implacable heart. Over the decades of married life a few of her secrets were revealed, but if he hadn't come to her hometown, how much would he have understood about her? Even though he'd come here, how many things about her did he still not understand?

Vincent raised his head and looked off into the distance. The encircling stone mountains spat out thick smoke like live volcanoes. The gray smoke gradually fluttered toward the small town. But it was no volcanic eruption, nor did it feel like an earthquake. Looking around at the nearby buildings, he saw that some oozed smoke, some did not, and none of the people inside came out. Vincent remembered the scene from when he had climbed out of Joyner's belowground rooms, thinking to himself, The people had gotten used to breathing within heavy smoke long ago. If he didn't leave, would the thick smoke occupy every open space? Regardless, he would be unable to get used to it.

Joyner stood coolly by the road, holding her broom. She was looking at the smoke too, her gaze clear, her features pretty. Most likely every traveler who came here was profoundly fascinated by her.

Vincent spoke without making a sound: "Joyner, Joyner, I love you." But he did not feel this love as a physical love. Why, considering her youth, full of freshness, was he not sexually excited by her? Surely there was something separating them. He worshipfully watched the girl, his mind repeating the question: twenty-eight years ago, how had he and Lisa come to love each other at first sight?

Joyner walked over to him, forcefully grasped his hand, and said, "I must go. What I'm saying is, soon I'll need to go below again. But Grandfather, what will you do? Look at this smoke, even the trains have stopped. I'll go underneath, no travelers will be coming, either on the train or by foot. Lisa's parents love you so much, why don't you go to their home?"

"Really? They love me? Why don't I sense it?"

"Because you've become unfeeling. Listen, no one here would let an outsider into the house because it's too dangerous. You are one of their family, so they let you stay at their home. For years they've been chattering away, saying, Supposing you came, they would save your life. So go to their home."

Joyner disappeared into the gray building. In Vincent's eyes, the small town became a genuinely bleak, desolate place, and that smoke, already slowly assembled, was now descending. Perhaps he could only obey what Joyner said. Perhaps at his wife's parents' house he wouldn't be in danger.

Against his will, Vincent stepped again through the door of the large house.

"This isn't a hotel, where you can come and go as you please," the servant said. He stood in his place as before.

Smoke still oozed from the mouth of the stairs. Yet the smoke didn't gush toward him, but rather took a turn and exited through an open window, as if something were guiding it. In a panic Vincent saw that outside there were rolling billows of smoke everywhere. Visibility was not even two or three meters. Because the doors and windows were shut tight, there was still no smoke where he and the manservant stood. The servant's voice sounded in his ears:

"Only the people whose desire for these earthquakes is strong can enjoy them."

That was to say, Lisa's parents were underground "enjoying," Joyner and her tenants were also "enjoying" this. In that place with no sun, an air-thinned place, flooded with stifling smoke . . .

He lay face up in a reclining chair, watching the magnificent, stately chandelier extend down from the ceiling. Near his ear someone was mocking him, saying he was a miser. Vincent sat up and looked around. Who was speaking?

"It's me, I'm Lisa's uncle!" The voice came from the open stove.

The parrot reached its head out. Evil words flowed from its mouth. It said Vincent didn't have a single redeeming quality. Vincent felt suspicious: why didn't it fly out? Even if it had lost its ability to fly it still could run away, and no one would block it. At the moment the servant wasn't even looking this way, he was facing the mirror to pluck the whiskers on his lower jaw with a metal clip! But the parrot didn't emerge, he only cursed like a gossiping woman.

"If you are Lisa's uncle, then we are related. Why are you cursing at me?" Vincent spoke with sincerity. He wanted to see the bird leave the fireplace.

But the parrot ducked inside and cursed even more ferociously, its wings fanning the charcoal dust inside so it poured from the stove door. Vincent didn't know why its most frequent imprecation was "Exploiting usurer!"

Vincent was just going over to the stove door to ask what this meant when he saw the servant race over, throw a large piece of burning firewood into the stove, and shut the door. Through the glass of the door he could see the parrot extinguishing the flames with its wings. The smoke inside obscured everything and he only heard its flapping, *pu tong, pu tong.* He could also faintly make out a shriek like an infant's.

Vincent's body broke out in goose bumps. He turned to face the servant's evil smile.

"Is it dead?"

"It can't die. It is a long-life parrot. It was here ages ago, when playing the slot machines was popular."

"Where are the slot machines now?

"They are all buried between the walls of the underground rooms. Those props aren't necessary any more. I won't go around in circles with you, I'll tell you everything: I am your rival in love."

"Lisa?"

"Yes. What a marvelous woman, burning between your legs."

Vincent furrowed his brow in disgust, which his adversary swiftly detected.

"You came here, but what use is it?" He stuck out his chin proudly. "You will never reach her heart because you don't understand the kind of woman she is. Look, she has such worthy parents! Even our parrot looks down on you."

"But I've already come here, and now I should leave?"

"Leave, this is the morality of people like you: you don't stay anywhere long, only in hotels, you have no home. Poor Lisa, she must regret you."

"I think Lisa has forgotten you." Vincent pricked him with this sentence.

"Maybe. I've heard that people who leave here lose their memories."

The servant was silent, thinking of his own problems. The parrot came to life again, walking back and forth in the smoke cloud with an apprehensive look.

Vincent walked over and opened the door of the stove. The parrot ran out all at once and jumped onto his shoulder. Now not only did it cease cursing, it also appeared attached to him, tightly holding his shoulder. Vincent sat in a reclining chair, and it jumped onto his knee. It looked serenely at him with its somewhat bleary old eyes. Vincent suddenly felt the bird's charm, but he couldn't say what sort of charm it was. He saw the servant looking himself over in the mirror. His mood seemed low, and he kept making grimaces in the mirror as if he were trying to adjust his mood.

"Vincent, Lisa has forgotten all about you." The parrot imitated his voice.

"Are you lonely, Uncle?"

"Is Vincent lonely? If he's lonely he should go practice his usury."

Vincent listened to what it said and laughed out loud. At this the parrot laughed, too. The sound of the parrot's laugh stopped Vincent's short. It was like the laugh of a ghost in an ancient tomb. The parrot laughed and laughed, its wings held straight up, as if it were possessed. Vincent was going to push it down off his knee when the servant turned toward him, as though he could see into Vincent's thoughts, with a cold, derisive expression; but the parrot suddenly shut its mouth.

"Why does it always say I'm a usurer?" Vincent asked the servant.

"Because in the gambling city we all have usury in our bones. Look at yourself, whoever makes you unhappy you push away. We look down on this kind of behavior."

When he said this, the parrot also stared at Vincent, and its bleary eyes suddenly shot out a cold light. It seemed to see through to Vincent's organs and its claws broke through Vincent's pants, catching his flesh. Vincent felt he must say something right away, and what he said was "Joyner."

The parrot was satisfied. It loosed its claws, jumped down onto the floor, and flew from the floor up onto the servant's shoulder.

"Joyner is the gatekeeper to the gambling city. After you go back from here, even if you lose your memory completely, you will still remember how she looked resting on her broom, standing in a cloud of smoke," the servant said.

"I wish for that, too." Vincent agreed from his heart.

He looked out at the window. The smoke outside was already dispersing. The sky broke through with a color pleasing to the eyes and the heart, like the colors of the frigid morning of a clear day, but even more beautiful than this, a beauty that didn't seem real. The gloom in Vincent's heart quietly receded. He walked to the stairway beyond the door and heard a nightingale singing. How could there be a nightingale in this sunny sky? In the garden opposite the house, a red apple fell from a tree laden with fruit. The apple didn't fall directly, but rather gradually drifted in the air before gently falling on the grass, where it lay like a miracle, giving off a red light.

"In fact, it's the middle of the night," the servant said lightly. He had also come outside. "Listen, your train is here."

Vincent heard the sound of a train entering the station.

"So I need to hurry? But I still want to see Lisa's parents."

"Don't worry, the train is stopped at the station waiting for you to make up your mind. But I don't think you need to see Lisa's parents. They are still underground, dreaming happy dreams. No need to deprive them of the happiness of their old age. Go see Joyner."

Vincent thought it was certainly out of envy that the servant didn't want him to see his father- and mother-in-law. However, now he wanted to see Joyner even more. He imagined the scene of himself and the young woman standing under that beautiful apple tree "spilling words from their hearts," and he grew a little impatient. And so he took his leave of the servant and the parrot on the servant's shoulder, and walked to Joyner's hotel. In the distance the stone mountains had stopped belching smoke and looked solemn in appearance. Before, Lisa had told him, the gambling city was small, only as big as a stone in a slingshot, but the residents had numbered several hundred thousand. The street was so crowded with pedestrians they could all smell each other's skin. In the casinos people were soaked in sweat. What led to the population's disappearance and their collective evacuation? What hidden nucleus was everything he saw aboveground and underground revealing to him?

"Joyner, I love you."

"Vincent, I love you, too. Ten years ago I fell in love with you. On that day you stood at the main gate of the Rose Clothing Company. My mother and I were shopping for clothes in the store opposite, and I took your measure carefully through the glass windows."

"Nonsense, how old were you then?"

"I was as old then as I am now. You still haven't realized, time stagnates here. So when I saw you this time, your aged appearance surprised me. That's why I called you Grandfather."

They spilled words from their hearts to each other. But the place they were standing was not under the apple tree. It was in a small room in the building where the cleaning tools were kept. The air in the room wasn't good, with the smoke from the basement seeping through wide cracks in the doors. Vincent choked and coughed. He couldn't open his eyes. When Joyner gently gripped his hand, an unfamiliar excitement rushed from his heart, a kind of feeling he'd never experienced with a woman's body, one that eliminated his lust for sex. Was it because Joyner called him Grandfather that his lust for her changed in this way? No, that wasn't it. The problem was with Joyner's body. From the start, Vincent had felt that this beautiful woman had nothing directly to do with sex. But how could he not love a woman like her? She was so beautiful and so affectionate.

"Joyner, I don't want to leave you, but I can't stand the smoke clouds anymore, I can't breathe. What should I do? I think if I leave your side now my life will become a stretch of darkness."

"Oh, no, it won't be like that. Go, Grandfather. If you leave you can always remember me. Go to where Lisa is, that is your normal life. But my life is also a normal life, don't you think? The gamblers always lead happy lives. Production and consumption proceed underground, and for many, many years we have been content. Your palms are so hot. That time when I first saw you, I assumed your palms would be hot. You're a warm-hearted man—how else could my younger sister Lisa fall in love with you?"

Vincent felt dizzy, that he had to go outside or he would fall to the floor. He wanted Joyner to come with him, but she was determined to stay inside the darkened room. He could only go out by himself. He walked into the living room, where there was no smoke, and had a fit of violent coughing. It seemed as though he would cough his organs inside out. When nausea overwhelmed him, nothing remained of his passion. He understood: he could not love within the poisonous smoke. This was why the parrot called him a usurer. How was this underground production and consumption mechanism operated? "Without entering the tiger's den, you can't catch the tiger's cub"—and since he couldn't breathe within the poisonous smoke, he had no chance of answering this question. Perhaps Lisa had agreed to his coming here in order to make him see where his own limitations lay.

He left Joyner's hotel, reached the garden at the center of the street, and sat down. Various species of bird drifted in the pure air. The birds weren't flying in a straight line or spreading open their wings, but were simply floating in the air, as if drifting with a tide, in a curvilinear motion. "The birds of the gambling city," Vincent sighed. He thought of the damp crows that dropped onto the steps of his house. Just at this moment the train whistle sounded, as if pressing him on. He suddenly remembered he'd left his luggage at Joyner's hotel, but he decided not to go back. It was better to return home at once.

At the end of the platform he could see the back of a woman wearing a skirt. She looked much like Lisa. He walked over to her, the woman turned around, and it really was Lisa. She was holding a leather suitcase in her hand.

"So you've come, too," Vincent said resentfully.

"Yes, I was just at my parents' house, in the underground rooms. Are you disappointed by my hometown?"

"No, I love this place."

"Then let's go to the underground rooms together."

"No, I'm not going back to the underground rooms, let's go back to our home. When night comes, I will search again, with you, and maybe we'll find the real casinos, the kind with slot machines."

A dove floated in front of them, followed immediately by a second one, a third, a fourth, peacefully moving past.

"I didn't think there'd be doves here," Vincent mumbled to himself.

"When I was little, the travelers who came from outside called this the land of doves. At that time, the entire sky was filled with doves flying back and forth in the rose-colored evening clouds. It's a pity you haven't seen this spectacle."

"So are doves the image of the gambling city's soul?"

"They probably are. At midnight, a dove sits on the shoulder of every person who comes out of a casino."

Long after the train started moving, Vincent and Lisa watched the doves outside the rail cars. Vincent couldn't figure out whether he'd stayed at the gambling city for one day or three because the sun had never set. Judging by his senses, it felt as though more than a day had passed. Yet in this elongated day he had only eaten one meal in Joyner's underground rooms. Now he understood why the slot machines were hidden in the walls and no longer played — in this region where nothing set apart the day and the night, the stimulation of the slot machines was of no use.

Lisa stared in a daze at the doves outside. Her heart was steeped in a recollection of happiness. Vincent had entered her past life at last. This illustrated the depth of love in their marriage. But her past was not limited to one kind of life, and this was something Vincent probably wasn't aware of. She had spoken to him of herself before, but what she spoke of was another of her lives. It wasn't fabricated. But now Vincent might believe that she had invented everything she'd told him before. Thinking this over, she grew faintly uneasy again. She leaned on Vincent's shoulder, holding his hand, and gently asked:

"Vincent?"

"Oh, Lisa! How could someone like you grow old? I know the mystery of why you are always young — a nightingale sings in your heart. My heart has no nightingale, so I cannot enter those underground rooms. Is that right? What your parrot said was right, I really am a shameless usurer."

Lisa was reassured. It appeared Vincent didn't intend to investigate her at all. He still had enough adaptability. He was so adaptable that Lisa still worried about not being able to predict his next step. A long time ago she had jokingly called him "mercury." The impulse like a riddle in the depths of his heart was, to her, truly like mercury.

There would always be a day when, because of this ungraspable poison, she would lose her life.

"Vincent?"

"Lisa, where did the people in the train all go to?"

"There wasn't anyone in the compartment. This train came specially to meet us. Look, the doves disappeared. Outside it's really night. Vincent, your whole body is cold."

"I feel like I'm spinning."

In his dizziness Vincent held Lisa's hand tightly, but what he held was only a hand. The owner of the hand was gradually moving away from him, and the hand gradually grew icy. In his drowsy state he sensed someone enter the train car and say to Lisa, "Snow is falling outside. This weather is an anomaly." Lisa gave an earsplitting laugh, clearly fake, then she and the person left together. Someone said in his ear, "Mister, where are you going?" "The Rose Clothing Company." He struggled to name this, the only place he could think of, his voice thin like a mosquito's whine. "Oh, so you are the usurer!" The man laughed an ear-piercing laugh, like Lisa's. Then he sat beside him. After a long while Vincent's eyes finally recovered their sight. He looked to the right and discovered there was actually no one there, only a cap placed on the seat. Maybe the man had gone to the toilet?

He stood to go find Lisa, walking from one train car to another. He felt as if the train he rode were passing through the dark toward the dawn. The carriages he walked through were all empty. Where was Lisa hiding? Finally he reached the tail end of the train, and Lisa was there at the back, curled up asleep in the last row of seats. When Vincent stepped in front of her, she opened her tired eyes in the faint lamplight. Vincent thought her eyes were beautiful! She made a sign for Vincent to draw near her, and he squatted down.

"That year I took the train away from the gambling city, it was the third day after my mother died. The gambling debt she owed was too great. She died of terror."

"The old woman in that large house wasn't your mother?"

"Of course she was. Even I have died many times."

"I don't understand."

"You'll get used to this sort of thing. Can you hear that? Outside it really is snowing. The places we're passing are all covered in snow, the same as that year."

Vincent could hear only the sound of the wheels of the train. He wondered what kind of hearing Lisa possessed. She shut her eyes as if she were going back to sleep. The underground rooms of her hometown seemed to have cost her almost all her energy. Now he was with her on this train, and the train connected the past and the future. What was the future like? Did the dwarf who came to their house in the middle of the night know the answer to this question? Vincent remembered how he and the dwarf had gotten drunk in the kitchen. The two of them climbed from the attic onto the roof. As they sat on the roof, a flock of bats brushed past their cheeks. It was then that the dwarf told him about the gambling city encircled by unbroken stone mountains and its rose-red sky. He said to Vincent, "It's a truly peaceful scene. No one would think of leaving that place. The stone mountains are only a picture: no one can really pass over them. The train connecting to the outside was something that came later. The train passes through long tunnels before reaching the city. The dark deep tunnels are like a passageway to death."

At first he wanted to ask Lisa why she had left her hometown. But then he remembered Lisa had explained this before, so he didn't ask. She wasn't the only person to leave. Wasn't there also the dwarf? The people of the gambling city had probably all left for some shared reason.

At daybreak the train conductor finally appeared. He was a fat man who yawned constantly.

"I dreamt of a large snowfall. It's absurd, how could there be snow now?"

He seemed to solicit the couple's opinion. Vincent smelled alcohol on him.

"When you live in a lonely town like this, how can you not depend on drinking to pass the time?" He kept speaking, as if uncomfortable, and as if he wanted to spill words from his heart toward them. He invited them to his conductor's office to sit for a while, because in half an hour the train would reach the station. He didn't want his guests to lack an impression of his train.

When he opened the door of his "office," Vincent and Lisa were surprised. The tiny room was just one meter square, with a small student desk attached to a metal chair. If *anyone* sat there for a long time it would be painful, let alone someone as fat as the conductor, who would have trouble squeezing into the seat. They didn't understand. Why was the conductor's office designed like this when it was such a spacious train?

The conductor seemed to have guessed their thoughts. He raised one leg, squeezed behind the desk, and sat down in an extremely painful posture, his stomach tightly propped on the desk drawer. He asked Vincent to give him the liquor bottle. A half-bottle of brandy sat on a separate shelf. The conductor greedily emptied it, drinking straight from the bottle. He threw it away, bent over the desk, and went to sleep. Lisa said to Vincent: "The train can indeed be called a lonely town, but why did he want us to see how he dreamed? He's a strange man."

"It's possible this is how he lives his life. We happened to become the landscape of his world."

When he said these words, Lisa stared at him for a moment. He couldn't say whether she approved of what he said or disagreed. The train had already entered the station. They surveyed the conductor and decided he had no intention of waking. Although he looked uncomfortable leaning there, he certainly slept soundly.

That day Vincent and Lisa sat in the garden for a long time. The sun was scorching. The scent of the green grass made them drowsy. He told Lisa that there were a few things he was now unsure of. He couldn't tell whether he should go to work. Maybe he should become a train conductor, or something like that? But he wouldn't like that journeying kind of life, and even more he didn't like loneliness. Yet he felt his career was now a yoke around his neck, because there were things in this world that still held interest for him, things he was unable to pursue. He chattered on. What he talked about seemed to have been suppressed for decades. The more he spoke the more direct his gaze grew, and the more he felt himself near but not touching on reality; but still he couldn't stop.

Lisa let him talk at first, looking absentminded. Her large brown eyes watching him appeared so remote it was as if he were a passing stranger.

"Vincent, when I picked brake ferns in the gully, where were you hiding?" she mumbled.

Vincent was surprised and shut his mouth.

Lisa made several odd gestures with her hands, appearing nervous. Vincent sensed that she was communicating with someone. With whom? There was not a single person in the vicinity.

"Vincent, I want to leave," she spoke again, her face turned elsewhere. "Every day I go to the same places. But why do you complain? I think you are complaining."

Yet she didn't move. She still sat there, staring into space. Later on she finally stood, circled around the stone table, and placed her hands on Vincent's shoulders, saying, "I've finally remembered. It isn't Maria going on the long march at night, it's me. Look how forgetful I am. You don't need to change jobs. It won't affect your pursuing those other things."

"I remember your going on the long march at night, too, but you said it was Maria!"

"The delusion probably emerged when I was in her rose garden. Now, when I'm speaking with you in this garden, I'm already gone, I've left. You see my shadow receding? Along with the cook's."

Vincent reached out his arms to embrace Lisa. The woman sat in his embrace as calmly as a kitten. He heard a strange noise. He listened carefully and made out the sound of galloping horse's hooves, with the sound of people yelling pressed in between.

"Darling, where do you think you can run off to?" he asked, kissing her ear.

"I am changing my habit of going on journeys at night." She stifled a laugh.

"Lisa, you're so light. Is this you? I saw the gambling city under the sun. It looked like it was coming toward us. Lisa, is this you?"

"It's me, darling. You can't forget the city, because it will always be in the depths of your heart."

They were talking in this mad way, and at the doorway of their house Joe, his features strained, was looking for Vincent. He had an emergency to report to him. The cook told Joe that the house's owner and his wife had already returned and were both in the garden. Joe walked into a large garden so overgrown even the path was obscured, but he didn't see the two of them. He saw doves. The white breed of doves, hidden in the thick grass. They were everywhere, making a lovely cooing. Joe was released from his anxiety. He felt no need to be nervous, and thought that spending an afternoon here wouldn't be too bad. A few nights before he'd passed through a street-corner garden and seen Vincent sitting on a bench drinking, worries written all over his face. He had come here to find Vincent and discuss a problem from work, but he'd already forgotten what he'd wanted to talk about. He vaguely remembered that it had something to do with an improvement to the style of the clothing. Now he was afraid of meeting Vincent, because he couldn't say what had brought him here. Joe squatted in the grass, listening carefully to the doves' coos. It was a few days since he had seen his boss. Joe wondered whether he himself still hoped to leave. If he hoped to leave the clothing company, why was he still laboring body and soul at the company's work? It had already developed into a giant corporation. Opportunities increased, and Joe's salary grew larger. Maria had renewed her habit of buying jewelry. In the midst of his pressing business at work, Joe continued his frequent reading. And so sometimes, when talking about work, he used literary language. Encountering this, his customers often nodded their heads to show complete understanding. What kind of people were his customers? He heard Vincent and Lisa's voices. They were walking past the other side of the peach tree beside him.

"How could you breathe in the underground rooms? I can't think of how. Could you teach me?" Vincent said.

"Vincent, dear, it is called summoning demons. I don't want to fill our everyday life with earthquakes."

Through the branches of the peach tree Joe saw Lisa's gorgeous skirt. The couple was walking toward the house. The cooing of the doves, the blue sky, and the green trees made one reluctant to leave the place. Joe sat down, taking out a novel from his briefcase. A train appeared in the chapters he read. One of the train's cars had no people in it, only two shadows showing on the glass window. The train conductor, a fat old man, came over to explain: "This is a newly implemented experiment, to see whether this special journey is possible. The two people who founded the Rose Clothing Company in the city belong to an elite class of people." Joe didn't like the tone of this description: it was oily and shifty. What elite class of people? Vincent wasn't that kind of man. Joe suddenly realized, How could things taking place in reality be written in the book? He looked again at the book's cover, where there was a picture of a bee along with the title in italics: *The Heroic Long March.* At this moment two real bees fell onto the page of the book. They were both comatose, one a worker bee and the other a drone, hopelessly moving their legs. Was Vincent passing information to him? He cautiously moved the bees onto a blade of grass, thinking of everything Lisa had said about the earthquakes. Yesterday there had been a real earthquake in his square. The statue in the center had toppled over a little at a time. Spring water rushed from the well. With a nameless impulse he ran to the well, wanting to see his own face. But he couldn't lean into it because he was drenched by a small waterfall, and he couldn't keep his footing because of the vibrations from every direction.

The couple floated in the air, walking as they talked, then fluttered into the large house. The door quietly shut behind them, then quietly opened again. The cook, a woman, put her head out. Joe stood up, clapping the dust from his clothes, and walked toward the cook. He wasn't sure what he could do to appear natural.

"I remember the cook they hired before was a man. If his employer lay drunk on the ground, the cook would carry him inside." Once he opened his mouth, this is what Joe said.

The cook didn't say a word. She looked at him briefly, then let him enter the building.

He had just sat down on the sofa in the spacious hall when husband and wife came to greet him.

Although they welcomed him warmly, Joe sensed that their thoughts weren't inside the house. He could tell this from their drifting expressions.

"Joe has come to settle accounts with us," Vincent joked.

Joe heard this with surprise. He thought, Was a foundational change coming to the Rose Clothing Company? The empty hall gave him an eerie feeling. Where had the original furniture gone? Vincent didn't ask why Joe was there, but thought it natural that he was. Later on Vincent invited Joe to go for a drink at a restaurant down the street. Joe said that if he drank before the sky was even dark, fear would fill his heart. Vincent laughed aloud, a skin-crawling laugh. Then he pulled Joe into the street by main force. Joe was a moderate man and not willing to oppose his boss. So although he hated the way Vincent went about it, he was compelled to go along.

In the car, Vincent told Joe his trip had left him uptight and he wanted to get drunk. At home if he drank too much Lisa would interfere, so he pretended to take Joe out for a drink. He really just wanted Joe to accompany him. He didn't have to drink. When Vincent said this, his voice became loud and piercing, like a parrot's, like an old parrot's. His brow twisted, revealing his ferocity.

Because it was afternoon there was no one in the restaurant, but the door was open and a single bottle sat on a single table. Vincent uncorked it and drank a few large gulps straight from its mouth. He then turned and told Joe that he wanted to go below. Joe asked him below where, and he replied that he meant the underground rooms.

"You're coming, too?" Joe agreed.

The underground room was full of wine bottles. People lay on the ground every which way, and appeared to be asleep. Joe saw a small door beside the liquor cabinet and couldn't help reaching out a hand to push it open.

"You will get free if you leave this place." Vincent seemed to smile. "You will make up your mind eventually."

Before Joe's eyes appeared the back garden of his own home. A ghostly woman wearing a kimono stood in the garden.

"Maria!" he shouted.

A strange man walked out of the building. Glancing back, Joe saw that the door to the basement was already shut. Joe scanned the walls for signs of rain, but there were none. Whose house was so like his own?

The woman said to the man, "I'm going to the square."

She finished this sentence and the sky grew dark. The man and the woman, one after the other, left the garden.

12

JOE RESOLVES TO LEAVE

Joe finally emerged from the intricate crisscrossing alleys. He told Maria that he had been in a heavy-headed state, but light-footed. He remembered only that he saw parrots everywhere—on the balcony, on the walls, on the trashcans. Everywhere, and moreover, the birds weren't afraid of people. When they saw Joe, they approached and spoke to him. The birds' voices scared him, sounding too much like Vincent's voice. Even the import of what they said was similar.

"Joe, have you made up your mind?" the old parrot swayed side to side toward him.

Joe looked up at a sky covered in haze, and answered dejectedly, "I want to find an exit."

The bird stood its ground, dissatisfied. But wild laughter erupted behind Joe from another bird.

Maria heard him attentively to the end, and at last responded: "Vincent truly is your kindred spirit. When you pushed that small door open, didn't you hesitate, even a little? It sounds so strange."

"I thought of it too late." He felt his will sinking.

The next day Joe took off from work. He began reading a book with only one page. The book was clothbound, with a drawing of a tall pine tree on the cover. Inside there was a single thick sheet of paper. This sheet could be unfolded to the length of the desk. The picture on the cover appeared to be of an anthill. The periphery of the anthill was densely written over with a miniature text, visible only under a magnifying glass. And once Joe looked with the glass, he discovered that he didn't recognize a single word. This book had sat on the lowest shelf of the last rack in a small bookshop on a noisy street in the city. When Joe went to pay for it, the elderly bookstore owner came over and told him the book was not for sale.

"It was on the shelf, but it's not for sale?" Joe was furious. He grasped the book tightly, almost afraid the shopkeeper would take it back by force.

"Fine, take it away, take it away! But don't regret it!" He walked away resentfully.

The book's price was unusually high, but Joe paid without hesitation.

Now he attempted to locate his own square in this anthill. Accompanying the slow movements of the magnifying glass in his hand, the floor under his feet began to rise and fall.

"Father, what are you doing in there?" Daniel shouted from outside the study.

"Be a good boy. Don't come in, it's a mess in here . . ."

Daniel evidently didn't dare enter. Joe sighed in relief and continued to wrestle with the book, which was flying around madly. At one point, he flopped down to the ground, his ear to the floor, and heard Maria's voice underneath the floorboards. She sounded irritable. Joe didn't care to listen to more, so he stood up, leaning against the wall. But he hadn't been on his feet two minutes before he fell down onto the sofa. He looked around from the sofa and saw that the anthill had disappeared from that remarkable book and turned into a blank white space. He felt as if the sofa were a small boat on the rippling water. Daniel pushed the door slightly open and stuck his head in. His neck and face looked fresh and healthy.

"The study is finally mad, too," Daniel said, looking pleased.

"Daniel, son, what are you planning to do?"

"Me? Don't blame me, this is because of you, you bought that book. And there's Mother . . ."

He closed the door, apparently to go downstairs. Joe was astounded: "Does Daniel really know everything?"

In the chaos of the study, Joe started to think calmly. A dove was cooing. There was an actual dove inside the heap of books on the floor. Had it flown in through the window or had Maria put it there? Many of the books were damaged, their pages strewn all over. Joe leaned against the wall and slowly moved out onto the balcony. Before his eyes a familiar scene reappeared.

Maria and Daniel sat among the bushes drinking tea. The two cats walked, stately, back and forth. The balcony was directly in the line of sight of mother and son. Joe waved to them, but they did not respond. Did they even see him? The room shook again with violent tremors. Joe feared he would fall from the balcony, and quickly went inside, crawling aboard the sofa, holding on with a death grip. "And so there are things as strange as this," he said to himself irritably.

Afterward the earthquake gradually subsided, although there were still aftershocks. The aftershocks continued until Maria called him to come downstairs and eat, when they finally disappeared. He went downstairs, disoriented, and sat at the dining table. Daniel wasn't there.

"Did Daniel go to work?"

"So you know everything after all."

"Of course. Doesn't he know everything about me, too? He's an ambitious young man. I just lived through an earthquake, damn it."

"Daniel and I saw. You were shaking with fear. But we couldn't have helped you, could we?"

A turkey was arranged on the table. Maria's face appeared almost bewitching in the rising steam, her cheekbones almost like two red halos. Joe couldn't make out her expression. It was as if she were covered by a membrane.

He had just finished eating and put down his chopsticks when an uninvited guest entered his yard. The man's head was wrapped in a turban. He seemed travel-weary. Maria told Joe that the man was his driver. Joe recognized the familiar face. It brought to mind the time he'd stayed for a night and day in the north at Mr. Kim's home. But when had Maria come to know the driver?

"I arrived a number of days ago, and I've been staying in the basement of the restaurant. You've seen me, you haven't recognized me, and you've walked away from me. At the time I was drunk, down on the ground, but one of my eyes was always open."

Maria called to him to put down the canvas bag he carried on his back, but he didn't, standing in the doorway instead.

"Mr. Kim wants you to come and relive old dreams with him," the driver said to Joe.

A vast pastureland floated up in Joe's mind, the mountain peaks piled with snow and the eccentric owner of the house halfway up a mountain. The driver stood in front of him without moving. His face under his turban was extremely handsome in the evening glow. Joe was drawn in by him, thinking that in the city one very seldom met a good-looking man like this one. Was he the descendant of a warrior from ancient times? But when Joe had first met him on the pastureland, he hadn't been handsome. Maria's eyes were fixed on the man. Joe remembered that she and this fellow had already been in contact, and jealousy unbidden leapt up in his heart. She, and him, and also Kim, what sort of connection did they share?

"How would I relive old dreams?" he asked.

"You're already reliving old dreams." His eyes were smiling.

"But I don't understand." Joe felt his whole body go hot and dry. "I'll go now."

He walked from the yard, through the main gate, and disappeared into the golden sunset. Maria's face glowed.

Joe couldn't stay sitting at home. He went outside. He walked aimlessly and unconsciously reached the small bookstore, where he saw the fearsome shopkeeper. People came and went in the shop. With the dim lamplight, the people coming in all appeared furtive, but the bookstore owner sat haughtily on a high stool at the entrance. Over many years, Joe had bought many fine books here. Yet before it had been an ordinary little bookstore, doing a lackluster business. Who would have thought such a bookshop could survive in the city for so many years? Joe suspected that the bookstore owner might rely on an occasional shady transaction to support his livelihood. Joe had never spoken with the bookstore owner, who wouldn't cater to people, as if he really were someone important. Nevertheless, his shop contained some truly interesting books.

Today was a little strange. After Joe entered the shop, the electricity suddenly shut off. He was shoved back and forth, and a bookcase was knocked over. All the books fell out. The bookstore owner cursed in the dark. Fortunately the lights were soon restored.

"Wherever you go, there are earthquakes," the bookstore owner said, gathering the books.

Joe helped, thinking to himself, How did he know? After the books were gathered up, he was too embarrassed to stay and left the shop. But the bookstore owner called him back. From under his buttocks he drew out the book he was sitting on and handed it to Joe, saying it was especially for him. Joe's heart pounded. He hid behind a bookcase, opened the book, and saw a portrait of Kim. But it wasn't Kim. Another man's name was written underneath the portrait. He read from the introduction. The introduction said that in the book the author described the minutiae of his entire life. It also contained an extensive daily record. "Because someone is willing to publish it, I wrote everything without scruple," the author wrote derisively. Reading up to that point, Joe resolved to buy the book. The bookstore owner wasn't willing to accept money for it. He said the book was left by the author with instructions to give it to Joe as a gift.

"The author came?" Joe was disturbed.

"He didn't come himself, he sent his underling. Look, he's sitting over there."

In the obscure light, Joe saw the driver's handsome face. He was browsing through a book in a corner. Joe's heart palpitated. He thought, "It really is still him."

"Sometimes the people one meets by chance were already by one's side." The owner finished this sentence after he returned to his high stool, recovering his haughty look.

Joe thought the driver was smiling at him, but evidently he didn't want Joe to disturb him. He seemed to be looking for a book. Joe left the shop. In the light of the streetlamp, he couldn't help opening the book again, and so he saw the photograph of Kim a second time. When he'd calmed down, he discovered that the man wasn't Kim after all. It was only someone whose face had a similar shape. The man's expression was cold and stern, even a little cruel. Joe didn't like cruel men. But wasn't Kim a bit cruel? Joe thought this strange: he rather liked Kim. A fellow who could write down his personal secrets in a book this thick, and who moreover wanted to give the book to him. Joe shivered, although he wasn't cold. So this driver, was he the driver he'd met at Kim's? Perhaps this book was what he called "reliving old dreams." But the man in the picture didn't really look like Kim. Even the color of his hair was different: Kim had black hair, black like a crow's wings, and this man's hair was a lighter color.

Then Joe thought: Could he write a book like this himself? If someone would publish it, would he write all the trivial things that happened in his life into a book? This way of thinking stemmed from a kind of avarice. Joe wasn't sure whether he would be able to do it. He honestly disliked the countenance of the man in the picture. Pondering this question, he carelessly ran into someone's back. It was a black woman, the beautiful street cleaner.

"Good evening! Why are you reading in the street, sir?" she asked cheerfully.

"Excuse me." Joe's face and ears suddenly reddened.

"This time of day is so beautiful, especially in the bookshops where the light is dim. Don't you think so?"

"Yes, yes, you are so beautiful, that's how it is." He spoke at random.

The woman walked away, smiling. Joe saw his own awkward, distracted look in the shop window. He clamped the book under his arm and hurriedly walked toward home. Without intending to watch him, he saw the driver leave the bookshop and go in a different direction.

"But in the evening the world outside is glorious. Why do you always stay in your study?"

Maria reproached him. What for? He carried this question back to the study. He was eager to know what sort of thing this author's "reliving old dreams" was, and whether it had anything to do with the web of stories he'd been constructing over the years. Because a man with a face like this one couldn't have given him the book without a motive. The opening of the book was the man's self-introduction. It seemed affected:

I was born in a mountain village of a small country in the East. The impression of this country in the mind of the average person is of an extremely cold place, where the long winters are insufferably dull. The reality of the matter is not like this at all. People there have extremely warm dispositions. The ivory snow of the mountain range is our paradise. There are numerous ice caves in the mountains, dug out by generations of tenacious labor. In fact, I was born in one of these ice caves.

Joe, reading this far, felt duped. Nor could he produce a corresponding image in his mind. Hadn't the author said he would write exclusively about the personal details of his life? This generalized background was like an old teacher's worn-out saws. He put down the book, growing distracted. There was a man in this book who wanted to say something to the people of the world, and so he had written the book. The man was much like Kim, the owner of the grasslands in the north whom Joe had met; but he was also entirely different. Yet Kim, his own situation hidden, had indirect exchanges with Joe through all kinds of connections. The result of these exchanges was that Joe sank into oblivion. Joe sighed and picked up the book again. This time he began to read in the middle.

The landscape of swirling snowflakes is a symbol of happiness. One only has to see the atmosphere of ardent collective labor in the ice caves to understand this. What is happiness? Sweating in the freezing winter, at 30 degrees below zero Celsius, is happiness. Each person holds an iron pick in hand, digging stroke on stroke into the walls of a thousand-year-old ice cave. We are extending our own space.

Joe shut his eyes and felt incredibly tired. Someone came into the hallway. Was it Daniel? Did Daniel know his father's spirit had fallen into a difficult place? Such a sensitive boy! When the web of the story in Joe's mind was about to reach a state of perfection, someone was sabotaging him, pulling the firewood out from under the pot. In recent days, the space Joe had constructed over a long period of time had been shrinking. His eyesight was also getting weaker. He held in his hand a book that fascinated him, but he simply couldn't read it; he only had a sense of being excluded from it. Was he already so old?

"Father, I love you." Daniel stuck his head into the room and then drew back.

Joe heard a cat meowing in the hallway. "A woman who builds up a home like this is admirable." Joe felt deeply Maria's intrinsic perfection and beauty. "I love you, too, Daniel," he said to himself. The loom sounded downstairs. Hadn't Maria stopped weaving a long time ago?

Daniel finally came in. He stood quite still against the wall, a long thin twig.

"Is something bothering you?"

"I'm happy."

His response startled Joe. When Daniel was little Joe took him fishing, and when a fish was hooked Joe had asked him what he felt. He said it hurt him. Now he'd become a gardener with a happy life.

"Daniel, why are you still standing there?"

"There are things in this room that I'm afraid of. Father, do you see the bone you hung on the wall, it's moving . . . What kind of bone is it? Is it human?"

Daniel stuck close to the wall. To Joe he looked like he was trying to bore into it.

"Don't take this to heart, child. Your thoughts are so serious."

Joe stood up and went to another bookshelf. From this angle he couldn't see Daniel. The boy made him restless. He sat down, still wanting to reason through his own train of thought. But he couldn't with Daniel on the opposite side, interfering with him like a magnetic field. Joe heard the sound of pages turning. Was Daniel looking at the book out on the table? Abruptly the study rang with the sound of Daniel reading aloud:

The garden in the air has no flowers, only wild grass. Who would garden in a place like this? No one. But when a gust of wind thins the dense fog, a straw hat appears.

Joe walked out of his hiding place. He saw Daniel holding the book. Joe moved in front of him and took the book from his hands. But somehow he couldn't find the sentence his son had just read aloud. He asked Daniel where the sentence was. Daniel said it wasn't in the book, he had just seen it. He'd strained to look and the sentence appeared. This was the kind of book you could see things in, but usually he didn't read because it was too hard on his eyes. He wished his father would read less of this kind of book.

"Father, you should just be a gardener, too." His look as he spoke was both simple and experienced.

Joe thought of the days and nights when he was immersed in the world of his books. There was also the story he had woven, a great undertaking soon to be completed. In comparison to Daniel, all of this was insignificant. He sank back into gloom.

"I don't want to be a happy gardener, son. My destiny is to work at the Rose Clothing Company. My life is under a spell. Maybe someday I will be able to leave. It's what my boss expects of me. Daniel, are you still afraid of that bone?"

"No, Father. It isn't moving now, so I can see it's a cow bone. I have to go. I'm even happier now, because you aren't opposed to my being a gardener. I haven't touched any books for years. Are you disappointed?"

"No, Daniel, I admire you." Joe spoke in sincerity.

The door shut. Joe heard Maria and Daniel talk in the hallway, then go downstairs together. Joe reflected that he had an admirable wife and an admirable son. He paced onto the balcony and saw the figures of mother and son floating out through the garden gate like ghosts. A cat squatted guard on a boulder, watching them go.

Someone was in his study. When Joe returned to his desk and sat down, the man walked out from behind the bookshelf. He walked up behind Joe with slow steps, then returned back behind the bookshelf. Joe heard him, but did not want to turn around to see him.

"Daniel, your father wants to come out of his cocoon. Will you move back in, darling child?"

"No, Mother. This way is better."

Maria looked at her son as he walked beside her. His long, thin body seemed to be near her side, yet also at a far distance. She thought of the young women who wore kimonos in Joe's story. It was possible that in Joe's eyes those girls were embodiments of Daniel. Joe was such a strange man. At the present moment her son was by her side, and yet wasn't by her side, and surely he was pondering some remote thing. When he came outside, Daniel had said he would bring her to see the garden he'd designed in the air, but they were already outside the city, where there weren't any gardens. They followed an embankment down into a dry riverbed. Daniel squatted, scooping the river's silt with his long, thin fingers, letting it run through them. Maria heard a groan from his throat. The fog gradually grew thicker, and after a bit they couldn't see each other's faces. Maria's mind grew confused.

"Daniel, I can't remember what I did yesterday."

Daniel's answer was scattered in the air with a buzzing *weng weng*. Maria had no means of understanding the disordered words. She breathed with effort. Surely she smelled the fragrance of a rose of Sharon. The blooms were invisible; probably they were running through her son's fingers. A vision of Daniel wearing a straw hat, sweating under the sun, appeared in Maria's imagination. She heard him saying two syllables, *Fa-ther*. But Daniel wasn't calling his father. It was like a preschooler practicing his letters.

Steps could be heard on the river embankment. Maria stood and the steps stopped.

"Is that Joe?" she shouted.

"Is that Joe . . ." The air vibrated, Daniel's voice echoing hers.

A magpie flew in front of them, toward the embankment.

"Mother, let's go back to where Father is."

Daniel stretched out his hands to restrain her. Maria saw that the arms he reached toward her were the branches of a Chinese redbud, with small flowers swaying cheerfully. They climbed together up onto the embankment, but Joe wasn't there. Maria's heart flowed with warm currents of happiness, because she heard again the voice of Joe in his youth. She was moved to tears.

"Joe, Joe . . ." she said.

Many years ago, she and Joe had climbed up from the dry riverbed. Over so many years, she had never thought she might return like this, in person, to old dreams. Maybe now she and her son truly were walking into Joe's all-encompassing story. He wasn't on the riverbank; he was inside her body. On such a day redbud flowers grew from her son's body. The year she became pregnant, she'd often seen Chinese redbuds.

Joe was on the embankment. He saw the mother and son in the riverbed, one standing, one squatting. Then they started to walk, groping like blind men, as if neither could see the other. Joe took two breaths of the limpid air. Then he saw a white-haired Eastern woman appear on the opposite shore. The woman's clothing was also white and looked a bit like a kimono, a bit like the short dresses of ancient China. She leaned on a willow tree, observing mother and son in the riverbed. Joe stared without shifting his eyes from the aged, beautiful woman, in a daze because he had never seen such a fine older woman. He felt his soul spirited away from his body. Someone clapped his shoulder. To his surprise, it was the shopkeeper from the bookstore.

"The person over on that side isn't real." The bookstore owner knit his brow, spitting out the sentence as if it hurt him.

"I had also sensed this. What a pity. Where is she from?"

"She is my former wife."

Joe looked in surprise at the ugly bookstore owner, and had nothing to say. He couldn't bear Joe's gaze. He hunched his back, broken down. Joe recollected an image of him sitting proudly at the bookshop entrance on a high stool, and suddenly understood the pain in his heart. In the riverbed mother and son, one before and one behind, climbed up to the bank. They hadn't seen Joe. Maria's legs were slightly lame. Seen from behind, her posture was still like a young girl's.

"Why isn't she a real person?" Joe asked the bookstore owner, his voice revealing his tender thoughts.

"Because whichever way you go, you still can't reach her. If you don't believe me, you can try it."

"I would like to make an attempt."

After Maria and Daniel climbed onto the bank, the woman opposite turned around, her back to Joe and the bookstore owner. Joe thought the woman's figure resembled the immortals in an Eastern myth. Was the East the place he should go? The shopkeeper walked down the riverbank, hunched over. He said he couldn't bear it any longer. He seemed to cry as he walked.

Joe went down to the riverbed, wanting to cross over to the other bank. As he walked he distrusted his progress, because the bookstore keeper had just spoken of how no one would be able to reach "her" face. Joe climbed the bank anxiously. He saw the woman slowly turning around. Her clothing was a dazzling white. The woman wore glasses. Joe had not imagined that she might wear glasses.

"Are you off work today?" she asked amiably.

"I never expected . . . I thought how much . . . Today I didn't want to go to work. Do you live near here? It's so nice here!"

"Yes, I live here. I've observed you, too. Someone is urging you to leave this city, isn't that right?"

Joe did not answer. He understood why the bookstore owner was crying. Above them, the heavens became like crystal. He wanted to ask the woman whether she knew Kim.

"Do you mean the man who has a pastureland, who lives halfway up a mountain? Of course I know him, there aren't many people who don't know him. He is not a real person. Have you sensed that?"

Her dazzling glance watched Joe. His blood bubbled.

"Your former husband said that you weren't a real person either. Why?" He drummed up his courage to ask.

"Some people are an unsolvable mystery to other people. If he lives with that sort of person, he will gradually disappear. Have I answered your question? If you go to Ito's bookstore late at night, you will hear him wrestling inside and the books falling from the shelves."

"Who is he wrestling with?"

"Who? I think it's a ghost. He has exceptional eyesight."

The owner of the bookshop was named Ito. Joe had never noticed this before. So he was Japanese? His wife, this woman before him, was Japanese? They came here from the distant East to start a business, then they separated? Human hearts are frightful. There was something he wanted to ask her, but he couldn't think of it. She seemed already to know what he wanted to ask, and moreover to be weary of answering it. She said someone was calling her, she must go at once, then she hurriedly left. "We won't meet again." This was the last thing she said.

Joe made up his mind to go to Ito's bookshop in the depths of the night. What relation did this strange divorced couple have to those young Japanese women wearing kimonos in his story? The woman he'd just seen, wearing white . . . it seemed that he had seen her somewhere before.

Joe looked up and down the pattern of a new tapestry Maria had woven. His head felt dizzy. There seemed to be no design at all, only changing layers of faint color. Perhaps even the changing of the colors was only in his imagination, and there was no pattern on the surface of the tapestry. His eyes began to hurt looking at it; even his temples hurt. He thought of turning aside his gaze but a magnetic force seemed to draw him into the tapestry. "Let me go, Maria," he begged in his heart.

"Joe, what are you wasting your thoughts on?"

Maria appeared in the doorway. A few wasps wheeled around her head, looking dangerous. The wasps made Joe's memory vivid and bright.

"You've come from seeing Kim, Maria?"

"As good as seeing him. I met the driver. Ah, that grassland! Did I weave it well? This time I began anew. It's a new beginning. Listen, Joe. It's so quiet. I mean the walls are quiet. After you leave, Daniel and I will miss you."

And so Maria expected him to leave, too? Joe thought of the bookstore owner's former wife, how years ago she and her husband had undertaken the journey here. The bookstore in the evening dusk and the riverbank during the bright day formed a contrast, so that Joe spontaneously felt the longing between the separated couple. But what kind of longing did Joe have for that woman? Maria was disappearing. Now she wove tapestries that gave him headaches, that left Joe's line of thought suspended in midair. Joe circled the room, discovering the walls hung with quite a few similar tapestries, only with colors that were even more shadowy, in layers even more difficult to tell apart. When he fixed his eyes on a tapestry with deep gray tones, Maria spoke again, from behind him:

"Joe, what are you wasting your thoughts on?"

Joe uneasily turned to face her, saying to Maria that he grew more and more stupid. He heard the household's two cats howling from the tops of the walls, and unexpectedly he glimpsed the pattern revealed in the tapestry. It was a hatchet. What hatred did Maria hold in the depths of her heart?

He heard Maria talking to someone, but there was no one in the room. She stood with her back to him, behind the loom, her voice low and hoarse. She was using a language that Joe didn't understand.

Joe quietly left the workroom and went into the garden. There were a large number of wasps flying around it. Where had they come from? Was a wasps' nest nearby? Daniel had also come out to the garden. A large group of wasps wound around him. He was wearing a sleeveless shirt, but he didn't mind the poisonous wasps. Joe thought of Daniel's girlfriend, the Vietnamese girl with a body as light as a swallow's, and felt that these two were truly a match made in heaven. Perhaps one day Daniel would go back with her to live in Vietnam. In that green country full of rainwater, Daniel would feel like he was returning home.

"Father, do you know who led the wasps here?" In the sun, the freckles on his nose were conspicuous.

"Who?"

"It was that driver. The moment he stood in the rose garden the wasps swarmed in, in a black mass. Such beautiful little things! The driver is admirable. Maybe he's in love with Mother. Will you be jealous, Father?"

"I don't know. Maybe I will be." Joe spoke without confidence. "Do you think your mother hopes I will leave?"

"Mother loves you," Daniel said earnestly. "Although that has nothing to do with your leaving."

Joe saw the wasps sting Daniel's head and face over and over. His face swelled rapidly, so that even his eyes were swollen into a single seam. Joe was afraid, but the wasps didn't sting him. Only one kept at his ear, menacing, making its *weng weng* buzzing. Daniel sat calmly on the stone bench, as if he had not felt the wasps attack him, and was indifferent to the red swelling.

"Daniel, where should I go?"

His manner was helpless. He knew Daniel couldn't answer questions like this, Daniel, who was bending down to investigate the roses, half his face swollen. He told Joe that the roses gave him evil thoughts.

Joe heard the loom start up again in the house. At the same instant, raindrops fell on his cheeks. How strange, when the sun was shining brightly!

"Daniel, did you notice it was raining?"

"I was just thinking about the problem of the soil quality, and I had a few thoughts about a tropical rainforest. What luck, Father, you seem to be able to feel my thoughts. Mother said there is a square inside of you, and a broad road shaded with trees extending all the way to the foot of snowy mountains. But why can't I feel it there?"

Surrounded by such an atmosphere, Joe felt suffocated.

Daniel pulled up a rosebush and said something to its roots that Joe couldn't hear. His hands were shaking. This boy, who as a child had shed tears at seeing a fish on a hook, had grown so violent. When Daniel was a year and a half old he fussed at night, and Joe held him in his arms, swinging in a circle outdoors, Daniel's cries reverberating through the whole street. But once he learned to speak he became a silent, prissy child. Maria wasn't willing to have Daniel grow up at her side and she sent him to a boarding school on her own initiative. For this, Joe had resented her. But now he felt grateful to her.

Joe needed to break something, to struggle. This boy, his face swollen, speaking to rosebush roots, and the headache-inducing tapestries in the workroom . . . he couldn't breathe. Also, there were the electricity-carrying cats. He must find a pure land to hide away in. Who could tell him where such a place was? Maybe the former wife of the bookshop owner could tell him?

A large clump of wasps circled Daniel. His face was swollen out of shape. He hadn't realized it. He pulled up another rosebush and studied it in his hand. He seemed to have forgotten Joe still at his side. The sun burned the sweat from his youthful body, its odor filling the air. Joe heard an ominous implication in the loom's shuttling sound. He had borne all he could.

He went inside and picked up his briefcase, telling Maria he was going to the office.

From her loom Maria fixed her eyes on him for several minutes, nodding her head. Joe sensed that her eyes were filled with expectation. Joe quickly walked into the yard before hearing Maria stick her head out and yell, "Joe, dear, walk to the corner and don't look back."

Joe, moving as if a generation had passed on, proceeded through the narrow streets. His own face reflected in the glass doors and windows was a stranger's, a long face, a somber man, with a head of white curling hair. If the change in himself was so great, what had Maria, and Daniel, and other people, too, known him by? The street cleaner stood at the corner. Even this beautiful black woman seemed a little weary. She leaned toward Joe to greet him, with an imploring look. Joe stopped in his steps, and at the same time remembered Maria's words.

"Can I help you?"

"The night is vast, I will fall into the tiger's mouth. No one can help me." The beautiful woman showed her teeth savagely.

"Oh! Oh!" Joe groaned as he walked, cold sweat running down his back.

"Don't come back again!" the beautiful woman screamed.

When Joe entered his office he saw the wasps. An enormous wasps' nest was tied to the air conditioner, where they massed into squeezed, black piles. But these little insects didn't make any sound at all, which was unusual. Joe opened a drawer, took out a Tibetan travel book, which he hadn't seen for ages, and turned to the middle. He couldn't read a single one of the Tibetan words, nor did the book have any pictures, but over a long period of time he had turned its pages one by one. What was inside this book? He didn't know. He only knew that perhaps inside there was a world, an unfathomed place. As he fixed his eyes on the Tibetan script, a wasp dropped onto the surface of the page. The Tibetan words suddenly leapt up like flames burning the little insect. It struggled for a few minutes and then didn't move.

"Joe, are you making an experiment?"

Lisa entered. She was still dressed gaudily. Her skirt even showed a stretch of thigh.

Even though Joe turned his face to the wasps' nest in embarrassment, Lisa walked over indifferently, lifting Joe's book, spreading its pages with a few shakes. Joe saw a layer of dead wasps lying on the floor.

"My old home was called the village of wasps. Every person's blood is permeated with their toxin. Vincent doesn't believe this, and so he suffered enormous hurt."

"Then what is inside my book? Do you know?"

"It's a place where you haven't been."

Lisa stepped underneath the air conditioner and put a hand in among the wasps. Joe saw her slender hand rapidly swelling. She laughed naughtily. Then she pulled back her hand, her fingers swollen like carrots. Walking away from Joe with a smile, she left.

He had just put the book back into the drawer when a customer entered. He was unannounced. Joe, furious, glared at him without saying a word. He was a skinny fellow with scars on his face. He said that when he came into the room he felt like he was returning home. Who still raised wasps in their offices today? Such a lovely idea. He praised this idea with his teeth bared while pulling a glass bottle from his pocket. It was full of dead wasps.

"Joe, I am a worker from Reagan's farm." As he spoke he wiped away tears with the back of his hand, because his left eye always ran. "The work clothes your company manufactures brought about the deaths of two more people yesterday."

"That has nothing to do with our company." Joe spoke coldly.

"Really?" He stepped closer, staring at Joe. "Really?" He also swung the bottle in his hand.

Joe discovered that the wasps inside the bottle were moving.

"I will make a business trip to your farm, to investigate the deaths of these workers."

The thin man looked at Joe curiously, rubbing his eye, and asked him whether he sincerely wanted to understand this matter. Would he be paralyzed with fear by the reality of the situation? He also said that if Joe wanted to go, he didn't need to go to the farm. He should go to Country C instead. Why should he go to Country C? Joe asked. The thin man became immediately active, walking back and forth across the office and jumping to pluck at the nest so that the wasps flew around, filling the room.

"Country C is the place where you should go. The boys we lost came from there. Two beautiful boys. Your clothing wrapped around them like snakes. But I must leave. Go there yourself, but don't go to the wrong place. If you see grapevines, you should stop and wait."

After he'd left, Joe spread out the Tibetan book on his desk again. He thought that the book should have a topographic map and an itinerary inside. Could those two boys have come from the snow-peaked mountains of the plateaus? Joe had one reverie after another, he couldn't help himself.

Two drenched black birds stopped on the windowsill. They were crows. Joe sensed the air of death. How could he get to Country C? He would take a plane, of course. But how would he tell Vincent? Say he was going to realize his aspirations? Say he would never turn back? Joe felt that web appear again at last. The broad road into his square led all the way to the horizon, and a woman wearing a kimono walked slowly ahead. Was he struggling out of chaos? Or would he jump into an even larger web of chaos? It seemed everyone was inciting him, forcing him to leave. Yet at the very beginning this plan had come from the boss who couldn't do without him. It seemed that Vincent, too, was forcing him.

Vincent hadn't shown his face. Joe searched for him in all corners of the office. He hadn't come, no one had seen him. Joe's co-workers stared at him in reproach, thinking he shouldn't search for his boss so anxiously. Someone even hinted he might pay attention to his own business. Unbelievably, everyone knew what was on his mind. Joe didn't dare keep on asking. He returned to his office like a stray dog, put his things into his briefcase, then sat down to make a phone call to the airport. He had just finished the call when Lisa slipped back into the room like a ghost.

"You're just going to leave without giving notice?"

"I couldn't find Vincent."

"He wouldn't be here, especially on a day like this. Look at those two crows, so black. That year I came from the gambling city all alone in the world . . . You have such good fortune, Joe, you possess everything!" She spread her arms in exaggeration, as if she would dance.

"Actually I have no place to even set my foot . . ." Joe grumbled and placed the Tibetan travel book in his bag. He remembered that he still needed to go home and pick up his clothes. What was he doing, was he possessed, that he'd obey a complete stranger's suggestion? Just because the atmosphere around him incited him to this crazy idea? Who was that thin man, and what made him say Joe should go to Country C, that faraway place not even described in books? Yes, he read many books, but he still had never read a book that described this faraway nation. In books he'd read of red palace walls and amber tiles, but he hadn't thought about Country C. Joe often traveled on business, for the most part to domestic locations, and sometimes also to Europe and to Mediterranean countries, but Country C, an ancient Eastern country, remained only a hazy recollection in a recess of his mind. He had a groundless intuition: perhaps what Maria had woven was that place? Perhaps he was also on a road with her, depicting those patterns that couldn't be seen? "Maria, Maria, you are so callous, you won't release me," he said to himself. The sun shone on him through the glass. A wasp flew faltering by, stopped on the back of his hand, and began to sting him. Joe's mind became a stretch of blank space.

He returned home as if moving in his sleep. Maria wasn't at home. Daniel had not returned either. Once Joe entered the house voices spoke from inside the walls, a sound both urgent and agitated, as if they were quarreling. He put his ear to the living room wall, but couldn't tell what the argument was about. He went upstairs to his bedroom and packed his suitcase. When he opened the bedroom curtains, two drenched crows sat on the windowsill! The crows did not turn to look at him. They sat unmoving, like statues. Their bodies were much larger than normal. They appeared to be a special breed of crow. Other than his clothing, what else should he bring? He couldn't make up his mind because he didn't know a single thing about that country. He had heard before, unwittingly, some familiar person, whose face he couldn't even recall now, say that poppies grew everywhere there, and that the men and woman all loved to smoke opium, floating like sleepwalkers in blue smoke. In that place, time could reverse, people could return to their childhoods, collecting a few pieces of testimony from their former lives to bring back. Since he had been inattentive at the time, he couldn't remember who had said this. He discovered that Maria had left a note on the desk. She said she was going to deliver a tapestry that had been ordered by that driver. He felt no need to leave a few sentences for Maria because she'd wished for him to leave all along. Of course, Joe was slightly jealous—he wasn't sure of the nature of the relationship between Maria and the handsome driver. But now wasn't the time to consider the matter.

He tidied his suitcase and went out the door. A tall woman wearing a black skirt stood at the front doorway of his house. Joe had seen her before. She had an Eastern woman's face, her expression detached. Joe greeted her; she merely nodded her head. Perhaps she stood there by chance. The two crows suddenly cawed. The sound reverberated through a vast sky.

At the intersection he ran into the beautiful black woman. She smiled at him with spirit, showing glistening teeth. Joe answered her with a smile, confusedly trying to avoid her, but she willfully moved to the side of the road.

He was troubled by the thought of the sordid action he'd just taken, because he was carrying away the better part of the family's savings. If he didn't return, Maria would have to sell her jewelry to live on. Yet it didn't matter, she always had ways to get through trouble.

13

JOE ARRIVES IN THE EAST

"Maria, Joe's gone to the airport," Lisa said as soon as she came in.

"Did he bring that book?" Maria had not moved her eyes away from the loom. She was following an image in the recesses of its pattern, her face flushed.

Lisa shot up from her chair as soon as she sat down. She felt Maria's sorcery growing stronger. Someday this house would be the residence of a demon. When she walked around the room she felt the soles of her feet tingling on the floor. The voices coming from inside the walls brimmed with menace.

"Was the book he brought his map?" Lisa asked.

"Yes, he's going to the country of poppy flowers. It's very beautiful. But is it really what he has desired for so long? I'm not too sure."

"He's a mild-tempered demon."

Lisa couldn't stand still inside the house. Her heart was under attack. She ran into the yard and stood gasping among the shrubs. The sunlight made a *weng weng* drone, and the loom inside the house still shuttled evenly.

Maria stopped the work under her hands, glanced at the empty chair beside her, and called out once, "Lisa."

Just at this moment the same image floated to the surface. It was a swiftly moving black wolf. Maria blinked her eyes and it disappeared, but she heard it give a long howl.

Lisa made a sign at the window, saying, "I can't come in. You are too severe, my heart can't endure it."

"It's because I am retracing Joe's journey. Tonight he will stay on a plateau, where there are wolves."

"Oh, and so your heart is full of expectations for him. If troops march there at night, what will it be like?"

Lisa raised her head and saw sparks exploding from the walls with a *pa pa* crackling. She hastily moved back a few steps. She tripped over a gladiolus, knocking against its sharp spike, and her face oozed blood. The two cats ran over from behind her, their bodies giving off electric sparks, *pa pa*. In her mind the scene of a trek on the plateaus appeared—soles rubbed to bleeding by boots and deep gullies swaying with white flowers. She wanted to leave, but she heard Maria screaming from the house. She rushed to the window and looked all around inside. She saw Maria staring at the unfinished tapestry, trembling.

"Maria! Maria! Are you all right?"

Maria didn't speak.

Lisa rushed inside and placed her hands on Maria's shoulders. There was nothing on the light brown tapestry. She heard Maria's teeth knocking. Her body ran with sweat.

When Joe boarded the plane he saw a woman board as well. He couldn't see her face because she wore a large straw hat pressed down low. On the gangway, the wind billowed her black skirt. She seemed to hesitate, and suddenly she stood still on the stairs. The fat man behind her pressed her on indignantly. Finally, as if waking up from a dream, she started forward again. "Damn, Irene," the fat man said.

On entering the cabin the woman disappeared among the seats. Joe suddenly thought, Could the Eastern woman he'd seen at the door of his house and the bookstore owner's former wife be the same person? Was she named Irene? Or did the fat man call all women "Irene"? He indistinctly remembered the bookstore owner calling his former wife something "__Mei." He was under the impression that the women of Country C were the ones called "Mei." Why was Daniel's Vietnamese girlfriend named Amei, too? After he took his seat, he stood back up and surveyed the entire cabin once more, but he still didn't see the woman. However, he hadn't seen her face clearly, either. So how could he find her? He fastened his seatbelt and shut his eyes.

Shit, there was a wasp spinning around his head. Had it come from his office? Would it sting him? Sure enough, it flew nearer and stung his eyelid sharply. Frightened, he felt his entire head go numb. Even his eyes couldn't shut all the way. He touched his face with effort. It had no sensation. Now he caught sight of the black-clad woman. He couldn't think of where he'd seen her before, because he couldn't concentrate.

The woman stood above him. She was speaking to the flight attendant.

"Once people are out of the cabin the freezing wind will bite their faces," the attendant said.

"I got used to it a long time ago. Every morning I draw water at the side of the brook," the woman said. "At noon, the grass bakes in the sun, and Mother speaks to me from the balcony. She asks me whether I want a drink of milk."

"You see this man, his face is swelling so terribly." The flight attendant pointed to Joe.

He wanted to move his lips into a smile, but they wouldn't move.

"His wife is a woman named Mei," the black-clad woman said, indicating him. "This morning, at home, she saw a wolf. It bit her clothing and would not let go. She grew agitated and cried out."

Joe didn't understand what she was saying. He felt the entire cabin begin to move. The man sitting on the inside seat stepped over him. People were gathering their luggage one after another.

"The temperature on the ground is 20 degrees below zero Celsius," the broadcast said.

Waiting until the cabin was empty, Joe at last picked up his luggage and moved outside. He was afraid. Outside the cabin, as expected, a freezing wind blew. It was fortunate Joe's face had no feeling, only his hands felt a little painful in the cold. He nearly fell down on the stairs. The plane was stopped on the tarmac. Joe saw dazzling snowcapped mountains in every direction, illuminated by the sun, as if on fire. He casually chose a door and pushed it open, walking outside.

Someone took hold of his suitcase. He loosened his hand without noticing, and let the man lift it. The man carrying the suitcase wore a straw hat. Joe couldn't see his face.

The airport was small, so he walked right out of it. A few men and women were out on the street. These people didn't mind the cold. They wore peculiar clothing that left their backs bare. The expression on their dark, ruddy faces was solemn. Their hair was worn very long. The man kept in front of him. When the street was almost at an end, he placed the suitcase on the ground, saying: "Now go ahead by yourself. From here you can't get lost." He spoke in Joe's language.

Then he turned and hurried back. Joe stood beside his suitcase and looked back. He saw a crowd of children coming, chasing each other, sweating in the cold sunlight. Suddenly he heard a girl (who was also wearing a robe that showed her bare back) shouting in the language of his country, "Maria! Maria! I'm choking to death!" She gasped painfully, suddenly spat out a mouthful of fresh blood, and squatted down. A large group of children, all ten or older, surrounded her.

Joe suddenly felt unsafe, because he saw many of the children holding daggers in their hands. A few watched him with shining eyes. He lifted his suitcase and casually turned into a shop beside the road. It sold silver ornaments and utensils.

The wolf quickly disappeared from Maria's design. Maria whistled, trying to call it back. She heard the loud noise Daniel made digging in the yard.

Mother and son bathed in the sunlight, attempting to return to an earlier time. Afterward they went to Joe's study and saw that all of his bookshelves were overturned. They entered, stepping on the books, and sat among the chaotic piles, talking about what things had been like when Joe was at home. Daniel casually picked up a book, browsed lazily through it, and told Maria about his father's frame of mind when he'd purchased it.

"How do you know this?" Maria asked, knitting her eyebrows.

"This isn't difficult, it's written in the book. Father is like you, a perfectionist."

Maria thought of Joe talking about business while immersed in his own stories, and nodded her head.

"Mama, why are there so many people who talk inside the walls of our house? I remember from when I was little, they came in one group after another. Are all these people our relatives?"

"Yes, this is a house built on its original foundations. Do you like these people?"

"Sometimes I do feel happy. Especially at the boarding school, when I couldn't sleep at night, so I talked to myself with my eyes still open. When I spoke children answered me from inside the walls. Are there children who passed away among our relatives?"

"Many. Your father is about to meet a wolf."

Daniel put the book in his hand in front of his nose and sniffed it, saying, "This is the wolf. It won't abandon its pursuit. I have seen it twice before."

Maria asked him if he remembered when they drank tea in the rose garden, and Father spoke with them from the balcony of the study. Maria called this conversation "exchanges in the air."

Daniel answered that he would never, ever forget, because that was the time he saw a ladder suspended in the air stretching down from the balcony.

"Only Father could have the skill to make the balcony send out a ladder, hanging straight up in the air without leaning on anything."

"A man like him can also disappear from us entirely, and run off alone to the ancient East."

After Maria finished this sentence, she felt a familiar disturbance emerging from inside her body. The checkered skirt she wore stretched tight. Her gaze was fixed on the wooden gate at the other side of the yard. A woman wearing a black skirt stood at the gate. This slender woman from an Eastern country always hung around here. Daniel was also looking at the middle-aged woman, his youthful blue eyes aflame with lust. The book in Daniel's hand fell to the ground, its pages trembling as if wounded. Maria saw an antiquated landscape illustration inside, a picture of a beach. On the beach a fishing net was spread open to dry in the sun. Maria reached to pick up the book but it was electrified. Her hand was struck back. A rending scream made her blood congeal. It was Daniel screaming, his face red from the pressure.

"Daniel, you're not well?"

"No, this is delight," he murmured, and walked out the door.

Looking down from the balcony, Maria saw Daniel, covering half his face with a straw hat, brush past the woman's body and run out. She could hear his elastic steps ringing on the road. The woman seemed to have no awareness of Daniel. She was there waiting for someone. Maria pitied her son. She shut the door leading to the balcony, drew the curtains, and stayed alone in the shadows thinking deeply. She wanted to whistle, and so she started to whistle, gently, a little like a cricket in the dark. Underfoot the mess of spread-out books started to shake their pages, becoming fan-shaped, but there was no wind in the house. Maria knew these were the original source of Joe's square, from which his stories extended, becoming a limitless web of stories. Now he had abandoned all this and become the story himself.

In the electromagnetic field of the books Maria began to recollect her life with Joe. She remembered that Joe was afraid of her grandfather, even after Grandfather had been dead many years. Since the house had been built on an ancient foundation, her grandfather's image occasionally appeared on the walls, most often at noon, when there was sun. Maria, in order not to frighten Joe, pretended not to see it, but she knew Joe saw. He didn't dodge away, but rather stared intently at the wall. Maria understood that he longed for this kind of fear. In her adolescence, her grandfather always sat inside the house and seldom went out. One time Maria bolted in and saw Grandfather dancing to soft music, his legs, stiff from arthritis, now flexible. His arms spread wide, embracing an imagined woman. "Grandfather, who are you dancing with?" "With her," he answered briefly, falling into an armchair in disappointment, painfully panting. Maria knew this "her" wasn't her grandmother, because Grandmother didn't dance. Of course it wasn't some other woman either, because Grandfather never met women socially. Who was she then? For several decades Maria thought about this question. Now that Joe had left, Maria felt it had a prospect of solution. After her grandfather was buried she'd searched the house from top to bottom for that recording, but she could not find it. Perhaps there was no recording after all? That music? Was it no more than their hallucination?

Joe had heard the music when he arrived at her home. Grandfather seemed pleased with Joe, but he couldn't say so. Instead he said he hoped Maria would stay away from this kind of man. Maria asked him why. He said there was no why. He also said he hoped she wouldn't live at home after she married. "The origin of our family line is too ancient." Young, energetic Maria didn't understand what her grandfather was saying. And it wasn't long before he passed away.

One night, when she and Joe were tired from lovemaking, she fell into a deep sleep. But at midnight she was roused by that music playing in the darkened house.

"Joe, are you dancing?" Maria felt suddenly confused and upset.

"No, I was watching, darling. Your family is so magical. I was wondering, am I your family's lost son?"

So many years later, this "lost son" had left the home once again. At the moment Maria felt gratified and a little worried. After all, she and Joe had never gone to such a place before. But she also reflected that earlier, before Joe had even arrived, she hadn't known he existed. Maria stood up from among the books, the haze in her heart dispersing little by little. It was almost as if she really had returned to former days.

"Oh, sir, you came so soon. We've had no time free the past few days." A young boy wearing a long gown walked from the interior of the shop over to where Joe stood, sizing him up from head to toe.

Joe's surprise can be imagined: he spoke the language of Joe's country.

The boy started to laugh, and led him toward the interior, saying: "My father is one of your people. He always talks with me about your affairs. Father is very lonely."

In the back there was an enormous, dark room. The boy lit a small oil lamp. Joe saw a spacious carved bed hung with linen mosquito netting. Someone apparently lay inside the netting. In a soft voice Joe asked the boy whether it was his father in there. The boy stuck closely to Joe, his nude back rubbing against him, as if he were afraid of something.

"No, my father is here, look!"

He pulled Joe over to the table and uncovered the lid of a bronze incense burner, scooping the bone ashes inside with his small hands.

"My father's name is Kim. He lived over where you come from, and I grew up there. This year I'm thirteen years old."

"He owns the pastureland?"

"Yes, I brought Father back by myself," he said proudly. "He always says the bosom of the snowy mountains is his home. I never met someone who thought of home so much. Do you want to listen to him speak?"

Joe put his ear to the bronze censer, but what he heard was only the moan of the man inside the netting.

The boy waved the censer. The moans of the man inside the netting were worse. The more the boy shook the incense burner, the fiercer the moans. Bone ashes spilled out of the censer. Joe asked the boy who was inside the mosquito net. He said it was a passerby who'd walked in and gotten inside the netting.

"Sir, can you help me?"

"Help you do what?"

"There's a large oven over there. It's lit. Hold onto me, throw me into the oven, and wait until I've turned to ashes. Then you can scoop me out and put me into the censer."

He led Joe to a door and kicked it open. Joe saw a blazing coal fire. A wave of heat attacked him and he drew back. The boy laughed piercingly.

"Coward, coward. Here, drink some of this scented tea."

He gave Joe an enormous cup. Joe drank a mouthful and was choked so fiercely he couldn't stop coughing. It felt as if his throat were being cut apart by knives. With difficulty he finally controlled the cough. Insane ideas sprang up in his mind.

"If you don't drink the tea, how will you climb the snow-covered mountain?" The boy put on the manner of an adult, his voice becoming melancholy. "I will go into the furnace anyway. But I worry about you, what you will do alone."

Joe didn't dare open his mouth. He thought that if he opened it blood would come out. His mouth was already filled with the taste of blood. The man inside the netting grew enraged and began to curse and roar. The boy wanted Joe to go outside. He said it wasn't safe in the room, and since Joe couldn't help him he would finish the task himself. He wanted Joe to go through the door and walk always toward the east, because "underneath the sun nothing can go wrong." When Joe passed by the large bed he smelled a strange fragrance, and another like the smell of a forest. His steps drew to a stop as if pulled by magnets and he stood still. "I didn't think you were interested in this," the boy said. He urged him to look inside the netting. Joe raised the netting, and the smell of mushrooms, of pine needles and of spring water blew against his face. A man lay inside the mosquito netting, or, more precisely, half of a man.

He was naked, with a seam dividing the center of his body. The left side was a normal man's body; the entire right side was rotting, the skin turned to a blackish-green with spots on it, and with mold growing on the spots. His enormous penis was erect. It was especially offensive to look at—one side black, one side red, on the scrotum where the testicle should be was a festering hole. He stared at Joe, not feeling the slightest shame at his nakedness. Joe heard him say several sentences—perhaps it was the local language, he didn't understand it. The boy crawled onto the bed, and he said in Joe's ear, "This year he is 103 years old. He isn't a passerby, he is the spirit of the earth for this region. His power is great."

The fragrance of wildflowers assaulted Joe's nostrils, and he sighed, saying, "I never thought, I never imagined."

That man raised the good hand on his left side and grabbed his right armpit. Flies tore crazily around the netting. His armpit was an abscess. Numerous flies sucked on the inside.

The boy, with a wild expression of joy, crawled over, lightly fondling the putrid leg from the foot all the way up toward the penis, where he stopped, kissing the putrid hole in infatuation, stretching his tongue to lick it. Inside the netting there was an indistinct sound of running spring water. The man, fondling the boy's naked back, moaned comfortably.

The boy turned his head to glance at Joe, saying, "Quick, get out! The lamp's tipped over and started a fire!"

Joe felt in the dark to the outer room. When he reached the shop front, the netting and the wooden bed had already kindled into a huge blaze. He heard the boy stamping his feet on the bed and yelling at him to get out quickly.

A number of people had already collected on the street. All were wearing the dress that exposed the back. This kind of clothing made them appear very easy and natural, especially when the wind lifted the lower hems and they looked like so many hawks. Now these people all stood surveying the fire in the silver shop from the street, excitedly craning their necks and sniffing the strange fragrance in the air. No one noticed Joe. Among them was a woman with one breast exposed who was especially beautiful. She lifted an arm, seeming to greet the people inside the silver shop. The fire grew larger, and poisonous smoke rushed into the street. Everyone began to cough violently. Joe hid far away, avoiding the smoke cloud. He saw all of them stooping to the ground to vomit, or they might have been spitting out blood.

The man who'd helped pick up his luggage at the airport appeared again.

"I said you wouldn't get lost and you didn't! My name is Kim."

He picked up Joe's suitcase, swayed a few times, and asked: "What's in your suitcase?"

Joe answered that it was clothing and toiletries.

"Very good. You are frugal. Come with me to King Street."

Joe tailed him as he turned onto a wide gravel road. In Joe's eyes, from behind Kim looked solemn and mournful. It seemed there were many stories inside him, stories that exceeded Joe's experience. All the people and things of this place had nothing whatsoever to do with the web of his past stories, with that square. With his mind occupied, he ran into someone. It was a local man, who pushed Joe away and continued to walk ahead. He wore only a thin green robe, his feet bare, and he walked along the road airily. Joe looked again at the stone road full of local people, all wearing thin robes, with bare feet, slowly, airily moving about. The man named Kim turned his head and said to Joe:

"These people all smoke opium. Every person's heart holds a ball of fire. Have you seen the flower gardens? The poppies in them are their lifeblood. A cold place like this doesn't grow poppies natively, but there are hot springs in the gardens, and the enormous ground heat changes the temperature. The poppies grow lush in those areas."

Joe didn't see anything because only businesses lined the two sides of the road. He thought, Perhaps this man named Kim smokes opium and is recounting his hallucinations.

"Where do you plan to stay? A hotel or the poppy plantation?"

"The poppy plantation," he blurted.

The man named Kim stopped by a low iron gate, saying, "You're already there."

He pushed open the door. Inside was a deserted compound. After a while, a side door opened on the courtyard's right side. A man with an ardent expression walked toward Joe. He reached out both hands, grasping Joe's hands firmly.

The man's mouth spit out a string of the local language. His gaze was firmly set on Joe, as if he wanted to remember his features. Joe thought sadly that he had no distinctive features—what could be remembered? Suddenly the man left Joe aside, walked off and sat down in the mud. He was thinking deeply.

Kim said in Joe's ear: "This man is an opium smoker, too. Stay here with him."

As Kim went out, he locked the gate of the courtyard from the outside. Joe at once grew nervous.

He leaned his suitcase against the wall, sat down, leaned his back on the suitcase, and from that spot observed the local man sitting opposite. He was a little weary, and his eyes soon grew dim. In a drowsy state he saw the man slowly stand up and move as if he were swimming in front of him, holding a bunch of poppies in his hand. The man was just opening his mouth when there was a confused sound at the courtyard gate. A terrified expression appeared in his eyes, and he threw the flowers to the ground. He seemed dejected. He put a hand into his clothing and felt around, as if he were stroking the painful region of his heart. Joe kept a concerned eye on him.

He stood in front of Joe, watching the wall beyond Joe as if absorbed in his thoughts. Joe looked up at him from below, curious about the hand always fumbling in his clothing. That weathered hand was very focused, but also a little hesitating. It seemed he was exploring a method to dig out his own heart. Joe waited.

"Oh, oh!" he said. He drew out a coldly glittering dagger from his chest.

Joe stared.

The man tested the knife point with his thumb, then squatted down, looking into Joe's eyes as if seeking his opinion. Joe felt a numbing chill in his neck. He involuntarily nodded his head. His last thought was: Why do people who smoke opium also have murderous impulses? But his judgment was mistaken. The man threw away the knife, stood up, and left him.

Joe fixed his eyes on the blood on the floor. Was it his blood? He touched his neck; it was fine. So it must be that local man's blood. Joe picked up the dagger from the ground and looked it up and down, yet did not discover any blood on the knife. Someone above him was speaking.

"This kind of bleeding is unconscious."

It was the man named Kim, who'd come back in. Joe saw that the courtyard gate was wide open and there was a rush of people outside. They all peered in, but why didn't they enter?

"Let me look at the knife," said the man named Kim.

He accepted the knife, pointed it to the heart in his chest and pushed it in. Then he knelt down, motioning to Joe with his eyes, asking him to help pull out the knife.

Joe's hands shook severely, but once he held the knife fast he immediately gained strength. He grasped the knife handle, agitated it a bit, then pulled the knife out. Kim looked gratefully at Joe. Blood gushed from the wound, but stopped in a short while. He covered the wound with his clothing. A row started outside the gate.

"This poppy garden is where our ancestors dreamed. People today, even though they smoke opium, cannot enter that territory. Someone who has the wrong intentions, like me, tries to achieve that end by slaughter, but blood cannot conquer those noble hearts. The result is predestined."

Joe saw Kim's face become extraordinarily white and fill with deep pain. He grabbed the yellow mud wall that circled the courtyard as hard as he could. Clay lumps fell in pieces to the foot of the wall. The row grew louder, as if the people all wanted to come in, but something blocked them. What was it?

"Where did the man go who was just here?" Joe asked.

"He's a fearless bastard. I've seen him swallow a knife with my own eyes. But even that is a futile effort. For many months he's stayed inside this poppy garden. According to him, no one comes out to drive him away, but no one admits him either. Opium's effect is mysterious. He draws support from it to survive these days of despair."

"What does he want to do inside the garden? Or is he waiting for something to come out?"

"No, it's not that. He only wants to become a worker in the poppy garden. This way the source of opium won't be a problem for him. His lazing around here will become an accomplished fact. How shameful!"

Joe could now carefully size up Kim. This Kim and the pasture owner Kim bore no resemblance to each other. The pasture owner had a northerner's imposing high-bridged nose, and this one had a flat face, roughly drawn. His nose was only two holes. But why was their speech so similar? They spoke like twins, and even their gestures were exactly the same. Joe remembered the Korean Kim who lived halfway up a mountain and a warm emotion sprung up in his heart. Because of his fond memory, he clung to this flat-featured Kim in front of him. He wanted to spill out words from his heart.

An old man was pushed into the courtyard by the clamoring people outside the gate. He was blind and wore dark glasses, and he carried a walking cane. He appeared very timid, taking great caution in touching the cane to the ground.

"The rays of light from the snowcapped mountains stabbed him blind." Kim's voice was dry.

"Does he also smoke opium?"

"Of course. If he didn't, how would he dare enter the courtyard?"

The wind sent the odor of the old man's body over. It was a dizzying, evil stench. He shuffled to the extreme end of the courtyard's circling wall. His gait looked like he might collapse and tumble to the ground at any moment.

The old man sat at the base of the wall. His feet showed from inside his robe. One was a fake foot made of wood. He took off his sunglasses, and Joe saw two deep eye sockets.

"Why doesn't he stay here with us?" Joe asked.

"This man loves cleanliness. He fears even a touch of foul odor on his body. Just now when he entered, he probably smelled a stranger in the courtyard—you came from far away, and you haven't showered—so he skirted us and walked over to that side. This old man is known for keeping himself clean and out of the muck. Look, one leaves and another enters." He meant the man who'd just left, and the old man who'd arrived.

Joe listened and nodded, and all at once began to feel himself inferior. He wanted to ask Kim if he could help him get opium. Then he felt it wasn't a suitable occasion for this question, because he was an outsider.

"I'm afraid the old man won't leave now. In that case, you'd better leave for a while. He can't stand you. Look how impatient he is, he's digging holes in the ground with his cane. He wants to monopolize the poppy garden. That way he can return to the beautiful scenery of the snowcapped mountains."

"Beautiful scenery of the snowcapped mountains? Weren't his eyes blinded by light from the mountains?"

"Yes and no. How can I put it? He reached a place where ice and snow were everywhere, and the landscape made him go mad. In order to forever keep that landscape in his mind, he blinded himself. Of course, I'm not sure if his mind is actually filled now with the light of those snowy mountains. Or if it's a stretch of pitch darkness. See how much he's suffering? It's because we are here. We should go."

Kim lifted Joe's suitcase without explaining further and walked outside.

One by one the people blocking the door gave way to Joe and Kim. A few of them lay down on the ground in fright. What were they afraid of? They lay prone on the ground and covered their faces with their hands.

"Do you like the women here?"

They stopped at the doorway of a bar, where Kim asked this question.

"I don't know. I haven't examined them. And I'm dirty, it's no time to think about that kind of thing." Joe felt himself speaking without logic. He didn't even know what he was saying.

"How can you be dirty? Didn't you just shower at the poppy gardens?"

Joe didn't understand. He raised his head and saw the signboard for the bar. He didn't recognize the blood-red script, but he felt that the red color was like a false display of power.

"Why is it so red?" He unconsciously spoke aloud.

"Hmm."

They went in. There was no one inside.

They had just sat down when they heard a hair-raising, bone-chilling scream from the inner room, followed by restrained weeping. It was a woman.

"It's sexual repression." Kim lifted his liquor bowl and drank a mouthful. "For a year already, everyone has suppressed their desire. Do you want to see her? She's waiting for you to go in."

Joe uneasily made an "ah" sound, and his face reddened. He saw Kim curl his lip in disdain, and avoided his glance in shame.

The door creaked with a *zhi ya* sound as a woman appeared. She was young, her body naked, her long hair worn to her waist. Her nipples were erect, and she watched Joe with eyes like a wolf's. Fortunately she swiftly went back inside. Otherwise Joe wouldn't have been able to sit still.

"I'm so ashamed . . ." Joe spoke haltingly. He wanted to say something to Kim, but Kim was nowhere to be seen.

Joe was enlivened. He stood up and went inside.

The woman lay on a felt cloth, as red as orangutan blood. She was moaning. She saw Joe approach her in the dim light and made signs for him to strip off his clothes. Joe complied. There was a deep riverbed, with a crowd of snakes dancing madly. The snakes entered into their bodies without friction and came out again from another side. In a state near to unconsciousness, Joe saw the woman, indistinct, above him. She put a dagger, flickering in the cold light, into his hand, and with infinite tenderness pressed it down on her wild breasts. Joe subconsciously took the dagger and cut into her left breast. His last thought was: how could there be waves in the deep, dry riverbed?

Maria was weaving the largest of her patternless tapestries. She felt some object about to bulge out from the weaving on which she concentrated her mind. Lisa had already quietly entered, and stood behind her.

"The entire Rose Clothing Company is in chaos." She spoke gently.

"Oh!" Maria shut her eyes. The hallucination disappeared from her memory. The room was deserted. She smelled something burning, so she jumped up and ran to the kitchen, with Lisa following her closely.

That cat ran through the door shrieking. Its fur was all burned away.

"Look, it opened the stove," Maria said anxiously.

Together they cleaned up the kitchen, sat down, and ate a chocolate cake. Maria stroked the burned cat. Its brown fur fell in pieces to the floor. Its eyes were bleary. Only Maria knew how much it suffered because it missed its old home in Africa. When people brought it here, it was only as big as a mouse. But Maria knew its body was filled with memories of burning heat.

Lisa told Maria that last night on the long march she reached Luding Bridge, the iron cable bridge in Chinese Tibet. She stepped onto the bridge, and cold wind spun up from the abyss. An idea appeared in her mind: if she came across Joe in Tibet, surely she would bring back a message for Maria. But she was trapped on the bridge the entire night.

"Is the day when two dreams will meet still as far away as before?" Her voice was contained within the kitchen.

Maria raised her head and saw the handsome driver standing next to the refrigerator, looking absentminded. He grabbed the chocolate cake and put it in his mouth, eating as he said, "This is for me? This is for me? Why can't I taste it?" He ate an entire large pan. Cake crumbs covered his face.

"Eating cake cannot solve his problems." Lisa watched him sympathetically.

He heard what Lisa said and nodded.

Daniel dug up earth in the yard. He'd gotten poppies from his girlfriend Amei's family. He wanted to plant them in all corners. Yesterday Amei told him that if he napped among the poppy flowers a book would spread open in the sky. Daniel asked her when she'd seen that book. She said it was aboard the ship on the way to Country A, and then afterward she'd seen it twice more. She also said that the book was not used for reading, because its pages were filled with revolving lotuses. Eyes could never endure it. Daniel was enthralled by the scene she described, and immediately asked her for poppy seeds. When Amei gave him the seeds she joked: "Daniel will run into his father."

Then her expression grew sleepy as she entered a kind of hallucination. She wanted him to come to her home at nightfall.

"At that time the magnolia tree at the door of the house will be in bloom. Your father will stand underneath the tree."

"Amei!" Daniel shouted, shaking her.

But she didn't hear. She slid out of his hands like a fish.

"Come at six o'clock," she said.

When Daniel stopped digging, his whole body began to tremble. There was no magnolia tree at the doorway of Amei's house. What metaphor was she speaking in? His sweat flickered in the sunlight. He felt that he was so young, so ignorant, while Amei, her body attached to an ancient spirit, had seen through him long ago.

He saw his mother put her head out at the kitchen window. Her face was covered with wrinkles like knife cuts and her gaze had the air of a tomb. How could she look like this, when she was with her lover? Daniel had just seen her lover. He was a glutton, ready to eat everything in the refrigerator. As the man ate, Daniel's mother and Lisa cowered into their own meditations.

A little past nightfall, when the sky was almost black, Daniel finally went to Amei's house. The lights were unlit and the door tightly shut. It seemed that all were sleeping. He stood on the broad stairs and knocked rhythmically on the wooden door.

Cursing came from inside. It was Amei's mother. She thought it was punks making trouble out on the street.

Then Amei came in a flurry to open the door.

"How could you come so late? It's terrible, the magnolia blooms all withered."

A strange sound came from her throat. The sky grew dark in an instant. Daniel thought the girl might disappear into the dark at any moment. He followed her closely as she went inside.

"Amei, Amei, you can't abandon me!"

He heard his own piteous voice. In the dark the arrangement of Amei's house was entirely different. He'd already walked far in behind her, but Amei still walked on ahead. Daniel remembered that the bedroom where Amei and her older sister slept was through the living room and down a small hallway, but where were they going now?

"Daniel, close your eyes. You will see a lamp in the rainforest." Amei's voice came from a distant place.

Now Daniel's surroundings were pure dark. He was slightly nauseated. He did not know how to proceed, but in short order Amei's voice came from in front of him, and he had to follow it.

"Now you've reached the outer edge of the rainforest. Do you smell the mist? That's also the smell of your father's body, so you must be used to it, ever since you were little." She chuckled, *ge ge*.

Daniel heard vague cursing somewhere. It was Amei's parents. They made him very uneasy.

"Your father has walked out of the rainforest. Didn't you know this? That place is in the East. It is our native place, us two. Listen, it's raining again there. Everything is growing."

Generally, what appeared in Maria's mind were always pictures, and very seldom words. But that morning when she lay on the bed, her eyes open and watching the waving curtains, a paragraph caught her by surprise.

"The traveler stands at the end of the bridge, the muddy yellow river water churning under his feet. He hears the distant call of wild geese. In his pocket he carries three silver coins, jangling, *ding ling ding ling*. The sounds of these strange things make him nervous, they make his body stiffen. When he can't go on, a vineyard appears before his eyes. 'Ah, wild geese,' he says, but not aloud. Someone pushes him and he bounces, like a rag blown in the wind, crosses over the barrier, and falls into the river. When he's still in the air he thinks: 'Who is pushing me?' Three silver coins scatter from his pocket, disappearing in the warm sunlight that illuminates everything."

She considered as she dressed: could "he" be Joe? Could the bridge be Luding Bridge? But Joe hadn't gone to China, he had gone to Country C. Ever since Joe brought home that book with only one page, Maria knew that a turning point in their lives had already been reached. Joe had put it in the refrigerator, telling her that he wanted to freeze the boiling din inside the book. Otherwise, if he put it on the bookcase, it would bother him until his mind became uneasy. When he did this Joe wore his usual conservative look, but Maria thought her husband was like a child.

She went into the workroom to look at the tapestry she'd woven yesterday. Yesterday she wove and wove, so vexed she almost cried. Every time the loom sounded it seemed to be saying, "Why can't you understand?" So now she first shut her eyes for half a minute, then suddenly opened them again. Those lines knit from lambswool were still lines, and no pattern protruded. Suddenly she discovered a small hole. She leaned in and saw two or three other holes. It looked like moths. Probably the newly bought knitting wool hadn't been processed correctly. She lightly smoothed it with her hand, and the knit lines surrounding the holes began to loosen and spread. Before her eyes, like a domino effect, the fabric was reduced within a short space of time to a pile of wool threads. An indignant shout came from inside the walls. Maria's head felt dizzy. "Joe, my head feels dizzy," she said as she sat down on the floor.

Someone helped her into a rocking chair. It was Daniel. The odor of his body was like an early morning mist in a forest.

"Where did you come from, Daniel?"

"Amei and I went to Vietnam. We reached the village of butterflies," he said excitedly.

He fell silent. After a while he finally spoke again.

"I love you, Mother. You're truly admirable."

Maria's eyes went dark. She said: "Did you see my fabric? Don't be discouraged. Things are much better than you think they are. I, I saw Luding Bridge!"

She grasped a pile of the tangled wool threads and put them to her nose to smell them. The threads inside began to smoke. Daniel wrested the wool from her, threw it to the ground, and stomped on it a few times.

Daniel saw the stories swimming in his mother's eyes. The stories called up once again in his heart the circumstances of the evening of August 15. On that night, the two of them stood on the stairs, leaning against a wall. A low *ni nan* chirping came from inside the walls. The Swiss watch on Daniel's wrist made *zheng zheng* clanking metallic noises. His mother's strong neck crooked to one side, her head leaning on his shoulder, and the moonlight swam swiftly under the osmanthus tree. For many years the walls of this house had tied Daniel's heart down firmly, and his wanting to throw them off was futile.

Without intention, Maria's gaze swept across the walls. She saw the two tapestries on the wall in their wooden frames fluctuating rapidly. Designs of mountains, reefs, solitary islands, and geese appeared in alternation. Maria's eyes were heavy with sleep, and they filled with tears.

"Do you like the women here, Joe?" Kim asked him once again. The two of them sat in a teahouse where they had a full view of the snowcapped mountains.

"I don't know. They're not much like what I expected. What is her name?"

"Xima Meilian. All the women here are named Xima Meilian."

"When I was at home, I saw an especially beautiful Eastern woman. Did she come from here?"

Downstairs someone called for Kim. He leaned over to listen carefully, seeming a bit nervous.

The man came upstairs as he called. It was the old fellow who sold silver goods. He stood by the table, glancing with eyes full of hate at Joe, who was drinking tea. His ornaments struck one another with a pleasant sound.

Kim approached the old fellow, the two of them speaking the local tongue.

Suddenly, Joe felt the light from the snowcapped mountain to be especially dazzling, an endless flow toward the dark little teahouse where he sat. In the room the two men changed into two pale shadows in the white light.

"This is Xima Melian's father," one shadow said to Joe, his head stretching and curving, both comical and a little distressing.

"What's wrong with my eyes?" Joe struggled to say.

Joe could still hear the silver ornaments as he felt the small building disappearing and his feet thrashing in the air. He became a man floating in midair. And those two shadows were also floating into the distance.

"Xima Meilian, Xima Meilian!" Kim said, as if threatening Joe with a false show of power.

But his voice floated far away. Now Joe was facing the snow-covered mountains. When he stepped ahead, the snow under his soles made a *cha cha* whisper. Aside from the snowy mountains there were no other colors or forms before his eyes. He suddenly experienced a feeling of being "crushed." He was crushed. His body disappeared. He wanted to touch his face with his hand, but he had no hand, and he had no face. So whose sense of hearing was this? In the *long long* rumbling of an approaching avalanche, who would witness it?

"Who?" he asked.

"Xima Meilian!" Kim said, his response echoing in the distance.

He wanted to step toward the place where Kim was, yet he didn't dare. He felt that it was an abyss. His lower abdomen tightened, and untimely desire made his organ harden. Where did Kim actually come from? He looked outwardly like a genuine local man, but he spoke the language of Joe's country. Joe thought of the portrait of Kim, the pasture owner, in that book. He thought of the owner of the streetside bookshop. He suddenly understood that the book with one page was a snowcapped mountain! The reason the owner wouldn't sell it to him was because he wasn't willing to sell the secret in his heart. Joe's thoughts moved away from these two books, and returned to those books he'd read before. He felt waves of emotion, his mind flickering with light. Now what appeared in his mind was no longer a square and a broad road with parasol trees planted along its side. The wild, heavy snow concealed everything, everything whispered secretly under thick layers of snow. He laughed with understanding: so this was that anthill! How many years passed while industrious worker ants constructed a palace underground, and already no one could see through to it? Should this be sad or joyous? The books existed. The owner of the tiny bookstore guarded them.

Joe, too, guarded them. Paper perhaps could be damaged by insects, could be scattered in all directions, but the stories inside the books entered the mind and were passed down generation to generation, preserved in secret places.

Now Joe's face was pressed to the surface of the ice. Perhaps the snow-covered mountain was kissing him? How unusual, he felt the bone-piercing frozen wind cut through his whole body—his body shook without stopping—but his desire was as before.

The snowy mountain leaned toward him, as if pressing against his body, but it wasn't heavy. Joe squinted. He saw butterflies flying in the ice and snow, masses of colorful butterflies mixed in with the snowflakes. Joe's organ was frozen by the ice and snow. Moaning, his spirit lost in rapture, he came.

"Xima Meilian!" Kim said in the distance.

14

IDA RETURNS TO THE FARM

Ida swam along in pain, like an injured fish. The lake bottom was lit by a dim gleam, and there were many shadows. After a short while she saw that these shadows were actually the shadows of plants. Ida had often gone to the lake bottom before, but she had never seen these plants. It appeared this place had undergone a transformation. What kind of plants were they? They looked like climbing vines, with huge egg-shaped leaves creeping along the silt like innumerable small beasts. Now was the time when Reagan came to fish. She leaned against the leaf blades, listening to his footsteps close by. Reagan's steps were filled with hesitation. He didn't stop, but like a man possessed he wound in circles on the same spot. Ida wondered, Could he hear the sound she made stirring in the depths of the water? Numerous small fish stopped to rest on her naked body, crowding especially on her back. When she swam, these small animals bit her back and shoulder blades lightly, causing her pain to shift.

She heard a loud sound on the shore. It was Reagan falling into a water-filled depression. Perhaps a snake had attacked him. The snakes had always been friendly with him before. How could they wildly assault him now? Ida felt a certain comfort.

Reagan really was wrestling with the snakes. The violent little bastards not only poured their venom into his body, they also got into his abdomen and thrashed around inside it, making him die and come back to life again and again. He told himself, "Die, just die." But he couldn't die. Then one of the deadly poisonous bastards went into the arch of his foot, and he finally passed out. The last image he saw was a red star exploding in the sky.

When he came around Reagan heard Ida crying. She squatted at a spot five meters from him, looking very much like an orangutan. Her long arms propped her up on the ground, and in the night's luminescence even her eyes turned red. Thoughts assembled in Reagan's extremely weakened mind: "Did this woman grow up among the orangutans?"

"I-da." He spoke the two syllables with difficulty.

"How good," Ida spoke from her heart. "A nightingale just flew by."

"Come here."

"No. I'm not used to it any more. I want to stay for a while on the farm. May I?"

"You may, Ida."

Reagan felt his body disappearing in the vanishing of hope.

Ida slowly left. Reagan saw her crawling away. She crawled ahead bit by bit. Reagan wanted to cry, but there were no tears in his eyes.

In that endless time before daylight Reagan sat unmoving in the water-logged ditch. The venom already flowed throughout his body, yet the great pain slowly brought him cheer. What he found astonishing was the way the snakes had suddenly disappeared, without leaving a trace. His surroundings were therefore tranquil. All the small living things were hibernating and did not stir. From the lake came the incongruent sound of singing. It was a woman, a bereft woman, but of course it wasn't Ida. She had already gone in the opposite direction. So who was it? He didn't want to move. Lightning flashed in his mind, flash after flash illuminating its most hidden corners until they were as bright as snow. White horses, red foxes, and spotted leopards sliced the air like comets. Tolling thunder surged, pressed by the black wind. Perhaps the pain made his imagination so keen. Reagan saw his own life turn into unimaginably clear lines of ideas, like veins. The path of his thoughts stretched out from the dark surface of the lake, slipping unimpeded along the ground. At this moment he couldn't help sighing like Ida, "How good!" What he saw wasn't a nightingale but rather the spotted leopards, white horses, and red foxes in his mind. He didn't want to separate himself from his great pain. This novel experience made him reluctant to pull away. Every time he swung his head, there were ever stronger flashes inside it, and from its hidden corners ever more incredible animals ran out. Ancient Chinese qilin, dragons, and so on . . .

Ida crawled far away before finally straightening up. She walked slowly. She wanted to return to the apartment building where she'd lived before, a building set among the banyan trees.

But the building had collapsed. Her friends Lara and Liang sat in the rubble of its broken walls.

Ida walked to the half-wall of piled-up debris and saw their small single beds spread with clean white sheets. The two girls were both orphans, and Ida knew nothing could happen that would surprise them. Reagan's farm had another name, "the orphanage," because a large part of the staff were orphans.

"Ida's come back," Lara raised her head. "Look, we have to sleep out in the open now. Liang and I have already gotten used to it. Will you be able to? Mr. Reagan tore down the building. His own home is torn down, too."

"How did he tear it down?"

"It's unclear. We were sitting inside when a thunderclap blew us to the ground beneath the building. It toppled backward before our eyes. Everyone heard the farm owner howling in the thunder. We think he did this in order to seek a better life. We should be patient."

It was only Lara who spoke. Liang stood stooped over the head of the bed playing with several white mice. She appeared to be training them to stand on their hind legs. Her mouth made a *si si* hissing, like a snake.

"They are survivors from the disaster. Liang wants them to work miracles," Lara explained off to the side. "When it rains, we prop up a tiny canvas tent . . ."

Ida felt that when she said "prop up a tiny canvas tent" her voice was filled with a certain bitterly sad memory. The mice started squeaking, *chi chi*, as if echoing Lara's speech.

"Ida, sit down." Liang was calling to her.

Ida sat on Liang's bed and saw the mice make their way into

Liang's arms. It was completely dark. Fortunately Ida's eyes could see everything clearly in the dark. But her two friends didn't possess her special eyesight. Ida thought of how in this rolling dark world, they were so lonely.

"Lara, where did all the other workers go?"

"They went to the mountainside and built a log cabin. Mr. Reagan wanted us to stay here."

"Stay here and do what?"

"Wait for you to come back. Look, there's another cot over there, that's your bed."

Ida followed the direction she pointed in, and to her great surprise she really did see a small white speck.

"Since you left, Mr. Reagan comes every day to change your sheets. We mock him, but he doesn't get angry."

Ida walked over to her cot. The bed abutted the trunk of a large banyan tree. When she spread out the quilt and lay down with her head on the pillow, the crown of the banyan hung down, protecting her. She shut her eyes and saw a calm, beautiful beach, the sea, and seagulls. A gentle breeze blew. Her dead friend appeared with a solemn face in the shallow part of the water. She was still wearing that work uniform. She was undoing the buttons on her chest but none of them would open. Her long, thin, agile fingers moved rapidly up and down. Ida sighed: "Oh Reagan, Reagan, how could you have ordered such unlucky uniforms for us?" A large flock of seagulls flew up, then dropped again near her friend. She was still undoing buttons, and above her the sun blazed down. Liang was also there, playing with her mice. Now she laughed cheerfully, and Lara was at her side, screaming. Ida's mood became calmer. For the first time in many days she entered a deep sleep.

She dreamed of rubber trees. She didn't know how, but the rubber trees grew on the mountain slope, and the farm looked as it had when it was still undeveloped. There were lotus pods in the lake and wild ducks drifted on it. The sun, unexpectedly, was black. "If the rubber trees are transplanted, their survival rate will be very low," she said to Mr. Reagan. Mr. Reagan was panting inside her. She struggled to open her eyes in her dream and saw the crows she hadn't seen for so long filling the sky. They flapped their wings and drops of water fell on her face. It was those soggy wet crows. They crossed through time and flew to the past. In tiny increments, her desire became a remotely ancient memory, in the process of reviving. This kind of desire lost its previous violent nature and came to resemble a silkworm's thread, both disarrayed and distinct. Now she reached the deepest place inside Reagan's body.

"Who's crying?" Ida asked.

"I am," Reagan said in the dark.

He stood behind the tree and spoke with Ida between the tree trunks.

"Ali and I live on a boat now, a sea vessel. In dreams, our boat reaches different places all over the world. One day I saw Ali eating durian fruit, and I asked her where she got it. She said it was from Malaysia. Then she asked me, 'Last night we got off the boat there, and stayed for a long time in a garden shaped like a triangle. Have you forgotten all about it?'"

"These past days I've lived at a bar, in a tower in the air. There are two bedrooms. The owner's daughter and I each had a room. Downstairs a group of musicians played folk music from the countryside the whole day long. There was no staircase to go downstairs, so we depended entirely on our thoughts to move up and down. They were unforgettable days."

The sky wasn't light yet, so Ida was still lying down. She tried as hard as she could to return to her dreamscape and converse with Reagan. She collected her thoughts by thinking of a tiny black door, and longed to hear its slight *zhi ya* creak. Owing to this excessive effort, she couldn't tell later whether she had actually been dreaming. She felt her mouth saying "ah, ah, ah." No matter what speech she came out with, it all turned into this "ah," and that small black door was in a place nearby, half-open, with a beautiful peacock passing in and out.

"On breezy nights I lie on the deck listening to the whales swimming. There is a shark that lives there, and when it arrives the whales grow restless. On the shore someone says, 'Is this the village of fruit?' Then a burst of running footsteps."

"We, the bar owner's daughter and I, later reached the point where we didn't want to get out of bed. We slept in the air. Gradually, the music downstairs changed into a dirge. The room was filled with women and elderly people dressed in mourning. Once someone led in a dog yapping *wang wang*."

Reagan saw that Ida didn't move when she spoke. He couldn't make out the face of the person under the quilt. He constantly suspected that Ida's body had already disappeared because the voice he heard sounded like it played from a tape recorder. Had Ida come, and now the sky would not grow light? Lara and Liang were lighting oil lamps. Reagan thought that the two girls seemed a little nervous, as though they were waiting for something to happen. The banyan's aerial root swayed above him with a *ge ge* creak, like the sound of a skeleton in a dissection room. He thought that maybe after Ida awoke she wouldn't remember that he and she had talked. This kind of misapprehension would be the pattern of their contacts after this.

Reagan didn't remember when he'd begun to change into a ragged drifter. He wore clothes that gave off the sour smell of sweat, and passed through the crows that crowded together. These drenched birds sometimes attacked him, leaving his body covered in droppings, but he didn't care about such things any more. If he saw any strange girl whatever on the farm he would go over and interrogate her, until people found him detestable.

Beautiful Ida was lying under the banyan tree, and Reagan hid behind its thick trunk, giving off a stink from head to foot. They were separated into two worlds, carrying on this strange kind of intercourse. Reagan felt that this woman had taken away all the vigor and weight of his body. He was as light as a mayfly now. His body rose and fell with currents of air.

"Is it better to change into a bird, or into a tree?" Lara asked from off to the side in a loud voice.

Liang let out a ringing laugh, playing in the dark with her mice.

Reagan came out from behind the tree trunk and walked toward the two girls. He felt as if he were swimming. The effect of the earth's gravity on him was reduced until it was miniscule.

"Girls, girls!" he said weakly, his voice like a cicada call.

"Is it better to change into a bird, or into a tree?" Lara responded to him with this question.

He couldn't walk. He sat down right there on the spot. He heard a section of the broken-off wall collapse. But rather than collapsing altogether, it fell down brick by brick, as though someone were knocking on it. He doubted whether he was sitting on the ground, because he couldn't feel the soil, only handfuls of dry leaves. He became very light, so light the leaves failed to crackle into pieces underneath his body.

"Is this that powerful man our boss? His body is breaking apart like pieces of tile."

It was still Lara who spoke. Her mocking tone made Reagan feel there was nowhere to hide himself away. He wondered how she could treat her own boss like this. She was caustic. He couldn't help feeling over his body to make certain he hadn't broken into pieces.

Liang was still laughing. He didn't know whether she was laughing at him or at Lara. Perhaps her laughter had nothing to do with the two of them.

The day a rainstorm collapsed the multistory building, Reagan had seen Liang searching for her mice in the rubble of the broken walls. Her movements were like lightning in the sky. Whenever her hands touched the small animals, they became obediently still so she could lift them one after another to carry in her apron. The sight moved Reagan greatly. He meant to commend this girl, but afterward he forgot about it because he was busy finding accommodation for all the people who'd lost their homes. There were many mice on the farm, but Reagan's attention rarely focused on these recluses as they traveled back and forth. Liang appeared to be someone who had a purpose, and perhaps her schemes ran deep. Every person here had schemes that ran deep, including the one who'd drowned.

"Girls, girls." His voice had no strength.

"My mice, my mice!" Liang, who hadn't spoken all along, suddenly shouted, then wailed with heart-tearing, lung-rending grief. The sound cut open the silence of the night air.

Reagan hung his head, repeating silently to himself: "Disappear, disappear." He saw his boat and a black river, so he went aboard, entered the cabin, and lay down in its narrow space . . . His hand explored underneath him, catching handful after handful of leaves, leaves he couldn't twist into pieces. Liang's voice grew more and more distant and finally couldn't be heard. A wild wind, its direction uncertain, blew across the surface of the river.

At daybreak the two girls finally came over. They saw Reagan's body buried in thick layers of leaves from the tree. His mouth was also stuffed full of leaves. His figure looked like a corpse.

"Our boss is pursuing pleasures of the mind," Lara said. "Look how content he is. I had a grandfather whose body was set into an earthen wall when he neared the end of his days. Other people believed he was suffering, but really it was pleasure."

At night Ida slept under the banyan tree, and during the day she drifted around the farm. One night she got up because she couldn't sleep, and without realizing it walked to the eastern slope of the mountain. There was a half-collapsed wooden house on the hillside. Ida knew the family of the farm manager Jin Xia lived there. Ida had known for some time that the house was eaten through by termites, and now, it seemed, one side had finally fallen in. In the several rooms that had not collapsed the lamps were lit. The inhibited howl of a wolf came from inside. The shapes of two people scurried in front of the window. What was the family busy with in the middle of the night?

That wolf's howl abruptly began again, a sound loud enough for the deaf to hear. Ida felt the ground under her feet vibrating slightly. Immediately afterward a window opened and a dark shadow flew out, landing on the ground. Ida simply stared. It was Jin Xia's older son, the one who cared for the wolf. The boy came over to Ida.

"They will kill someone," he told Ida, pointing to the window.

"The wolf is chained, but even an iron chain can't hold it. Mama puts the blame on me, and now the whole family wants to kill me."

"Where will you run away to?" Ida was troubled.

"Yes, where will I run away to?"

The youth wrung his hands. The green light shooting from his eyes terrified Ida. She sensed that although he was shy, he was a bit like the chained wolf. Was it possible that he did change into a wolf, and that was why his family wanted to kill him? When she looked at the window again, the lamps were already out. Inside all was quiet.

"What will you do?" Ida asked him.

"Hey," he was suddenly relaxed. "I will sleep in the forest near here. I'm already used to it. Father told me to raise the wolf. I was taking care of it before I'd been on the farm very long. In the end they wanted to force me to leave. My wolf ran into the house and it collapsed. It was my fault. But I worry about my little brother. Father might also order him to take care of the wolf. My brother is weak, he'd be done for."

"Don't worry too much, he can change," Ida said, to comfort him.

"Maybe. What good is it to worry?" The young boy was suddenly impatient. He walked off by himself into the bushes.

The wind blew as Ida continued to climb up the mountain. Something tripped her, and she almost fell down.

"Manager Jin Xia! Why are you here?"

"I'm looking for my son. I want to catch him and bring him back. The boy's very destructive, and I'm afraid something will happen."

"I think not. Just now he was fine."

Ida and Jin Xia stood side by side next to a rock projecting out of the ground. The moon hid behind the clouds. Dark surrounded them. Jin Xia lit a cigarette with his lighter. "Mr. Jin Xia, do you think your son should grow up like a wolf?"

"Yes, but he has to be fastened with an iron chain."

"It's too cruel."

Jin Xia laughed piercingly. That green light shone in his eyes. "People here are all like this, right?"

When Ida lowered her head tears fell down. She left him, her spirits low, and walked back down the slope.

The sky began to lighten with morning haze, the lake water in distant places shone with white light, and birds sang on the mountainside. Some object in Ida's heart was also little by little reviving. Was this the farm where she'd lived before? Why didn't anyone work? In several days she hadn't seen a single person in the rubber trees. Only one day, she saw in the distance an Eastern woman wearing a black skirt, walking alone in the woods. Ida had heard that her companions from work all lived on the mountain slope, but when she went there she didn't see a single building, or even tents. She had also gone once to Mr. Reagan's home. The building hadn't fallen down after all, but it looked like there was no one inside. The jeep parked at the entrance was covered in dust so thick its color couldn't be seen. Last month, Ida had tried to make up her mind to pass the night in this building. Originally she had planned to enter through the back door in the middle of the night, but Mr. Reagan changed his mind. He told her his home wouldn't suit her. If she came, he would be hurt. Now he didn't appear to want this home himself.

She heard people speak of the farm's boundaries. It seemed the farm had already expanded to the neighboring counties. And their farm, which made up its center, was deadly quiet. The only lively things were those drenched crows. No matter where she walked Ida would run into them. It was also possible that the farm had disbanded and her fellow workers were already returned home. When Ida thought of this, the future turned into a stretch of desolate beach extending all the way to the horizon. Lara had told her that the other workers all lived on the mountainside, but probably she'd said this to keep Ida's courage up. Not far from where they slept there was a canteen, and a black cook who made food there. All three of them went to the canteen to eat, but they never met any other workers, not once. Behind the canteen there were toilets and showers. All of these appeared to have been finished only recently. There was an employee responsible for sanitation. Canteen, toilets, and showers constituted a small civilized world. Why had Mr. Reagan arranged this strange life for her?

"It's because of love," Lara said to her. "His inner heart is a waste-land now."

Ida panicked at discovering a nest of dead snakes in among the reeds, large ones and small ones, more than ten altogether. It was the striped kind of snake most common to the farm. The site showed no signs of a massacre. It might be death by poisoning. She stood to the side for a while with a *weng weng* buzzing in her head, as though someone kept on saying something to her. The lake water became so bright, so insidious. She gazed a moment at her face in the water of the lake. That youthful face made her think of her dead mother, espe-cially about the eyes and brow. She thought that it might have been her mother's wish for her to come here, poor and vagrant. Crows flew past, and the wind fanned by their wings made ripples on the water's surface. Her face dispersed.

"Miss Ida, don't you have a home?"

Someone in the water spoke to her. It was a child. She stared at-tentively, searching, but could not see anyone in the water. The per-son was behind her. It was Jin Xia's older son.

"Little one, what are you doing following me?"

Ida looked into the child's shining wolf eyes and began to smile.

"You have a home, but you won't go back to it," she said.

The youth stood there bashfully, looking at the water-logged ground, as if he wanted to say something, but hesitated.

"Miss Ida, tell me, will my dad kill my little wolf?" he finally said.

"No, why?"

"Last year I saw him sharpen his knife and then he cut off one of the little wolf's paws. His left hind foot. The little wolf howled for three whole days and three nights. He covered the house in blood. Afterward my father cried, and I cried, too. He cried when he told me that this way the little wolf won't be able to run away. Did you know that little wolves always want to run away?"

He squatted gloomily by the watery ditch, poking at the leeches in the water with a stick. Ida observed from above his fiery-red, babylike hair. The tremor in her heart was indescribable.

Someone rustled in the reeds. It was that Eastern woman again. She appeared in a flash and then was gone.

The boy didn't raise his head.

"That women has no home. We call her the lunatic, poor woman. One time she lost a shoe at the door of our house and ran away barefoot. Maybe our little wolf scared her."

"What is your name?" Ida finally asked him.

"My name is Little Wolf. My dad says our family has two little wolves."

"It sounds nice," Ida said sincerely.

Little Wolf was suddenly infuriated. He stood up and spoke with hatred: "You woman, why are you complimenting me? I don't need you to say nice things about me." He threw the stick, abandoned her, and walked into the reeds.

Ida thought that maybe the manager Jin Xia's whole family was frightening. Mr. Reagan had brought him in to be the manager, so surely something in Jin Xia's temperament must have appealed to him. Living in their wooden house eaten by termites, caring for a wolf, this family was not, in reality, a threat to anyone except themselves. Where had Mr. Reagan found this man? Thinking about the family, Ida did not notice her pain easing. It was truly a miracle cure. She stretched her long arms, jumped twice, and filled her lungs with fresh air. Mr. Reagan's making her live under a tree was a brilliant idea.

Ida stopped drifting around. She felt there were a few things she wanted to do.

A long time ago, when Ida was still at her old home, she'd often watched the people there making bricks out of yellow clay. They baked the bricks in the scorching sun, then built houses with them. Now there happened to be this same clay beside the forest where she was staying. She started by making a brick mold with her hands, then industriously began the manual work. Her sweat dripped into the clay bricks, and her hands became extremely rough. Every day, in the setting sun, she heard the mountain flood scream past in her ears.

"Ida, don't you like your home to be everywhere and to live out in the open?" Lara asked her.

"I am a wasp, surely you've seen how a wasp makes a nest."

As the walls rose, Reagan looked on from a distance with overwhelming emotions. Ida's movements were so harmonized, so rich in musicality. She was an innately skilled builder. The original detached wall now became the back wall of her new building. This new building had two rooms, front and back. Lara also took part in the work. She had done carpentry before, and now she was helping Ida make the roof frame, which they prepared to cover with thin strips of Chinese fir.

And so Reagan watched Ida move the cot into the small house she'd built. He knew the crude small building had no electricity or running water, or even a window, and there was only a low wooden door. At midday Jin Xia's older son, the "wolf child," always came to the front of the small house and knocked on the door. Ida would make warm welcoming sounds. But the wolf-child never went in. They would chat at the door, and then the wolf-child would bounce away. Reagan took notice of all this. Reagan's home wasn't the boat of which he'd spoken. It was an abandoned trailer. Every day Ali brought him simple meals and water.

"Why does Ida want to live in that building?" he asked Jin Xia.

"She wants to become the farm's witness. The farm is ceaselessly expanding, the borders change and change again, and in her heart she's uncertain about it." Jin Xia's expression revealed satisfaction when he said this.

Reagan saw Jin Xia's wife holding a basket of clothes as she tottered up and down the stairs. She was going to the backyard to dry the clothes. Her purple swollen feet shuffled. She did not appear to be in a good state of health. Jin Xia went with Reagan to stand under the tree. He smoked one cigarette after another, squinting his long narrow eyes and plotting some affair in his heart. A feeling of uneasiness skimmed across Reagan's mind as he thought of certain rumors about Jin Xia. "Never mind what they say, this man's driving ambition isn't a menace to anyone," Reagan thought.

Jin Xia's wife finished drying the clothes in the backyard and came out. When she went up to the house Reagan saw her bare feet running with water, each step a damp print on the stairs.

"Every day my wife and I make up vain dreams inside the house. She tells me our farm could occupy more than half of a country. She wants me to expand into diversified production."

"I worry about the termites," Reagan blurted out, then felt a moment of remorse.

A nauseating odor filled the trailer. It smelled like decomposing sea creatures. Reagan didn't know where it was coming from. He lay on the sofa bed in the dark with his eyes open, waiting for the Eastern woman to arrive. She'd altered her pattern and no longer lay entangled with him. She stood outside the window of the trailer, poking her head in, breathing forcefully, making reveling sounds. So she *liked* the stench inside the truck. Reagan remembered that the woman walked back and forth under the burning sun all day, coating her clothes with dust, but when she was entangled with him he had never smelled a bad odor on her body. You could say her body had no smell. Even her body's odor couldn't be smelled. Then what about her body excited him? When Reagan was with her, he had never managed to attain a clearheaded judgment. Her flesh was like a fish in water, relaxed and smooth, but at the crucial moment it always lacked substance. One time, when Reagan was faint from climax, the woman's body actually disappeared. His whole body was rapidly dispirited. He felt only dread. Fortunately the situation lasted only a few minutes, then she reappeared. He began that hungry, thirsty lingering with her again. She very seldom spoke, only once, when she told him she came from a small, little-known island in the Pacific called Yellow Fruit Island or some such. Reagan had never heard of this name. At all other times, her speech was just two or three words: "oh my," "I never thought," "look," "love," "keep on going," etc., in a thick foreign accent, but Reagan couldn't guess her meaning. It was as if she were practicing saying these phrases for fun.

"Seabed, seabed!" the woman said to him from the window, blowing out air with her mouth.

"Dear, come here!" Reagan called.

Futile thirsting tormented him. Inside the trailer the evil odor grew thicker. Reagan was astonished: how could a quiet, lithe woman like her enjoy the odor inside? She stopped by as if it were merely the smell which drew her there. An enormous whale skeleton appeared in Reagan's mind. A few pieces of rotting meat stained the skeleton. A tsunami was pushing this prop, spinning it around.

He sat up with an effort and saw the woman leave the window and walk into a patch of forest that was billowing with smoke.

"Ida." He strained to say these two syllables then returned to the sofa bed.

The farm's territory was reaching into the far distance under the cover of darkness. The enormity of its scale drove Reagan mad. Now he entered Jin Xia's insane path of thought, changing into a crow circling in the sky over the loess, with no way to alight. He meant to set a boundary, but this intention became an obsession over a vain dream. Thirst, hunger, fear—he flew in rings, flew on diagonal paths, then made a spiral descent. He thought that perhaps he had stayed at the same spot and was not really moving around. At one moment he glimpsed a breakwater, and thought mistakenly that it was the border. But it wasn't a sea beyond the breakwater, it was a field of maize extending beyond the horizon—a test site for launching Jin Xia's experiments in diversified production.

When the sky was barely light he heard Jin Xia talking to someone. Apparently it was a police officer questioning Jin Xia about the issue of buying land. Jin Xia stuttered and his voice trembled. He would say something and then immediately deny it. Reagan guessed that he was already white in the face, his forehead sweating.

Reagan walked to the window and glanced outside to discover one man there, Jin Xia, standing under the tree and staring into space.

"Jin Xia, who were you just speaking with?"

"Oh, no one. I was talking to myself," he said awkwardly.

"Talking to yourself? Then why is there a rumor going around saying you take bribes?"

"Mr. Reagan, I tell you, I started the rumor myself."

"Oh!"

Reagan was greatly surprised and didn't speak for what seemed like half a day. Crows cawed suddenly in the trees. A whiteness appeared in his brain. In the trailer the stench had disappeared, but his keyed-up nerves still could not relax. What Jin Xia described, too, exceeded Reagan's anticipation. He thought of the wolf Jin Xia was raising, his house eaten through by termites and half of it in rubble, his wife's edema dripping water, his older son drifting around like a wild wolf . . . Reagan stepped out of the trailer. He wanted to speak with Jin Xia.

"Jin Xia, how many years is it since you came here from your original home?"

"Me? Oh, let me tell you, I don't have a native home. I was born on the road, and after that I was always on the road, in a troop on the march . . . Look at me, do I look like someone who has a native home?"

As he spoke he stared into the distance. Reagan followed the line of his sight and saw a hawk drop slantingly through the air, at first managing to hold itself aloft, then plunging into the lake.

"I have no native home," he said again. "Your driver Martin knows all about this."

"Martin?"

"Yes. I met Martin at a picnic—a young man who took care in his dress, with an elegant manner. It was at his suggestion that I came to your farm. At that time I was enjoying successful promotion in my career. Martin said I should come here, where I would have a place to exercise my talents. He also called your farm 'a wasteland.' An intelligent young fellow. The scenery here is especially beautiful, particularly the green sky. It makes me enlarge my outlook."

After a while, Jin Xia told Reagan he needed to go.

"Going back home?"

"No, to make the whole world my home. My family will leave at night when it's dark. I already found someone to replace me. He was formerly a monk."

"I'm very surprised."

Reagan passed another night without sleep. He was at the lake, sitting on the small bench fishing. The boy sat on the ground at his side.

"Little Wolf, will you be leaving?"

"Yes, Uncle Reagan. Aren't I saying good-bye to them now?"

"To whom?"

"Them, the leeches in the water ditch. I'm good friends with them. Once every week I let them drink blood from my leg. Look!"

He smoothed his pants leg, showing Reagan his slightly swollen and inflamed calf.

"I love you, Little Wolf. Are you really going to leave?"

"I really am going to leave, Uncle Reagan. Dad says we won't come back again. My heart's already flown to that place far away in the mountains. I heard all the buildings there hang from the cliffs. My dad is a hero, isn't he?"

"Yes. Is your wolf going with you?"

"Hmm."

His mood darkened. He kept kicking the small bench where Reagan sat until he could no longer fish. Reagan didn't know why the boy was so unhappy. Maybe he shouldn't have brought up that wolf. He'd never understood why Jin Xia had lamed the wolf. He packed up his fishing rod and sat down on the ground with the child, holding his little hand, wanting to speak with him. The child's hand was extremely skinny. It gave Reagan an unusual feeling. He remembered the child had been eating and sleeping out of doors all these days.

"Uncle Reagan, will I die?"

"No, you won't. You are a child."

"Children can die, too. I was just thinking about the buildings hanging from the cliffs. When our wolf starts to howl, the buildings might fall down. Last time when most of our house collapsed it was the wolf that did it. It wasn't the rainstorm at all. My dad told everyone it was the rainstorm. He was fooling people. Uncle Reagan, do you think I should go? I want to stay on the farm with my wolf. I already found a good place over there in the forest. I could put up a house and live there with it. I wouldn't have to live in that termite nest any more. But I also wonder if living on a cliff would be more interesting, only if you don't fall in. I think and think, and I can't make up my mind. I'm still a child, I don't want to die. My dad is a hero."

Reagan pityingly rubbed the child's small hand, although in his heart he understood that the child needed no pity.

"Little Wolf, you don't have to go. You could live here with me in the forest. What do you think? In the future you would grow up to be like your father and come help me manage the farm."

"Things are good here, but I also want to go live on the cliffs. Uncle Reagan, what do you think I should do?" He looked seriously at Reagan.

Under the moonlight Reagan thought his eyes looked like two deep caves, as if there were no eyeballs in the sockets. A feeling of cold scudded across Reagan's heart, and for a moment he couldn't speak. Someone swam by in the lake with a noisy gurgling, *hua hua*. Reagan could tell it was someone else, not Ida. Ida was rhythmical, while this person slapped the water carelessly, almost willfully. "It's the forest keeper," Little Wolf told him.

The forest keeper came ashore naked. His clothing was on the bank, and he walked over to dress. The old man's silhouette looked strong and healthy, not at all like his downtrodden appearance in the daytime. Reagan thought: Maybe the forest keeper believes this lake and farm both belong to him? Look how confident he is. His movements are so poised. Little Wolf suddenly ran over and hugged the forest keeper. The pair walked away, speaking warmly in whispers.

Without blinking Reagan watched their old and young figures as they left. A kind of regret sprung up in his heart. Without knowing why, he sensed that the forest keeper was the true owner of this land. Every tree and blade of grass was probably in his dreams, and this child was a free bird flying back and forth. It was said that the forest keeper's family had lived here for many generations. Formerly it was a true wilderness. Suddenly, the silhouette of a deer appeared within Reagan's view. The deer were on the opposite bank, a great herd of them. He had never heard of there being deer in these mountains. What sort of monk had Jin Xia hired to replace himself as the manager of such a large farm? Seeing the deer suddenly emerge from lower ground on the opposite shore, Reagan felt that the future was uncertain. At this very moment Jin Xia might have already packed his bags.

He returned to the trailer, unable to lift his spirits, lay down, and shut his eyes to its stinking odor.

"Mr. Reagan, I will start my job today." The forest keeper's voice came from inside the trailer.

"You?"

"Of course Jin Xia didn't tell you, that bastard!" He clapped the trailer window so hard it rang.

"He said it would be a monk."

"I used to be a monk. That bastard, playing tricks on us!"

"Come in and talk."

"No, I need to get to work. Mr. Reagan, yesterday I dreamed I saw our farm extending to the eastern seacoast. Jin Xia had great momentum."

Reagan shut his eyes and reflected for a long time, but he was unable to think of the forest keeper being the manager of the farm. In these past few years, everyone viewed him as a dirty, strange old man who lived alone on the undeveloped land. In these years there were countless times when Reagan had burst with the impulse to speak with him, but once he got to the keeper's door he was held back by dread. How was Reagan not a plunderer? This stretch of earth was formerly a wilderness. The forest keeper's family had lived here for generations, and the forest keeper was the only descendent of that clan. Naturally he saw this land as his. Now Reagan had transformed the land into a farm and him into a forest keeper. Who knew what grudge he might still harbor in his heart? Looking in through the broken door, Reagan always saw a snow-white triple-edged scraping knife lying out on the table.

How many years might this old man have been matching his strength with Reagan's in the dark? There were many times when Reagan had heard that the forest keeper would die soon, or was at his last breath. Apparently this was all a smokescreen. It was as if this strange man controlled everything here from a place deep in the earth, and was now, finally, bit by bit, encroaching, retaking the things that belonged to him. Jin Xia's sham expansion was no more than a means to divert Reagan's attention. Damn Jin Xia. Where had he come from? What was he doing? Reagan thought back, but his first meeting with Jin Xia was always a blank. He couldn't recall anything. It seemed to have been in some underground walkway in City B; it also seemed to have been at home in the kitchen, at midnight, when he went to fetch brandy. Had he invited Jin Xia to work on the farm, or was it Jin Xia who wanted to come? Or was there some third party who introduced him for the job? Reagan no longer retained the slightest impression. His distinct memories all came after Jin Xia started at the farm, and these were all connected to the wooden house on the mountainside that was eaten through by termites. Now he decided that, very possibly, this was a scheme plotted out a long time ago, a conspiracy relating to some few ancient, untraceable wishes. Even his driver, that young fellow, played a role. From the beginning it was like this . . . And Ali? At this thought, Reagan felt like a drowning man, like that girl, except he didn't wear a work uniform and could get to the water's surface to breathe.

Ali quietly came into the trailer. She was making him breakfast. Reagan, trusting to his luck, thought that maybe nothing had happened. She was so serene!

"The new manager does not intend to move. He will still live in his old cabin."

Ali finally spoke the fearful truth. Was this possible?

He must open his eyes, must get out of bed. The world had not disappeared in front of him. He saw a drenched crow plunge from the window into his trailer, dropping into the washbasin. A warm, damp animal smell spread everywhere inside the trailer. The bird's half-shut eyes seemed to stare at him. Ali ever so carefully cupped the injured bird (perhaps it was not injured) in her hands, stepped down from the trailer, and walked it to a growth of grass, where she put it down. She kept saying, "Little fellow, little fellow, you're so rash!"

"Mr. Reagan, you should get moving!" she said when she left.

When he stuck his head out the window, the violent sunlight temporarily blinded him.

Ida left her own small house and came there. Now she saw him clearly. He didn't look like a farm owner any more, only like a man who was down and out. He was extremely thin, so thin that his old clothing appeared empty on his body. The trailer was behind him, and the black-clad woman's skirt flashed behind the trailer. What was that woman doing hiding there? Two days earlier Ida had seen that Jin Xia's wooden house had completely caved in. A few wild dogs moved around in the ruins. She didn't know where the family had gone.

She thought, "Today the sky is green. It's so strange, how is the sky green first thing in the morning?" The road she'd taken passed through the rubber tree plantation. There was not a single worker there.

Mr. Reagan evidently saw her, but his expression was hollow. He had sunk into distraction. "Mr. Reagan!" Ida called out in an exploratory way. The woman behind the trailer was nowhere to be seen. Ida ran over to look, but there was no one behind the trailer. She looked back inside the trailer, but she saw only Ali sweeping.

"Ida, what are you looking at? Everything has changed now." Ali spoke without raising her head.

"I'm still not used to it. Can you teach me, Mother?"

"You don't need me to teach you. Isn't this what you hoped for all along? Try calling him again, I think he will answer. He answered you before, but you didn't hear."

Ida called to Reagan again. Her voice was rending and shrill. Suddenly she felt that there was nowhere to hide, and she ran away, cradling her head. She ran to the lake and then through the groves of trees, running until her eyes went black and she fell to the ground. She indistinctly remembered falling on a space of open ground.

"You run back and forth, but it's still the same piece of land. The young lady's heart is like the morning dew."

Ida heard the forest keeper close by. He was wearing the same clothing and leg wraps. He hugged a wild pheasant to his chest.

"Mr. Reagan handed over the farm to me. I want to change it into a territory of the night. Ida, your eyesight is so good at night. You will have a place to develop your talents."

His voice came through his beard with a *weng weng* droning. He'd already grown a beard.

"With the first light of morning, I saw Ida running toward me. My heart was truly moved." His snow-white brand-new beard shook.

"But I didn't . . . Oh, the sky this morning was so beautiful. Where did our convoy go? Doesn't it usually travel along this road?"

Some object in her heart revived. She felt herself eager to do something. She stood up and stretched her body out, appraising the forest keeper's cabin.

The forest keeper laughed heartily and said in a loud voice: "Convoy! Convoy . . . There's no convoy any more, dear, only a pack of wolves tearing through the wilderness."

But at noon large crowds of workers appeared on the road. To the south there was a road-repair bulldozer pushing earth. The forest keeper stood underneath the machine giving orders. Ida knew he wanted to construct a new road. This was the pack of wolves he talked about—those workers. Among the workers were both new hands and old hands. Ida asked one of the young men where they lived. He said by the sea. They slept on the beach under the open sky. He also said their manner of living now was "better than we ever imagined." Ida saw that he was holding a pheasant in his arms and asked what he was going to do with it. He said he was going to domesticate pheasants. "Everyone's job will change. This is what the new manager says."

Ida thought of Reagan's unfavorable situation. One moment she thought it was the end, but the next moment she thought it was a turning point. As if in a trance, she came to the seaside. A breeze was blowing and the fish smell of the water excited her. There were many people on the beach with their bodies buried in the sand. She approached them and chose a stretch of sand to sit on. She began to bury herself. The middle-aged woman next to her said that lying like this you could hide from a landslide, and you could also speak directly with your ancestors. "You are crushing my hand," she complained. Ida thought this was odd, because the woman was more than two meters away. How could her hand be underneath Ida's body?

In the sky numerous hawks stared greedily, but they didn't dare take precipitate action. Maybe they thought that these people with only heads showing were a bit unusual. You couldn't say what snare might be hiding underneath. After long, hesitant wheeling above, one large gray bird made a fierce dive at a young boy. Grappling and struggling began. They all held their breath and looked on intently. Ida wanted to look, too, but the sand got in her eyes. She couldn't see anything. She heard the woman calling her.

"Ida, Ida, I am your mother!"

"Mama, Mama! My eyes, I can't see you!" Ida began to cry.

"Never mind, stupid child, it doesn't matter. When the flood came from the mountain you couldn't see, either, but didn't you escape? And not seeing is better. It's tragic, tragic, the child broke the old hawk's wing. There's so much blood."

Some object was underneath her, pushing at Ida's back until it hurt. She thought of sitting up, but didn't move. The woman beside her said there was a person underneath. It was Mr. Reagan. Ida pressed down on him so that he couldn't get out. No matter how much he tried, it was a waste of his strength. Ida felt blood running from her eyes. The grains of sand cut her eyeballs like needles. "Mr. Reagan, I love you," she said. Then the person stopped pushing at her so hard.

"How nice, Ida found a beau!" The woman's voice was piercing. "And he's a landowner."

Ida remembered that Mr. Reagan had already given his farm freely to the forest keeper. Now he had nothing at all. But who had told her this? Was it him?

In the midst of the stinging pain, which was hard to bear, Ida began to ponder.

15

VINCENT AND THE FIVE DRAGON TOWER

Joe had already traveled through so many countries in the East that he could no longer remember where he was. He stood in front of a stone tower. The tower was on a plateau, and beside him was a local yellow dog that had been following him. He'd spent one night in a small town and now the dog followed him everywhere. Perhaps it meant to lead the way for him, but Joe didn't have a destination. He was only walking at random, and the yellow dog seemed happy with this procedure. Whenever they reached a new place it would let out a burst of yelping, *wang wang*, in its excitement.

The interior of the stone tower rose in a spiral with stone steps for climbing. Because the tower dated to a time ages ago, its stone steps were broken and fallen in some places. It looked dangerous to ascend. The yellow dog kept barking, begging Joe to climb up quickly. Joe looked up and saw the high roof marked with numerous round holes. They were put there so people could lean out of the tower. He estimated that the stone tower was about thirty meters high. The terrifying steps did not look very solid. He hesitated a while, then decided to leave. The yellow dog barked behind him indignantly for a long time. He felt guilty.

That night he rested in a hotel in the small town. It was a fairly high-class hotel. The rooms had French windows with hanging bamboo screens. Outside the windows a natural mountain spring flowed into the courtyard. But there were lots of mosquitoes. Even though he shut the window they got into the room, dancing and singing and making Joe irritable. Since he couldn't sleep, he opened the door and walked into the courtyard. It was large and full of yew trees and rose of Sharon. He hadn't walked very far when he heard someone talking. A man and a woman sat under a yew tree. They didn't mind the mosquitoes biting. The topic they discussed seemed to be extremely significant.

"And so Vincent came here, but how did he find out where I was staying?" the man said.

"You're his older brother, of course he would do all he could to find you. Where can you hide?" The woman laughed gently. She spoke leisurely and looked pleased.

Joe's heart leapt in his chest. He stared at the blurred silhouette he threw on the grass, trying with futile effort to recall exactly where he was. On the route of his journey, with its planes, wooden sailboats, trains, long-distance buses, he'd changed from one means of transport to another, passing from one country into another, and the borders melted little by little in his mind until he no longer took note of them. The old story inside him had already melted. His eyes were empty. The only thing in view was the yellow dog running at the edge of the horizon. These days he was accustomed to the life of a man traveling the globe alone, and now he suddenly heard familiar names. It was like the report of a tragedy communicated from another world.

"Someone saw him climb to the top of the Five Dragon Tower. That was yesterday." The man spoke again.

"It's the highest point in the world. Anything might happen there. Doesn't the proverb say, 'the higher you stand, the farther you see'?" The woman's voice lowered, as if sinking into thought.

"It's frightening. We shouldn't have come here to begin with."

"You regret it?"

"No, forever no."

The mosquitoes bit so severely Joe had to leave. He took off his jacket and wrapped it around his head, then put his hands in his pockets and walked back and forth. The mountain spring made a rustling *sha sha* as it passed through the rockery. From the garden he could see all the way to the outside, where tiny spots of light swam in the darkness. Could this place be "the roof of the world"? Joe couldn't believe it. He recalled that "the roof of the world" was in China. He decided to go back to the Five Dragon Tower tomorrow and climb up to look around.

Inside the hotel building there was a sudden confusion. All the lights were on, and someone yelled "Fire!" Everyone rushed into the garden. He hadn't imagined there could be so many people inside. Joe was squeezed among them and carried along as everyone rushed out to the street. He turned around and saw the small five-story building already roaring with flames. The people around him talked all at once. "It's dangerous!" The same alarm issued from different mouths. "Was it a plot?" One man raised this question, but the surrounding uproar drowned out his voice. This was when Joe finally thought of his luggage. Several books he'd carried with him were inside, the most important being the book about Tibet. Fortunately he still had some cash on his person, otherwise this would have been a disaster. The small building was still burning. People gradually dispersed. Joe didn't know where they were going. The street grew cold and deserted. A dog rushed over from the street corner. It was the yellow dog that had been following him.

The dog reached him and held his pants leg in its mouth, pulling him to the left. Joe had to go along with it. They came to a quarry. Several workers labored in the dark. The yellow dog circled to a temporary work shed behind the quarry. Joe saw that the door was open and an oil lamp lit inside. A man sat at the table holding his head tightly in both hands. The table was piled high with various objects.

"Joe, you've come. Sit down." To his surprise the man was Vincent.

Now Joe saw that the things piled on the table were human bones.

"This is Lisa," Vincent raised his head and seemed to smile. "Lisa followed the route of the Red Army's Long March and reached here, where she fell into the great gorge. It's unthinkable."

Joe's body shook in spasms. He didn't dare sit down at the table, so he just stood there. The dog hid at his feet whimpering with a *wu wu* sound, as if it were crying.

"Vincent, we meet again," Joe said, his teeth chattering.

Vincent lifted a bone and placed it against his face, with an expression of intoxication.

Joe became aware of a group of people surrounding the work shed, slinking about in the dark and talking in excited low whispers.

"Someone's here," Joe said.

"It's always like that in places like this, thieves everywhere."

Vincent blew out the oil lamp. He wanted Joe to talk about his happy adventures over these past days. Joe said there hadn't been anything worth remembering. He was simply roaming. Because Vincent wanted to hear more, Joe made up a story about planting opium poppies on the plateau. Joe thought his narrative prosaic and dull. In the middle of telling it he heard the people outside closing in and beginning to knock on the windows. He believed he saw a knife blade gleaming in the moonlight. But Vincent pressed him to keep talking. He didn't want Joe to stop.

"I wanted to smoke opium, but no one would let me. I'm an outsider here," Joe said, feeling slighted.

"You were an outsider to start with, you come from the West. That's what's interesting. Look at Lisa, she had an obsession. She threw all her strength into it."

Joe couldn't speak because two dark figures had slipped into the room. Unsettled with fear, he calculated how much money remained in his wallet. He saw the two shadowy figures take seats at the table. In this way, the four of them each occupied one side of it. Vincent still talked about Lisa as if nothing had happened. He spoke about his wife's pursuit over a long course of time. But Joe had stopped listening because the person on his right was stamping on his foot so hard he shouted in pain. He thought his bones might be broken. Should he give this man money? He was unable to determine whether the fellow wanted his money or his life, perhaps both. The man on his left lit a cigarette. In the spurt of flame from his lighter Joe saw the face of an outlaw.

Vincent was also smoking, and speaking unhurriedly. It looked as if he'd long since put life and death out of his thoughts.

"The gangs of thieves are as common in the plateau region as home-cooked meals. Many of the thieves live inside the Five Dragon Tower. Actually, some of them are also local, people who aren't willing to do honest work, or who are lonely. But the thieves didn't plot to murder Lisa. She wanted to take risks, she was obsessed. She'd been like this ever since she was young, and it's hard to change your nature. I regret not going with her. I was too slow, always a step back. Joe, these two guys aren't out for your life. If you want to go, you can go."

Joe tried to stand up. He tried to leave the shed. And they didn't prevent him. He saw the yellow dog standing at the work site waiting for him. Several spectral workers were carrying stones. Joe hadn't gone very far when he stopped and thought of going back again. A face appeared under the work-site lamps. It was Xima Meilian, the indigenous woman he'd met on the first stop of his journey. Joe thought of going to meet her, but the yellow dog bit into his pants with a death grip. Joe became aware of something. He stopped struggling and stood in place, dumbly watching the woman.

There was a black shadow behind the woman's body. Half of her beautiful face was blocked by the shadow, so Joe could only see one of her eyes. Her narrow eye still burned with the desire he'd seen in it before. She raised a hand, as if to welcome Joe over. The black shadow slowly enveloped her. Joe couldn't see her. He wanted to call her name, but he didn't know how to pronounce it. Looking once more, he saw the shadow already absorbed by the darkness of its surroundings. The work site's sole lamp shone quietly. Joe sadly recalled that river.

Inside the work shed Vincent struck the bones on the table with a wooden stick. He'd gathered them inside of the Five Dragon Tower, the bones of wolves and dogs. He didn't know why he'd wanted to say they were from Lisa's skeleton, perhaps in order to give himself something to feed on. To search out Lisa's tracks he had gone to many places across thousands of kilometers. The farther he went the more his heart lacked assurance. The Long March was only a long march, Vincent had learned this point profoundly. After she went missing Lisa never reappeared. One time, in a temple, Vincent saw a woman who looked like Lisa. But when he went over to her, he discovered it was a woman of a different race altogether. Although he couldn't find Lisa, Vincent had never felt so close to her. Yes, he felt that he had already become Lisa. A longing sprang up in his heart to trek from one place to another. His soul melted into the landscape, strange to his eyes, of the Eastern world.

Lisa had disappeared from his side in a crowd of people. They were coming out of the largest department store in the city, and Lisa had told him to wait for her a moment because she saw a girl from her hometown. She squeezed through the spaces between people and soon disappeared. Vincent waited, but she didn't come back. At last the black woman named Joyner came. Joyner told him she'd seen Lisa at the train station. She was rushing to catch a train. The night before, Lisa had told him she wanted to make an inspection in the field, to get a clear idea of the makeup of the troops who constituted the long march army. Vincent asked her whether she would journey to countries in the East. Equivocally, she made no answer.

Vincent didn't start his journey until the second day. He understood that Lisa was using her action to point out a direction for him—to go to a place where he'd never been, a place of which he had no perception. So his first intention wasn't even to search for Lisa, which was almost impossible anyway because there were no clues. His first intention was to throw off everything he had now and go, as Lisa had hinted to him, to try another kind of life. Of course he didn't plan to abandon his clothing company. He only meant to let this long journey make him lose his way and become a different man, then afterward he would return. He thought it was probably the same with Lisa. When he passed the high-rise building in the car, the Eastern woman was standing at the doorway. The infinite emptiness of the expression on her face left him once again deeply shaken.

The first conveyance he chose for himself was an airplane, not a train. He thought that at high altitude he would recall Lisa's appearance from their early years together. Before, he thought, he had not paid enough attention to many critical facts. These facts had revealed themselves to him many times in the early years. But on reaching high altitude, he discovered that his plan had come to nothing. People cannot return to the past through recollection. Not only did he fail to recall all sorts of details about their life; he couldn't even call up the image of Lisa in those early years, as if when he met her she was already a woman of a certain age. He grew dejected and stopped trying to remember. Later he went many places, and Lisa's face grew vaguer in his mind. And not only her face from earlier days. Little by little he forgot even her more recent appearance. On this point he was both anxious and upset.

One day he slept in a large courtyard belonging to a family of farmers. He slept until midnight, when he was startled awake by the repeated crowing of a rooster. He walked to the threshing floor and saw shadows in the landscape of the paddies where the water and sky met as one color. At the time the moon was bright, and a busy scene, very much like the Eastern markets he had seen many times in the previous days, appeared in the sky. But it was only an image, there was no sound. After careful discrimination, he made out that those shadows were all attempting to enter a structure resembling a casino, but a ferocious tiger stood on each side of the door. On top of the dome of the structure, an enormous hawk looked majestically over the shadows underneath. All the shadowlike people were blocked at the doorways by the tigers. Vincent wanted to look closer, but the old farmer, named Xiao (some people called him this), came out from the house. Xiao was smoking a pipe, his creased old eyes alive with vigor. He spoke a foreign language Vincent didn't understand, and he seemed agitated. He talked and talked, making all sorts of gestures with his hands. Suddenly, Vincent's mind opened, because when he stared at the old man's face, he unexpectedly grasped the import of what Xiao was saying. The gist of the old man's speech was: do not watch the scene in midair. It is extremely frightening. It kills people daily. Xiao painted a large circle with his hand, to show that there were human corpses buried in all the paddies in front of them. As he spoke the illusion in midair disappeared and became a ghostly atmosphere. Xiao abruptly shouted at Vincent. Vincent heard him say, "What did you really come here to do?"

Vincent turned and ran into the house. In the large courtyard he saw that everyone had gotten up. They stood at the doors of the rooms watching him. The halls and corridors were lit by pine torches. He couldn't find the room where he had been sleeping. Every room had changed to look exactly alike. He went in and retreated again, ridiculed the whole time. Later a boy walked up to him, making a sign that he would show him the way. Vincent followed as they rounded one turn after another and at last reached a large chicken coop. All the birds inside were roosters. Once Vincent appeared they started to crow, so loudly even the deaf would have heard. The young boy ran away. Vincent was tired and scared, so he simply stayed in the coop. He didn't know how it had gotten there, but an old sofa sat in the corner. He fell onto the sofa and went to sleep. There was a kind of extremely small mosquito that bit his skin painfully, but he paid no attention to their bites. In a dream, he marched heroically through cannon fire. Shrapnel bloodied his whole face. Blood ran into his eyes until he couldn't see anything.

In a fishing village by the sea Vincent came across a man from his own country. He was an elderly tourist. He wrapped his head in a white turban like the local men. This man sat in a wicker chair on the beach every day. They conversed facing the distant waves.

"There are people from our country everywhere here. I don't think this is by chance," the old man said.

"I hadn't thought about it closely." Vincent felt slightly ashamed. "But you, do you live here? Don't you intend to go back?"

"I want to pass the last day of my life in this little fishing village."

The old man's face revealed a smile. To Vincent, his expression seemed to say that he was the only one who knew the mystery of the way of life in this fishing village, but he didn't intend to communicate it to Vincent.

Vincent was disheartened because in this boring little place his thoughts were already frozen. During the day everyone went to sea to catch fish. Only a few children and the elderly were left in the village, along with four or five of the women. And at night people went to bed early. Once the moon came out there was no stirring in the village;

it was profoundly dark. Yet the old man had adapted to this simple, almost primitive, life. He went to the beach every day and stayed there. Vincent saw him sometimes talking to the seagulls, sometimes exclaiming to the sea, but the better part of the time he sat silently dozing in his wicker chair. Vincent had no way to leave. This place received no messages from the outer world. A long-distance bus came once a month. He could only calm his heart and while away the days. Sometimes he realized that he didn't remember things and he couldn't think clearly. It was more or less as if he had been born and raised in the fishing village, a loafer eating the food of idleness. He was still able to indistinctly remember his own past busy life, and remember that Lisa was his wife, but the details of his life were like a kite with a cut string. No matter what he did, he couldn't remember. One boring day he asked the old man, since he'd been in the village so long, why none of their countrymen had come here. The old man answered him:

"That is because you are here."

After Vincent returned to his room at the hotel he thought again and again of the old man's statement, and suddenly he understood it. So in his remaining days Vincent no longer sauntered all over, but instead brought a wicker chair to sit by the sea like the old man. Once the sun came out the two men went to the seaside and sat there until the people who'd gone to sea to fish returned. Halfway through the day a worker from the hotel brought them food.

As they sat idly, the old man seldom spoke. Vincent came to know from a few scanty words each day that the old man was from the northern part of Country A. He'd worked for several decades in a timber mill, and was now retired. He had a wife, children, and grandchildren, a large family. He said he'd received an invitation to come to this fishing village. One of his uncles, his mother's brother, wrote a letter from here inviting him for a brief visit. Although the whole family was opposed, he came. The day before he arrived his uncle fell ill and died. He was only in time for the funeral. He still remembered his agitated emotions on arriving. He had now lived in the fishing village for two years. Because he had no way to communicate with the outside world, his family might already have forgotten him. He felt that in his family's eyes this would be a good thing. Sometimes Vincent wanted to talk with the old man about life in Country A, but every time, before he opened his mouth, his mind went blank, and he couldn't think of anything to say. And the old man immediately saw this, always telling him, "There's nothing to say, let's not talk about it."

When heavy winds blew they had to stay inside the hotel. But the old man had something in his heart he couldn't let go. He made one trip after another, running outside to look at the sea.

"A stranger may come to find me, a local man. I worry about missing him." When he said this to Vincent, Vincent thought of him on the shore, waiting.

One night at midnight the old man knocked anxiously on the door of his room. Vincent opened the door and saw him standing outside in his pajamas.

"Can you be my witness?"

"What's the matter?" Vincent already vaguely sensed what it was.

"I need a witness. I'm afraid people will forget me in the same way I fear death."

"Let me think a bit."

"So you can't make up your mind. I need to wait for you to make up your mind."

He looked a little disappointed. Vincent didn't know how to console him.

After daybreak, when they met once again at the seaside to sit together, the old man told Vincent that the visit in the night had only been a moment's impulse. Now his mood was tempered. He shouldn't be so hasty, he should "let the flow of water make its own channel." That day a boat arrived. When the boat came, the old man glanced at it with drowsy eyes, then lowered his head, mumbling about something. Vincent guessed what the old man was saying. He felt his heart brought closer and closer to the old man's.

The atmosphere in the fishing village seemed primed for something to happen very soon. Day followed day, and no one took notice of the two men. Most of the villagers just stood at a distance observing, none of them ever displaying excessive interest. And news from the outer world never reached here. The boats always sped past in a hurry, so that they could not see who was on the deck. When the sea breeze blew through the old man's white beard, Vincent noticed that his face became more and more expressionless, like a mask. Vincent couldn't help thinking, Was the coming event happening inside the old man?

He arrived. He came at noon, rowing a small wooden boat over from the coral island. The man was probably a little over forty. He had a face a little like a spider. He was holding a leather bag in his hands. He used the language of Vincent's country to explain that his leather bag was filled with "precious blood." The old man stood up from the wicker chair. Vincent noticed his relief, as if he were putting down a heavy load. He realized that the old man wanted to free himself.

They were to set off on a journey. The old man eyed Vincent with a questioning gaze. Vincent opened his mouth and said, "Yes, I saw. I remember."

In the bright sunlight the fishing village began to seethe with excitement because news arrived that someone had died in an accident.

After the old man was gone Vincent stayed in the fishing village by himself. Every day he went to the beach. Facing the sea, the sky, the blowing wind, he also unconsciously pondered this matter of "witness." Who could be his witness? Could the ignorant villagers count as his witnesses? Could the wife whose husband had died count as his witness? Could the young boy over there picking up crabs by the sea count as his witness? That there was no true witness proved his time still hadn't come. Vincent began to long anxiously for the long-distance bus.

The bus arrived on a Wednesday. The whole fishing village, men and woman, old and young, stood by the road to watch him leave. The women held their children and looked into the bus with slightly open mouths. What were they searching for? The driver nodded coldly, signaling for Vincent to board the bus. Then, without turning his head:

"Are you ready?"

Vincent's heart was in a confused state. He waved his hand to the driver in despair and shouted:

"Go! Go!"

Once the bus started moving, the days and nights in the fishing village came back to life, playing like a movie in his mind. The month hadn't passed as drearily as he thought. He remembered going out roaming with the old man late at night. They saw will-o'-the-wisps at the grave of a villager who'd met with an accident. There were explorations of the coral island, where he and the old man discovered people sleeping inside a deep cave. They lit pine torches and sat talking with these people for a long, long time. These dreamers knew the answers to nearly all questions; they understood the language of every nation; and their thinking was extraordinarily dynamic. The two of them also visited a fisherman's home — the family had caught an unmentionable disease. Although each of their lifespans was only forty-one years, they hadn't turned into gamblers or drug addicts. Their method of coping with the menace of death was to abolish sleep. And so Vincent saw that the family had no beds. The brothers and sisters went about their own work late at night, while their parents sat at the table next to a tiny soybean oil lamp and kept accounts. Vincent and the old man also attended a celebration in the village. Everyone went to the beach and began to dance in the moonlight, to intense drumbeats, until no one could dance any more, until they all fainted on the ground . . . There were many other events, Vincent remembered them all. But when he was at the fishing village he'd forgotten all about these things. Why? Probably because they took place in the middle of the night. After passing through sleep and reaching the next day, he forgot them entirely. Now recalling these events Vincent suddenly understood. The old man had entered another kind of existence which he'd desired to attain — an existence he'd desired for several decades. Many years earlier, when he felled trees in the tall mountains and ancient forests, when he heard the long sighing sounds the trees made as they fell before him, he'd planned for that existence countless times. The mysterious uncle had helped him realize his aspiration. But the uncle? Was there such a person? Why had the old man never mentioned him later on? They had gone together to see the village cemetery, and there were no graves of any outsiders. Yet according to his previous narration, the old man's uncle was buried there. It seemed quite possible that his uncle was inside the deep cave on the coral island. Along the route many travelers boarded the long-distance bus. These people resembled one another. Their expressions were both weary and active. Vincent felt that they all must have come from the same place. In his mind he called that place the village of dreams. It was his firm but ungrounded belief that the village of dreams was the destination of his own journey. Perhaps the old man by the sea had promised him this?

"Are we there, Dad? Why is the view along the way so sad?"

"There are happy ducklings swimming in that lake, child. You need to look harder."

Vincent listened harder, and to his surprise he understood their language.

When Vincent left the work shed the sky was already bright. He once again came to the Five Dragon Tower.

Joe was also there. His eyes were suffused with threads of blood. It looked like he hadn't slept all night. Walking into the tower, both men felt a chill wind spinning inside, causing them simultaneously to look up. There was a patch of white light on the roof. They couldn't pick out the round holes any more. At the midway point of the tower of stone someone was climbing, someone elderly with fluttering white hair.

"He came from the banks of the Ganges. He had raised a lion in the village," Joe said to Vincent. "Afterward he went mad. It was a very beautiful village. Standing at the riverside, you could hear the ancestors speaking in the starry sky."

"Was that place really the Ganges?" Vincent asked.

"I don't know. I've been to too many places, they're all muddled together. But I want to think so. Such a wide river, where elephants stood towering on boats. The Ganges, the Ganges."

"But it's really cold here." Vincent sneezed a few times in succession.

The old man had already climbed to the roof and disappeared into the patch of white light.

"He worked during his lifetime as a cooper. Raising the lion was his secret occupation. He did this using pheasants he'd captured. The lion hid in the forest, only appearing in the village in the middle of the night. The relationship between the lion and the man was unknown to others. He left riding the lion's back. That day, the woods were full of noise and the water of the Ganges overflowed both banks. The elephants, the elephants . . ."

He couldn't continue speaking, because he heard a loud violent sound, like a rock smashing to the floor. Could a stair have fallen down? But there were no traces of it on the ground.

"Are you speaking of this old man?"

"Yes, I know him."

"But he just fell down. Think of how heavy a man's soul is."

That day they did not climb up. They stood underneath in the tower's shadow, watching the patch of light at its crown and discussing those irrelevant things that don't touch on reality. In the afternoon they went to eat at a small restaurant, then returned to the Five Dragon Tower and continued talking. Time silently slipped away and night fell again. Joe sensed that Vincent seemed to be waiting for something. He went up to the doorway, over and over, to look around outside. Finally, a woman appeared. As every step brought her nearer Joe saw clearly that she was the bookshop owner's aged, beautiful former wife. But in Vincent's eyes, she was that weightless woman from the twenty-four-story high-rise in City B. Vincent had remembered agreeing to meet her at this spot.

The woman walked in, nodding familiarly to the two men. She said, "At dusk there was so much fog I could hardly make out the road."

Vincent and Joe opened their mouths at almost the same time and said to each other, "So, you two arranged to meet here."

At this they were both embarrassed. But the woman wasn't. She walked over and clasped both their hands, shaking them forcefully a few times. Joe saw a figure beyond the wavy white hair of her elegant head. It was a rare breed of white tiger. In the dim light the tiger's eyes were two lamps.

Soon the three of them couldn't see one another's faces.

Joe pressed the woman's hand. Her hand didn't give him the slightest feeling of reality. He thought of something.

"You'd said we wouldn't meet again, didn't you?"

"Yes, I said something like that. This is like fate . . . If Ito were here . . ."

Her voice was so ethereal Joe felt she must be floating overhead. But her slender hand was still held in his own, although it grew icy cold. Joe tried to warm it with one hand, while he clasped it with the other.

"Joe, why can't I see the things I want to see?" Vincent's dejected voice came from the dark. "I look harder, but on the beach there is only a boot the sea has pushed onto the shore."

Vincent seemed to be crying. Joe thought that his tears probably fell on the palm of the woman's other hand, because the hand Joe held in his was regaining its warmth little by little. The woman took back her hand and walked out through the door with quick steps. Joe heard her voice still inside the tower.

"The work in the bookstore increased every day, while Ito grew old."

The white tiger walked into the night behind her.

Joe wanted to follow after her, but Vincent blocked the doorway. Vincent said, "She wears that black skirt and shirt all four seasons of the year."

"Oh," Joe was surprised. "Wasn't she wearing a white kimono? She's the former wife of the owner of a bookstore. I've met her before."

"We saw the same person." Vincent sank into tangled thoughts.

Someone came down from the top of the tower, then went through the side door and walked away. They couldn't see the person, or maybe it wasn't a person: the footsteps sounded like horse's hooves.

"Joe, you go on ahead. Tonight I'll sleep inside the tower. There's a felt blanket here. Everyone says this is the highest point in the world."

Once Joe left, Vincent shut the heavy door. As Joe walked he imagined Vincent scaling the tower inside. He thought that Vincent wanted to climb alone. Vincent wouldn't be sleeping.

Outside there were no lights, and no stars in the sky. The night was deepening. He could dimly see the white tiger appearing and disappearing nearby. For the first time in many days Joe remembered Maria, and remembered he had a wife and a family. On this remote plateau someplace in the East a dim part of his lost memories reappeared. He remembered passing rich busy little days with Maria in City B. The two managed a restaurant that offered Western specialties. Their son was a long-distance truck driver, speeding along the highways of other regions year-round. Joe said to himself: "Such a wonderful family life." He saw steam rising in the kitchen. Outside, the dining room was filled with seated guests. The thick smell of fried shrimp was everywhere. Maria bent over in the food cabinet looking for something, then she straightened up and walked over to Joe, asking, "Joe, did you finish seasoning the shrimp?"

The voice saying this sentence dropped, and the white tiger darted in front of him. Joe sobbed like a child.

He returned to the hotel and lay down on the mildew-smelling folded quilt. His mood quieted and he began to dream.

Midway through the night he woke up once and looked at the yellowed wallpaper on the wall of the hotel. A question flashed briefly across his mind: Was the bookstore's volume of business really increasing? Then he quickly went back to sleep.

Vincent was inside the tower. It was so dark that when he stretched out his hand he couldn't see his five fingers. He heard that person walking down. The man was probably feeling his way one step at a time. Proceeding was strenuous. Vincent imagined the fear in the man's heart and unconsciously made a *ge ge* creaking sound with his fist. After a while the man stopped. A stair might be loose. Vincent remembered the loud sound inside the tower earlier. Perhaps a section had fallen down and there was a large gap between the stairs. Or could the white-haired man's strength be used up? He'd looked so frail, he must be ancient. But he began to move again. His footsteps came even closer. Did he have wings to fly over that gap? Or was there no gap?

The footsteps sounded in front of Vincent, but he had not seen the old fellow face to face. Perhaps these footsteps were the sound of his heart? What was the white light on the roof after all? Vincent hadn't ascended because in a dream the old man from the village clearly told him, "Do not go to the top of the tower." Last week a beautiful little wolf had died inside the tower. Vincent thought that the little wolf must have died from exhaustion. It appeared quite serene and had no wounds on its body. The color of its fur was very light, almost a light yellow. It was at the age of dreams. But who had taken away its corpse?

Vincent touched the blanket on the floor with his foot. He wanted to lie down. Just at this moment, someone outside knocked on the door of the tower. Vincent went over and opened the door. This person brought in a smell of dew.

"The hotel is all full, I had to come back here."

It was the black-clad woman.

Vincent and the woman lay down together on the blanket. He asked her whether she'd heard the sound of footsteps descending. The woman smiled and said, "That was me, I went up and came back down. All the people who ascend lose their weight. Don't you see that I'm as light as air?" Vincent thought she truly was as light as air. He asked her what was on the roof of the tower. "Ten circular holes, you've seen them. From the round hole you lean out . . ." She didn't speak. "What's there?" Vincent pressed her to speak. "I don't know," she said, "I haven't done it, I came right back down."

Vincent embraced her tightly and entered a dream. In his dream he was at his home in Country A at Christmas. Thick snow fell outside the windows. Lisa was adjusting the logs in the fireplace. The blazing flame made her face shine like a ripe apple. She turned her face to him and asked, "Vincent, when do you plan to set off?"

"Tomorrow," he blurted out. "Otherwise I'll be too old."

When he woke in the morning, his eyes were dazzled by the strong sunlight from above and wouldn't open. He reached out a hand to the woman by his side. She wasn't there. When he raised his head again to look up, he discovered that the patch of white light was moving downward. Maybe it wasn't moving, maybe it was expanding. Yes, it really was expanding! In a short time the whole inside of the tower was bright and dazzling. For Vincent it was as if he were looking directly at the sun. He couldn't see anything. He felt hot and began to sweat. Nearby he heard the voice of a local person, it was very indistinct. He tried reaching out his hand, felt the edge of a knife, and shrank back at once. Someone was pulling his hand. Vincent caught at the hand, feeling that it was an old man's, damp with cold sweat.

"Yesterday the sun came out. Today heavy snow seals off the road. You couldn't go back even if you wanted to. Life at the top of the Five Dragon Tower is the same as a brush with death," he said. He was probably from the same country as Vincent.

"And me? What is my life at the bottom of the tower the same as?"

"Your life is the same as watching a play."

He laughed hollowly, then flung Vincent's hand away, turning to climb the stone steps.

Vincent groped his way out of the tower. His eyesight immediately returned. The plateau was bright and clear. Green grass, trees with pink leaves, gray wolves racing along, cottages with thatched roofs beyond the woods. But this landscape didn't seem real. Vincent imagined that if he stamped the ground everything before his eyes would disappear. Now that he had placed himself in the beautiful, ill-intentioned landscape he felt deeply that the Five Dragon Tower behind him was the single sight within this scene that was firm and would not collapse—and he'd left it.

He followed a road trampled into the grass by people passing back and forth on foot. He reflected that the plateau changed its face quickly. Over these past days he had become extremely familiar with this area, but now every blade and tree was wholly transformed. Was there some power at work? Was it to make people who came here cherish the Five Dragon Tower with yet greater reverence? He turned to look. The tall tower had already turned into a small gray triangle, just like one of the wooden building blocks he'd played with as a boy. Perhaps the tower was a building block?

Vincent stepped forward alone, anxious and fearful, into this false landscape. His legs were a little shaky. He thought it might be because he was so hungry. He asked himself: Had he made up his mind?

A long time ago, on the beach, watching the distant coral island, he had thought about that question. In truth it was an imponderable question. So how could he ask it? He didn't ponder the question's essence. Instead, he only circled around the question, opening many passages to it, setting an ambush.

When these sentences appeared in Vincent's mind, his whole body felt a little feverish. Energy filled his gaunt and exhausted body. His footsteps gradually became steady. He was no longer nauseated by the false landscape extending in every direction.

Beside the forest an old man collected firewood, catching dry branches with a long hook. After Vincent walked past him, he shouted a sentence in the local language at Vincent's back. Vincent suddenly understood that he was shouting, "Taking a boat or a plane?" Vincent returned to the old man, but his eyes were lowered as he tied his wood into a bundle with a vine, as if nothing had happened. The old man's big-boned, able hands looked familiar. Vincent felt a few things inside him swiftly die, but at once a few other things grew.

The old man shouldered his load of firewood and walked into the depths of the woods. Vincent stepped forward along the road heading in the opposite direction.

16

LISA AND MARIA'S LONG MARCH

Maria came to Lisa's house for the first time. She cautiously looked all around. Lisa didn't ask her to sit in the spacious living room. Instead, she invited Maria to go upstairs into the bedroom she shared with Vincent. Maria saw that their bedroom was much more spartan than her own. Aside from a wooden bed there were no furnishings. The walls were bare, without a single picture. It was out of keeping in such a high-class residence. The windows were the strangest part. There were two of them, both very small and set high up, making it difficult for light to enter the room.

"I designed our bedroom myself. What do you think of it?"

"Oh!"

"At night we should shut ourselves up in a prison cell, that was my thought initially. Vincent approved of the idea. Since I didn't come here alone—I brought a large crowd with me. Their maneuvers usually take place in the corner where you're standing. I prefer to have the long march unfold in a closed-off space."

Lisa was walking back and forth across the room as she spoke, both hands constantly pushing out from her chest, as if she were pushing something away, but these things kept rushing toward her, and would not let her push them away. Maria saw what seemed to be thin smoke rising in the room.

"And Vincent? Where does Vincent go at night?" Maria asked.

"I don't know. Maybe he sits on the windowsill. The windowsill is so high, it's a good spot for watching the battles."

"How are things between you now?"

"You mean since he left? Ha, he comes here every day. He

is always among the army troops. So long as I'm patient a while I can see him there. Last night he also had me meet a new friend of his, a retired lumberman. He's an old soldier, an expert at breaking through enemy lines."

Someone knocked on the door. Lisa said it was her driver. She lowered her voice and told Maria she could not let the driver know Vincent had left, otherwise she might be seduced by him. Maria asked her how she managed it. Lisa said that provided the spectacle of the long march continued, the young man could not enter the room.

Sure enough, the driver knocked quietly from the outside but did not shout or push the door open.

Maria couldn't help wanting to laugh.

"He looks down on himself terribly." Lisa evaluated him. "He wasn't like this before. Before he was unruly, and he didn't take notice of me at all. But once Vincent left, this big house became an empty city of desire. Listen, there are two men, the other is the cook, A Bing. The cook is already half-mad because his homesickness torments him. These two poor orphans, I want to take them into my arms!"

At Vincent and Lisa's home in the center of the city, Maria saw with panic the desolate and fallow inner world of the married couple. It was a residence progressively neglected and forgotten by its owners. She circled the property in Lisa's company. Although Lisa presented the home to Maria with enthusiastic words, reviewing the romance of former days, in every installation and every corner Maria saw unsalvageable, dead things. It all belonged to the past, to the wreckage of passion. The untended garden, regressed back to nature; the swimming pool emptied of water; the wooden pavilion with its paint peeling; the large house with rooms that had been locked for years were in Maria's eyes products of a period of impulses. And now these things were all hidden, disappearing into the darkest depths of their hearts.

The cook A Bing was cleaning birds' nests out of the enormous swimming pool. Why did the birds build nests there? It was a complete mess. A Bing's movements seemed full of hatred. Maria saw fragments of birds' eggs spread on the ground.

"A Bing! A Bing!" Lisa's voice revealed her pain.

A Bing was dazed for a moment, then he threw down the broom and climbed out. He stood in front of Lisa, rolling his eyes with a scoundrel's smile on his face. Maria was angered.

"At night this swimming pool is busy as hell," he said.

"A Bing, you aren't a young man any more. How can you still enjoy acting so willfully? Since you live here, you must get your life in order. If you have so much hatred in your heart, how can you arrange your life properly?"

"My life is arranged properly," A Bing interrupted Lisa impatiently. "Each person has a different ambition. You have missed me every time. I'm in the long march army, too."

Lisa was in a predicament. She silently lowered her head, pulling Maria away.

Maria and Lisa sat in the roomy kitchen eating the tasty potato pastries A Bing had made. Lisa said A Bing was a priceless treasure. She also said that if he didn't have those impulses of hatred, who could say he wasn't a man "who would do great things"? Maria answered, smiling, that perhaps the cook didn't want to do great things. He saw through all earthly things.

"Just like Vincent?" Lisa asked in a mischievous voice.

"No, Vincent will never see through things. He travels everywhere and looks and looks. This has no end."

The two women laughed aloud. They hadn't laughed so freely in a long time. A Bing walked over gloomily to take their plates, intentionally making the cups clatter.

"He often loses his temper at me. In this house, it seems he is the master," Lisa said. "Look, he's going, he doesn't want to speak with us."

Maria watched the cook go down the steps into the yard. He was shaped like a black bear. He appeared to be breathing angrily, but why?

"Maria, I want to make an experiment. Can we dream together in that bed tonight? To see if we can communicate with each other in our dreams? Then we can search for Joe and Vincent together."

Yet after the lights were out the house became a large graveyard. All the graves were earthen mounds piled up with soil. Lisa sat on one of the mounds hugging her knees with both arms. Maria stood at her side. There was no moon or stars in the sky. Someone was carrying a lantern toward them from a place off in the distance. He walked and stopped, walked and stopped again, beams from the lamp shining on the grass on top of the earthen mounds. Maria turned around and saw another man carrying a lantern. He was also searching for something between the graves. She looked again and saw yet another one, just catching up from the road in that direction, who also held a lantern. And behind him was a fourth.

"It's busy in the graveyard," Maria said.

When she spoke the first man had already reached her. He raised his lantern up high, giving Maria a very strange feeling. Lisa pulled Maria down to sit with her, quietly saying, "He is making a signal. You haven't realized yet? A regiment is coming. In a little while this will be the military camp. This spot where I'm sitting is actually Vincent's grave."

"Vincent is inside this mound?"

"Not yet, he is still roaming outside. I sit on top of the grave and my heart is at peace."

Maria raised her head and saw that there were already eight or nine lanterns in their vicinity. The faces all looked familiar. She recognized one of them as a neighbor from her own street. More time passed, and she saw Daniel and Zhenya arriving.

"There's Maria!" Zhenya said happily to Daniel. "I see the members of your family can hold in their emotions particularly well! Your mother looks positively sedate sitting there."

Maria couldn't see Daniel's face clearly. His body was like a long, thin twig.

"Daniel!" Maria shouted, her heart aching.

Wind blew through the graveyard. Daniel's voice sounded as if he were inside an urn. She couldn't hear what he was really saying. Maria saw that her son was shaking his head as hard as he could.

"Daniel, what do you want to say to me?" Maria was disheartened.

"He's talking about his father." Zhenya answered for him. "He's always saying that even I'm affected by him, nearly falling in love with your Joe."

Maria reached out to embrace Daniel's long, thin waist, but she was shocked because her son's back bulged out in a protuberance.

"What is this?" her voice shook.

"It's Joe," Zhenya said. "Your son now carries his father everywhere on his back. See, isn't Daniel much sturdier? He is a grown man."

Maria took off her son's shirt, touching his deformed back. Several mad ideas occurred to her. Lisa comforted her, saying, "It's a good thing, you see, your son's outstanding." Daniel grumbled another sentence.

"He says his father is speaking inside him, so we can't hear him clearly," Zhenya interpreted again.

Maria relaxed her hand and Daniel immediately hid behind Zhenya's back. This left Maria almost disconsolate.

Quite a few people had already gathered in the graveyard. Maria smelled a faint odor of horses and even of gunpowder. The people holding lanterns appeared to be going to a temple fair. How could they exude such smells? Zhenya and Daniel vanished into the dark. Lisa said she was going into the army to find someone. She had Maria take her place on the grave mound to avoid missing anything. She walked away as she was speaking.

Now Maria sat alone by herself on the mound. Some small animal pushed underneath her foot. Oh, it was her African cat! The brown striped one. In the dim light she discovered that the cat's claws were dripping. It was injured, with its right front paw almost cut off. It was unable to transmit electricity. Maria grew extremely anxious. She wanted to bring the cat back home to treat its wound, but she could not break her promise to Lisa. She waited helplessly for Lisa to appear. People were rushing around the graveyard; everywhere there were points of light. Another of Maria's neighbors passed her, carrying a lantern. Maria called out to the old woman to stop:

"Karen, can you help me find Lisa? It's urgent."

"Ha, it's Joe's wife here." Karen's elderly face smiled. "How can you have time to sit here? It's urgent for all of us, it's life and death. We come to the last opportunity, the time is now!"

She raised the lantern to size up Maria's face. Maria felt the old woman's eyes like a hawk's on her. She cowered in fear. And even though it was injured the cat struggled out of her arms. Maria was annoyed and gave the cat a slap. The cat didn't move after that.

"Just give it up," Karen's mouth shriveled. "Who can find anyone on a night like this?"

The old woman walked far away, her back hunched. Maria saw seven or eight women curiously surrounding her to get a look. Probably her speaking with Karen had drawn them over.

"This is Joe's wife? Oh my!"

"Poor Joe, gone and not returning."

"He's not stupid. He can figure things out for himself, that usurer."

"He is a real pangolin!"

The women, heads close together, mouths to ears, dispersed again like a swarm of wasps.

A premonition grew in Maria's heart. She felt that something had happened to Joe. What was it? Perhaps he would return home soon? Did he have a grave here too? Just at this moment, Lisa returned. She carried a yellow lantern on a pole. Far away there were joyful shouts:

"Maria! Maria, dear! Joe's come back! Listen, listen!"

Lisa's head and Maria's were close together. They listened carefully. All the neighboring people were surely saying "Joe, Joe, Joe . . ." Casting her eyes into the distance, Maria saw them squatting one by one on the grave mounds, placing their lanterns on the tombstones. The graveyard seemed vast and limitless. Lisa said that each one squatted on the grave of his or her "beloved."

"I want to go back home, my cat is hurt," Maria said.

Maria passed through the grave mounds hugging the cat. She still heard people saying "Joe, Joe, Joe . . ." Warmth sprang from the desolate depths of her heart. She smelled a faint odor of tobacco and the rusty smell from the cables of the iron bridge.

"The forms of the long march are many and varied," Lisa said, sitting in Maria's flower garden.

Maria saw that Lisa's spirits were roused, and she thought of the events of the night. She was distracted.

"Daniel! Daniel! Don't trample your father's books!" she stood and shouted.

Daniel's voice carried down the stairs, muffled. His throat seemed to be squeezed by something. The study windows quivered. Maria sat back down in her chair, disappointed, and continued talking with Lisa about Daniel's days at middle school. As they spoke a three-legged African cat jumped onto her knee. "Is this happiness or suffering? Is this happiness or suffering? . . ." she repeated. The cat trembled nervously on her knee.

"There was a yellow butterfly," she finally recalled. "At noon, Daniel came back from school. All around it was very quiet. But why did Joe return home at that time? I was staring at a yellow butterfly, my mind brimming with good fortune. Joe opened his mouth wide and called to me, but he couldn't make a sound. He pointed to the blood running down on Daniel's forehead. He looked crazed. The yellow butterfly spun in circles and stopped on the top of the stove. See, Lisa, having a son is such a troublesome business."

While she was speaking, another cat, the yellow-and-white one, came over. Lisa felt her calf tingle, like an electric shock.

"So could the long march take place here?" Maria asked, hesitating.

"Of course. Daniel has already begun."

That night Maria went to the study because she couldn't sleep. Although she hadn't turned on the light, she could see that Joe's bookcases had turned into a dark forest of books. The books had grown large, one book set next to another vertically on the floor, the pages of the books opening and closing. She couldn't feel the wall of the room, and so she didn't know where the light was. Her voice was a little ghastly as she shouted: "Joe? Are you there?" Then she stopped shouting. She felt that Joe was nearby, sitting behind a book, beside a little stream. He had taken off his shoes and stretched his bare feet into the black water. Maria thought, Joe would not leave her again. How good. In the house built on the foundations made by her ancestors, she, Daniel, and Joe, this family, were starting their own long march. They were going to bring back to life those long-ago stories. This would be a fine thing! But she feared her husband's body was forever disappearing from their home. Daniel, because he couldn't find his father, was losing his way. It was Daniel who had pushed down all the bookcases. Was he also sitting behind a book now?

"Mother, I'm here."

"Daniel, what do you think of this?"

"I'm truly happy, Mother. Soon we will reach the end of the bridge. Do you hear the roaring of the river?"

Maria couldn't see Daniel, but she knew he was nearby. This mutual searching and pursuing in the nighttime sent a warm current through Maria's heart. After so many years, she experienced for the first time the way blood kept relatives together. Maria touched the enormous book pages with a shaking finger. She touched one after another of the letters protruding from the pages, and those letters jumped slightly, giving off electricity. Suddenly she comprehended the book's meaning. The book told of an ancient, deserted beach. Someone climbed onto the bank from the sea. Sea birds cried ominously in the air. "That man is Joe," Maria spoke quietly. Then her finger touched the word "Joe." "Joe, is it you?" she asked.

"Of course it's Father. Why don't you believe it?" Daniel spoke in the dark. "Touch it again, everything is inside that book."

Next Maria touched the description having to do with her African cats. The book didn't tell of her cats in the present, but rather of long ago when they were still in Africa. They had just been born then, and were two little kittens. The sun of the African continent irritated their eyes so they could not open them. But why did the light-brown cat have only three legs? It had lost its leg later, in the graveyard.

"It always had only three legs. You just hadn't noticed," Daniel spoke again.

"Daniel, can't you come over here?"

"I can't, Mother."

Maria touched the surface of another book. This book had an illustration of small snakes. Her hand kept touching them, and the snakes began to slither. Maria feared the desire inside her body and circled around behind the book, her back to its spine. She thought, over several decades of uninterrupted reading, her Joe had created this forest. And he hadn't removed her from it. Once she entered, she blended into this place. In the *su su* rustling sound made by the pages, a world of writing appeared in her mind. She realized that for many years everything she'd woven was this writing. So familiar, so pleasing—was this happiness? She began to walk from one book to another. Dry leaves made noise under her feet; her feet touched a few small stones; she even heard the song of a nightingale. It was inside the pages of the largest book, singing and then pausing.

"Mother, you should speak with Father. In the square his ears are listening carefully. That ear hung on a tree is flapping ceaselessly with thirst."

"Joe, your story has come back."

"Wonderful, Mama, Father hears and is contented."

"Daniel, if a man expends a lifetime of energy changing himself into a forest of stories, then does this man still belong to us?"

"He doesn't belong to us, but is with us every day."

"Thank you, son."

"But Mother, you don't belong to me and Father either. I saw you walking in the woods, your silhouette so long and thin, so unreal, your entire body full of electricity."

There was a dim light in the forest of books, but when Maria looked up she couldn't see the sky. Was there even a sky? There were grass, stones, a path, and she heard water flowing from a spring. But the air was filled with the fine smell of old books. This was Joe's story. This story belonged to her, forever. Maria's heart was full of gratitude. She pricked her ears, awaiting the nightingale's singing again.

She waited till it sang, but it wasn't one call, it was many, many calls. One rising as another fell.

Lisa did not go home after she left Maria's rose garden. She turned into a narrow street and stood at the door of Joyner's flower shop. Someone waved her into the shop, but it was dark and she couldn't see who it was. Once her eyes adjusted she finally saw Joyner. However, this wasn't the same Joyner as before. Except that her face gave Lisa a slight feeling of familiarity, she'd changed completely—she'd become a fat middle-aged woman. The main difference was in how her movements were hampered. She strained and sat down in a wicker chair, placing herself among the tulips. The darkness of her surroundings made her face look even more pallid.

"Did you come to see Vincent?" Joyner asked sternly.

"Yes, I'm looking for him."

Lisa felt dizzy, because it was suddenly dark inside the room. She couldn't see anything.

"These are tulips from the Netherlands. On your right are yellow roses, and also violets. Did you come to see Vincent?" she asked again, her tone even more severe.

"Yes. Vincent . . . Could he be here?"

"Step over my body, and you will be able to see him. You need to step boldly, raise your foot!"

Numerous giant lightbulbs, as bright as snow, suddenly turned on. They shone in Lisa's eyes and she still could not see. She felt that she had been placed in a square, perhaps a competition arena. No matter what direction she went in, she didn't bump into anything. Should she go on? As she was thinking this, she had already raised her foot.

"Vincent, I want to speak to you!" Lisa shouted, so excited her face grew pink.

An ocean of light spread in all directions. Her voice reverberated for a long time. She still couldn't see. She was moving ahead, but she couldn't even see her own feet. She suddenly thought, Maybe this was a snowcapped mountain? Long ago, Vincent had said to her that letting the light of a snowy mountain become the light inside one's eyes would surely be fascinating. Lisa wanted to speak to him now about her own feeling of "blindness." Joyner had not deceived her. Vincent was nearby. In the midst of the light she saw his inner heart. This light was a cold light, but her eyes were suited to it.

"Vincent, I want to speak with you!" she shouted again.

She felt profoundly that Vincent had transformed into this light. At this very moment he was touching her neck, her eyes. She recalled the events that had just happened. Wasn't she in the flower shop not far from the office, where she'd met the black woman, Joyner, and then come here? Lisa didn't like flowers, and she didn't plant flowers, so why had she gone to the flower shop?

"That kind of story is concealed in every corner of the world."

In her mind this line of words appeared distinctly.

At the end of the ocean of light a shadow appeared. It looked like a crowd of people, or of beasts. Lisa sensed a bugle sounding in the darkness of her abdomen. Her feet stumbled on something and she almost fell over, but she didn't fall. She spread her arms like a giant bird trying to keep its balance, then, staggering, flapped ahead. The more anxious she grew, the more slowly she advanced. But she made out that the distant shadow of the army was growing stronger, and it was expanding by degrees in her direction. She even saw the corner of a red flag, guns, and litters, and gunpowder smoke slowly rising into the air. A memory of her childhood revived in an instant. On the solemn grounds of a large mansion, she and her mother were summoning their courage to attack a mud frog. Her mother pounced into the pond and climbed back out, drenched. She made Lisa listen to the violent, sudden sound of drumbeats. They were army drums. Thereby their home became much darker.

CAN XUE is the pseudonym of Deng Xiaohua, author of many novels, short works of fiction, and volumes of literary criticism in Chinese. Can Xue's books in English include *Five Spice Street* and *Vertical Motion: Stories.* She lives in Beijing.

ANNELISE FINEGAN WASMOEN is an editor and a literary translator. She is pursuing a Ph.D. in Comparative Literature at Washington University in St. Louis.